SPICE ROAD

SPICE ROAD

MAIYA IBRAHIM

DELACORTE PRESS

Text copyright © 2023 by Maiya Ibrahim
Jacket art copyright © 2023 by Carlos Quevedo
Interior art used under license from Shutterstock.com

All rights reserved. Published in the United States by Delacorte Press, an imprint of Random House Children's Books, a division of Penguin Random House LLC, New York.

Delacorte Press is a registered trademark and the colophon is a trademark of Penguin Random House LLC.

Visit us on the Web! GetUnderlined.com

Educators and librarians, for a variety of teaching tools,
visit us at RHTeachersLibrarians.com

Library of Congress Cataloging-in-Publication Data is available upon request.
ISBN 978-0-593-12696-7 (trade) — ISBN 978-0-593-12698-1 (lib. bdg.) —
ISBN 978-0-593-12697-4 (ebook)

The text of this book is set in 11.25-point Adobe Garamond.
Interior design by Michelle Crowe

Printed in the United States of America
10 9 8 7 6 5 4 3 2 1
First Edition

For Jason and Soleil

THE KINGDOM OF ALQIBAH

Al-Bawaba Pass

TAEEL-SA

SIDI SHARIF

The Azurite River

BASHTAL

Lake Azurite

GHAZALI

The Spice Road

Zeytoun Forest

BROOMA

Gulf of Fire

Bay of Mist

1

WE WILL FIGHT, BUT FIRST WE WILL HAVE TEA.

Not quite the motto of the Shields, but just as apt. Ordinarily I would be outside Qalia's walls with my squad, defending our lands from a never-ending onslaught of monsters: djinn, ghouls, sand serpents, and whatever other nightmare one can only conjure in the clutches of a fever dream. But even now, when we are home on mandated rest, we are facing a hard day of training—and I am certain Taha ibn Bayek of the Al-Baz clan can't wait.

Whenever we are in Qalia's barracks together, Taha's squadmates challenge me to spar him. It is a pathetic attempt at settling which of us is the better Shield, but Taha himself has never commented on the ongoing rivalry. In fact, for the two years I've known him, Taha has acted as if I don't exist, apart from the occasional snide comment. I've no doubt his squadmates will try again after the tea ceremony, but I have rejected their other challenges as a waste of my time, and I am not about to have a change of heart, even with him coldly staring at me like that from across the tea room. If one knows his reputation, and who in Qalia doesn't—a talented archer and beastseer who can control the minds of falcons—one would be forgiven imagining a young man with a keen gaze. But Taha's eyes are troublingly placid, the washed-out green of grasslands that have seen too much sun and not enough rain.

Tea ceremony etiquette is to watch the person preparing the Spice, but I wish he would deviate from tradition just this once and stop tracking my every move. I untie the drawstring on the silk pouch of *misra* and remove ribbons of bark. They have been carefully stripped from the ancient misra tree standing in Qalia's Sanctuary a few buildings over, as it has done for a millennium. I have led tea ceremonies enough times that I could do it with my eyes closed, but I still marvel over what is in my hands. Magic.

The light of the overhead lanterns winks in the gold-veined bark as I hold it to my nose and inhale deeply. Every Shield in the room does as well. Perhaps they too hope to decipher what scent the misra possesses. Once, I thought it smelled like life itself. Another time, stars and dreams. This morning, it is as bitter as the old ash of a fire long burned down to dark. Of someone gone, but not forgotten. It reminds me of Atheer.

It has been a year since I last saw my big brother and best friend. I was kneeling like this, preparing the misra, but I was at home and the Spice still smelled pleasant then. He joined me, seeking conversation with that faint, mystifying air of desperation about him.

"There are things in life greater than duty and rules, Imani," he said.

"Like what?" I asked. His eyes took on a somber gleam, as dry as dying light reflecting off a dull blade.

"Truth," he said quietly. "The truth is greater than everything; it is worth sacrificing everything for. And I have seen it." He waited then, for what, I don't know. Felt like it was all he did in those last few months before his disappearance, wait for something. But I said nothing, and after a time, he left home and did not return. I never asked him what it was, that truth. I didn't want to know.

My fingers tremble as I place the bark in the stone mortar. I clench my fists to steady them, then take up the pestle and grind. The aroma floods the room; it wafts up to the ceiling and weaves through the rug fibers. My nose wrinkles; the back of my throat stings. I restrain a cough. My squad leader, Sara, kneels in the front row, inhaling the scent in appreciative drags. For her, the Spice is agreeable, like savannas after rain and her mama's jasmine perfume. Not withered things and words left unsaid. Once I asked my auntie Aziza, who commands the Order of Sorcerers, why the Spice smells different from person to person, ceremony to ceremony. "For the same reason different sorcerers possess different affinities: magic is a mirror," she answered. I wonder what this bitterness reflects about me when it is all I have smelled of late.

The tea must be taken in silence, allowing the drinker to dwell on the Great Spirit's gift and prepare to receive the magic. The two dozen Shields in the room are silent, but it is my mind that chatters defiantly, and I am strangely afraid they know it, as if my thoughts are leaking from my ears. While I scoop the Spice into the silver teapot, I think of Atheer. While the tea steeps and the others meditate, I imagine the rough wilderness he mysteriously disappeared into. Which of the elements did he succumb to in the end? The unforgiving sun, the howling sandstorms, the freezing nights? Or perhaps it is like some cruel people whisper, and it was none of those, for he took his life before any could claim it.

Taha clears his throat. I open my eyes. Everyone is watching and waiting. My ears burn; heat swims under my leather armor. I pour tea into the small cups lined on the tray and take it around the circle before settling back in the center with my own. It is customary to wait for the one leading the ceremony, and everyone follows suit only when I put the cup to my lips. Then we drink.

The hot tea goes down biting and belligerent. The magic in it is an ancient gift from the Great Spirit of the Sahir, granted to protect our people, on the promise that we will in return protect the Sahir from monsters and outsiders. For a time, misra allows its drinker to manipulate one affinity of the land that the Great Spirit presides over. For some, it is the affinity of sand, or wind. In my late brother's case, he was a skin-changer, capable of transforming into a lion. For me, it is the affinity of iron, specifically the dagger I keep on me always. The duration that a cup of misra lasts depends on the sorcerer—the more skilled one is, the more efficient they are in the use of the magic.

"The tea will awaken in you an affinity that accords with your natural strengths," Auntie explained in our first private magic lesson. "Think of the misra as a seamstress who takes a sheet of silk and fashions something with perfect measurements, unique to you. At first, the silk will not look like much, but in time, it will be something new and yet entirely expected. So too will the affinity that the misra stirs in you. And if you wish to hone it, you must dedicate years of study, training, and reflection."

I am halfway through my tea when a fast rapping interrupts the quiet and one of the arched doors to the ceremony room bursts open. Dalila, my younger sister's best friend, stands on the threshold. Her sweaty mahogany skin and pitching shoulders immediately set me on edge.

"Sorry," she gasps, looking across the solemn gathering.

"Why are you interrupting our ceremony?" asks Taha, getting to his feet.

Dalila shrinks half a head, holding on to the brass door handle for dear life. "I'm sorry. I just . . . Imani, may I speak with you?"

I quickly drain my tea as Taha strides over to her. Like his infamous father, he is imposingly tall and muscular, and he liberally uses his frame to intimidate. It doesn't help that he is attractive, at least outwardly, with his burnished ebony hair and hard-cut jaw—and he knows it.

"Silence is sacred to tea ritual," he says in a pitiless voice. "Don't you know that basic tenet, girl? Shut the door and wait outside like you were supposed to."

"Easy, Taha. There's no need to berate her," I say, standing as well.

He turns and glares down his straight nose at me. "The rules apply equally to everyone, including you and your friends. Shocking, I know."

His squadmates trade smirks; the other Shields in the room

look as uncomfortable as I feel. It's strange, I used to feel offended when Taha pretended I was invisible during lessons, given we share unique things in common. At seventeen, I am the youngest Shield in recent history, but at eighteen he is the second-youngest, and we both have family members on the Council of Al-Zahim that governs our nation. His father presides over the Council, and my auntie is Master of the Misra. Regardless of one's opinion on *how* Taha's father became Grand Zahim, I thought a boy from a modest clan, now the son of the most powerful man in the Sahir, would want to socialize with others in similar positions, like me. The sting only worsened once our squads began venturing out on missions. I would hear secondhand stories of the many people he heroically saved and the terrifying monsters he vanquished against impossible odds, and although I did the same, he never once acknowledged my existence. Perhaps that was a blessing in disguise.

"Dalila, why are you here?" I ask, turning my back on him. "You should be in school."

She shifts on her feet. "Well, yes, we were *supposed* to be, but Amira . . . she's in trouble."

Not again. I have lost count of how many times my sister has played truant this past year, and I have dreaded the moment her truancy leads to something worse.

"Honestly, when are Imani's siblings *not* in trouble?" remarks Feyrouz, one of Taha's beautiful but mean-spirited squadmates.

Snickers chorus behind me. I pivot and scan their sneering faces for even a hint of shame, but I would have better luck finding guilt amongst thieves. They are too emboldened by Taha's position as the Grand Zahim's eldest son to fear getting in trouble for mocking a Councilmember's niece. Happily, my squad leader is not cowed. Sara descends from a proud, wealthy clan of merchants, and there have been more than just a handful of famous warriors among their ranks.

"Word of advice, Taha, seeing as this is still very new to you: encouraging nastiness is unbecoming to someone of your station." She snatches the tea tray off the floor as if she means to strike him with it. It isn't necessary; her riposte seems to have sprouted a hand and slapped Taha across the cheek, judging by how sour he looks. She nods at the door. "I can finish up, Imani. You go."

I salute her. "Thank you. Please tell Captain Ramiz I'll return to training as soon as I can."

"Don't worry about it," Taha interjects. "I'm sure this situation will be kept hush-hush, the way you're used to."

My pulse stutters. The other Shields frown, several exchanging confused glances.

"What are you talking about?" Sara asks.

I cut Taha the most murderous look I can muster, hoping he finds in it a promise to shut his mouth if he is incapable of doing it himself.

He calmly stares back at me. "Oh, it's nothing. Right, Imani?"

I can hardly believe it. The first substantial thing Taha has said to me in two years, and he makes it about my brother. After Atheer disappeared, it was discovered he had been stealing misra from the Sanctuary, a telltale sign of magical obsession. By a majority, the Council determined to keep the matter secret to protect my clan's reputation. Judging by how chafed Taha is about it, I doubt his father was pleased with the verdict. But this is neither the time nor the place to address it.

"Yes, nothing," I mutter as I shepherd Dalila out and close the door behind us. The lightness I should have felt escaping his intimidating presence is swiftly substituted with dread. "What happened to Amira?" I ask.

Dalila breaks into a jog down the sandstone corridor. "We were riding outside the walls, and when we stopped for a break, her horse—your brother's horse, I mean—he snapped his tether and bolted."

My chest twinges at the second abrupt mention of Atheer this morning. "You mean Raad, the black stallion?"

She nods. We descend the ceremony hall's main spiral stairwell and cross the shadowy, lantern-lit vestibule, enveloped in the clashing scents of burning incense and the tea ceremonies happening upstairs. The sunny quadrangle outside is wall-to-wall with Shields grouped around their sparring squadmates, their stern-faced seniors watching on and barking advice. Magic fills the air alongside the strident quarrel of swords—in the middle of the large group before us, a Shield shoots a ball of fire from his palms, but the onrushing flames are smothered by his opponent manipulating a cyclonic gust of wind.

"Amira sneaks him away from your place whenever we go riding," Dalila breathlessly explains as I carefully navigate her past a surge of superheated air. "He's always been a little unruly, but today was something else. You'd think a devil was in the saddle caning him! When he started for the Forbidden Wastes—"

My eyes bug. "The *Forbidden Wastes*?"

"Hey, I *told* her to let him go, I warned her of the evil things living in there, but she refused to listen."

"Of course she did." I bite my tongue before I curse my sister in front of my fellow Shields. It was months of hurtful speculation after Atheer died. The last thing I need is people realizing Amira is on a wayward path of her own and deeming it a worthy topic of conversation.

I signal the smoking stable hand to fetch my horse. "So you let her go on her own?" I ask, turning back to Dalila.

"*Let* her? No, Amira almost killed me shoving me out of the saddle when I refused to go any further. She stole my horse!"

"Please, lower your voice." I feign a casual smile at a group of Shields marching past.

"Sorry. Just, please save her. Amira's not been herself since . . . you know."

"I know." The stable hand emerges with my silver filly, Badr, shining in the morning sun. I hoist into the cool saddle. "Go back to school, Dalila. I'll make sure she's safe."

Or I will die trying. I snap the reins and ride to the barrack gates.

2

MY HORSE GALLOPS THROUGH QALIA'S TWIST-ing streets, dodging crowds fanning in colorful silks between carriages agleam with brass and gold fittings. The enormous city is a sun-splashed labyrinth of date palms and sandstone minarets; long, breezy arcades; and spacious villas with verdant gardens on their roofs. But I was born and raised here, and I know it like the lines in my palm. I quickly navigate the quieter back lanes and leave the gilded gates behind, travers-ing grasslands west to the Forbidden Wastes.

It is almost an hour's ride before I crest a hill and find Amira hurtling across an arid plain on Dalila's chestnut mare. With her dusky-rose cloak and ribbons of wavy brown hair billowing be-hind her, my fifteen-year-old sister resembles a subject from the dramatic, bleak paintings of Mama's favorite artist, Hadil Hatra. *The Girl Who Flees,* this portrait might be called. I dig my heels into Badr and rapidly close the gap.

"Amira," I call after her.

My sister's head twitches, and she glances over her shoul-der at me, revealing a full, flushed face under the hood of her rough-spun cloak. I have been home for two weeks and have seen her every day, but it still strikes me how different she appears since Atheer died. Under her hard, angry exterior, inside her burning-coal eyes, she is a wilted flower.

She slows to a stop and slides out of the saddle. "Imani, why are you here?"

"I could ask you the same thing." I jump down too, gesturing at the vast plain. It is little more than rusty grit and mounds of stone, as dead and deserted as a field of toppled burial cairns. "You know you're to stay away from the Wastes. It's unpatrolled land."

She cartwheels a stone across the sand with her pointed slipper. "Oh, so Dalila found you. That was fast. She has a big mouth on her, that one."

"And you have thieving hands," I retort. "You stole her horse."

"I had to! Raad bolted. See?"

I follow her pointing finger. Sure enough, our solitary vista is intruded upon by a trail of hoofprints stubbornly traveling toward jagged red mountains. I wave a hand.

"Let him. He always misbehaves outside the walls, which is why he's not supposed to *be* outside the walls."

"Great." She climbs back into the saddle. "If I'd known you hadn't come to help, I wouldn't have stopped."

I close my fist on her horse's lead ropes. "You must let him go, Amira."

She shoots me an unnervingly furious look. Once upon a time, my sister was doe-eyed and smiley, enamored with herbalism class at school and wearing bright makeup; clever like Mama but blessed with a creative flair, her head always buried in a fantasy book about brave kings and braver queens. How gentle she was, meeker than a mouse in a thunderstorm. Then Atheer died, and she took on some harsh edges I can't seem to polish out.

"Raad is the best of Baba's stock. Why should we abandon him?" she asks.

I wasn't talking about Atheer's horse, but I don't have the heart to correct her. "He is neither my horse nor yours for us to have a say. He is Atheer's."

She nods at the hazy sun. "And Atheer will expect us to take care of Raad while he is gone."

Something unexpectedly hot aches behind my eyes, presses like a fist on my throat. "It's been a year."

"So?" She studies my grip on the lead ropes. "Raad knows Atheer is out here. *That's* why he keeps trying to run off whenever he is outside the walls. He's trying to tell us something, if only we would listen."

I concede a flat laugh, as sad and deflated as an old cloth doll with not enough hay in its belly. "That's comical coming from someone who never listens to anyone."

She purses her lips. "I do so."

"You feign illness to get out of school, and when Mama forces you to go, you pick fights with your classmates, you talk back to your teachers, or you skip lessons entirely. Principal Imad doesn't know what to do with you anymore, and neither do I."

Amira's features are gently curved, yet they manage to take on an unkind rigidity. "And you're better than me, are you? Running off with your prestigious Shields all the time, risking life and limb even though you know Mama doesn't want you to anymore."

"I swore a sacred oath to protect the Sahir from exactly the kind of monsters you'd find in there," I say, gesturing at the Wastes.

"You barely took a day off after Atheer disappeared!" she erupts. "Did you even care about him, or us? Me?"

It is magic, how words can be deadlier than daggers. Agony rises in my chest, rending it; my heart is ready to tumble out and shatter on the grit. Despite training myself not to, I am already hopelessly lost in the soft glow of memories I usually keep locked away. The memory of Atheer teaching me to spar the same afternoon I announced that my dream was to be a Shield, like him. The memory of him showing up at my Trials to support me, or him comforting me with soft words and a hug after I returned from my first mission, distressed over the giant sand serpent I'd witnessed devour an occupied carriage. He would have a joke ready for me every morning; if not that, he'd tug on the end of my braid whenever he passed by me in the house or the barracks, and when I'd flash him an annoyed look, he would innocently point at anyone nearby, even our dog. My brother, the pride of our clan, the jewel in Baba's crown, Mama's heart and soul . . . How could my own sister think I never cared about him? Perhaps because she did not see the tears I shed, she did not count the hours of sleep I lost.

"Amira, you know I care about you, but I dealt with Atheer's death in my own way," I say.

"You didn't deal with anything, Imani. You *ignored* it. Those long missions you agree to go on couldn't have anything to do with you wanting to be away from us, could they? You don't have to hear Mama cry at the door to Atheer's room or Teta praying for the Great Spirit to guide him home; you don't have to deal with Baba getting angry over the smallest thing; you don't have to listen to him and Mama argue for hours on end. . . . You don't have to talk to me."

If there were words to say, they've abandoned me. I am feeble in my leathers somehow, a rope laden with too much and stretched too thin, little more than a feather's weight from fraying. There has been more silence than conversation between Amira and me since Atheer died, and yet, I find myself incapable of changing course and getting close to her again. Close to anyone, really.

"Or maybe you do your own searching for Atheer when you're out there and you think nobody is looking," Amira says, softer now. "Maybe you know in your heart that I am right, and something more was going on with our brother."

I gently untangle her hand from the reins. Her skin is hot, her nails stained messy red with henna. She looks as if she's been poking pomegranate jam, or blood. "It is a comforting thought, but there was nothing more. He was stealing misra from the Sanctuary and abusing its use for months. All sorcerers are at risk of developing an obsession with magic, and things were harder for him, being of the Beya clan—magic, the drive to master it, it is in our blood. I'm sorry, Amira. Excessive magic has a debilitating effect on the body and mind, even that of a healthy, brilliant sorcerer like Atheer."

"No!" She snatches her hand away. "I don't believe you or any of those fools on the Council parroting the same tired excuse. Apart from stealing misra, Atheer showed no signs of magical obsession—"

I interrupt her with a long sigh. "You don't know the signs."

"I read about them at the library," she snaps. "He was not aggressive, erratic, or irrational."

"He was different—"

"Yes, and he left for a *reason*. It's up to us to find out what, and damn the Council if they don't want to investigate further."

I am suddenly shaky all over, like a tent pitched on shifting sands facing down a gale. "These are words too big and angry for you."

"The truth is the thorn, not the rose."

"You learned that from Atheer, didn't you?" I ask.

She stares at the shimmery waves rising off the grit. "He had things to teach us, but you refused to listen, then and now. Let go of the ropes. I'm bringing his horse back."

I tighten my grip. "You won't. This is dangerous territory."

"Then it's lucky my sister is the next-best Shield we have," she says with mocking cheer. "What did Atheer call you? Bright Blade? I hear everyone is going with 'Djinni Slayer' nowadays."

"I am not joking, Amira. Atheer is gone. There is no sense risking your life corralling a stallion who wants to be free. Come, return Dalila's horse and go back to school. You've some hours left to make."

She glares at me. "If you do not release the lead, I will run you over."

"You wouldn't," I say, but it comes out sounding like a question.

"I will, and short of you killing me, *Bright Blade,* you won't stop me." She snaps the reins, sending the mare barreling past in a cloud of sand.

I step back, shielding my eyes. "Abandon this folly, Amira!"

She pushes the horse faster. Nothing I say will stop her now. Either I abandon her to this perilous errand, or I go with her and keep alive the only sibling I have left.

"Damn it." I race back to my horse, clamber into the saddle, and set off after her.

3

SOMETHING HAPPENED TO ATHEER THAT CHANGED HIM. I don't know what it was, and the mystery has bothered me since, like a sharp rock in my boot that I can't shake out. For years, he had been investigating the source of the monsters that plague the Sahir. One day, he returned from a long mission, and he was . . . different. I couldn't decipher how. He was the subject of a portrait who'd had his features altered slightly, enough to disconcert you, not enough for you to know why. He was intense, but then, hadn't he always been? Charming, funny, clever, devoting to any subject or person who interested him the utmost attention. It was something poisonous that seized his attention in the end.

One evening at home, he asked what I thought lay across the enchanted Swallowing Sands that protect our borders. I told him what the Council has taught our people for a millennium: nothing is beyond the Sahir. It is a cursed, magicless wasteland populated by scattered, savage peoples who would devastate us if they learned of our existence, and that of our magic Spice. Though I was serious, Atheer laughed to the verge of tears. I asked him what was comical about well-accepted facts. He sobered and said, "If the world is dark and you are the only one with a flame, what do you do?"

"Share it," I answered. He smiled, touching a scrap of paper to the candle flickering between us on the coffee table.

"Yes, Bright Blade, for light not shared is light diminished." He placed the flaming paper to the wick of an unlit candle. Together we watched it come to life, but I did not understand.

I don't understand the Forbidden Wastes either, but they puzzle me just as Atheer did. The land is inscrutable, every stretch of sand and stone exactly the same as the last, but somehow different, and new, and indecipherable. It's like trying to read a language composed of symbols that have all the familiar curves, dots, and dashes of Sahiran, and realizing in the same breath that it is not a language I know at all. Time loses its grip here, or perhaps strengthens in the secret way only it knows how. One moment is wet dye bleeding into the next, and crossing the enormous plain is easier and faster than moving from one side of a small room to another. Like wading through a dream. I only know time has passed when I look up at the sky and see the sun has declined.

Between two heartbeats, the mountains locked on the horizon leap up from the sands to envelop us. They resemble the curved bodies of giant sand serpents, their surfaces painted with brown and red lines, glass-smooth from millennia of relentless erosion. Raad's tracks dimple the sand along a pass threading between towering rock walls, leading us away from what is familiar and safe.

Amira and I travel side by side in grim silence. It swelters here, but my skin is bristled stork flesh, and she keeps rubbing her arms through the beige sleeves of her tunic. I do my best to focus on the tracks lest I lose them in this confusing maze. Earlier Raad's steps were spaced out with the rhythm of a galloping horse. Now they meander along.

Noticing, Amira points. "See how he's slowed? He must've neared his destination."

"He's an escaped horse, not a carriage driver going from Dahabi Bazaar to Afrah Pastry Shop." I tilt my chin to the late afternoon sky. "It's not long until sunset."

"Is it?" She gawks up too. "But how? It hasn't felt that long."

"This is why the Shields issue travel warnings," I say. "Monsters are spreading across the Sahir, but in many pockets, like the Wastes, their hold is especially strong. There's no telling how much farther off Raad is, and I am not eager to discover what lurks in these mountains at night."

"Then we need to be quick," she says. The passage ahead is too narrow for us to ride parallel. She moves to take point, but I stop Badr in front of her.

"This place isn't right. Don't you feel it? As if *we* are the ones being tracked."

She swallows, looks about us. "Perhaps. But Atheer told me once that fear is like water. If it is not contained, it leaches across any part of us it can, pooling in our lowest aspects and letting harmful things fester in its well. Maybe you're just afraid. Let's push on a little further."

She gestures for me to move. I don't. It's curious: despite our vastly different interests and hobbies, my sister and I were never contrary in childhood. Yet here we are, butting heads again. Arguing seems to be the only thing we do together anymore.

An eerie whinny echoes down the passage, interrupting our impasse. Amira's face lights up. "*Raad.* He's close. Hurry, we can continue on foot." She tethers her horse to a withered root poking from a fissure in the wall and takes her woven bag with her to the passageway.

"Stay here while I investigate," I say, fetching my lasso from my saddlebag.

"No. I'm not some low-rank Shield you can boss around."

I hop down and tether Badr. "Haven't you grasped how unsafe the wilds of the Sahir are yet?"

She makes a big show of shrugging. "We've not been attacked, and you're with me. As far as I'm concerned, I'm the safest I can ever be."

"I appreciate the vote of confidence." Sighing, I go over to her as I loop the lasso around my shoulder. "You said before that I don't talk to you. Well, let me tell you something, then. A few months ago, my squad leader received word from a small walled town out by the Jeyta Salt Flats. The town was being plagued by a ghoul that had abducted a local man mere hours before we arrived. The man's family led us to where the ghoul was lurking in the town's burial grounds. The creature was tall, about seven foot, but hunched over, its gray, leathered skin rippling with muscle. Vaguely human, except its wiry arms were so long, they could brush the ground when fully extended." I hold up a hand. "It had five fingers with long curving talons in place of nails, same on its feet. In its face, two red-yellow eyes glowing in the moonlight, a huge grin of razor-sharp fangs dripping with saliva. It had pointed ears, and lank strands of straight black hair falling around them. But for the rags around its hips, it was naked, and every time it drew a breath, its ribs strained through its skin." I stop in the passageway. "It killed and devoured the young man before we could stop it. Right before my very eyes. Do you know what a ghoul can do once it has killed you?"

She presses her body against the wall and whispers, "No, what?"

"Take on your likeness. One moment, the man it had killed was bones picked clean on the ground, hair and all. The mist rolled in, drifted aside a moment later. The ghoul was nowhere to be seen, but the young man was upright again. Living and breathing as you and I. But it was no man. It did not act as a man, could not speak as one, only howl. I killed it with one blow, for if you strike a ghoul twice, it rises again with renewed strength. But that young man? He died twice, and his mother did not forgive me for it. You think the Sahir is safe because you have not been hurt yet, but I assure you, many others have, and there is no end in sight to this war. It is a poison seeping across the land that we are barely beating back."

Amira stares down the passageway. "I'm sorry you had to endure that, Imani, that you even have to fight in this war, but I . . ." She draws a deep breath. "I will face what I must to save our brother's horse."

I take her hand again. "Please, reconsider, for your own safety."

"I'm old enough to make my own decisions," she says through an obstinate pout.

Yes, foolish decisions, I think, but I resignedly step past her into the narrow passage. The hungry sand sucks at our shoes, each of our steps sounding like a gasp. In moments, the nickering of our horses fades; the air settles, stuffy and tomb-stagnant. The world hushes save for the sigh of wind over the peaks, and the pebbles rolling off edges and bouncing down steep cliffs. It feels as if we are totally alone, the last beings alive in the Sahir. But we aren't.

Around the next bend, we are confronted by an archway carved from the stone, once barred by a rusted bronze gate now hanging open. Beyond it, a courtyard with a stone pond. Raad stands beside it, watching us.

"Yes," Amira breathes, rushing ahead. "See? I knew we'd find him."

I drag her back. It is not only the sight of Raad that gives me pause, nor the peculiar sense that he has deliberately led us to this place, but the place itself: an ancient dwelling cut from the rocks, once grand, long worn down by time's unrelenting hand. The opposite wall of the courtyard is a spectacular façade of helical pillars carved around an open archway. Elsewhere in the courtyard's walls, asymmetric windows peer out, and eroded staircases with spiral balusters meet caved-in doorways, though some remain open, beckoning to the mountain's secretive depths. Stone benches and urns bearing dead vines dot the cracked cobblestones around the courtyard's border. The only new thing is an inverse-conical messenger tower next to the pond, about half my height, constructed from wood and brass. When in use, the fragrant smoke of burning spices would waft from it in a sky-tickling pillar, catching the attention of messenger falcons who are trained to recognize the distinct scents from far away.

"That's out of place," I say.

Amira scrunches her face. "Why would someone receive letters out here?"

I don't want to know. And though I am impatient to secure Raad, our Baba, Qalia's most eminent horselord, taught me never to approach a runaway horse hastily, lest I spook it. I take a measured step through the gateway, then hesitate at the howl of the wind.

"Hold on," I whisper.

We wait, listening to the wind rushing through the channels and crevices of the mountains toward us, growing louder, clattering furiously as it stirs loose rocks. Suddenly it bursts across the gateway with the momentum of a thrust spear, dragging a swell of sand in its wake that obscures the courtyard from view. I step back, protecting my eyes with my hand as something emerges from the gust.

No, not one thing. Several. Immensely tall, shaped like people. But in place of flesh is throat-stinging smoke, shuddering and simmering, the wispy edges of their silhouettes licking the air in decayed tongues. Faces with hollow eye sockets, the slits of serpent nostrils, and no mouths.

Amira grabs my hand. "Are they . . . ?"

"Yes. Djinn."

4

THE TALLEST DJINNI GLIDES FORWARD ON A SHEET of black smoke. I hear rushing water; I feel a chill colder than any desert night.

"Leave," he hisses over the whining wind.

"Get away," I tell Amira. She digs her nails into my palm and continues staring up at the djinn. It is impossible to know how many there are. They keep flickering, doubling, and then scattering, before re-forming. The only constant is the one in the middle, floating toward us. I prize Amira's fingers off and shove her.

"Go, *now*."

She blinks several times and scrambles behind a nearby outcropping of rock.

"You do not belong here," says the djinni.

I draw the dagger strapped to my thigh, through which I am able to channel my magical affinity. With its polished hilt and watered steel blade, it is a precious family heirloom, a gift from Auntie when I joined the Shields and was initiated into the Order of Sorcerers. It is also the perfect weapon against djinn, who fear steel most. At the same time I draw it, I call upon the magic of the misra. Having had a full tea this morning, I feel it rush readily through my veins. The dagger glows white-blue and lengthens to a longsword. I point it at the djinn.

"Leave or suffer ruin by my hands."

Their malign laughter skates across the back of my neck, summoning shivers. "We shall see about that," says the leader.

He thrusts a diffuse arm of smoke; the arm hardens to a spear with a point so sharp, it need only whisper across my neck to steal my life. I dodge left; fabric shreds where the spear impales my cloak. The spear retracts and the djinn consider me keenly. Time stretches. Waits, almost, with bated breath in the lengthening shadow of suspense. Then it exhales.

The djinn descend upon me in a flood of smoke. One swings a lance at my chest. I duck as it slices the air above my head. I spring up and thrust the sword through the djinni's body, scattering wisps of smoke like frightened baitfish. The djinni's scream inflates in my skull, which throbs, yearning to fracture with the pressure. Distantly Amira groans in pain.

Another is on me, swiping with something resembling a claw. I sidestep the strike and put my shoulder into my swing, and sever the djinni's head from its body. The stump of its neck sprays inky black blood before the djinni crumples to ash. More and more emerge from the smoke around me, all sneering eyes and rolling laughter. I burn through them, and they keep coming, these rapacious insects swarming from the darkness around a torch. My blade is part of me, wielded as intuitively as my own limbs. It lengthens to a pole-arm when I need to slash in a circle; it shortens to a dagger when the gap between me and a djinni is too small. It impales as a spear and severs as a sword, the djinn crumbling to heaped ash around my boots. Using my affinity makes me feel whole, complete, as if I am ordinarily composed of fractured pieces and magic is the only glue that can seamlessly unify them. The misra courses through me, my magic surging when the blade changes and ebbing in the wake, gradually being spent. I pour my rage into the battle; it is all I've done since Atheer died. Harden my heart until I have become more steel than flesh. Fight my way from the wretched feelings I cannot defeat, the angry fear that my big brother abandoned me for reasons he didn't consider me worthy of knowing.

A djinni screams. The mountains groan, and fractures finger through the rock walls. Warm blood oozes from my nose onto my lips, from my ears too. I cut the djinni down, freeing my vision of the smoke. I turn to attack another, but only the leader remains, striking my weapon hand. A fierce burning takes up in it; my fingers spasm and I drop my sword. He extends a grotesque limb and kicks the blade away.

"No," Amira yells from her hiding spot. "Stop it, don't hurt her!"

"You will not pass, Djinni Slayer," he says.

"So you've heard of me." My longsword is discarded in the grit several meters away. I keep my arm down, but I stretch my hand as I mentally call to the blade. It's like reaching out to a lost part of myself. I am me, but I am also the blade, and both aspects seek reunion across this divide.

The djinni raises a spike primed for my heart. "Word of your savagery has spread far. Word of your death will too."

"One day," I say through clenched teeth. "For all who live must die." The sword shifts, turns slowly; the hilt pops off the grit. I thrust my hand out. The sword spears through the air and lands in my fist. "But today is not that day."

The snarling djinni drives the spike. I dodge and thrust my shining sword through his chest. He screams and drops like a curtain of silk, decaying to an ash mound. The wind stops howling; sand and pebbles rain on me in a dreamy whisper. I transform the sword to a dagger and sheathe it.

Amira sprints over as I collapse onto hands and knees. "That was the most *brilliant* thing I have *ever* seen! I'd be dead if it weren't for you."

Sweat slides off my face and splashes into the sand between my fingers, carving little pools. A drop of red joins them, then another. Amira kisses my forehead, hugging me so tightly, I think my heart is about to pop out of my mouth. I don't complain; this is the most affection she's shown me in months.

"The Djinni Slayer all right. Even that djinni knew who you are. Are you hurt?" She brushes the stray brown hair that has escaped my braid and examines me like a healer, with puckered lips and furrowed brow, first my throbbing ears, then my bloody nose.

"I'm fine," I say, peeling my glove off my hand. It is already blistering.

She steals a sharp breath. "That looks painful. Here." She pulls a flask from her bag and pours water onto the inflamed skin. I wince but gratefully keep it there until she is done.

"Thank you," I murmur.

She begins dabbing the blood off my face using a scarf, trying to catch my eye. "Why do you think Raad has come here? And how did he enter without being attacked by those things?"

I push up to my feet. "I don't know, but I want to find out."

We walk under the arch into the courtyard. Raad stands by the pond, watching Amira press her nose to the open top of the messenger tower. She recoils.

"I've smelled this incense blend before . . . in Atheer's room. Am I wrong?"

A passing breath confirms her suspicions. "No," I murmur, bending to examine the bed of burned coals at the bottom of the tower.

"And look at this."

She has found a chair beside the tower and collected something that was piled in the sand around it. I recognize the pale coils in her palm: wood shavings. Could it really be? Atheer used to carve statuettes in his spare time and gift them to us on special occasions. I have a small, lifelike lion at home, stuffed into the bottom drawer of my dresser because I can't bear to look at it. Even when resting, Atheer busied his hands with something productive. He'd sit on the back veranda in the evenings, fashioning an animal he had seen while out on a mission, curls dangling over his eyes, fingers deftly manipulating the carving knife as he lovingly poured his soul into the creation. He took many short hunting trips in the months before he disappeared. Were they really hunting trips, or pretexts to conceal his visits to this place?

I rake my gaze between the chair and the tower, imagining him in my mind's eye. "He sat here, whittling wood while waiting for a messenger falcon to arrive . . ."

"But why not do that in Qalia?"

"Perhaps he didn't want anyone knowing he was receiving

these letters." I start toward a silver lantern waiting on the ground by the main archway.

Behind me, Amira brushes Raad's mane. "You brought us here, didn't you? Hey, Imani, where are you going?"

"You have a tinder box in that bag of yours?"

She jogs over and places a box in my hand, peering over my shoulder at the entrance. "Do you really think Atheer went in there?"

I light the lantern with a match and raise it above my head. "Only one way to know."

We enter the wide corridor. Light washes over a vaulted ceiling, revealing motifs of date palms and reed bunches. The walls are engraved with faded scenes of the Sahir: grasslands, mountains, a dune sea. The corridor opens on a columned hall, but darkness cloaks the ceiling and walls, giving the sense that we are in an unfathomably large space. Fragments of broken columns litter the stone tiles at our feet. I carefully navigate the debris, scouring what little area the lantern reveals.

"I don't like this place," Amira whispers.

Neither do I. For each step I take, reason begs me to make it my last, but I continue anyway. Something far more forceful than reason is compelling me. Intuition, the same that has kept me awake many long nights since Atheer died, wondering if it could really be over. Now I sense it isn't.

A few moments more of cautious shuffling, and the light melts across a bedroll, an empty water jug, and a wooden chest on a rug pushed against the base of an intact column. The edges of my vision pulse as we creep over and kneel on the carpet. The fibers shift under us, releasing a breath of apple *shisha*, sand, and wood. Amira gasps.

"Atheer was here," she says, running her fingers over the rug.

I drink in the mélange in melancholic gulps. The same scent is embedded in Atheer's blankets and pillows, his tunics and *sirwal* still hanging in his closet back home, in the room nobody dares change. The room time forgot, the day of his funeral when Baba shut the door and it never opened again. I envision Atheer's smiling face, more lucidly than I have done in a year: his kind brown eyes tinged amber, the sun forever shining in them, his wild brows nigh perpetually raised in surprise, the impish grin that would steal along when he poked fun at Baba. And Baba loved him so dearly, the serious man would take his son's sly jibes with only a rumbled laugh. But I don't only see Atheer's face. I feel his magnetic presence too, here, in this place. *His* place.

I set the lantern down and sweep away the dust that has dared settle on the wooden chest's surface. My fingers shake; I fumble to unlock the hooked bronze latch and lift the lid on a small heap of items. At the very top is one of Atheer's smoking pipes, its polished wooden stem etched with the graceful stroke of his name's first letter.

"Baba gave that to him," says Amira; then she turns away and sobs into her hands.

There is no use fighting my grief. I hold the sweet-smelling pipe to my chest and weep. I am embarrassed to do it in front of my sister—me, the damned Djinni Slayer, bleating like a lost babe, but I do, out of sorrow so unexpectedly intense, my tears are neither strong nor spacious enough to convey it in its entirety.

It crowds in my chest, pointed and painful, rioting for a release I fear it will never find.

The other items I explore carefully, as if we have uncovered an ancient artifact and even the slightest breath or too-firm grip will crumble it to dust. We find quills and loose papers, a half-full inkpot, a wax stamp and tinder box, candles, a blend of incense for the messenger tower, a pouch of spiced tobacco, a half-empty snack bag of Atheer's favorite colorful *kdaameh,* even a few grains of misra heaped in the corners of the chest. I unroll a large scroll.

Amira leans in. "It's a map . . . I think."

But it is unlike any I have seen before. Instead of the Sahir, it depicts the world outside it, or at least part of it. A world I have never seen, nor imagined to be so much like ours.

"The Kingdom of Alqibah," I read aloud, tracing a finger along the gorgeously rendered details: the cities with lofty defensive walls protecting stately castles; the sprawling farmlands and tree-covered mountains, replete with fluffy clouds wreathing their highest peaks; the squiggly forking line bearing the name *Azurite River.* Weaving between towns and cities across this enormous landmass is a thick ribbon. The Spice Road. There is only one place in Alqibah not connected to the Spice Road: a sprawl of desert marked by a skull symbol and the word *Sahir.*

Amira cranes so close to the map, her nose brushes it. "Spirits, is that where *we* are?"

"It can't be," I say, though my churning gut feels differently.

Where our maps of the Sahir show villages, towns, and the city of Qalia, this one depicts nothing. And where our maps of the world beyond the Sands depict nothing, this one shows villages, towns, and cities. I stare at the map for a long time, trying to accept how the outsiders must see us—they don't. We are invisible, and the world is invisible to us. Since I was a girl, I have known that our people made an ancient, unbreakable pact with the Great Spirit: magic was granted to us to protect the Sahir, but protecting both magic and the Sahir required hiding ourselves from the outsiders. I know this, yet it has struck me now with a significance I cannot measure. Perhaps because what lies beyond our borders looks nothing like the harsh wilderness we are taught about from childhood.

It is painful, tearing my eyes from the Sahir's lonely corner of the map, but there are more things to examine. Atheer has made notations. Cities are labeled *fallen,* sections of the Spice Road are circled, arrows point at landmarks, others are marked with crosses.

I sit on my haunches, staring into the dusty dark. "This map cannot be real."

"It must be—"

"Think on what you are saying. This is not the outside world the Council told us of."

"I know, but . . ." Amira chews her lip. "Why else would it be made, and so detailed, if it were not real? And by whom?"

They are questions I cannot hope to answer with the scant information I have. "It's impossible," I mutter. "Just impossible." I pick up the scroll again. "If this map is indeed real, it means Atheer cannot have purchased it anywhere in the Sahir."

"He got it outside the Sahir, in this Kingdom of Alqibah?" Amira's wide gaze roves over the map. "But only the Council knows the secret paths through the enchantment of the Sands."

"Only the Council, and our brother."

At that, she leans in and conspiratorially whispers, "I must tell you something," as if there is any possibility we may be spied on. "Mama and Baba were once talking about how the former Minister of Land had to be replaced after he fell ill. Do you remember that? Atheer overheard them and told me the Minister wasn't ill; he was *corrupt*. A worker in the Sanctuary discovered he had been taking coin from the coffers, and that was the real reason he had to be replaced. Atheer warned me never to heedlessly trust the word of the Council. He said they lie to us about many things." I follow her gaze to the map. "I think this is what he meant," she says. "For some reason, he had to be secretive, but he still tried to tell us the truth about the outside world. We were taught that the Sahir is its own territory, but this shows we are part of Alqibah. And look. There are roads, cities, a kingdom. . . ."

We exchange a grim look before returning to the chest. I search it for answers, something to order this vortex of chaos dragging me under. I pull out a few scrolls. Letters, inked in a strange language, though it bears enough similarities to Sahiran that I can read it. They are addressed to Atheer and are only a sentence or two long.

The Empire has claimed everything north of Innareth's Shrine. Any who resist are caught and executed in the streets, which run as a red river, reads one.

Taeel-Sa is not long to fall. When will you return? Our supplies dwindle, and the others lose hope in your absence, says another.

Then, dated much later: *Your idea for another ambush has much support in the ranks. We will move forward with the plan when you return.*

The sheet quakes in my grip, and my breathing turns shallow.

"This is too much to be fabricated. It is proof Atheer went into Alqibah, proof that Alqibah even *exists*. And somehow, he found his way across the Sands and met outsiders."

Amira's hands tremble as she unrolls the last letter. She has scarcely finished reading it before she is doubled over, crying. More than any monster, more than death itself, I fear confronting the terrible truth waiting in that letter. But it is as she said: the truth is the thorn, not the rose, and I cannot hide from its wound forever.

I take the scroll and skim the message written in slanted script.

A.,

> *Three more of us were caught last night. Rima was among them. We desperately need a resupply of the Spice— and I need you. You know where to find me.*

> *Journey safe, my love.*

F.

"Spice," I whisper.

The letter floats from my slack fingers and comes to rest at my knees, but my gaze searches the space it just occupied. Every second I endure is anguish; I am trapped between walls I cannot see, fighting to expand my lungs to enjoy one full breath. I don't want to read that letter again and force myself to accept what it holds. Doing that will draw the already shattered sky down upon me and destroy the crumbling remains of my world. But what alternative remains? Leave and forget this ever happened? I would have an easier time swallowing the moon than banishing the memory of what we discovered here today. So it isn't with courage that I take up the letter—it is resignation. I reread it a dozen times, until the ink swims and fat tears veil my vision, and I could not read it again even if I wanted to.

"Spice. . . . You shared misra with the outsiders," I say, as if Atheer might hear me from the afterlife. "Why? Had things become so bad that you forgot everything that mattered to you?"

Amira bolts upright. "Bad? Didn't you read the letter properly?" She takes the scroll and points at a scribble in the top right corner. "Look."

I squint. "What's that?"

"The *date*. It's barely a week before he vanished. Don't you see what that means?"

I try to decipher it, but my mind refuses to cooperate, and my heart pounds my ribs, the war drum of my pulse growing louder in my sore ears, so loud that I am drowning in it and can hardly hear Amira or my own thoughts. She shakes me.

"Imani! Do you understand—"

"He's alive." I find my voice finally. "It means he didn't get lost or end his life in the Sahir. It means he is alive . . . in Alqibah."

"*Yes!*" she shouts, her unbridled joy echoing through the hall. She throws her arms around me, weeping, but these are the happiest of tears. "Our big brother is alive!"

5

AMIRA'S ELATION IS A WAVE CARRYING ME high—too high, dangerously so. This letter is not salvation—it is the mirage of an oasis, beckoning me not to safety but to death.

"Atheer *might* be alive," I say loudly.

She clasps my cheeks between her hands, mimicking Baba; he does it whenever he encourages me to be brave, bold, indomitable—to embody everything that has made our clan great for over a thousand years. The familiarity of the gesture only weakens me.

"Our brother is the cleverest young man in the Sahir," she says. "He is alive, out there, waiting for us."

I try to shake my head, but she is squeezing my cheeks. "Stop. You're raising your hopes on nothing but speculation."

"No, I have always known he is alive. Between us three exists an invisible thread stronger than steel. It connects us, and I feel in my heart and soul that I am still connected to Atheer's thread. This letter proves it." She studies my face, the deep red protest that must be scrawled over it. She sighs, releasing me. "You don't want him to be alive."

"Don't say that, please. Look around, Amira." I run my hands over the items scattered on the rug. Each is a baffling puzzle piece; none fit together. "Atheer had ink and paper; he had a messenger tower out there. He was sending people letters. Why didn't he ever send us one?"

Spirits forgive me for the light dimming in her eyes. "There is an explanation," she says tightly.

"Yes. He died long ago."

"You don't *know* that!" A thick vein bulges in her neck. "Until a moment ago, you didn't even know there are cities outside the Sands!"

I hold my hands up. "Assuming these maps are accurate, then Atheer was clearly not himself when he left the Sahir. And an un-well person cannot look after themselves as well as they should. We know he left for this Alqibah, but we don't know if he made it. If he did, we don't know if he survived the terrible violence these letters speak of."

"We also don't know if he died."

I raise the scroll between us. "Amira, he was sharing misra with outsiders. He knew we have a sacred duty to the Great Spirit to protect the magic from them. Instead he abandoned his family and people to *help* them! Does that sound even remotely like the Atheer we knew?"

She rubs her red nose. "It sounds like someone who needs our help, even if he doesn't know it himself. Someone who needs us to believe he is alive so we can bring him home to his family, where he will be safe." She wriggles closer. "You value reason, logic, things you can see—but just this time, hold on to hope. Please? We are bankrupt without it."

"Hope," I whisper. How is it possible for one person to feel so wretched? An intense fire has ignited in my chest, and it hurts to even speak. "I am only trying to prepare you for the very real possibility that he may be gone. I don't want to see you grieve him a second time."

Her gaze hardens, the warmth in her coffee-brown eyes frosting over. "Don't fret for me. You're the one who fears grieving him."

"No, I—I don't," I stammer quickly.

"You really thought that if you returned to duty so soon after he vanished, it meant you'd accepted his death? You were only delaying the heartache."

The fire blazes, pinching the air from my lungs. "That's not true," I choke out. But if it isn't, why can't I stem my tears?

"You act as if you are certain Atheer is dead, but in your heart, you believe he is alive. There was never any evidence to the contrary."

My pulse hitches. "Enough, Amira. I don't want to discuss this."

She takes my shaking hands between her warm, steady ones. That upsets me more than it should; my baby sister stands fast where I waver.

"You fear that if you commit to finding him now, you will be forced to learn his fate. And if he is dead, you don't know how you will deal with the pain, because you never really did. You returned to the Shields and pretended none of it happened and nothing had changed. You thought . . . Oh, *Imani*." Her voice cracks; I feel it splintering my heart. "You thought that if you never grieved him, you could never truly lose him. But don't you see? If you never grieve, you may never find him again either."

Her words distort in my ears. A dense, dark cloak cascades over me, as cold and oppressively shrouding as death's veil. It takes me fully, and before I know it, I am transported home to our sunny backyard, where I am three years younger with a heart so light, it soars. I am practicing sword stances for the Shields' candidacy exam; a baby-faced Amira lounges nearby, tweezing her brows in a handheld mirror. Soon she tires of that and takes to weaving flower crowns out of lavender flourishing in the garden bed.

"Princess Imani," she announces, traipsing over to me with a crown in her fingers. I am sweaty and dirty, midway through swinging my sword, but I bend anyway so she can place it on my head. Atheer is on mandated rest and helping Baba train a new horse. He comes down a side walkway that moment to fetch something from the shed.

"Ah," says Amira gladly, taking another crown. "And here is our future king."

He glances over with a cocked brow, but when he notices the flower crown, he solemnly lowers to one knee. "Imani, coronate me with the sword. It's only proper," he says, waving me over.

I roll my eyes, being far too mature for that, but I am chortling a minute later, gently tapping the sword to his broad shoulders. Amira lowers the floral wreath over his disheveled curls.

"All hail King Atheer," she says, and I ululate.

Baba comes round a few minutes later, mopping his sweaty brow with the tail end of his checkered keffiyeh. "Atheer, where are you?" he calls, looking over the garden, where Amira is brushing her brows with a fine comb and I am fighting my invisible foes again. Atheer bustles out of the shed, spare bridle slung over his shoulder, crown still adorning his hair.

"Got it here, Baba."

Baba's eyes round. "What's that on your head, Son?"

Amira and I peek at each other, our cheeks inflating with stifled laughter. Mischief gleams in Atheer's honeyed eyes.

"It's a new style, Baba. Haven't you heard? All the guys are doing it." He half turns to wink at us, then casually strolls up the side of the house, whistling. And dear Baba stares after him in comical confusion, scratching his bristly black beard.

The memory burns more than it brightens. Sorrow sears me to my edges, confused anger blisters and curls them inward, and I only know to scream for relief. How I scream, pained and hoarse, baying into the murky light while Amira holds me and assures me everything will be fine. I scream until my lungs ache and my throat burns and I am on the verge of retching. I scream until spots dance in my eyes and I no longer hear myself. When I stop to breathe, air howls in my tender airways and my head spins. I collapse onto my back, gasping, crying. Then, in the darkness, a foot falls.

The bitter smell of fire and ruin floods the hall; it soaks my clothes and skin. My tears cease; even my breathing abates. If it weren't for that smell, I would wonder if I were imagining things in my state. But that scent makes every warning bell toll in my head—something accursed is here, and close. In this very hall with us.

I jump to my feet and arm myself, Amira scrambling up behind me. I point my radiant longsword at the shadows. I still smell the monster, but it hasn't parted from the gloom.

"My, my, such an impressive blade." His voice is sharper than the sword. Oddly hypnotic. He must be a djinni, for no other monsters are so renowned for their eloquence—or their danger.

"I will find you, and when I do, I will end you." I position my body in front of Amira. "Pack the chest. Hurry."

She kneels and clumsily sweeps papers into a pile. The monster utters a laugh, as nimble and free as wind toying in an olive tree.

"And wielded by the infamous Djinni Slayer no less. So, you're Atheer's sister. It seems a rather predictable development now, given his magical prowess." He pauses. "The resemblance is truly uncanny."

I breathe faster, but I am more suffocated than ever. "You speak as if you knew him."

"I did, very well."

Behind me, Amira stops packing. I glance at her over my shoulder. "Ignore him. He lies; it's in his nature."

All djinn deceive with their speech. They try to convince us they are not our enemies, even though a millennium of historical accounts tells us the opposite. One of the first lessons I learned as a Shield was that it is better to cut off one's ears than listen to a djinni speak. Better still to kill it and never give it the chance.

This one sighs. "You are cruel in your ignorance. Do you believe your brother found his way here of his own accord? It was sheer luck he spent so much time in my abode unscathed? No, Atheer and I were friends. He even spoke of you during our conversations. His beloved sister Imani."

"Stop lying," I order. "You didn't know our brother; you're using the meager information you gathered from spying on our conversation to trick us. You are a fool if you think it will work."

Silence. Then, as calm as a summer's night, he says, "I know your mother, Zahra, is an Arch-Scholar in the Qalian Archives. I know your father, Muamer, descends from a famous line of horselords. I know your auntie Aziza is Master of the Misra. Remind me, were those details mentioned in your conversation?"

Amira slowly rises to her feet. "You really knew Atheer."

The possibility is nightmarish. I have faced many monstrous things in the wilds, but standing here, talking to this shadow that has done nothing but utter the names of my family . . . I am weak with juvenile fear.

"May we see you that we may talk?" Amira asks.

"Quiet," I hiss at her, but she appears at my side, reaching a blithe arm into the dark.

"Imani won't harm you. We are only seeking answers about our brother."

I steady my blade, bracing for a wicked thing to come springing out of the shadows. But it is a boy, about my age yet simultaneously ageless, who trades the darkness for the light. He is unnaturally striking, possessing a slim vulpine face, the commanding centerpiece of which is a pair of sleepy eyes under straight-dashed brows. They are ominously entrancing, fit to have been stolen off a striped hyena, black and impenetrable in that they do not speak anything of his nature, not that he is friendly or malicious, or even alive. Wavy ebony hair dangles playfully to his jaw, complementing smooth, brown skin reminiscent of sand basking under an afternoon sun. He has clad his slender frame in a simple but fine black tunic over midcalf-length black sirwal. And he is barefoot, a thin string of black beads adorning one ankle; in appearance, he is one simply lounging about at home on a day of rest.

"My name is Qayn. I mean you no harm, if you mean likewise."

"We don't mean any harm either." Amira has forgotten her fear, and I've no time to warn her that powerful djinn assume attractive forms they think will trick us into complacency. "How did you know Atheer?" she asks.

"I found him despairing in the Wastes. He had recently returned from a scouting mission in Alqibah, a place he was regularly sent by the Council since he was eighteen."

Something odd happens to my heart; I think it's turned sideways. "You don't know him at all, then," I say, with much less conviction than I want. But I am thinking of how noticeably long Atheer's missions became once he turned eighteen, and he started taking them alone.

"Our brother was a Shield," says Amira.

Qayn bows his head. "He was, and the Council knew his secret secondary duty—to routinely venture to and fro across the Swallowing Sands, reporting on what he found. Unlike their predecessors, the Zahim wished to be kept apprised of world affairs." Qayn juts his chin at the map on the floor. "Not quite the barren wasteland you envisioned, is it? They are peoples much like you. Related to you, in fact. You share ancestors."

"Lies." My sword brushes the front of his tunic. "We are different peoples."

He seems fascinated both by the blade and by me, and studies each as he speaks. "Yet you can read Alqibahi. It belongs to the same language family as Sahiran, did you know? The Alqibahis do not possess the Great Spirit's blessing of magic, of course." He flashes a dry half smile that dimples one cheek.

"Atheer was right," Amira says to me. "The Council was lying when they said nothing is out there."

I am suddenly recalling everything Atheer said and did before he vanished, reframing it with this new, terrible knowledge. The exercise only displaces me, Atheer having successfully wrenched apart my world and scattered the laws that preserve its order. I drift in his wake, caught in an updraft, longing for something to fasten me.

"So what," I challenge, pawing the sweat off my brow. "There are cities and a kingdom beyond the Sands. If Atheer was a Scout like you say, he knew that well enough. What does that change? The people in Alqibah weren't chosen by the Great Spirit like we were. They are cursed, and he should not have involved himself with them."

Qayn shrugs. "Atheer did not share your opinion. During one mission, he witnessed the arrival of the Harrowland Empire. As we speak, these foreigners are pillaging Alqibah and violently oppressing its people, all to control the Kingdom's lucrative spice trade. Spices power Alqibah, you see, in much the same way that misra powers the Sahir. They are the Kingdom's lifeblood, and so whoever controls the Spice Road controls the Kingdom itself.

Colonizers, the Harrowlanders are called—those who seize control over a land that is not theirs, often by force."

Amira paces beside me. "How could Auntie have kept the truth from us? We're family, for Spirits' sakes."

I cut my eyes at her. "Don't be ridiculous. None of this concerns us, and that includes Atheer—Scout or not."

"It concerns the Council, yes?" Qayn tilts his head. "Atheer informed them of the bloodshed he witnessed. He hoped they would lend aid to Alqibah—supplies, medicines, food. Anything. They selfishly decided not to."

"On what grounds?" Amira asks.

"That such an interference would upset the Great Spirit, and any large-scale movement of goods across the Sands could jeopardize your people's secrecy."

"And they were correct, you fool," I snap. "The outsiders are not our people, for us to be risking our oath and our well-being. I can only imagine what might happen if the Harrowland Empire learns of what grows at the end of the Spice Road, across the Sands, and what it can do."

"The same reasoning nearly ruined your brother," Qayn replies quietly.

I try to swallow the hard rock that has somehow lodged itself in my throat, but I don't have much luck. "Nearly?" I croak. "I daresay it succeeded."

"Perhaps." Qayn pensively looks off into the dark depths of the hall, revealing a pleasing, symmetrical silhouette. "The Council's apathy distressed him, left him hopeless. . . . He was attempting to end his life when I found him."

"Oh, *Atheer*," Amira whimpers.

I use my free hand to swipe the tears tumbling down my cheeks. "He didn't, though, did he?"

"No, I saved him. Brought him here, gave him shelter and water, a place he could return anytime he wanted to correspond with his allies in Alqibah."

"Allies? You mean the wicked outsiders who manipulated him into giving them misra."

Qayn considers me with a look that could freeze the Wastes twice over. "I listened to Atheer without judgment, and he treated me like a friend."

I am too furious to respond. Atheer was *my* best friend, yet he didn't talk to me about how he felt. He was influenced into choosing the company of outsiders and a djinni over his own sister.

Amira takes the crushed scroll from my fist. "This says he left for Alqibah. Is that where he would be now?"

"Yes. The last time we spoke, he said if your Council would not help the people in Alqibah, he would. He left to join the rebels in their fight against the Harrowland Empire."

My heart plummets into my heels. "Spirits, he is more troubled than we knew. Those letters seem to indicate he was making trips back and forth to Alqibah, transporting misra to the outsiders. They must be low on supplies by now. He might be readying to return to Qalia this moment."

Qayn scoffs. "Perhaps, but Atheer *did* steal a rather impressive quantity of misra from your Sanctuary over the years."

Amira's eyes bulge. "*Years?* That can't be right; we thought it was only a few months."

It is a marvel I am still standing under the weight of these revelations. "If he has been drinking misra without any breaks ever since, rational thought will be long beyond him."

"Hardly," Qayn sneers. "Atheer was an avid sorcerer, certainly, and his tolerance for magic was higher than I imagine is typical, but almost all the Spice he stole was hoarded and smuggled into Alqibah. Are you certain you knew him as well as you think?"

The question abrades me. I dig the blade into Qayn's neck, relishing the onyx dome of blood that pools around its tip. "Don't dare be so familiar, snake. Atheer wasn't your brother—"

"He was my friend."

"Plaything," I growl. "A vulnerable, misguided young man. And rather than encourage him to return to his family for help, you led him further astray. It amused you, didn't it, his pain."

"Did it?" Qayn replies in an ambiguous lilt. His gaze is impersonal, unyielding, like peering into a grave—and the soil never gives anything back.

"You must tell the Council about this right away," Amira says to me. "Only they know the way across the Sands."

I don't lift my eyes from Qayn. "Agreed. But a matter here needs dealing with first."

His lips stretch into a smirk; the slit resembles the two faces of a coin, alluring on one side, repulsive on the other. "I hope you don't mean me, Slayer. I am, after all, the only one who knows your brother's clandestine activities in Alqibah, the full details of which he divulged to me during our conversations. The Council may know the way across the Sands, but what then? Only I know who he interacted with and where to find them—a group of rebels led by the young woman who signs as *F,* if you are curious." He unveils a smug grin of fatally sharp canines. "You see your predicament now, don't you?"

"What do you mean by that?" Amira asks.

"Shields are duty bound to the Great Spirit to kill every monster they come across," he answers. "But if Imani does that, Atheer will be lost to you forever."

I adjust my sweaty, blistered grip on the hilt. "Tell me what I need to know, and I will spare your life."

He roars laughter, heedless to his indented throat scraping the blade. "Oh, a *very* likely tale, from who else but the one they call the Djinni Slayer. No, I rather think *I* am the one making the threats and offers here." The shadow of something malevolent passes over his beautiful, angular face, writhes like a snake in his eyes before prowling on. "I would like to check on my old friend in Alqibah, so I will take you to your brother's last whereabouts. You may think you can find him without me; I promise, you cannot. The rebels he is holed up with are most practiced in concealment, and I imagine they would be reluctant to give up their prized sorcerer when he is the only hope they have."

"You can't take me anywhere," I say, seething. "The enchantment over the Sands confines monsters to the Sahir, whether you know the secret paths or not."

"Correct," says Qayn, nodding. "I cannot cross them unaided. But with the mediating help of a human such as yourself . . ."

My brows meet; a drop of sweat slides down my temple. "You . . . you're asking to *bind* to me?"

He waves a hand. "A tale as old as time. In the happier ones, the djinni willingly binds to the home, granting wishes to the chosen master in exchange for safety and material comforts."

I studied the ancient ritual in my first year with the Shields. Binding monsters to oneself, sometimes against their will, dates back to the early years of our people's magical history. But once the Order of Sorcerers was established and all magical practice consolidated, the Council forbade the act as contrary to our oath to the Great Spirit. Djinn, like all monsters, are enemies of the Great Spirit, but it is especially dangerous keeping one close for any length of time, given the creatures' proclivity for deceit.

"Binding is outlawed," I say.

"Don't believe the lies; it is entirely harmless to you," Qayn counters easily. "Though, I am rather ashamed to admit I am not powerful by any measure. You will have little magical benefit commanding me, but I will give you my liberty and a promise to aid you in your quest. Once you have saved your brother, release me."

I squint. "Why are you offering this?"

"Well, perhaps by then you will have become convinced of my goodwill and truly honor your word to spare me. I quite like living, you see?" He stifles a rogue smile. "And I suppose this *is* a ripe opportunity to see beyond the Sands. It is exceedingly dull being trapped in the Sahir for as long as I have been."

I can't help but laugh through my contempt. "Of course, everything you do is in service of your own whims. You manipulated my brother for fun, and now you want to bind to me so you can go sightseeing around Alqibah." I jab the blade. "If you refuse to tell me what I need to know, I will force the answers out of you and have you begging for death's mercy."

"Silly girl, I never speak idly," he drawls. "Torture me, and I will flee, leaving you no choice but to kill me, and me no choice but to take your brother's last whereabouts with me. Best of luck retrieving the information from wherever it is I will go."

"Alard," I supply. The underworld, the Land of No Return.

He grins, but his eyes are untouched obsidian. "Alard, then. You have my offer, Slayer—it is the best you will receive."

"Take it," Amira says instantly.

"What? It's not safe—"

She tugs my tunic. "Neither is Atheer! He is out there fighting a war, for Spirits' sakes. We must ensure he is all right."

"What do you mean, *we*? You're not getting involved—"

She stomps her foot. *"Ugh,* this isn't the time, you stubborn donkey. If you're too much of a coward to do it, I will. Qayn, bind to me."

I yank her back. "Stop at once. As your elder, I forbid you."

She claws me off. "Being older doesn't give you claim over my free will. Qayn, tell me what I need to do—"

"Amira," I bark, but Qayn interrupts my fury.

"I appreciate the offer, my dear, but I will only bind to Imani."

I don't know whether to feel triumphant or aghast; neither appeals. Amira is crestfallen.

"Why?" she asks.

He smiles at me, and something deadly devious dances in his eyes. "The Djinni Slayer binding a djinni to herself is an irony I cannot pass up."

My hand burns with the urge to kill him, but I must grudgingly consider his offer. "How can I trust you're being truthful?" I ask.

"If I am not, unbind and kill me. But I speak the truth, Slayer.

Under your blade, I have nothing else. And if I am not mistaken, you have nothing else either."

"Curse you," I hiss. The devil is right, what choice is there? He won't tell me what I need to know otherwise. I could kill him and lose the answers; I could free him and watch him disappear into the Wastes. Will I deny Mama and Baba the joy of being reunited with their son again? Or Amira, who has never given up hope that he is alive? What of me? I haven't slept a full night since Atheer left, not gone a single hour without thinking of him. If he is dead, nothing will change. The pain I have dammed for a year will break the levee and drown me, and I will pray to emerge on the other bank with a lungful of air left. But if there is any possibility Atheer is alive, it is my duty to pursue it. Great Spirit forgive me, but I will break a thousand laws and risk my life if it means I can finally put the pieces of my broken family together again.

"Fine," I say, looking back at Qayn. He smirks, and Amira exhales a sigh of relief. "On one condition: you will be bound to an object I possess, not to my soul. Do not argue. I will not have you peering through my eyes and listening through my ears to everything happening around me, nor having access to my thoughts and memories. At least in an object, your perception will be limited."

He gives an exaggerated sigh. "You trust me so little. I suppose that will be acceptable."

"Good. I have an oil lamp we can use—"

"I will only bind to your blade."

I start to chuckle. "Why? Does the self-confessed 'powerless' devil fancy himself above dwelling inside a common oil lamp?"

"Forgive me for not wishing to remain captive to a misplaced oil lamp for eternity." Qayn lowers his voice until it slinks along. "But that blade, as old as Qalia itself—it never leaves your side, does it? Your affinity for it has become legend, even amongst my kind. I'd wager you keep the blade on your bedside while you sleep."

"Under her pillow," Amira amends.

He finds that greatly amusing, and a chuckle rolls deep in his chest. "Even better."

All my love and fear for Atheer, and I am still tempted to drive this sword through the devil's belly. *"Fine.* Your terms are satisfactory. Hurry up before I change my mind and my hand slips."

He reveals a small, private smile. "Lovely. Repeat after me."

I reluctantly recite the words back. "Qayn, to this blade I bind your soul, your liberty to command and release at my will. Do you accept?"

He runs his bright red tongue over his lips, seeming to prolong the moment only to worsen my nerves. "I accept."

A great squall stirs, howling in my ears and lashing my cloak. The warmth drains from the air, frosting my sweat and blanching my exhalations. I hold my ground, squinting as the sword burns a blinding light. Glassy black swallows the whites of Qayn's eyes; then a pulsating shadow cloaks him and he loses all form or semblance of a boy. The shadow collapses and spirals around the sword's length; it shakes in my fist; my heart thrashes; the squall rises, my eardrums throbbing with its protest. I fear the storm will never abate, but the shadow absorbs into my blade with a snap. Warmth returns, and silence reigns.

I lower the sword to my side, breathing fast. There is only a moment's relief before my shoulder aches from holding my arm up for so long.

Amira creeps over. "Is it done?"

I turn the sword in my hand. "I don't know. . . . Qayn, I command your presence."

"My presence you shall have."

We jump, finding him next to us, hands dug into his pockets. "The binding was a success."

I train the sword on him again. "Prove you were truthful. Who is the woman calling herself *F,* and where did Atheer go to meet her?"

"Her name is Farida," he answers, eyeing the blade with palpable disgust. "She lives in the capital city of Taeel-Sa. Your brother confessed to me he had fallen in love with her."

"Infatuated people can be manipulated into doing anything," I say defensively. "Where in Taeel-Sa did they meet? I need details."

Qayn swings his head. "Mm, no. In the interests of my survival, I think that is enough for now."

"You vowed you would help me."

"And I will, in time," he croons softly.

"By the Great Spirit, I ache to kill you," I say through clenched teeth.

He laughs with vexing ease. "And you wanted me to believe you would spare my life."

"I command your absence, devil," I snap, adding in a grumble, "Though, better the order was a spike lodged between your eyes."

"*Go away* will suffice, Slayer." In a blink, his smirking face is gone.

The sword burns bright, then pales, shortening to a dagger and sapping the last of my magic. Goose bumps scurry across my skin; with them comes an overwhelming desire to leave the Wastes and never look back. I sheathe the blade and kneel on the rug, throwing items into the wooden chest. Out of the corner of my eye, I notice Amira watching me. I secure the chest under my arm and head to the corridor.

She follows with the lantern swinging in her hand. "Are you all right?"

The lamplight paints our distorted shadows on the walls. They melt over each other; in one glance, we are two, but in another, we are three. I fight the irrational fear surging in me—I control Qayn, not the other way around. He is bound to my blade, not me, not my soul, and he will only be bound until I save Atheer. Then I will kill him and fulfil my duty.

"Imani?"

I clear my throat. "I'm fine. We have little time to waste."

6

LASSO RAAD AND LEAD HIM AWAY FROM THE COURT-yard. The stallion follows easily, seemingly satisfied that he has achieved what he set out to do this morning. Back in the passageway, I stow Atheer's wooden chest in Badr's saddlebag and start the journey home.

"I am so happy," Amira sighs as we trot down the winding path. "Our brother is *alive*. It's a dream come true."

The words *may be alive* are on my tongue, but I keep them unsaid. This all certainly feels unreal, and I don't know what to do next. Do I mourn the long, lonely nights I endured, or rejoice for the bright days ahead? A blissful future where Mama and Baba no longer argue, Amira has grown out of her rebellious streak, and no one gossips about my brother because he is back and as brilliant as ever. But other worries, ones that thrive in the shadows, hastily tow me back from the lofty heights of this daydream. They ask me to fear for Atheer's well-being; they coax me toward an undercurrent of anger that demands answers for his actions. Grief is a puzzling thing, the most; it is mangled love persisting in spite of the world's best efforts to hinder it.

"I still can't fathom that he was sharing misra with outsiders," I say, a long time after we've left the mountains' confines.

Amira shrugs. "Atheer has his reasons. He has seen a world we haven't."

"But our brother isn't like that," I say. "Something must be gravely wrong. He must have suffered some kind of—I don't know—internal crisis."

Her peach-hued cheeks inflate with a snort. "If by *internal crisis* you mean he fell in love with someone and wants to help them, then I agree."

"This isn't a joking matter." I swat a sand fly off my thigh, and accidentally crush it. "His 'falling in love' with an outsider is only further evidence. Our ancestors hid us away because we were chosen by the Great Spirit. Us, not the outsiders. They couldn't be trusted with the magic, meaning Atheer wouldn't give them misra unless he was manipulated into it." I nod steadily. "That is precisely what I must tell the Council. They always listen to reason, and Auntie will advocate on his behalf."

Amira's cheeks deflate. "I suppose."

I lean over in my saddle toward her. "We *know* our brother, Amira. This is not him. It isn't."

But she doesn't say anything to that. We quietly cross grasslands tinged gold under the late, indolent sun. This is one of the few monster-free zones left in the Sahir, where things are safe and familiar. On the near horizon stand Qalia's majestic walls, overgrown with climbing jasmine and rosebushes. The sight of the city, like a graceful, spontaneous sprouting of the earth, stirs an intense melancholy. Atheer has been trapped in a war that isn't his for a year. An entire year he hasn't seen home. I wonder, does he glimpse Qalia in his dreams? Are we there too?

"Imani." Amira interrupts my reverie. "I want to join you in finding him."

I tug the reins and slow Badr. "You can't."

"Why not? Atheer isn't your brother alone."

"I didn't say he was."

"So why, then?" Her gaze darkens. "You want to avoid my company, don't you?"

The untethered upset I've felt all day suddenly coalesces. "This has nothing to do with your company, Amira," I say sharply. "Recovering Atheer will involve journeying through dangerous parts of the Sahir, crossing the Swallowing Sands, entering cursed lands. You're not equipped to deal with any of that. At your age, I was already in the Order of Sorcerers, not skipping school any chance I had—"

I bite my tongue. Amira's lower lip wobbles, and in the fading light, I spot fresh tears in her eyes.

"Forgive me," I mumble thickly. "I say it only for your safety. Please, go home and don't speak about this. I will explain the situation to Mama and Baba when I finish with the Council."

"Fine," she mutters, hanging her head. "Sorry I'm not as perfect and accomplished as you." She takes Raad's lead rope and canters toward the city, weeping softly.

"Amira, that's not what I meant," I call after her, but she has already gone.

I watch her leave, my heart galloping in my chest. I want to catch up and apologize for my harsh words, but an angry voice inside wishes she would stop being so defiant all the time and upsetting our already distraught parents. Things are difficult enough at home without her causing trouble, like wanting to come on this dangerous mission. If my being harsh encourages her to be better, then perhaps it is the right thing to do. This person Amira has become is not really her, just as the Atheer we learned about today is not really our brother. But if I can bring him back home, the true Amira might return too.

That's what I repeat hopefully to myself, over and over, yet the words do little to soothe my guilt or make things feel any less out of control.

I WAIT UNTIL AMIRA HAS FALLEN out of sight before continuing to Qalia's open gates.

Wrapped in gold, they stand in a huge archway of black-and-yellow stone, their surrounding ramparts manned by archers in gilded helmets and cerulean cloaks. The city within is no less wonderful or welcoming. Smiling people go about their evenings in every pristine street; the crowded coffee shops and shisha lounges hum with laughter and the music of *ney* flutes, *darbuka* drums, and oud guitars. The bazaars are still open, illuminated by magical light and sustained on the shouts of merchants selling everything from fresh fruits and meat to dates and nuts, silk carpets, perfumes in colorful glass bottles, and much more. Between them stroll Sentries of the City Watch, longswords hanging from their belts. They patrol in pairs, but their manners and conversations are easy. Qalia has always been safe, with very little crime. A city of plenty.

"This place is too much," Atheer said when we were walking to the bakery to buy *manakish* for breakfast one day. I asked what he meant, but he only shook his head. I understand now. He was comparing Qalia to the places he saw on his scouting missions, where this foreign Empire plunders and tyrannizes. It pains me that he couldn't see the impossibility of the situation, that he could not win the war on his own, nor was it ever his responsibility to try. His place is here, as a celebrated Shield in the blessed Sahir with his people and family who love him. And it is up to me to bring him back.

I make my way to the Sanctuary, but instead of taking the route that leads to the barracks, I follow the winding, grass-lined Noble Path up to the main entrance. Constructed in white marble, the Sanctuary sits on a hill overlooking Qalia, and it is the heart of our magic, governance, and knowledge. An enormous marble-and-gold dome marks the center portion of the Sanctuary, with smaller domes over the wings. Illuminated minarets guard each corner, giving Sentries vantage over the grounds and city beyond. At the very back is a garden that houses the ancient misra tree. The magic was a mercy bestowed upon us by the Great Spirit to help us fight the Desert's Bane, a malevolent monster that terrorized the Sahir a millennium ago. After we defeated the Bane, the Great Spirit allowed us to keep the tree and its magic, both as a reward for our sacrifices and so we could continue as custodians of this sacred land. I have never been permitted inside the garden—only Zahim may enter—but it is grace enough to spy the tree's tallest branches peeking from behind the gold dome as I approach.

A Sentry standing outside the front gates raises his gloved hand. "Halt! Identify yourself."

"Imani." I stop Badr in the circle of light issuing from a brass lamppost. "I must see the Council."

His squinted glare relaxes and he bows his head. "Ah, Djinni Slayer, welcome. The Council is in a meeting—"

"This is urgent." I nod at the Sanctuary. "Send word to Aziza Zahim."

"Right away." He rushes inside the gates, leaving the other Sentry to catch my eye and smile nervously. After a few awkward moments, she risks conversation.

"I never had a chance to say this before, but I am very sorry for your family's loss. Your brother was a great man."

My chest trembles. *He is a great man. Is.* I hope.

The first Sentry returns and gestures me inside. I pass through the gates, stable Badr, and cross the rambling gardens with Atheer's wooden chest tucked under my arm. The round-top Sanctuary doors are open and waited on by another pair of Sentries. One accompanies me into the entrance hall and left across the white tiled floor. Despite the number of times I've been inside, I still eagerly drink in the rich details. The Sanctuary's interior is a masterpiece of archways and keyhole windows; honeycomb, vaulted ceilings; sprawling rooms of silk carpets and cedar furnishings with inlaid marble; elaborate tile mosaics that span the walls of spacious halls; and long arcades upheld by columns of stucco relief fashioned into date palms, wrapped in gold leaf and precious jewels. There is no room or alcove that does not smell of myrrh and aloeswood, gathered fresh from one of the many gardens, and the entire Sanctuary is brightly lit by decorative silver lanterns that hang from the ceilings in complex arrangements.

The Sentry rings a bell hanging on the wall outside a pair of closed doors. A moment later, he opens one and ushers me into a circular room. Its walls and domed ceiling are covered in murals depicting significant historical events, such as the Sanctuary's construction by sorcerers who mastered stone affinities and could lift enormous blocks with their minds alone. A long, rectangular table in the center is piled high with platters of fruit and syrup-glazed *baklawa,* steaming cups of black coffee, and tall, jewel-encrusted goblets of juice. Seated in six ornate chairs around this feast are the Council of Al-Zahim.

At one end is Auntie Aziza, Master of the Misra. The imposing, stony-faced man towering over the table beside her is none other than Bayek, the Grand Zahim and Taha's father. Yasmeen occupies the next chair—the Minister of the Land is as renowned for her power to manipulate the rain as she is for the curly brown hair she keeps shaped in a tall beehive; tonight, a sparkling veil is pinned to it, draping to the floor in a sheer wash of slate and blue beads, reminiscent of a storm. Peeping over the table beside her is Treasurer Aqil, a small, wizened man with a powerful affinity for gold (evidenced alone by the thick rings concealing his quick hands). Occupying the last two chairs are Nadia, the Grand Scholar; and Tariq, the Grand Physician. Even in countenance, they are eminent individuals, variously attired in silk and linen dresses and tunics, finely woven robes and camel-fur *bishts,* and all manner of gold and jewels. I have seen them at events before, but never so intimately, and never after having broken the Council's sacred law regarding magical bindings, let alone carrying a djinni into such a hallowed place. Rather than feeling excitement, I am sick with nerves, and an irrational fear that somehow they will be able to detect my wrongdoing.

Auntie rises from her chair. She is a beautiful woman in her midthirties—extraordinarily young for a Zahim—slender with tawny skin, a cascade of wavy brown hair, and the same umber eyes as Mama, though Auntie's possess a foggy wistfulness.

"Come forward, Imani," she says.

I shuffle over to the table, uncertain who to look at. Armed with a gold-plated fork, Aqil is chasing a fat red grape across a platter; Yasmeen refills her goblet with fresh *jallab;* Tariq is glancing over some papers; and Nadia is polishing her slim spectacles using a silk tissue. Only Auntie and Bayek give me their undivided attention, so I direct my announcement to them.

"Forgive me for interrupting your meeting, but I've come with urgent news."

"Oh?" Auntie settles into her chair again. "Please, tell us."

I draw a deep breath. "I believe my brother may be alive in the Kingdom of Alqibah."

The room is thunderously silent. Above, the magical light flickers in the crystal chandelier; one after the other, the distracted Zahim look up at me.

"Speak again," Auntie prompts in a controlled voice.

Another breath. "I have evidence Atheer may be alive in the Kingdom of Alqibah. I found some of his belongings in a place he frequented in the wilds." I tap a sweaty palm to the wooden chest. "His horse led me there."

My heart pounds harder as the Zahim exchange confused glances.

"The wilds? His horse?" Aqil says through the thick white mustache curtaining his mouth. He scratches at his thatch of hair; as always, it refuses to remain neatly contained beneath his black silk keffiyeh. "I am afraid I do not follow, my dear."

Bayek is staring at me too intently for comfort. The stern warrior supposedly possesses an unrivaled lightning affinity. He can create an electrical barrier capable of repelling sword and arrow, and in his days as a Shield, he wielded a solid beam of energy that cut many a giant sand serpent in half. The veracity of such tales is questionable, but there must be some truth to them, given that Bayek is both Grand Commander of the Noble Sahiran Armed Forces and Grand Zahim, chair of the Council. He is an intimidating individual, one I must respect whether I want to or not. I bow my head only to break eye contact with him.

"Forgive me, Aqil Zahim. I am not explaining myself well." I pause and run through the story I have concocted before trying again. "One of Atheer's horses was lost outside the walls. I tracked it to a place Atheer must have been using during hunting trips. There I found this chest, containing letters he exchanged with outsiders from Alqibah. I gathered from them that Atheer was manipulated into fighting the Harrowland Empire alongside rebels he met during his scouting missions, as well as sharing some of his misra with them."

I place the wooden chest on the table. The Council marvels as if it were made of solid gold, but Auntie is the first to move. She opens it and slowly rifles through the scrolls, then pushes it aside and drops her head into her hands. To my shock, her shoulders heave on a thin sob. I have never seen her weep before, and perhaps neither have the other Zahim, because suddenly the table is chaos.

Yasmeen leaves her chair and comes around to console her. "This is troubling news, certainly, but what matters is that your nephew is alive."

Aqil cranes his short body to peer past Bayek. "Yes, think of your sister. She will be elated!"

Mousy, puckered-face Nadia tuts. "Indeed, this has been a trying time for Zahra and Muamer."

"And for us." Aqil knits his bushy silver-flecked brows. "It was a terrible shame to lose such a talent as Atheer. Oh, but the young can be so vulnerable to manipulations."

"The war shook him," says Tariq, to which Nadia responds, "He had never seen such a thing before," and Aqil adds, "His excessive use of the misra could not have helped matters," and Yasmeen exclaims, "Certainly not with accursed outsiders in his ear," as she returns to her seat.

On they go like that, chattering over the scrolls. Bayek watches Auntie with something disturbingly close to amusement. I've no doubt he perceives her tears as a sign of weakness. It is irrelevant that Auntie is Master of the Misra, overseeing all sorcerers and magic-related issues; it is irrelevant that, prior to her election, she spent several productive years as an architect and inventor, and is the greatest source of magical light throughout the Sahir, having mastered the sun affinity. All he sees is a vulnerability he can exploit. She has always insisted they are on good terms, but I have never been less convinced of that fact than now. And Taha's antipathy for me must stem from somewhere. What better source than venomous words uttered in the privacy of their household?

Suddenly Bayek swivels his gaze to me, and it is as if he is looking through me. His eyes are not like Taha's, big, jeweled, and sedate. They resemble a crow's, small and calculating, and a scheme is being hatched within them, I am certain.

Auntie's coughing mercifully draws his attention. She comes over to me, dabbing her cheeks with a silk tissue. "Forgive me, Imani. Of anyone, learning the truth would have been hardest on you." I mask my confused frown as we hug. "My wise fellows, please accept my sincerest apologies on behalf of my nephew." She sweeps back to the table, her shimmery dress trailing along the rug behind her. "I fear the stress of his responsibilities made him susceptible to the outsiders' influence."

"An apology is unnecessary," says Aqil. "No harm has come of the matter."

"That we know of." Bayek does not look up from the letter he is examining. He has a deep, commanding voice and a gift for crafting a fatal edge to each word.

Aqil's mustache curls around his pinched lips. "Do revive my memory, Bayek. Have we received reports suggesting outbreaks of *hysteria* over magical sightings? Are the outsiders running through their streets screaming about sorcerers?"

Nadia and Tariq drop their gazes to the table, but Yasmeen boldly titters into her goblet. "No, I don't believe I've heard such things."

"No, we have not." Aqil folds his arms. "Atheer imprudently shared misra with several lowly rebels, most of whom have been strung up by their necks already. I understand you are of a military background, Bayek, but please, do leave the fear-mongering in the barracks where it belongs. It is not helpful to this discussion."

I am astounded by diminutive Aqil's pluck, even more by his acerbic remarks. Does his defense of Atheer stem from his closeness to my family (several of his kin have married into the Beya clan), or his personal dislike of Bayek? After all, Bayek is something of an outsider himself here; he does not descend from a long, esteemed lineage, like the other Zahim. The Al-Baz clan have always been humble hunters and pelt sellers, who only rose in social prominence thanks to Bayek's accomplishments in the armed forces. Everyone in this room would know he wasn't initially selected for the position of Grand Zahim, but the Elders' first choice met with intense public outcry. Supposedly some clans felt Bayek had been unfairly passed over in favor of a less experienced candidate from a better clan. Mama speculates that the furor was drummed up by the Al-Baz clan itself. Whether that is true or not, the uproar caused the Elders to change their selection and name Bayek the Grand Zahim. The furor this caused was so great on both sides that a few outspoken critics of the Elders' new selection even met untimely fates in the subsequent months, though it was never conclusively determined that they were the targets of foul play. And given that Grand Zahim is a lifetime position, the Council—and the Sahir—is now stuck with Bayek. But if the Grand Zahim is offended by Aqil's comments, he excels at hiding it.

"Stealing misra, abandoning one's post, sharing the magic with outsiders—Atheer has committed grave crimes, and grave crimes require graver punishments," he says.

Aqil makes an affronted choking sound. "Be reasonable, Bayek, will you? The boy was experiencing emotional distress."

I spot a narrow window of opportunity. "Respectfully, my Grand Zahim, I must agree with Aqil Zahim. These actions are atypical of Atheer. He was deeply troubled in the months leading up to his departure. He requires treatment, not punishment."

"I daresay the boy's trying experience in Alqibah has been punishment enough," says Yasmeen, "but certainly, he will hear stern words if we can return him."

"Perhaps a lengthy suspension from duty too," suggests Tariq.

"That seems fair," says Auntie, and all but Bayek are in agreement.

"Need I remind you, Atheer knows multiple paths through the enchantment," he says. "It only takes one outsider crossing the Sands with his help to endanger the entire Sahir, as well as the peace and security we have worked hard to maintain for a millennium."

"Hyperbole," Aqil mutters.

"The brush fire that consumed the town of Ayadin began with a single, insignificant spark, did it not?" Bayek coolly retorts.

He is right. If Farida manipulated Atheer into sharing his magic, is it implausible to think she might ask to enter the Sahir too? What of her family, and those of the other rebels? They may seek shelter from war in the Sahir, and if they do, they could be spotted and followed by other outsiders—by the Harrowland Empire even. I shut my eyes as hot sweat leaps onto my skin. *Great Spirit help you, Atheer.* I need to save him before he unwittingly does something that threatens us all.

"I know where Atheer went, sir, and where he will be, if he is indeed alive," I say, moving toward the table. "He met a young woman named Farida in Taeel-Sa. She leads a group of rebels, and she is the one who sent those letters. The best thing for all of us is that he is brought home immediately."

Without lifting his narrowed eyes from me, Bayek pushes his chair back and stands. He resembles a column now, tall, straight, and impassable. "You are offering to go after him."

I bow my head. "Yes, sir. Atheer is misguided and may be prone to rash behavior, but he trusts me. I will convince him of his folly and return him to Qalia. You have my word."

Bayek stalks behind the other Zahim. "And I'm to take your word on face value, am I? I'll leave the security of the Sahir to your promise, shall I?"

It makes my skin crawl how similar in manner he is to Taha. Or rather, how fastidiously Taha has been molded into the spitting image of his father.

Aqil heaves an irritated sigh. "Reluctantly, my dear, I also do not think it wise that you embark on this trip."

"I agree," says Yasmeen, and Nadia and Tariq nod.

Numbness seeds in me, slow but steady, in my extremities first, then rising up my limbs. "Why?"

Bayek turns his broad back to me; I hear papers shuffling on the table. "You lack training, experience, and the correct constitution necessary to safely complete the mission."

"Correct constitution," I echo slowly.

"And you are too close to the situation. Others will be sent in your stead." He pivots and points at a quill in an inkpot beside a sheet of paper. "Write Farida's whereabouts, everything you know. A team will be dispatched in the morning to retrieve your brother."

My shoulders rise and pitch. I struggle to hear the other Zahim over my labored breathing.

"Do not worry, my dear. Atheer will be returned safely," comes Aqil's distorted voice.

"I will personally see to his treatment," Tariq offers.

"Yes, a period away from the Shields would be both remedial and an opportunity for Atheer to reflect on his mistakes," says Yasmeen.

The numbness has spread across my entire body. "Please—" I whisper.

"That was an order, Shield," Bayek says.

As I shamble toward the quill, my fingers inadvertently brush the hilt of my dagger strapped to my thigh. Moments later, deep hatred has leapt off it into my fingers and soared up my arm into my chest, filling me with a raging fire. I slow to a stop and speak before I consciously realize what I am doing.

"No, sir, I will not tell you where my brother is."

A tangible tension swallows the room, making the luxurious space feel stuffy and cramped.

Bayek glares down his strong nose at me. "Refuse again, and I will have you arrested."

An apology comes rushing up my throat. I quickly place my hand on the hilt again, stealing the resentment that must belong to Qayn and using it to steady myself. I have come too far down this path to abandon it now, sacrificed too much to the Shields to have Bayek treat me like an incompetent warrior; I have spent too many sleepless nights grieving Atheer to be turned away from the door to salvation. Atheer is *my* brother; his absence created fractures that are trying to swallow *my* family—if he is alive, I must be the one to save him from the chaos he is lost in. I must restore order to our world.

"Nobody else knows his whereabouts but me," I say.

Bayek turns sharply. "Won't you intervene, Aziza? Your ill-mannered niece is trying to threaten us. Has she no shame before her aunt?"

"Leave her out of this." I don't even need to touch the dagger now. This defiance is all mine.

"What do you want?" Bayek growls at me.

I force myself to face him. "I am not asking much, sir. I only want to bring my brother home."

I swear lightning crackles in his dark eyes. "It is your fate, Shield." He sweeps his black, gold-trimmed bisht and returns to the table. "You will not go alone, and you will answer for your contempt on your return."

The river of defiance surges. Grand Zahim or not, does Bayek really believe he has standing to punish me for wanting to save my own brother? My clan helped *build* this city. My clan was on the very first Council a thousand years ago, facts he would do well to remember if he wishes to maintain his tenuous foothold here. I am so sorely tempted to voice this cruel warning that I have to bite my tongue.

Bayek jots something on a paper and hands it to Auntie. "Briefed and geared first thing in the morning," he mutters.

Tomorrow. I expected to leave soon, but hearing him confirm it . . . my rib cage suddenly houses a dozen fluttering shrikes.

Auntie stiffly leaves the table. "I will have them meet at the barracks at dawn. Come, Imani, I will escort you out."

7

I EXPECT AUNTIE TO SHOW ME THE DOOR. SHE ASKS ME to accompany her deeper into the Sanctuary instead. I expect her to scold me for my impudence during the long walk, but she keeps silent, and soon we emerge in a place I have never been: the Garden of the Misra.

I stop on the marble path, slack-jawed. The ancient tree is easily as tall as a minaret; despite it being regularly stripped for Spice, the smooth brown trunk is pristine, its gold veins gleaming in the moonlight; its boughs are handsome and evenly proportioned, supporting elliptic green leaves on which silvern light frolics with the fluidity of water. The tree occupies the center of a garden that has, in parts, been left long and unkempt in nature's delightfully wild way. Elsewhere it reveals the thoughtful mark of a human hand: stone paths meander between manicured beds of flowers and precisely shaped hedges; ornate stone benches are arranged near fountains spouting water in mesmerizing patterns and wrought-iron lampposts from which bloom perpetual light—the creation of a team of sorcerers who work under Auntie to maintain light throughout the Sahir year-round. Between the hedges peek granite statues of archers, falconers, scholars, and that is only what I can see from where I stand. A melodious whistle vibrates the air; my gaze is drawn to a blue-and-purple oasis bird with trailing feathers as it sails overhead and comes to rest somewhere in the misra tree. And though it is just a tree, it is not. The Great Spirit's magic emanates from it, invisible but tangible. This is the beating heart of the sacred Sahir, land of magic and prosperity; it is the sun, the moon and stars, the sands, grasses, the mountains and rivers, the heat and chill, the diverse birds and beasts. All of it, I feel in the soil under me, in the air, in my soul. And I am moved to tears.

"It is beauty beyond imagining," I say on a low breath. I look up at Auntie. "Why have you brought me here? I am thankful, but I thought only Zahim are permitted to look upon the tree. And after how I behaved before the Council . . ."

"I have permitted you to look upon it," she says in a tone that does not invite questions. She approaches the tree in long gliding steps, pulling her sheer veil loosely over her hair. The crystals embedded in its length catch the light; she seems to be wearing a swathe of the stars. Her gaze is as distant as they are.

"Today is a significant day for you, Imani. You glimpsed what exists beyond the Sands, the civilizations and the people within them. The Spice Road too, upon which disparate cultures trade spices and other goods: silk, horses, steel, art. Conflict. For those in what we call the 'cursed' lands, the sight of magic is life-changing. The things we do without second thought are to others the actions of divinity. And the magic *is* divine, gifted to us by the Great Spirit, though I fear we easily forget this and rarely appreciate it. For us, the people of magic, it is the truth of the cursed that shakes our core. The truth of uninhibited poverty, pestilence, war."

Truth. Atheer spoke of it that last time—he said the truth is worth risking everything for. What did he mean? I wish I knew, but I turned my back on his conversation for fear of discovering how troubled he had become. Is that why he took counsel from Qayn, because I wouldn't listen? I should have. I could have intervened and helped him see that his generosity and compassion were being exploited by the outsiders. All the times he guided me to the right path, and I never returned the favor. It is my fault he left, dissolved in the haze of heat like a mirage, never to be seen again. It is my fault he is in danger.

"We have never had to concern ourselves with such plights, for we are capable of acts like this." Auntie snaps her fingers and pulls together a swirling ball of light. "Records tell us the Council a millennium ago heeded the Great Spirit's warning and feared the destruction that would befall us if the outsiders learned of our magic. So—" She grasps the hovering light in her fist. "The most extraordinary sorcerer cast a powerful enchantment over the Swallowing Sands, trapping monsters here, and save for a person precisely following one of the secret paths, the Sands would induce terrible confusion, dooming travelers to wandering and death. The enchantment severed the link between us and Alqibah—indeed, the world. Our people were assumed extinct in the Sahir, our society never connected to the Spice Road." She closes her fist and extinguishes the light. "We were forgotten, considered the stuff of myths, alongside djinn and ghouls."

"We must remain forgotten," I say. "We shouldn't even send Scouts into Alqibah. We have nothing to learn from the outsiders, and as unfortunate as their situation is, we have no capacity to help them either. We have our own troubles to worry about." My chest pangs as I imagine Atheer in that strange land by himself. I am suddenly itchy with impatience; tomorrow can't come soon enough. "Being amongst them, seeing their violence and war, it broke something in Atheer. I only hope Grand Physician Tariq can heal him."

"Perhaps seeing the Kingdom of Alqibah will affect you too," says Auntie.

"No." I cut the air with my hands. "I have the 'correct constitution,' despite what Bayek thinks."

"I have never doubted the goodness of your constitution." She considers the fireflies twirling between the tree's boughs, the oasis bird preening its luxuriant wings. "We endeavor to shape the world, Imani. But now and again, the world succeeds in shaping us."

"If we let it. Magical practice centers on forming a strong will and imposing it on the world through our affinities. You taught me that."

She shuts her eyes as a breeze drifts through the garden, bending grass and bough to its rustling song. "Very good. But an iron will has no power—"

"If it is not shaped into a sword. I know."

"Or a shield, should the circumstances call for it. Never forget, my niece, that all life is sacred. If we can, we must lay down our own in defense of it. Come, I have something for you." She smiles, though I must look as witless as dirt.

I follow her back into the Sanctuary and up a lonely spiral

stairwell. On the landing, she unlocks an ornate wooden door into a shadowy room. It does not remain so for long. As she gracefully moves through it, the stained-glass globes strung overhead imbue the room with light. They reveal a circular space walled ceiling-to-floor in dark bookshelves. But Auntie owns so many books that even valuable, ancient-looking tomes are stacked on her cedar desk, between quills, inkpots, and piles of parchment. The tall, narrow window behind the desk has the best view in the entire Sahir: it overlooks the Garden of the Misra. Even the moonlight dancing through it shimmers as if made of crushed diamonds, and the wind wafting the white curtains brings the subtle perfume of jasmine, roses, and *magic*.

I stop my dirty boots at the edge of the fine purple rug. "Your office is beautiful, Auntie."

"And cluttered." She flashes me a dry look on her way to a chest of drawers.

I sweep my eyes over her desk, recognizing one of the open tomes. "Mama was reading that not long ago."

"Ah, yes. Zahra has been researching our clan's lineage. She believes there may be ancestors of historical significance we have not yet discovered." Auntie clears her throat. "I expect you will want to inform her and your father that Atheer may be alive in Alqibah."

"It's only right." I falter, the thought having only just occurred to me. "They didn't know he was a Scout."

"No. The Scout's identity was known only to the Council. I regret to admit I kept Atheer's appointment to such a new and perilous position a secret from my own sister."

I catch her sad frown before she turns to the chest of drawers. I edge closer. "You mustn't be hard on yourself. You had no choice."

"We always have a choice, Imani," she says curtly. "Tell them what you must; they have suffered in ignorance long enough. Tomorrow I will answer my sister's wrath." She shuts a drawer and returns, clutching something. "I do not know what awaits you on this journey, but a lamppost in the dark is often all one needs to find one's way." She places a crystal vial in my palm; it looks more like a star freshly plucked from the sky.

I admire the coiling white orb housed within it. "What is this?"

"Undying light, bound by a thread of my soul. If ever you are lost, release the light. It will guide you true."

My eyes widen. "But if you created this, it means you have mastered animancy."

It is the rarest of magical practices, to combine one's soul with one's affinity for any number of purposes; the most commonly known is to leave a lasting, complex enchantment over something, as is the alleged case with the Swallowing Sands.

"*Mastered* is a strong word," says Auntie. "This alone took years of practice, study, and meditation. And a bit of luck, I think."

"But what of the risks to you, to your soul?"

She rests a hand on my shoulder. "Take heart, Imani. The soul is neither static nor finite; we feed it our entire lives through our choices. Injustice shrinks one's soul; generosity expands it. Acts of selflessness fortify it."

I thrust out the vial. "Still, I cannot accept this, Auntie. It is too precious."

"I have no use for it." She closes my fingers around it. "After all, light not shared is—"

"Light diminished," I whisper. "Atheer said that to you too?"

She smiles, but her gaze is far away. Without another word, she leaves the office and descends the stairwell. I slide the vial into my pocket and hurry after her, back through the Sanctuary and across the gardens to the stables.

"See you in the barracks at dawn," she says when I am climbing into Badr's saddle. "Good night, Imani."

I ride to the gates, my insides twisting into mysterious knots. Auntie waits in the shifting shadows under a cypress tree, watching me go.

8

NIGHT'S COOL ARRIVAL HAS USHERED MOST people indoors. I trek through the gently lit cobblestone streets with only a tangle of thoughts for company. Binding Qayn's soul to my dagger allowed me to feel what he felt—a byproduct of the forbidden practice—but rather than keeping distance from the devil, I delved into his emotions, undoubtedly sharing some of my own with him. I drew us closer.

Auntie's puzzling words only intensify my worries. Her riddles circle my mind, begging to be solved, and the crystal vial weighs heavy in my pocket. She would only give it to me if she thought I would need it—if she believed I may get lost. Strangely, I think I already am.

I take the long route home, hoping the city's quiet will soothe my troubled mind. Qalia is something out of a dream. In appearance, no luxury is spared: gold, silver, and a rainbow of precious jewels adorn alabaster statues, highly decorated archways, and columns. The cobblestones are cut perfectly and laid flush; the buildings are constructed from solid sandstone and marble and are unmarred by age or wear; the laneways are fragranced with incense trees; the water in the fountains flows pure and free for all. They are blessings made possible by the Great Spirit's gift of misra—blessings I never truly appreciated before today.

I never fully basked in the peace of my home either. I try to do it as much as I can now, on the eve of my departure from this oasis. I ride past my childhood school, then the bookshop I used to walk Amira to in the afternoons, the hospital where Atheer had his dislocated shoulder mended after he took a tumble from Raad, the beautiful garden where we threw Amira's twelfth birthday party.

I arrive on the hill overlooking the lantern-dotted burial grounds. This is the closest I have come to them in a year. I didn't even attend Atheer's funeral; I couldn't bear looking upon the wall where his name is etched and accepting he was truly gone. I stayed home, feigning illness, but I was there later when Baba shut the door to his bedroom. Pressed up against the corridor wall, heart in my throat, watching the warm ribbons of sunlight that turned his room sleepy-afternoon-yellow slowly vanish from view. Feeling the corridor—my body—steep in cold shadow. Half expecting him to appear and stop the door, grinning as he revealed that this whole situation was a misunderstanding. That he was here all along, playing one of his jokes. But the thud of the door arrived with the finality of a sealed crypt, and I was left in darkness. It still sounds in my ears, that thud, now, during sleepless nights, sometimes when I am out on a mission and the Sahir is too quiet. It haunts me. And I still cannot go down to the burial wall, though it may not matter anymore. If I succeed in bringing Atheer home, we can go down there together and rub his name from the stone. Then it will be as if nothing ever changed. The door to his room will open again, and the warm sunlight will flood the corridor, the home, all of us.

I find the gate to our family's large stone villa already unlocked. I stable Badr and go up to the front door, but it is a long while before I have the courage to venture into the entry hall. Everything is as expected: frankincense burns in a brass urn, a lantern flickers on the console table, and my parents are in the midst of an argument. As I remove my cloak and boots, the commotion in the courtyard ceases, and Mama appears at the door.

"Finally, you're home."

With their dark hair and eyes, Mama and Auntie are often mistaken for twins. They could not be any more different in disposition: where Auntie is pensive, Mama is firmly rooted in the practical. Auntie plumbs the misra's most enigmatic depths; Mama researches and writes about how magic changed Sahiran society on an everyday level. And while I usually find their physical resemblance comforting, if not comical, it unsettles me now. I am reminded of Auntie's vial and cryptic words, and Mama is behaving even more curiously than her sister was: she steps into the lantern light, and I realize she's been crying.

"Mama, are you all right?"

She pulls me into a tight hug. My insides pinch even tighter.

"What's happened?" I ask. "Please, tell me."

"I forbid it," she says thickly. "No more missions. You have done enough, Imani."

I know she is referring to the Shields, but don't know what has spurred her. Initially both my parents supported my joining up, but since Atheer's disappearance, Mama has been opposed. I overheard her once telling Teta that the reality of losing a child changed her mind, and she couldn't survive losing another. Baba, on the other hand, encourages me. My exploits as the Djinni Slayer are integral to his Saturday morning conversations at the barber and coffee shop; he tells anyone and everyone about me, and owing to our clan's fame, people are only too happy to listen. My parents are different like that. Baba openly acknowledges his son's "death" for the perplexing tragedy it was. Mama is quiet on the subject, and only cries when she thinks none of us are awake or around to notice. Baba doesn't cry at all, although sometimes I catch him gazing into the distance, and I think he is reminiscing about his golden boy, all the times they spent together, praying, hunting, working the gardens, rearing the horses, smoking shisha, and discussing politics. Wondering where his son went, and where things went so wrong. He is about to find out.

Sniffling, Mama tugs me through the door into the open-air courtyard. In traditional Sahiran architecture, our villa has few street-facing windows; instead the home turns protectively on this courtyard, its heart. It is in a nearby alcove where we entertain guests; it is here where we draw fresh water from the well by the tiled fountain; it is here where we break fast, at the large dining table set amidst stone arches and citrus trees that were planted when Teta's mother was a girl.

Seated at the dining table are two figures. Teta, Mama's mother, a petite woman who peers at me through Atheer's same warm brown eyes. The other is Baba, and with his barrel chest, swarthy skin ruddy from a life training horses under the Sahiran sun, and the fierce scar beneath one eye he got from a falconer's bird when he was a boy, he is the very picture of *tough*. Simsim, our dog, curls at his feet, but perks an ear when Baba stands to greet me.

My heart pounds as I approach him. Red threads the whites of his eyes—he's been crying too.

"What's going on, Baba?" I ask, though instinct has me scanning the courtyard for Amira's specter. I spot her at the second-floor window overlooking the courtyard, gazing down at me, showing neither smirk nor scowl. *Why?* I wish to call out. She readily broke my order to keep this a secret. I dread discovering the level of detail she shared with our parents . . . if she mentioned Qayn.

"I must hear it from you." Baba's thick brows rise in the center, his carob-brown eyes searching me. "The Kingdom beyond the Sands . . . and Atheer . . . is it true?"

The courtyard is as still as a painting. Mama hovers by the fountain; Teta's wrinkled fingers stop counting prayer beads. I look back at Baba, and everything in me folds. I rush forward, and collapse into his waiting arms. "Yes, Baba, all of it."

Mama conceals her face with her hands; Teta's misty eyes look to the stars as she gives a silent prayer of thanks. To my surprise, Baba laughs loud and victorious, his broad chest quaking against mine.

"My mighty boy lives! And my brave daughter will bring him back to us!" He plants a kiss on my forehead, but the joyous moment is cut short.

"Imani will do no such thing." Mama pours a glass from a jug of water and mint leaves on the table and shoves it into my hands. "I will not lose another child to those cursed lands."

I stand between my parents, sipping water very slowly, even though my throat is parched. But I have this silly notion that if I am too busy drinking, I can't be dragged into their argument.

"Zahra, please," says Baba, shuffling after her as she begins setting the table. "Who else will go if not Imani?"

"Anybody else. Imani is a child—"

"She is a Shield."

Mama slams a plate down, shaking the table and almost up-ending the jug. "Yes, and it is unbearable enough that she risks her life fighting this never-ending war while everyone else puts their feet up, instead of figuring out *why* the monsters keep coming, *why* the waters are drying up. She will not enter another meaningless war. I will see to it that my *irresponsible* sister and that oaf who calls himself Grand Zahim send the best Swords to save our son from the mess *they put him in*."

"Come now," Baba implores, pinching his fingers together. "It is not appropriate that a stranger is sent in the stead of Atheer's sister. What would people say?"

"People won't say anything. This situation is to be kept secret; it is the least the Council can do for us. How dare Aziza steal my boy and throw him into danger without my consent?"

"Calm, my girl, calm," Teta soothes.

It is futile. Mama is the angriest I have ever seen her; it is almost perplexing that steam is not whistling from her ears yet.

"I will not calm down. Aziza must explain herself. And so help them on that Council if *any* have the cheek to question why Atheer has behaved as any young, confused person would in his situation."

I shoot a glare at Amira still skulking by the second-floor

window. If only she had waited for me to come home and explain, this row could have been avoided, and my parents wouldn't be speaking as if Atheer being alive is a confirmed fact. I look back at them.

"There is no need to argue. The matter has been settled with the Council. I am leaving tomorrow as part of a group."

"No!" Mama gathers my hands. "Do not misunderstand me, my girl, please. I am grateful to the merciful Spirits that my beautiful Atheer is alive, but this is not your responsibility, and neither was it his responsibility to investigate the outsiders to satisfy the Council's—my *sister's*—curiosity. If that is a problem with the Council, I will march up to the Sanctuary at dawn and order that bigheaded fool, Bayek, to assign someone else."

"That isn't the problem, Mama." I bob on my heels. "I *want* to go."

"And I want you to stay. It isn't safe, Imani. Those lands are called 'cursed' for a reason. *Please.* Look what happened to your brother."

All at once, I am horrifically tangled up inside, like forgotten yarn left knotted and jumbled in a bottom drawer. It will burden Mama if I leave tomorrow, but I must be the one who brings Atheer home. There were too many times I turned my back on him that I must make up.

"Forgive me," I say weakly. "I must be the first person Atheer sees. It will be a great comfort to him, and me. Please, let me go, Mama."

Tears slide down her face, tears I want to catch but can't.

"Then know this," she whispers, "if anything happens to you or him, I will never recover. *Never.*" She hurries across the courtyard and vanishes inside the kitchen, taking my broken heart with her. I make to follow, but Baba stops me.

"Let me speak to her, Imani. You are doing the honorable thing by your family and your clan. Go, tell your sister to come down for dinner, eh?" He glances at the second floor. "I'll have a word with that one later."

"Yes, Baba."

As I drag myself up the stairs, he enters the kitchen and shuts the door behind him. It does little to muffle Mama's hoarse shouts, nor can I ignore Teta murmuring prayers over her beads again. I sprint the remainder of the way upstairs. Being with the Shields may be dangerous and lonely, but at least out there I am not a length of rope being tugged between the two people I love most.

The second-floor corridor is empty, the door to Amira's room closed, just like Atheer's at the end. I don't bother to knock on hers; I fling the door open and let it crash against the wall. My sister's room is arguably the most lavish in the villa. *That's fitting*, I think angrily, *given how selfishly she is behaving*. A four-poster bed inlaid with crystals stands by a desk similarly adorned and dangerously laden in expensive books she hasn't opened for a year; beside that, a cream-painted wardrobe bursting at the joints, stuffed full of fine clothes she hasn't worn in a year either, then a bookshelf, similarly burdened. A makeup-smudged mirror rests against the wall, its outer frame of pearls coated in dust. My sister is curled up on the windowsill, occasionally concealed by lacy curtains swelling and waving in the night air. Compared to the room, she is painfully cheerless in her black dress.

I shut the door behind me. "You could have waited."

She shrugs, gazing down at the fig trees instead of at me.

"Damn it, Amira, you defied my order just to upset me." I drag a chair to the window and plonk down in it. "When will you give up this disobedient act? It's not you—"

"Not me?" She laughs, tilting her head against the window-pane. "Like you know who I am."

I could argue and curse until the sun rises, but what good would that do? A trip into Alqibah will take me weeks, if not months—months of Amira causing trouble for my parents. I have to try a different tack with her.

"I know you are my sister. You love reading fantasy tales, clothes, makeup; you love school—"

"I don't love any of those things," she snaps.

I sigh, sliding down in my chair. "Then what do you?"

"What does it matter? You don't need to pretend to care about me now that you're leaving." She twists away and rests her knees against the window.

"Where has this come from?" I exclaim. "I have always cared for you. I care that you're upsetting our parents and ruining your life."

"Oh, *ruining*. I'm sure. As if someone in our clan couldn't easily pull strings and fix everything for me. Nothing I do has any consequence."

My lips drift apart. Surely she is saying these outrageous things to incite a rise out of me. Surely she doesn't mean them.

"Listen to me, Amira. I understand you were acting out after Atheer's death, but there is a chance he is alive in Alqibah, and if he is, I am bringing him home." I pull my chair closer. "You do not need to fight the world anymore. Everything will return to normal soon, and once it does, you will wish you could pick things up where you left them."

She laughs again, barely a bitter rasp. "You worry me, Imani. How can someone so accomplished be so naïve? Life isn't a strip of steel you can bend to your will. Things change. *People* change. Accept that, or one of these days, I promise, something will upset you terribly and you won't know how to deal with it."

I lower my confused gaze to the rug. My body is still, but everything in me moves anyway. I've become a container for the river, and it's washing about, trying to knock me off this chair.

"I may not think or act like you, but that doesn't mean I don't have something of value to contribute," Amira says. She turns toward me and dangles her bare feet. "I am coming with you tomorrow."

Honest to all the Spirits, I would have a better response negotiating with a brick wall. I shove my chair back and stand up. "Do you even listen to me when I talk, or do you simply wait until you hear silence to open your mouth?"

"Are you describing yourself?"

I clench my fists. "We have been *through* this, Amira. The answer is no; it is not safe."

"I can follow your group," she insists. "Atheer is my brother too; it is my right to see him."

Fury possesses me, marching me up to where she perches on the sill. "No, it is your *duty* to obey your elders. Fulfil your duties, and you will earn your rights."

Her breathing quickens to a frenetic pace; she reaches for me. "*Please,* Imani. You might need me out there."

I push her hands away. "I *won't*! Your presence will only endanger me, and your absence will only hurt Mama."

She sweeps away a tear, shrugging again. "It won't be any worse than how she feels about you leaving. She and Baba only care about you and Atheer anyway. You're both perfect, unlike me." Her voice breaks, her posture sags. She looks ready to fall off the sill.

My chest pangs, and I quickly coax her into a hug. "Hey, hey, Mama and Baba love you, as do I. If we didn't, we wouldn't care if you went to school or sold onions by the side of the road. Please, Amira, give me your word you won't follow me, and you will do your best to improve things here. For me."

"I won't follow you," she mumbles after a long moment. "I will stay here and go to school. Promise."

Her surrender is relief beyond measure, but I am careful not to look too glad. "Thank you. Come, dinner will be ready."

For once, she doesn't argue. We join our family at the table downstairs, but despite the day's good news and Baba's attempts at conversation, the mood remains deflated. Mama keeps her bloodshot eyes down; they avoid me even when she is spooning *bamya* into my bowl. I don't taste the ordinarily delicious okra stew and hardly register time passing.

Later I float up to my room and lie down in my cold bed. And though I shut my eyes, sleep eludes me. I have only my thoughts, ceaseless and unforgiving in the subjects they are willing to explore. Atheer, out there. The strange boy in the stranger world, the lion without his pride. I wonder what he has seen, what visions haunt behind his eyelids at night, whether he can sleep or if he has no choice but to stand watch during the dark hours as I do. But most of all, I wonder if I will make it to him in time, or if it is already too late to save any of us.

"Atheer," I whisper to the dark. "Hold on."

9

A STRANGE, RESTLESS DREAM PLAGUES MY NIGHT. I find myself walking barefoot in a shady, lush walled garden nestled within a magnificent city of white stone; sunlight shimmers between the foliage of a mighty tree, landing in a warm dapple on my face. I am happy and at peace here, listening to the birds sing, enjoying the balmy breeze that ushers along the aroma of frankincense. But in flashes, the garden succumbs to a hot, raging fire, the day turns to a bitterly cold night, and in my happiness's stead festers a lethal resentment. Upon waking, there is little time to ponder the meaning of the dream. I must bid my family goodbye before dawn, and though I fear Mama will be cold, she holds me tighter than she ever has before.

"I cannot convince you to stay," she whispers tearfully into my ear, "and I will fear for you every moment. Please, be safe, Imani. You have burned me deeply, but you are my daughter. You will always have my love."

I take my leave shortly after that; if I don't, my guilt and homesickness will destroy the small courage I have left. I ride up to the Sanctuary with a full heart and heavy head, wondering if today is the last I will ever see my family.

Auntie Aziza greets me at the gates. Although she presents well in a formal, beige belted tunic, her drawn face is somber. "Did you manage any sleep?" she asks as we follow a cobblestone path through long grass.

"Little. I take it you didn't have much luck either, Auntie."

"Rather difficult to rest one's mind, given the circumstances." She glances at me. "How did my sister take the news?"

I wince, remembering Mama's ire. "Not well," I admit.

Incredibly, her expression hardly changes. She nods and says, "The group assigned to the mission is assembled in the barracks."

I frown at a black falcon soaring overhead. "Already? The briefing was scheduled for dawn."

"They wanted to squeeze some training in first."

"They?" I ask, still following the falcon with my eyes. It is too big and distinguished to be a messenger bird, more like one used by beastseers.

"Scouts, like Atheer," Auntie answers, drawing my puzzled attention. "You see, after he disappeared, I suggested we choose another Scout, but the Council had to acknowledge that the stress of his missions coupled with the isolation of his role likely contributed to his disappearance. We decided to train a group of three Scouts this time, rather than one. They will be accompanying you." She clears her throat. "You should know them, actually. . . . The group leader is Bayek's eldest son, Taha."

I stumble over my own feet and go sailing for a nearby hedge. Auntie grabs the back of my tunic and pulls me upright.

"Are you hurt?"

I clumsily straighten my tunic. "No, no, I'm fine. Did you say *Taha*?" To my misery, she nods. "Taha," I repeat to myself. It avalanches upon me, this abhorrent realization that I must venture into cursed lands with someone who plainly dislikes me, and I must rely on him for survival. What a laughable concept. I'd fare better relying on an empty pistachio shell. And given how little Bayek seems to think of me, I am certain Taha will obsessively watch me for any rule-breaking, like my conferring with a djinni I absolutely should not have bound to my dagger. Reflexively I brush a hand over the blade's hilt. A shiver snakes up my arm in response, and for a sprawling moment, I am wading through a sea of foreign, conflicting emotions. Anger, pleasure, impatience— the will to bide my time for as long as the sun burns. . . .

"Bayek put Taha forward as a candidate, and we found him suitable," Auntie says, interrupting my reverie.

"You found *Taha* to be suitable?" I narrow my eyes. "Be honest, Auntie. The Grand Zahim threatened a riot if the Council didn't elect his son."

She frowns. "Not at all. I can only imagine your skepticism stems from not having witnessed Taha for yourself."

I am unexpectedly cross at that. *My* auntie, Master of the Misra, impressed by Taha like everybody else in this city, as if he is the only accomplished Shield who exists. I run a restless hand along the nape of my neck. "Well, no, truthfully we only shared theory classes. *Ugh,* but why *him,* Auntie? Why not me? I am more than qualified."

"And so is he." She opens a gate for me. "The remaining Scouts are from his regular squad."

My jaw cannot physically drop any lower than this. Auntie obliviously continues past me.

"Yes, after Taha was selected, he proposed putting forth his own candidates, given the unit must work cohesively in a very stressful environment. We found it a suitable solution too."

I stomp after her. "How wonderful that it turned out so swimmingly for all."

"Well, as the proverb goes: the tree who heeds the typhoon endures the longest," she replies mysteriously.

I don't get the chance to query her meaning. The double doors of the sandstone barracks are pulled open by junior Sentries in leather armor, allowing us passage through a covered hall onto the quadrangle. It is already busy with training Shields. I follow Auntie between them. As soon as they notice the Master of the Misra, they bow and respectfully part.

She slows her pace and nods at something. "There is your group."

I follow her gaze to the archery range. A lone figure, tall and powerful, fires arrows from the range's farthest point. As each arrow effortlessly splits the center of its target, another is already drawn from the quiver and nocked. Keenly observing from a nearby post is the same sleek black falcon I saw earlier. The disparate links suddenly connect, and I realize the ebony-haired young man behind the recurve bow is Taha, and the falcon is his mindbeast. The impressive display leaves a sour taste in my mouth, so I shift my attention to a young man and woman locked in a fierce duel a few paces away, their longswords clashing loudly.

"That is Taha's cousin Reza." Auntie nods at the wiry midtwenties man with the half-shorn hair, a thin braid trailing down the nape of his neck. "He qualified in the candidacy exams a few years before Taha. He has a most impressive affinity for earth. And she is Feyrouz, though she prefers to be called Fey. Her affinity is for fire."

"Yes, I know her. *Unfortunately,*" I add under my breath as I study the pretty girl who is slightly younger than Reza. Bronze, blond, and aggressive, Fey accompanies each strike with a haughty "Ha," but never is she unsteady on her feet or imprecise in her posture. Confident in all things, including when she insulted me in the tea room yesterday morning.

Noticing Auntie's arrival, Taha slings the bow over his shoulder and whistles; the pair sheathe their swords and line up by his side.

"Taha, Reza, Fey, I'm sure you've met Imani before," says Auntie as we approach.

I am better with a blade than all three, but that doesn't stop me from feeling small and threatened, like a hare between hounds. I force myself to wave. "Good to be properly acquainted."

"Likewise," says Reza. Fey only nods while considering me from head to toe. Judging by her puckered lips, I have not met her standards.

"Shall we?" Auntie takes the fore and leads us into the blockish Abishemu Hall, named after a founding Shield. But rather than joining his friends, Taha lets them pass and walks beside me.

"At long last, I shall see the so-called Djinni Slayer in action," he says.

I study him out of the corner of my eye. He focuses ahead as he walks, his smooth face as unreadable as polished stone, his voice similarly betraying nothing. Most distracting are the glossy locks of hair dangling over his forehead and shifting in the morning breeze. It irritates me, the number of Shields I have heard openly gushing about Taha's looks, as if this arrogant boy was sent to us by the Spirits themselves. With the shorn sides of his head and that long hair on top, he resembles a puffed-up rooster to me.

We head down a corridor of empty rooms, usually reserved for Shields to study magic, monsters, and battle theory.

"I trust your father informed you of the situation," I say. It is only too easy imagining Bayek fuming to his son over last night's dinner.

"Yes. Suppose it's as I suspected, then: simply being of a distinguished lineage doesn't guarantee you a distinguished future," Taha replies. "So which is it, do you think—is your brother mad or bad? Perhaps a bit of both?"

I was wrong. Taha is no young man; he is a ghoul wearing the flesh of one. "Consider trying to hide how much this situation pleases you."

"Pleases me?" He knits his brows as if he is perplexed, but his reed-green eyes are as dull as ever. "And why would I be pleased that the welfare of my family and people are being threatened?"

"Nobody is being threatened by anything," I say defensively.

The others enter the room ahead, leaving us alone in the corridor. Taha shakes his head. "You wouldn't feel the same if it weren't your brother involved."

"And you wouldn't be a Scout if your father weren't Grand Zahim," I retort.

He is maddeningly impervious to the insult. I am not someone he should consider a rival; I am an irrelevant gnat he can look through. "If your auntie were Grand Zahim and I implied she was corrupt, you'd have me expelled from the Shields," he says.

I feel oddly askew then, as if he has kicked out one of my feet. I dress my upset with a sneer. "Is that how you intend to claw your way to the top? By banishing me?"

"No, of course not." He laughs, the first time I've seen him do it, and it is an intimidatingly handsome, self-assured gesture. He plants a hand on the wall over my head and leans in, making me shrink against it. "Unlike you," he says in a low voice, "I am not thin-skinned."

He pushes off the wall and marches into the room. I hang back to compose myself, but my insides refuse to stop somer-saulting. I impulsively reach for my dagger. It works as intended: I quickly trade my unsteadiness for cool confidence. Qayn's. It takes over, stilling the rapid beat of my heart. I step into the tea room and sense Taha glance back at me, but I manage to main-tain an aloof expression. I know it is wrong to use the djinni's binding like this, but if I am to survive this mission, I cannot appear weak in front of Taha or the others. And if I am going to forge ahead with breaking a sacred law, I may as well derive some utility from it.

The room's center firepit is ablaze, and an ornate silver pot of water has already been boiled. Bayek waits for Taha and me to kneel at opposite ends of the circle before beginning the tea ceremony. Taha rigidly watches his father grinding the misra be-tween us, but I watch Taha. I only do it out of the hope that it will infuriate him, and after a few minutes, I think it is work-ing. He wants to glare at me—his bright gaze keeps wobbling—but ceremonial tradition dictates he should not lift his eyes from

Bayek, and given who raised him, Taha is predictably incapable of disobeying the rules. The whole thing is petty of me, but that's all right. Petty is the most Taha seems to deserve.

Bayek serves a tray of tea around the room. The misra tastes the bitterest it ever has, and the magic is lead in my limbs. After the ceremony, Aqil, Yasmeen, Nadia, and Tariq Zahim sit in a row of chairs at the back to observe. I line up with the Scouts before Bayek and Auntie.

"Time is short and the matter is pressing," says the Grand Zahim. "We have evidence that Atheer, Imani's older brother, may be alive in the Kingdom of Alqibah. It appears he is fighting the Harrowland Empire alongside a rebel movement and has shared misra with them."

The ensuing silence is damning. Reza and Fey were never friendly to me before, but I read the total disapproval in their eyes now. Whatever chance I had of ingratiating myself with them, it's gone, and I am certain that if they ever discovered I've bound a djinni to my dagger, they would show me no mercy. This necessary evil is a secret I must guard jealously, or else I will be ruined.

Bayek paces before us, hands bunched in the small of his back. I see the famed warrior in his imposing frame and grim face that has never known the act of smiling. He may be Grand Zahim, but it is in the role of Grand Commander where he shines, and where I've no doubt he is most comfortable.

"You must understand the following: Atheer is a highly experienced Scout; he possesses knowledge of multiple paths through the Sands; he is sympathetic to the outsiders and actively involved in their affairs; he has revealed our magic to them, whether willingly or as the subject of a campaign of manipulation. At any time, his sympathy for the outsiders might extend to leading one across the Sands to the Sahir. It has not happened yet—this does not mean it never will. This is a very real, very serious threat, and without knowing Atheer's intentions or state of mind, we must assume the worst and move quickly to intercept and recover him. Questions?"

I have one I dare not utter except in my mind: *Could my brother really do something to hurt us?*

Taha raises his hand. "What is Atheer's location, Father?"

I slide my eyes over to him. Bayek told him the scandalous answer last night. I know it is so because even Bayek seems confused by his son's question. The Grand Zahim's temple pulses, and he holds a palm out.

"Imani, care to explain?"

Taha turns to me expectantly; Fey and Reza do the same. This is a ruse, one Taha has engineered to shame me before the Council and Scouts. But even if my tongue wasn't impossibly knotted, I still couldn't tell them Atheer's location. I only know he is in Taeel-Sa with a rebel named Farida. Beyond that, the answers belong to Qayn, and *he* refuses to tell *me*.

"Time is of the essence," Taha prods.

The sight of his exposed neck makes my hands tingle with an unspeakable urge. "No," I say through clenched teeth.

He tilts his head. "What?"

I want to slap the question out of his garish, vacant eyes. He *knows* what, but he is slickly putting on this show for the benefit of the others. Or is it for his own perverse pleasure?

"*No,*" I repeat. "If I tell you where Atheer is now, you will have no use for me on the mission."

"Forgive me for speaking out of turn, my Grand Zahim." Fey steps forward so she has an unobstructed view of me and plants her hands on her hips. "Imani, do you mean to say you are *extorting* the Council in order to come with us?"

"That's precisely what she is doing," Taha answers.

Reza turns to Bayek. "With respect, Uncle, this won't be permitted, will it? Imani isn't a Scout—"

"She has no experience," says Fey.

"—and she is a risk to the mission's integrity."

I've had enough of wearing their insults. "Why?" I demand. "What exactly makes me a risk?"

In the quiet that follows my outburst, my heavy breathing is excruciatingly loud. Taha is still placid. Like a river, I realize, and regardless of what shakes his depths, he is safe in the knowledge that he will continue to stubbornly, arrogantly flow until he has eroded everything and flattened the earth.

"It's very simple," he says. "Your brother may resist returning with us and require forceful capture. Moved by pity, you will be incapable of taking the necessary steps to ensure his return. You may even be induced into aiding him against us."

"Bayek," Aqil calls from the back of the room. "These are very serious accusations your boy is making."

Bayek doesn't just know it; he revels in it. The Grand Zahim is the closest I have seen to smiling, and this is the closest I have come to understanding his true, terrifying nature. He is a spike driven through the Council, and even with their collective wisdom and influence, they do not actually know how to deal with him.

Suddenly all that I fear and need possess me; they twist and wring in their quest to tear me apart. I am angry, but my cheeks burn. I am committed, but I stammer as I say, "T-tread lightly, Taha. I love my brother, but I am not beholden to my emotions. My duty to our people and the Great Spirit comes first."

"Yet you extorted the Council. Prove that your brother's welfare does not come above ours. Tell us his location and let us protect the Sahir from his madness or his malice—"

I suffer an awful squirming, like I am an apple with a worm in my rotten core. I lunge to the tune of the Council's gasps, and grab Taha's tunic. "My brother is one hundred times the Scout you will ever be, lout. Question his or my loyalty to our people again, and I promise, you will regret it."

Something, at last, moves in that sedated gaze of his. "Don't come with us if you know what's good for you, Imani," he says, so soft that only I can hear it. "I mean it."

"Aziza, please," Bayek is saying. He glances at the other Zahim for help, as if small Aqil could better prize me and Taha apart than the Grand Commander himself could. I am no fool. This is a golden opportunity to portray him and his son as principled, and me as little more than a menace, and Bayek has seized it with both hands and all his teeth. The theater has worked on Auntie.

"That is enough, Imani. Unhand Taha."

The first thing she has said at this infuriating meeting, and it is in defense of this beast. Not me, not Atheer. She wields mighty sway over Qalia, yet she cannot see fit to use it against Bayek? I don't understand her; I don't understand anyone anymore.

"Now," she orders.

Taha deserves to be disposed of from the window, and the only reason I don't perform the civil service is because it will make going after Atheer harder. I release Taha and kneel before his hateful father, uttering words that scald my tongue.

"Forgive my unacceptable behavior, my Grand Zahim."

He sighs. "This is the niece holding the security of our people in her hands, Aziza. Speak sense into her, I implore you."

Damn him and his son to the Land of No Return. Whatever shame cowed me into kneeling, resentment brings me to my feet again. "Nothing anybody says or does will change my mind. The arrangement is settled. Sir."

"I am afraid my niece is very stubborn," Auntie says to him.

I wipe the hurt off my face as he glares down his nose at me. "Pride is a dangerous thing, Shield," he drawls. A stifling moment passes like that; then he turns his attention to unfurling a map across the table. "Gather round, quickly."

I stand at one end of the table, Auntie on my right, Taha on my left. Bayek points at the map.

"You will cross the Swallowing Sands into Alqibah here, using this path."

The others lean in to inspect the route. Auntie lightly touches my arm, and I almost recoil out of annoyance. "You are the only one in the group who has not crossed the Sands before," she says. "Should you leave the path, even a step, you will be lost forever. Follow Taha unerringly, do you understand?"

My head twitches. I glance over at him, expecting a smug smirk, but he is intently focused on Bayek's instructions, acting as if I don't exist again.

"I understand," I mutter.

"This is a matter of great urgency, requiring you to reach the Sands as soon as possible," Bayek continues. "This leaves one route most viable over the rest. The Vale of Bones."

My eyes widen; I flit them at the Scouts, but if they are afraid, they have convincingly hidden it under steely veneers. How? Have they not heard the stories? The Vale of Bones is ancient, unpatrolled wilderness, home to many monsters, chief among them a giant named Hubaal the Terrible, who, at the behest of the Desert's Bane, raged through the Vale, destroying tribes and desolating the land. He vanished after the Bane's defeat, and is rumored to slumber somewhere in the Vale; old tales warn of the horror that will ensue should he rouse.

"There must be better routes," I blurt out.

"They will cost us days we cannot afford," Bayek answers shortly. "I have provided Taha with an ancient map of the area, and Aziza and Yasmeen Zahim have graciously plotted a course through. Spirits willing, you will traverse the Vale unharmed. Questions?"

The Vale of Bones. I can't believe it. I have never been through there, never so much as set foot over its threshold. Never dreamed I would have to one day. I glance at the window on our left, at the wide, open sky and the safe Sanctuary grounds. Home isn't far. In an instant, a small, trembling voice grows very loud in my head. *Abandon this folly,* it urges me. *Go home, apologize to Mama—*

Then Taha says, "No questions, sir. Nothing shall stop us," and his bullish arrogance lances the fear from me. He has shown how hungry he is to sully my clan's honor, hungry enough that he will risk staring into the grisly, gigantic face of death to do it. But letting Taha of the Al-Baz clan drag *my* brother back through the Sahir like a lost, rabid dog is a disgrace I will not abide. I am saving Atheer, whether I must go through the Vale or Alard itself to do it.

Bayek rolls the map and slides it into a leather pouch. "Very well. If there is nothing else, Aziza, please take them to their supplies."

We bow to the Council rising from their chairs. "The Spirits guide you," says Aqil, waving to me as he files out of the room with the others. Perhaps after Taha's offensive comments, he has had a change of heart about me going.

Reza and Fey follow Auntie into the hall through a different door. I deliberately potter after them so I can sneak a glance at Taha hanging back with Bayek. Curiously, they don't behave as father and son. There is no warmth or informality, certainly no physical interaction between them. No hug, not even a touch on the arm or a brusque handshake. They are more akin to superior and subordinate: Bayek, Grand Commander, rattling off instructions, and Taha, dutiful warrior, nodding.

He appears at my side when our group has neared the armory. I sense he has something to say—I do too. I slow my stride, leaving space between us and the others.

"I don't know whether you believe the ridiculous accusations you made back there, but I do know that you did it on purpose."

He furrows his brow. "Did what?"

"Provoked me in front of everyone to make me look bad."

"Oh." He considers me seriously. "Now is not the time to learn humility, Imani. You're the one who did the hard work tarnishing your reputation."

He strides off before I can retort. Just as well. I can't think of a single thing to say.

10

ARMORED AND GEARED, WE SET OUT FROM Qalia at midmorning, journeying north in a tight corridor along the Al-Ayn River. Safe, patrolled villages crop up and fall behind, and the Sahir yawns before us. Soon seamless blankets of grass sprawl to the horizon, threaded occasionally by stained-glass waters singing odes to untouched skies. A beautiful, sweeping vista, ruined by crass chatter.

I ride at the back of the group, captive to yet another of Reza's vulgar jokes. It's just my luck Taha's cousin is terribly fond of them and possesses an endless supply.

"A boy tells his baba he wants to marry his teta—" he starts.

"Oh, *gross*." Fey pokes out her tongue, despite the fact that she is red-faced from giggling at the rest of Reza's daft jokes. We've only been gone from Qalia half a day, and I have already noticed the pair exchanging winks and coy smiles. Taha knows of their romance too, though like everything else, he considers it with little more than a listless gaze. Even now, rather than acknowledge them, he aloofly feeds the huge black falcon named Sinan perched on his leather gauntlet. Unlike the smaller messenger falcons kept in cages tied to our saddles, Sinan is extraordinarily loyal to Taha and does not require confining.

Reza's eyes twinkle. "Yes, that's what the boy's baba said. 'Aren't you ashamed that you want to marry my mother?' 'No,' says his son. 'You're married to my mother, and I've never complained.'"

Fey folds in her saddle, shrieking laughter; the high-pitched sound pleases Reza enormously, judging by the inane grin spreading from ear to ear. Taha's chuckle possesses no enthusiasm. He sends his falcon off and twists to look at me.

"What's the matter, Imani? Reza's jokes offending your sensibilities?"

So he is seeking entertainment elsewhere. I roll my eyes. "Hardly. They're sidesplitting. Pity I am not here to be amused."

"Pity you're so insufferable," Fey remarks through a glossy smirk.

"No, no, it's *my* fault. I forgot." Reza flaps an apologetic hand. "The Best, Youngest, Smartest, Wealthiest, Most Popular Shield doesn't have time to laugh at jokes."

I muster a sneer, though my heart has started to pound. "Careful, Reza, your jealousy is showing."

He rounds his lips and looks at Taha, who nods and says, "Told you, they're all the same."

"Excuse me, who are *they*?" I demand.

Taha ignores me. "There is no such thing as criticism in their world. People can't be disapproving; they can only be *jealous*."

I pull the reins taut. "If you had a single shred of honor, you'd address me directly."

He flicks his brows at Reza. "See?"

Fey turns in her saddle, dramatically swishing her perfectly curled blond hair along her back. "So it's true, then. The poor thing really doesn't have a sense of humor."

"Don't I? Curious." I look at Taha. "I happen to find you very funny, because I know exactly what you're doing."

His ordinarily slack gaze hardens like crystallized syrup. "Oh, what's that?"

"Trying to get rid of me. Let me save you the trouble, Taha: nothing will turn me back from bringing my brother home, least of all a couple of bullies."

I squeeze my heels around Badr and ride past, catching his eye. He frowns at me, confused, and this time, I think he is the one who can't think of a single thing to retort.

WE MAKE CAMP BEFORE NIGHTFALL. Using her affinity, Fey generates dancing flames between her dainty palms and creates the campfire. Taha and Reza gather kindling while I take responsibility for securing our perimeter. I string a thin rope around the trunks of the trees surrounding our campsite, and from it, hang warning charms: little clusters of stone, metal, and glass that rattle together should anyone—man, beast, or monster— trip the rope during the night.

Afterward the three of them head off together into the dusk, Taha armed with his bow, Reza with a brown woven sack, Fey holding a torch. They don't bother informing me of their venture, but I overhear that they are going hunting, and by the way they're ignoring me, I am clearly not invited. Soon their figures melt into the twilit grassland, leaving me alone with my thoughts. Ordinarily I would welcome the peace and quiet, but my thoughts make for rotten company. I can't stop wondering whether Atheer has already perished and I am too late. What if I have given my family false hope, propping them up for an even greater despair?

I try to distract myself from my worries with a falafel sandwich—Teta's input to my supplies—but it doesn't work. I feel horribly lonely and isolated, and it's only been one day. Given how the others are treating me, I know that feeling will worsen as the journey goes on. Sighing, I set my sandwich aside and reach for my dagger, despite a voice inside cautioning me not to do it. But right now, I would rather confront this devil than my own.

When I am certain the others aren't returning, I whisper my command to the dark. "Qayn, I request your presence."

The djinni materializes in a breath of wind that makes the campfire leap. I instinctively draw a sharp breath, having forgotten his striking appearance. Most startling are those large eyes, evoking dark, depthless pools, and the perfect balance of his face.

"How may I be of service, Slayer?" he asks.

My mouth is a dry riverbed coated with tahini from my sandwich. At least, I think that's what is causing it. "I wanted to talk," I say grudgingly.

His lips are already curling. "Certainly. You can talk to me whenever you desire." He slides his gaze over the dark grassland before pulling up the knees of his sirwal and settling on the fallen log beside me. "What shall we talk about, then?"

Somehow the campfire before us intensifies in strength and illuminates his beauty—the flames frolic along the regal crests of his cheeks, the fine cut of his lips; they glimmer on the impenetrable surface of his black ocean eyes, burning so gladly that they must feel they are being beautified in the exchange too. I understand the sentiment well. With how close he is sitting to me, I find myself fighting to control the impulse that has me taking a deep, primal pleasure from admiring him. He is only a mirage, I remind myself, a nod of the head at something too lovely to be real. A liar and deceiver who helped lead my brother astray.

"I don't know," I admit, lowering my gaze. What conversation is there to make with a devil? I had been thinking of Atheer, but I don't want to discuss my brother, nor the terrible fate that may have befallen him. I crave distraction. "You," I say, looking up again. "Let's talk about you."

He gazes at me sideways, a glimpse of surprise softening his sharp features. I take my dagger in my hand and start twirling it.

"Tell me, why is it that when I touched this during my meeting with the Council, I felt hatred and anger from you?"

He considers the fire now, but I have the distinct sense he is avoiding my gaze. "Suppose I am not fond of a Council that seeks to eliminate me, that is all."

"Can you blame them? You are malevolence given flesh."

He tuts softly, but a devious glint shines in his eye. "Come now, Slayer, there's no need to be hurtful. I am but a simple djinni trying to make his way in the world."

"Simple, I'm sure," I scoff. "Be honest and tell me: who are you really, and why are you insisting on coming to Alqibah?"

He gives a grimacing smile. "I'd rather not. I am terribly opposed to talking about myself."

Snorting, I stand and begin pacing around the fire. I am more invigorated now, less dejected. Perhaps just glad to discuss something other than my troubles.

"You don't like talking about yourself," I echo, flicking my dagger with a twist of my wrist. The magic I have left in my veins from this morning's tea ceremony eagerly floods down my fingers into the blade, lengthening it to a short sword. This is perhaps my favorite pastime, absently playing with my magic while I think, using the lull as a chance to practice and master the various weapon transformations. Pride swells in my chest when I pause to admire my handiwork. "For some reason, I find that hard to believe," I murmur to Qayn, turning the short sword so the firelight rolls red and bright along its perfect edge. "Seems more like a liar's excuse."

Qayn is fascinated too, watching me nimbly toy with the blade, turning it into a small, gleaming axe, then a deadly razor that could kill with one slit. Seeing his expression only intensifies my pride.

"When you've been around for as long as I have, the subject of oneself can become rather tedious," he says.

I consider his slender frame elegantly draped in black linen, his smooth, appealing face that belongs to a boy of nineteen, if that. "Why? How old are you?"

He shakes his head, his black, chin-length hair shifting in the breeze. "My age? In years? Apologies, I am afraid time doesn't really *work* that way for individuals like me."

"What do you mean?" I transform the blade to its original form. "Once you weren't, now you are, like everybody else, djinni or not. How long has it been?"

He looks away again, this time to a lone firefly twirling between the blades of grass. "I don't know, really. I have always been this way."

"A pretty boy? Don't be trite," I blurt out. My gut instantly churns with regret as Qayn's mouth lifts at the corners. Suddenly he is on his feet and coming over to me.

"You think I'm pretty, do you, Slayer?"

My cheeks flush. I point the dagger, though admittedly, I like how much my unintended compliment delights him. "You play as if you don't know the form you've taken, devil."

He halts a step away, barred by the presence of the dagger. I've no doubt he would come closer if he could. He'd leap into my very soul, and right now I don't know if I am entirely opposed to the notion.

"A form you like, it seems." His sharp mouth curls around the teasing words. "Though I am sorry to disappoint you. I haven't *taken* a form. This is truly me."

"Ridiculous." I begin pacing again, twirling the blade only to disguise how flustered he makes me. "Djinn don't look like humans naturally. You've only chosen to take that form hoping it will persuade me to do what you want. It won't work."

"How curious," he murmurs behind me. "Perhaps I am not a djinni after all."

Goose bumps descend the length of my arms. I slow at the edge of the campfire's light and peek over my shoulder. "What are you, then?"

I find him staring at me, and I am confronted by the void in his eyes again, the limitless hunger of the grave, the unfathomable gulf of the universe; I am fully engaged in the act of looking into nothing. It is paradoxical—how can one *see* nothing—an enigma that only puzzles me the more I think on it. Then he flashes a jackal's grin and the intense moment passes, as blithe as clouds scudding across a summer sky, content to have come, likewise content to go.

"I jest, Slayer. I am a djinni, an old one by your conception of time."

"And a weak one too," I say, but my jibe is cut short by distant voices. Taha and the others, returning to camp. My heart leaps into my mouth. If any of them catch even a glimpse of Qayn, I will be dragged back to Qalia to face the Council, and Atheer's fate will be left in Taha's hands. I hurriedly point my dagger at Qayn. "You must go, now, before the others see you."

"Pity," he says through a pout. "We were only beginning to have fun."

He vanishes in a blink. A moment later, I feel him heating the blade's hilt. Something else arrives, a jumble of temptation: Qayn wants me to call out to him again, to throw caution to the wind and leave the others behind, but this time, he wants me to steal their misra and supplies first. To embark on this journey after Atheer, he and I and nobody else.

"Spirits, what am I thinking?" I murmur, shaking my head.

I sheathe the dagger on my thigh and grab my bag just as Taha emerges into the firelight. For a moment, I nervously scrutinize his expression to see if he's noticed anything amiss. His solemn face is flushed with sweat, one of his fists tightly clutching the brown woven bag. Bloody red splotches mark the bottom length of it.

"Dinner," he says, holding it up.

So my secret is safe, for now.

"I've eaten," I say. I catch his gaze as I march off to find a place to sleep. There's a look in his eyes I can't quite place—disappointment? I don't know, but after how he's treated me, I am not giving him the time or benefit of trying to decipher it.

11

FOR SEVERAL DAYS, WE JOURNEY THROUGH PA-trolled lands sprinkled with scenic sandstone towns and long ribbons of trading caravans carrying spices, coffee, nuts, and dates, their enterprise protected by squads of Shields. It is a calmer excursion now that the trio have collectively decided to ignore me. Mornings fill with solemn tea ceremonies, stamping out campfires, and saddling horses; afternoons belong to meditative riding toward red dusk, occasionally disrupted by Reza's jokes, Fey's giggling, and Taha's tedious monologues on the subtle but important differences between two identical types of recurve bow. Nights are cool and mercifully quiet, but I spend them tossing and turning. When I do sleep, I am haunted by nightmares of that mysterious grand city I do not recognize; over and over, my dream-self helplessly watches the walled garden surrender to frenzied fire as my joy burns to ash on my tongue. The dream does not relent, arriving every night, and no amount of contemplation helps me unravel its veiled meaning.

I rouse often too, plagued by grief that sits on my chest, caving it into my sleeping mat. Other times, it is not grief for

Atheer that weighs on me, but hurt. Desperation to know why my brother never sent us a letter saying he is alive, leaving us to mourn instead. Fear that he has become someone I won't recognize, that perhaps his kindness will have hardened to cruelty, his generosity become not so unconditional, his ready wit and easy smile replaced by something severe. Whatever I end up feeling, I use the solitude to ponder what I will say to my brother when we are finally reunited—if I will demand answers out of anger, or I will be silently overcome by sheer relief.

More pressing is the problem of summoning Qayn for directions to Atheer without Taha noticing. I took a great risk calling Qayn out that night where Taha could have easily seen him and reported my wrongdoing to his father using one of the messenger falcons. Yet knowing this has done little to temper my desire to see the devil again and learn more about him. But I can't, not yet. Even when Taha isn't watching me, I sense I am being observed. Followed, even. Or perhaps my unease over nearing the Vale of Bones is taking its toll. We are still days away and crossing a safe, scrubby plain at an easy trot, yet I still feel I am on the precipice of a fatal drop. And if I didn't have enough reasons to be tense, Taha has decided this morning to break our tentative peace.

"The foreigners in Alqibah speak a language called Harrow-tongue," he announces, looking to me riding on his right. "You need to learn some phrases for your safety."

This is an uncharacteristic display of civility. Perhaps I should ask if he is all right, if he has accidentally eaten poisonous wild berries, or fallen off his horse and struck his head. Intuition warns me this is a trap. With him, it must be.

"Why? I don't intend to speak to any colonizers."

"They may speak to you, and it would be unwise to ignore them," he says.

"Have you all been into Alqibah before?" I ask.

The three of them nod, and Taha says, "Yes, once."

"What was it like?"

Fey wrinkles her nose as if she smells something foul. "Dirty, busy, poor, violent—"

"Unremarkable," Taha cuts her off. "Listen closely. The word I am about to say means 'halt' in our tongue."

Fey and Reza lean forward to observe our impromptu lesson, like a pair of hungry pigeons waiting for scraps on the edge of a baker's roof. I ignore them and concentrate on Taha instead, but that isn't any better. In contrast to melodic Sahiran, Harrowtongue is a flat, clipped language. It doesn't roll over my ignorant ears; it bangs and crashes.

"Did you get that?" he asks. No, but I nod regardless. "Good. This phrase translates to, 'State your business.' A soldier might ask you it at a checkpoint or city gates. Listen."

I try—it is indecipherable from the soup of other words. Either Taha has noticed and doesn't care, or I am masking my bewilderment well, because he continues. "If you are asked your business, state your name and say you are a hunter from a town called Tull. It'll sound like this . . ."

I listen, still nodding, still completely lost.

"Try it for yourself. I'll play the part of a soldier and ask you to state your business." He recites the phrase in Harrowtongue. I only know he has finished because he raises his brows. "Now you say . . ."

"Oh, right." I squeeze my eyes shut. "Um . . . My . . . Imani . . . I . . ."

Fey smirks at Reza, who is muffling his laughter. Taha slows his white colt to a walk, slowing the rest of us too. "Listen carefully and copy me," he says. I am tempted to ask if he thinks my ears are painted on. He speaks in Harrowtongue and nods. "You try. I will order you to halt and ask you to state your business."

"Fine," I say, though I am put off by how frantically my insides are fluttering. I excel in studies and the practical application of theory, and I have never had any trouble giving speeches. Why am I so nervous? I certainly don't care for Taha's judgment.

He says his phrase in Harrowtongue and gestures at me.

"All right. Then I would say . . ." I clear my throat and deliver the answer, but I don't even need Fey's snorting to know it sounds wrong. Clunky and ugly. How else would it turn out? My tongue feels like a fat strip of leather, about as useful as one too.

Taha raises his voice. "*Listen,* Imani. Watch my mouth this time."

Scowling, I lower my gaze to his parted lips, my pulse quickening. He repeats the phrase slowly and clearly. I bob my head.

"All right, I have it. Ask me again."

He does and gestures expectantly, Fey and Reza craning even farther forward in their saddles. I hesitate. Is Taha smirking or smiling encouragingly? *What does it matter? Focus.* I swallow a deep breath and give my best shot in a steady, confident voice.

"My nome Imani. My hanter frem Tule."

A faint blush stripes his cheeks. "Close," he says, but he is drowned out by Fey's gut-busting cackle.

"You are *awful* at this," she cries, and almost topples off her horse. Meanwhile, Reza can't catch his falling tears fast enough.

I have never experienced humiliation so intolerably suffocating. It makes me want to flee, or find a tunnel to disappear down. I growl in my chest. "Go right ahead, laugh until you choke. I suppose you two are perfect and mastered every skill the first time you tried?" I sigh and look to Taha. "If this is as important as you say, let me have another go. I know I can get it with practice."

Our eyes meet, and his linger a moment too long. I am waiting for a mean quip about how I will never learn Harrowtongue, when he twists in his saddle and barks, "Shut your mouths already. I can't hear myself think over you hyenas."

I blink at the back of his head. Did he just *defend* me? Impossible. Taha can't possess an ounce of sensibility, or else this world has lost all sense. A more probable answer is that we are delirious from riding under the harsh sun for too long.

Whatever the reason, his rebuke has a delightful effect. Fey's laughter triggers a coughing fit, and when she finally lapses into silence, her eyes are streaming and her usually pretty face is an ugly radish red. She and Reza sit rigidly on their horses, resembling the wooden toy warriors Atheer and I played with as children.

"Good." Taha faces me again. "Repeat after me, Imani."

And so, our lesson continues.

12

ANOTHER SLEEPLESS NIGHT, SICK WITH SORROW.
The Sahir is cast in pale twilight blue, and I have
been awake for an hour already, hopelessly trying to fall
back to sleep. But once my mind begins churning, it is a brass
coffee grinder with a very committed shopkeeper at the handle.

I sit up. Fey and Reza are still asleep around the low-burning
fire, but Taha's bedroll is empty; he's probably gone to relieve
himself behind one of the terebinth trees quartering our campsite. As I quietly climb out of my bedroll and pull on my leather
armor, I jealously imagine him groggily stumbling back over the
long grass, already asleep before his head hits the mat. Stifling a
yawn, I take my water flask and a few plums and step over the
thin rope I've strung low between two trees, being careful to
avoid the warning charms hanging from it.

Outside camp, I find a rock to perch on while I eat. A wild
dog, big-eared, lean, and ginger, digs in the grass by a nearby
terebinth. It sees me and goes on its business. I finish eating and
begin stretching the knots out of my arms and legs while softly
reciting some of the Harrowtongue phrases Taha taught me.

"My name is Imani. I am a hunter from the town of Tull. Thank you, sir. Thank you, ma'am. Pardon me. Yes, sir. No, sir. Good day."

Once limber, I pull the dagger off my thigh and swing it around for a little while, until my shoulders are loosened up too. It is a familiar act, assuming a fighting stance and pretending a ghoul is in front of me, preparing to attack. Whenever I can't sleep on a mission, I practice sparring, with or without my magic. It is the only thing that truly clears my mind.

I dart forward and spear the imaginary ghoul. Howling, it swings a long arm ending in deadly-sharp claws. I duck as the arm sails over my head; then I shoot up and stab. Energy warms my muscles and speeds my heart rate. I parry and dodge; I hop back and lunge into the attack. Before long, I am thinly coated in sweat, breathing fast, and feeling capable. No matter what I find in the Vale of Bones, the Swallowing Sands, or Alqibah itself, I will deal with it and get to Atheer.

"Never took you for an early riser."

I whirl around, my confidence evaporating. Taha is propped against a tree, strong arms crossed, hair dangling over his brow. It looks handsomely disheveled, almost purposely, despite my certainty that he does not own a comb.

I focus on sheathing my dagger. "I expect you take me for one who sleeps in until noon and never attends training."

"Yes. In fact, I've long suspected that the tales of the Djinni Slayer were embellishments, if not outright fabrications."

I cut my eyes at him, face hot. *So that's why he never acknowledged me or my achievements.*

He saunters over. Without his leather armor, his white tunic has a *very* open neck that flashes his muscular chest whenever he swings his arms.

"There's something I've always thought curious about you," he says. "You're so proud, yet you never accepted people's offers to settle which of us is the better Shield."

I should've known. Taha didn't find me to make polite conversation or practice my Harrowtongue. No, either I am invisible to him, or I am someone he is actively besting. There is no in-between.

Groaning, I kneel to gather my water flask. "And I refuse to accept them. They're foolish. Akin to comparing pears and figs." I make to walk past him, but he steps into my path.

"I can accept that. So, how about we settle on deciding who is the best, respectively: me, as a beastseer; you, as a duelist."

"Oh, come now. You truly think you're the best beastseer in the ranks?"

"Ever," he amends.

"Ever! Ha!" I sidestep him. "And here I thought arrogance had limits. Next thing, you'll be claiming you're a better beastseer than Mera Urabi."

"I am," he says seriously, following me.

Mama's apt description of Bayek comes back to me: *bigheaded fool.* It's just as fitting for his son. "Perhaps you are not well acquainted with the history of the Shields," I say over my shoulder, "but Mera Urabi, *my* ancestor, did a lot more than use her lion to scout ahead for danger. She was once trapped in a bad storm and had a tree fall over her, and she was able to command her mindbeast—"

"To fashion a lever and use it to lift the tree off her body,"

Taha finishes for me. "I know the story; I'd wager a bag of misra that I know Shield history better than you do."

I pivot to squint at him. "Doubt it. My mother is an Arch-Scholar in the Archives. While your mother was telling you bedtime stories of the conniving fox and wise falcon, mine was relating detailed historical accounts of Qalia's founding."

A shadow passes over Taha's face. "My mother succumbed giving birth to my little brother. I stopped hearing stories when I was shy of seven."

The revelation is confronting, like a slap to the face. Even Taha blinks several times, seemingly upset by his own honesty.

I wipe the sneer off my face, stammering, "I'm sorry. I didn't realize she'd— It's only that I'd seen your mother around—"

"Stepmother," he corrects, a soft blush banding his cheeks.

"Sorry," I repeat, softer. I never imagined Taha might have endured a grief like the kind I am experiencing with Atheer. The realization leaves me askew—Taha seems to regularly have that effect on me. I am about to ask why his father didn't tell him bedtime stories in his mother's stead, but a passing recollection of Bayek talking *at* his son in the barracks is answer enough.

"I know the exploits of every famous beastseer," Taha continues. "I'd still wager I could convince you I am better than them."

I am curiously relieved by his return to being a conceited ass. For a moment, I imagined I was seeing a chink in his armor, and something about that made him seem—I don't know—more human than he really is. Still, this feels wrong.

"You've spent two years acting as if I don't exist, and now you want to prove yourself to me?" I dare ask.

Surprise widens his eyes. "Didn't think you cared, to be honest."

I didn't think I did either, I realize. "I don't," I lie quickly, and then give a petulant sigh to prove it. "But if you must be so insistent . . . A tea ceremony, then?"

He leads the way over the enclosing ropes into camp. Fey and Reza are still asleep, even though dawn is making its blush-pink approach. I expect Taha to rouse them, given the time, but perhaps he prefers for our competition to take place without an audience, in case he loses.

He works quietly around them, placing a teapot on the fire. While the water softly bubbles, he grinds strips of misra to a fine powder using a mortar and pestle. Kneeling this close to him, I see that old bruises crown the peaks of his knuckles, the faded olive-brown rising and falling with the strain of his hands. They look like the kind one gets from punching hard surfaces.

As the ceremony goes on, the blush in Taha's cheeks makes a gradual return. We are meant to be meditating on the Great Spirit's blessing of magic, but I sense he is focused entirely on my presence, which is only magnified by the immense, silent landscape around us. It's curious, but I am almost certain he is even *nervous* having me watch him so intently. He hands me my steaming cup, and I am pleasantly surprised to find that the wisps rising off the tea aren't bitter as usual; they carry the ever-so-faint scent of freshly cut grass, log fires, and rain. The tea even manages to taste distantly sweet, and I am glad for the reprieve.

We leave camp after the tea ceremony, Taha lugging one of his bags with him.

"What's that for?" I ask, eyeing it.

We return to the space where I was training earlier. He drops the bag onto the grass and pulls a small pouch from it. "You'll see." He whistles several times, and the musical sound echoes around us endlessly. A few moments later, Sinan soars over the plain toward us from a cluster of trees.

"Before we begin," I say with growing nerves, "let's agree on the terms of this competition."

Taha removes a strip of hare meat from the pouch. "I guarantee you will be more impressed by what you're about to see than any dusty story about Mera Urabi."

I stifle an incredulous laugh. How much pomposity can one person physically contain without popping?

"Right. And if I am—*if*—what then?"

The falcon lands on Taha's bare forearm. I instinctively wince, but his mindbeast is surprisingly careful with his talons, and there is palpable trust between them. "Then," says Taha, feeding the keen-eyed bird, "you will declare me the best beast-seer you know of, and you will hand over a pouch of misra."

I consider him closely. "Allotments of misra are strict because of the risk of magical obsession—we're not meant to exchange quantities, even amongst Shieldmates."

Taha seems to mull over my words, his blush leaching down to his pulsing jaw. "I won't tell if you don't." He lifts his arm, sending the falcon flapping off. "Anyway, it's not like you'd see any punishment for it if you were found out. Shall we begin?"

I am less concerned with punishment than his unusual recklessness. Taha has always been known for doing everything by the book. *Perhaps getting my approval means a lot to him.*

I extend a hand. "Go ahead, please. Outdo Mera Urabi."

A faint smile touches his lips. He marches away from me and the bag on the ground, and takes position on the rock I sat on earlier. His eyes, both irises and whites, glaze liquid gold as he shares minds with Sinan. I try to predict what is about to happen, but what could possibly surpass a Shield who had such control over her mindbeast that she commanded it to fashion a complex lever?

Sinan turns and flies back toward me. I stare at his gold eyes, somehow sensing Taha in there. I expect he will turn away to some new direction, but he remains arrowing for me. I almost yelp as I duck out of the way and the falcon circles on my right. He tilts into a gust of wind, black feathers rippling, and lands next to the bag. Slowly I straighten up again to observe. Using his long beak, the falcon opens the bag, withdraws several neatly kept items, and places them on the grass: a leatherbound stack of papers, a clean quill, a pot of ink. My eyes round as the falcon frees the knot holding the papers together and pulls a blank one free. Then he uses his talons and beak to *unscrew* the inkpot, dip the quill, and—

"No," I breathe. "Impossible."

The falcon touches the tip of the quill to the page and scrawls a message. A moment later, Sinan lifts the paper with his talons. I take it from the enormous bird.

"Could Mera Urabi do this?" I read aloud.

The falcon's eyes return to their duller yellow, and Taha's are green again. He strides across the plain, smiling. My ears burn hot, my fingers tightening on the page. *This* is why Auntie was so impressed by him, enough to appoint him to the position of

Scout. She even said it to me: "I can only imagine your skepticism stems from not having witnessed Taha for yourself." Now I have, and I cannot begrudge her decision. To exercise that much control over one's mindbeast is unheard of—it makes me wonder how many hours of practice Taha has poured into honing his skill, when other teenagers are out having fun with their friends. It reminds me of *me,* training with my blade at the barracks, late into the evenings, even on days of rest.

"Let's hear it, then, loud and clear." He holds his arms out. "I am the best beastseer you know. Say it."

If pride were physical, it would be occupying the free space in my throat. "Well, to say you're the best *ever* based on one act—"

He folds his arms, laughing; morning light catches his bright eyes and straight white teeth. "Of *course* you're too sore to admit an Al-Baz boy bested someone of *your* clan."

"No." I scowl. "I am not too *sore*." I finally manage to swallow my pride; it sinks to the pit of my gut like a brick. "Based on this act alone"—I huff—"you seem to be the best beastseer I know of."

The words are like glue, how hard they are to pry off my tongue. More than satisfaction radiates from Taha's bloomed pupils and open-mouth grin. He is elated, and something about that thrills me deeply. My stomach drops.

Oh no, I think. *No, no, it can't be. It isn't.*

We've been spending too much time together, that's all, especially after he ignored me for so long, and he *is* so imposing with his swagger. He knows everyone thinks he is handsome and brave and remarkably talented with his affinity, and because he acts like it's the irrefutable truth, it's hard not to get caught up in his current. Anyway, back in Qalia, I was regretting not pushing him out a window. One doesn't go from thinking that to *liking* someone, do they?

Suddenly a breeze rushes through the grass, plucking the paper from my hand and scattering the others from their leather casing. Taha curses, and we both chase after the contents before any more can fly off into the golden ether. I collect a map, several lists of supplies—and then my fingers fall on a letter wedged between two long stalks of grass. *Dear Father,* it opens, penned in an uncertain hand. *I write to assuage your concerns.*

I glance over at Taha. He is kneeling with his back to me, replacing the pages in their binder. He doesn't know I've found this letter, and there are still others that have escaped our grasp. He may think it lost to the wind. Whatever possesses me—curiosity, worry, malice—I crumple the letter and stuff it down my tunic.

"Here," I say, going over to Taha with the other pages.

"Thanks." He replaces them too, but before he loops the leather cord around the binder, he pauses. His head turns and he looks across the plain.

Heat rises in me. "Something the matter?"

"Missing some things," he murmurs.

"Ah. Hmm." I fold my arms over my chest where the letter is hidden.

He sighs. "Anyway, what about you?" he asks, looking up at me.

I start on the spot. "Me? What do you mean?"

"Well." He slides the binder into his bag and gets to his feet. "We've determined I am the best beastseer ever. Let's settle whether you're the best duelist."

"*Oh.*" I exhale a soft, relieved laugh. "Well, no. Unlike *you,* Taha, I make no claims to being the best ever."

"Better than me, surely," he goads, a slight raise in one eyebrow. "Unless . . ."

That's enough to make me forget my theft. "No, there is no *unless.* I am better than you with a blade, even more using my magic."

"Prove it. Let's spar."

I roll my eyes as my gut flips. "No. I'd be too afraid of accidentally murdering you." Or intentionally.

"Worry about yourself," he says, a faint dimple denting one cheek. He is joking around with me. *Taha,* the boy who had to be constantly reminded of my name during classes. "Help Imani collect the Almanacs from the cupboard, Taha," the teacher would say, and Taha would blithely reply, "Which one is Imani?"

"Hold on. I'll grab my sword." He leaves me shifting on my feet and returns in his leather armor, sword in fist. He nods at the dagger on my thigh. "Ready up."

"A fair warning to you, Taha," I say as I send magic surging through my veins, "I will not hold back. If a fight is what you want, a fight is what you'll get. Mind your neck." The magic filters out through the glowing dagger and lengthens it to a sword, simultaneously hushing my clamoring thoughts. I settle into the comforting state of completeness and focus that I always experience when using my affinity. In the blade, I feel Qayn's presence like a curious bystander at a brawl.

"Good." Taha runs his tongue over his lower lip. "Let's dance."

He advances first, fast given his size. I am faster. I block his strike; our swords connect with a metallic *clang* that sings across

the gilded plains. Our eyes meet, and his twinkle in the intensifying morning light. The moment of peace is fleeting. He withdraws and strikes again, and this time, he doesn't stop when I
parry him. He moves like an enraged viper, striking high, to the
side, attempting a brazen jab at my chest. I back across the grass
in a light shuffle, swiftly countering each assault. He goes low for
my shins; I hop over the blade as it slashes grass, and land out of
his reach. We pause, breathing fast; his skin shines, dewy with
the first beads of exertion, his brows pointed over his vivid eyes.
Slowly he rises to full, intimidating height.

"You fight defensively."

We regain our footing, squaring up like two wolves prowling
around contested quarry.

"No, I let my opponent reveal their weaknesses first," I reply.

His lips twitch in a smirk. "That's unfortunate. I have none."

He attacks again, with a frenzy he didn't possess before. But
he is determined to prove that statement and best me. I parry his
assault, the sword crashing on mine violently, a tremor racing
through the steel into my arm and between my ribs, where it
dances around my pounding heart. I kick him in the chest. He
grunts and stumbles back, sword sinking, brow knitting in a perplexed frown. I use the lull to turn on my heel, transforming my
sword into a club. On the outer swing, I whack him in the face,
just hard enough that his head jerks to one side and he collapses.
Magic sizzles in my veins; exhilaration fires my limbs. Another
surge and the club becomes a spear. I stand over Taha with the
tip pressed to his neck. He is on his back, blinking up at me.
Carefully he maneuvers a hand around the spear and runs a finger along his lip. It's split, and blood is dribbling down his chin.

"Is that enough for you?" I ask calmly, despite my heart skipping like a spirited child.

Honest to the Spirits, it's tempting hunger that shades his gaze. "More than enough. Help me up, would you?"

I transform the spear to a dagger, sheathe it, and pull him to his feet. I notice the touch of his warm hand on mine more than I should. Clearing my throat, I drop his hand and step back. "Let's hear it, then, loud and clear."

I wait for mumbled denials and angry excuses. Instead he looks me in the eye and earnestly says, "You are a better duelist than me, Imani. Perhaps the moniker 'Djinni Slayer' was earned, not bought."

"Perhaps?" I groan, but I am secretly pleased by his declaration. At last Taha has noticed my skill and achievements, although in truth, I owe much of my success as a sorcerer and Shield to Atheer, who tirelessly trained me at home and in the barracks in his spare time. And whenever I worried about the speed of my progress, comparing myself to him or even Auntie, he would be there with encouragement and an unshakable faith in my ability.

"Believe in yourself, Imani," he said the morning of my first Proving Trial at the Order of Sorcerers, both of his hands fixed firmly on my shoulders. "Self-confidence is the real secret to success, yes? That, and the willingness to get back up after you've been knocked down, again and again."

A lump forms in my throat. "I suppose we're even when it comes to bags of misra," I say, dragging myself from the precious memory.

Taha paws the sweat off his forehead. "Suppose we are. How about some breakfast?"

Taha and me amicably eating together. I never thought I'd see the day. But I am tired and hungry, and the speckled eggs he gathered from the nest of a red grassfowl two days ago sound very appealing right now.

"What's going on here?"

Startled, we turn to see Reza ambling over the grass. In a heartbeat, the line of Taha's shoulders hardens, and so too does his expression.

"Training," he answers coldly as Reza arrives.

I am careful not to betray his lie with my confusion. Reza looks between us curiously—suspiciously, even. "You were sparring? Who won?"

I spot an opportunity to dispel some of Reza's dislike of me. If he can see that Taha has accepted me, he and Fey may give up their enmity. But before I can open my mouth, Taha is speaking.

"Me. Obviously." He doesn't even look at me. "Imani has a few things to learn."

I stare at him, stunned, as Reza snickers. Whether or not it was attraction in his gaze before, he is completely aloof toward me now. It's as if he's realized he was never interested in me at all and was only looking for a way to pass the morning. Whatever tiny island of understanding Taha and I discovered today, it has vanished beneath an ocean of hostility. An ocean we will never cross, no matter what he says or does.

"Lying to save face in front of your cousin, are we?" I say sharply, but Taha only rolls his eyes and hoists his bag over his shoulder. He nods to Reza, whose previously smug expression is being threatened by a confused frown.

"Ignore her; she's a sore loser. Is Fey up yet? You two slept in. We'll take a short breakfast so we can make up the missed time."

He guides his cousin back toward camp, and Reza doesn't argue, sealing the matter. I follow, silently fuming, half seriously wondering whether I should have taken the opportunity and driven the spear into his neck. Instead I reach down my tunic and make sure the letter to his father is still there. If I was going to regret prying into Taha's privacy before, I won't now. I will find the weaknesses he says he doesn't have, and if he dares get in the way of me saving Atheer, I will use them to destroy him.

13

I DON'T GET A CHANCE. OVER THE FOLLOWING TWO days, Taha watches me closer than ever. He rides beside me, sleeps near me; he observes my every move. Where I was once invisible to him, I now seem to be the only thing that exists in his world. I even once got up in the middle of the night, hoping to read the letter, but he roused at the faint sound of my bag buckle and considered me queryingly. He hasn't spoken to me, though; that, he seems to be avoiding. I am almost certain he doesn't want to address what happened between us or, more important, how his behavior changed the instant Reza came around.

We reach the Vale of Bones the following morning. A violent dawn meets us; sheets of red shatter on the horizon, and splinters perforate the purple sky and draw blood. We stop our horses to study the stark valley clutched between jagged mountains. When I was a girl, Mama told me the Sahir used to be a land of neither magic nor monsters. Then sentient darkness appeared—this darkness was the Desert's Bane, and it has been a point of academic contention for a millennium where exactly the monster came from. Some scholars believe the Bane was a malevolent cavern Spirit; others believe the beast simply fell from the skies. Regardless of where the Bane came from, the end result was the same: one day, this unfathomably powerful monster decided to rain destruction upon anything it could find. It devasted towns and villages; it annihilated entire tribes; it drained the moisture from swathes of the Sahir, like the Vale. Before the Desert's Bane scarred this land, the Vale was verdant, as green as the sky is blue and home to many communities, this path playing host to wagons, carriages, and trading caravans. Now it is empty. Dead. The only thing that lives here is the past, and Hubaal the Terrible, somewhere.

"Aziza and Yasmeen Zahim's course through the Vale would take us two nights and three days," says Taha, considering the map open across his thighs.

"Three? Surely not." Reza, chomping on an apple, leans over in his saddle for a look. "Oh, if our horses are walking and we take that route instead of . . . that one." He points at the map. "We could do that in two days if we rode hard."

"We crossed Anzu's Pass that time in half a day," says Fey, not looking up from buffing her nails on her tunic.

"It isn't a good idea," I chime in, attracting their leery attention. "If my auntie has written three days—"

"My auntie," Fey taunts. "She isn't a Shield."

"No, she's only Master of the Misra."

"Yes, we're well aware of your clan's accomplishments, thank you, Imani. We're only reminded of them every waking moment." The airy animosity she was putting on suddenly congeals to something personal, and angry. "It's the objectionable details about the Beya clan that we're never told about, isn't it? You, for example . . ."

Taha glances up from the map. My hand instinctively floats down toward my dagger—and Qayn—as my entire body suffuses with heat. *Has Fey somehow discovered my secret?*

"Yes, me," I prompt quietly, pressing my tremoring hand flat against my thigh instead.

"You're the youngest person to be initiated into the Order of Sorcerers," she goes on, and I am careful not to exhale in relief over the fact that whatever is going on right now, it doesn't concern my entering a binding agreement with a djinni. But I don't know where Fey is taking this, and I don't like it.

"Your point being . . . ?"

She walks her horse in a circle around me. "You hardly needed time to practice with the misra before you took the Initiation Trial. I wonder, you didn't have access to misra at home *before* the legal age, did you?"

"Good point," Reza comments.

My hard mask threatens to slide off my face. Auntie *did* permit me to drink misra at fourteen, a year before anyone else, but I was ready for the magic by then. The fact that I took the Initiation Trial and passed on my first try is proof. Few others would be capable of that even if they started practicing with the magic at ten. Auntie understood that; they can't.

"No, I did not," I lie.

"You wouldn't tell us if you did anyway. What we do know is"—Fey ticks items off on her fingers, still circling me—"you are extorting the Council; your brother stole misra and is betraying the Great Spirit *and* his people's safety for filthy outsiders; and your sister, well . . ." She whistles, pulling up on my left. "I've heard Amira is *quite* the mean thief—"

"How dare you speak ill of my sister," I say, but I am shaken by Fey's accusations. About five months ago, I received a letter from Mama while out on a mission. In it, she said Amira skipped school and stole a bottle of rose perfume from Souq al-Attareen. The perfumer, a family friend, visited my parents at home about the matter, and they managed to smooth things over. Amira returned the bottle without ever surrendering an explanation as to why she stole it in the first place, when Baba could easily have purchased it for her, and the perfumer promised to keep the incident a secret. Either the perfumer lied or Amira has stolen items we don't know about.

"Anyway," Fey sighs. "Your auntie isn't and never was a Shield. She probably won't be Master of the Misra for much longer either." Fey falters, casting a nervous glance at Taha.

Dread gnaws at me. "What does that mean?"

"Nothing," he says, sliding the rolled map into his saddlebag.

"No, not nothing, Taha. What aren't you telling me?"

His temple pulses; then he exhales. "Fine, you want to know? There are rumors about your auntie."

Cotton dandelions begin sprouting in my lungs and throat, stealing my air. "Rumors?" I squeak.

"That she knew Atheer was stealing misra months before everyone else found out, and she didn't stop him or report it."

"She might have even assisted him," Fey elaborates with patent glee.

I swipe my tongue along my lips. They are parched, as rough as the surface of sandstone. What was it Qayn said back in the

Forbidden Wastes? *Atheer did steal a rather impressive quantity of misra from your Sanctuary over the years.* The statement soars back at me like a spear and hits me square in the chest. I hunch forward, pressing a hand over my pounding heart. Years. Spirits help me. Could Atheer's theft really have gone undetected for that long? But if it wasn't, does that mean . . . An angry vise pinches my temples, interrupting the thought. *Qayn is lying,* I tell myself, *and people like Taha, Reza, and Fey wish for nothing more than my clan's downfall.*

I straighten up. "Your attempts at discrediting my clan are laughable. Atheer was only stealing misra for a few months, and my auntie found out when everyone else did."

"And as Master of the Misra, she alone determined how much was missing," Taha says.

"Yes, and . . . ?"

He studies his falcon circling high above us. "It's nothing, Imani. For you and your kind, it is always nothing. But for everybody else . . ." He looks down at me. "Did you know, a hunter once stole a single pouch of misra from a Shield camp and was imprisoned for two years for the crime?"

I falter, my insides shifting like I have the river in there again. "I did not know that, but if the hunter knowingly deprived Shields of vital misra, he deserved his punishment."

"The hunter was a poor man prone to spells of madness."

"One of yours, then," I impulsively retort, despite knowing it is an awful thing to say. But I am too edgy to halt my tongue in time.

Reza shakes his head, looking away in disgust, but Taha turns his colt toward me, rage blazing in his eyes.

"How long do you think Atheer will be imprisoned for? Stealing misra, sharing it, jeopardizing our safety and our promise to the Great Spirit—certainly longer than two years would be fair, don't you think?"

"No, no, some stern words and suspension from the Shields for a month is *much* fairer," says Reza, while Fey nods with feigned sincerity.

Council meetings are strictly private matters; it is one thing for Taha to know what was said through his father, another entirely for him to then spread gossip to his cousin and Spirits know who else. I should keep my mouth shut to avoid prolonging this confrontation or turning it even more vicious, but the self-preserving instinct is too slow and weak, and my lips are already moving.

"Do you want to talk about bias, Taha? Why don't you ask your father how he became Grand Zahim?"

"He was chosen for the position."

"Chosen?" I toss my head back. "Ha! Yes, of course, after he had his mob *strong-arm* the Elders into changing their initial selection, and by the sheer grace of the Great Spirit, some of his most outspoken detractors passed away."

Taha's face contorts. "Is that what you call the Citizen Assembly, a 'mob'?"

"She would," says Fey. "Wealthy clans have never needed to rely on the Citizen Assembly to get a fair opportunity."

"Enough of this," I warn them. I am feverish with fury, and sick with something else, something I cannot and do not want to understand about who I have been raised to be. "We are leaving this wicked subject behind. My auntie and Yasmeen Zahim want us to ride slowly on a certain route for a reason: at a gallop, the strike of our horses' hooves will vibrate the earth and betray our position. We do not want to draw out Hubaal the Terrible or whatever other monsters lurk in the Vale."

I recall Mama's warnings about the Desert's Bane, how it was said to have spawned (or some argue, *invited*) the monstrous creatures that continue to plague us today. Some scholars believe the Bane committed the carnage for pleasure, others because it thought humans a lowly life-form unworthy of existence. If it had not been for the Great Spirit mercifully granting us misra to fight back, none of us would be here today, and the monsters trapped by the Swallowing Sands would be ravaging the world. But even though we defeated the Desert's Bane, its impact is still being felt throughout the Sahir, including in the Vale. Monsters are still here, their numbers only increasing; many people believe the ancestors themselves are restless. Auntie once described the situation as a sense that something remains out of balance—there is a loose end somewhere.

Fey flops in her saddle. "Oh, *please*. Those are children's tales, Imani. You're old enough and have seen enough real monsters to know Hubaal doesn't exist—"

"Quiet, Fey," Taha mutters. "Hubaal and the Desert's Bane aren't tales. They are historical realities backed by every Grand Zahim for a millennium, including my father. They are the very reason we were granted magic in the first place. Treat the matter with some respect."

She takes on a sickly watermelon hue that clashes with her flaxen hair. "Of course, I know they're true—"

While she blathers on apologetically, Reza casts an irritated glance Taha's way. I can't believe my eyes. Is Taha a young man with a mind of his own, or a sketch of an unthinkingly dutiful son brought to life by Bayek through some magic we've yet to know?

"My point stands," he says. "Better to get through the Vale as quickly as possible than linger around, waiting for Hubaal to find us."

I push Badr forward. "Would you listen to me, Taha? This is a very bad idea."

"You're welcome to return home if you disagree." His eyes turn gold as he shares minds with Sinan. The falcon arcs and soars over the Vale for a long minute, inspecting the area. Taha's eyes fade to their languid green. "The way ahead is clear."

"A good leader listens to his Shieldmates," I say at his back. "All of them."

"And a loyal Shield puts the welfare of her people over one sibling." He pivots his white horse toward the Vale. "We ride hard, we ride fast. Single file to reduce our area of impact. Go."

His colt launches into a trot. Fey follows him, then Reza, then, reluctantly, me. And as I ride for the scorched path snaking between mountains, something occurs to me, a truth that has arrived far too late to be of any use. Here, at the mouth of the Vale of Bones, I realize I am not heading into a war—I am already in one.

THE DAY OPENS IN PURE CERULEAN; the rocky ground rises around us in bulbous bald knolls baking beneath a relentless sun. At Taha's direction, we alternate between galloping, cantering, and walking long enough for our horses to recover some stamina. I warn him the beasts need more rest than that, but he ignores me. After that, no one speaks; they want to ride loud, but it seems we've secretly agreed to maintain silence otherwise. I accept it at first, glad to sort through the jumble of my thoughts, though I have little success. My mind races, my emotions keep tangling, and I swear I have heard another horse or several behind us. I am so convinced of this fact, I keep glancing over my shoulder, only to see an exhausted riverbed ribboning out of sight.

Then, in the late afternoon, the first vestiges of an ancient medina peek over the crown of a nearby hill. I make out crumbling granite walls, scattered limestone boulders, cracked marble pillars. In the shadow of these ruins, I hate the silence and all it keeps. I yearn for the comforting bustle of Qalia, the merchants poetically exalting their wares, the ceaseless creak of carriage wheels, the squeals of children playing in the fragrant laneways; I even wish for the commotion of my arguing parents and Simsim's barks. Spirits, a scrap of birdsong would do. Nothing sings here.

"Whoa," Taha hollers.

I look down from the medina to his horse, reared on its hind legs. Fey and Reza scatter left and right to avoid a collision, the falcons screeching in their rattling cages attached to the saddles. I am at the back of the group and have to sharply tug Badr sideways. I only narrowly miss them, but Badr moves awkwardly, stumbling over rocks and dipping. Suddenly I am askew, but Badr is still running, now squealing. A heartbeat later, I am flying from the saddle.

The world blurs around me, rusty orange, late blue, and all haze. I hit the ground. Dull pain blasts through my back and rings in my ears; sharper pain sears somewhere under my ribs. I slide down the grit, groaning at the setting sun, asking myself why I am here and not in bed at home, safe near my family. Asking myself *where* I am. A few swallows and blinks, and reality hastens back. The others are locked in a heated argument. Fey demands to know why Taha stopped, Taha doesn't know what startled his horse but something did, and Reza is shushing them.

"Quiet! *Look.*"

"Oh no." Boots hurriedly crunch over the grit, and a tall shadow shields me from the harsh sun. "Imani, are you hurt?" Taha. I feel his hands on my shoulders, my face, lightly patting my cheek. "Imani? Can you hear me?"

Groggily I turn my head left and right. I move my arms, I wriggle my toes, and then I sit up. My back is sore and a graze is throbbing hotly under my ribs, but as far as I can tell, nothing is broken.

"I'm fine," I grunt.

"Are you sure?" He extends me a hand.

Any other day, I would be loath to do it, but I take his hand and gingerly get to my feet. "Yes, fine. I've taken tumbles before, you know?" I brush the dirt off my tunic rather than look at him. I have trouble believing he honestly cares for my welfare. "We need to keep moving. It does us no good loitering around those ruins."

"We have a problem," says Reza. He and Fey are standing in a field of scattered foodstuffs and pouches that must have fallen from my saddlebags—and Reza is pointing at a large, toppled form on the ground. My heart seizes.

"Badr."

I sprint over to the filly sprawled on her side in the dirt. She is wheezing hard, weakly kicking one of her front legs. The other is still, bent awkwardly, and something white is protruding from . . . I tear my eyes away. "You're all right, girl, you're all right."

"Her leg is bad," Reza tells Taha, but he sounds distant. They all do, like they are speaking underwater an ocean away.

I brush Badr's flank. "It's fine. She just needs a moment's rest, don't you, girl?"

Reza sighs and leaves, and Fey's shadow drifts away with him. Time passes, how much I don't know. Taha kneels beside me.

"Imani . . ."

My vision distorts. "I said it's *fine*. Badr will be fine; she always is."

"She has an open fracture."

I fold over her, willing myself not to cry in front of Taha, but it is useless. I am back there on that sunny midafternoon, Baba calling me over to see the new foal Atheer helped deliver. "She's all yours, Imani. What do you want to call her?" I looked at her a long time, that vulnerable bundle nestled in the hay, searching for the perfect name for my new friend. Atheer said, "She's silver, like a full moon. How about Badr?" And how I liked the name the instant I heard it. I knew in my heart it was hers, made all the more precious because it was my brother who suggested it.

The golden memory fades; others jostle into the drab absence.

The missions we went on together, as if they weren't months of time but seconds stacked atop each other, viewable in an instant. All the occasions when she saved my life, bearing me from danger with speed and bravery; all those long, hushed rides through the Sahir's expanse. Sometimes I would leave my squad to venture to a nearby village, but I would never be afraid or lonely, even if it was only us two. I would sing, knowing we were alone for kilometers all around. Nobody there to laugh at me, and Badr certainly wouldn't. I'd sing, and she'd bop her head in time to the beat.

"We need to leave right now." Reza jogs over the rocks to us. "Something is stirring in the earth under those ruins."

"Imani," Taha starts.

His voice is a match to my wick. I become an inferno of anguish and rage; my brother's face flashes in my mind, and for this one, fleeting instant, I resent Atheer; I *hate* what he has done to me, my family and world. To my horse. A forlorn voice within howls for answers, pleading to know why he carelessly led me down this path.

I lunge and tackle Taha to the ground, straddle his chest as I strike him with my fists. "This is *your* fault!" I shout, ignoring Reza's pleas to keep my voice down. "I told you we should've slowed. I warned you the horses make mistakes when they're exhausted. I warned you!"

Taha grabs my arms. I wrench one free, almost wrenching my shoulder from its socket in the process. I don't care. I hit him in the jaw. His head jolts to one side, dark hair tossing over his eyes. He manages to seize my wrists and hold me still.

"*Stop*, Imani. I know what you're going through, do you hear? I *know*."

"You don't!" I fall limp and sob. If he were not holding me up, I would collapse.

"I do." He gently maneuvers me onto the grit. "When I was seven, I went on a hunting trip with my father and uncles. One night, far from any towns, a pack of wolves attacked our family dog, Rashiq. I helped chase off the wolves, but the damage . . ."

I raise my heavy eyes. Taha is kneeling so close to me, I can smell the sweat on him. I notice the ring of startling orange encircling his dilated pupils, the way his dark lashes defiantly stand up, the faded razor scar by his ear where he cut too close once. I see something in him other than pride: sorrow, and I am torn by the sense that I may have been wrong about him.

"I'd only ever cried like that once before, when my mama died," he says. "Rashiq was a gift from her. I'd already lost her. I couldn't lose him too. I was begging everyone to help close the wounds, but my father told me there was nothing we could do. We had to put Rashiq down, and if we didn't, he would suffer unnecessarily. But how can you do that to a dog who has slept at the foot of your bed since you were born? A friend who put food on your family's table and kept your feet warm while you ate?"

I look at Badr, her wet brown eyes fixed on the distance, her broad lungs heaving, that front leg still kicking but with less vigor, always less.

"I know you can't put your horse out of her misery." Taha sighs and gets to his feet; I hear him draw his longsword from the scabbard on his belt.

I blink the tears from my eyes. "What are you doing?"

"What must be done, for her sake and ours." He takes the sword to Badr, now resting resignedly on the ground, and trains the point over her head. "Go to your ancestors."

"NO," I scream, but I am powerless to stop the horror in time. The blade hits. The sound is awful, wet and thick, but over disconcertingly fast, with not even a grunt of pain from Badr. Just silence and all the wretchedness it keeps. My full moon, stolen from the sky forever.

I scramble to my feet and run over to her, shrieking, "How could you do that, you cruel, ignoble *monster*!" I stoop and brush her silken mane; I hopelessly search for a glimmer in her eyes. They are the painted glass lamps one would find in a bazaar back home. Beautiful but hollow without the light. "Oh, Badr," I whisper, "why did you have to leave? Our adventures were not yet finished."

Things happen around me in an agitated blur. Taha unbuckles and carries off some half-empty saddlebags. Fey and Reza try to recover our scattered items. I don't help; I don't even move when the soil trembles under me.

"Forget the food. It's too late!" says Reza, pushing Fey to her horse.

Taha climbs into his saddle. "Imani, you've no choice but to ride with me. My horse can best bear the weight."

I can neither ride with him nor shake the vision of him killing Badr. How foolish am I, thinking there could be anything but conceit and cruelty to that boy?

"I swear on the Great Spirit," he says in a raised voice.

A guttural snarl floats over the hill. It is an animalistic sound accompanied by the stench of rotting flesh. In a distant part of my mind, I recognize the signs of—

"Werehyenas," Reza shouts.

Staggering out from between the crumbling pillars of the ruin on the hill are eight-foot-tall beasts, neither man nor hyena, somehow both. At least a dozen of the monsters, hungering for flesh—they were people once, lost souls said to have been cursed by the Desert's Bane to never know redemption. And if a person is killed by a werehyena, she joins them, doomed to roam in their adrift clans for eternity.

The pack begins loping down toward us. Their patchy fur camouflages them amidst the debris scattered on the hill; they bounce and spring off the debris as if the land is glass and they are made of light. The monsters laugh and growl and snarl. They utter sounds that may have been words once, but I could only know in a nightmare what they might be saying, whether they are threatening us or pleading with us for help. The notions terrify me equally.

"Imani, *please*," Taha yells at me.

But I can't move. An irrational part of me doesn't want to. It wants to stay here with Badr; it would rather go where she has gone than ride with Taha.

Fey snaps her fingers and summons bright flaming orbs into her palms. Reza holds his hands open over the dry earth; the ground trembles and cracks under him as deadly shards of stone lift and hover in the air. As Fey begins shooting immense plumes of fire at the werehyenas, Reza barrages them with the stone spikes he pulls up from the ground. The monsters fall down the hill, singed, crushed, and skewered, but even more take their place in a swelling horde.

"This is useless. We're too outnumbered," Fey snaps, shooting a glare back at Taha. "Just leave her. We need to get out of here!"

"No, we need her." Taha leaps off his colt and sprints over to me, as behind him, Reza and Fey make for their horses. "Come *on*," he grunts, dragging me up by the back of my cloak. He tugs me to his colt and practically throws me onto it before hoisting himself into the saddle and snapping the reins. *"Yah!"*

I've no choice but to hold on to him, so I bunch his riding cloak in my fists. We charge through the valley, our harried beasts kicking up dirt and gravel, the shadows of their thrashing limbs stretching colossally over the hills. The pack of werehyenas sees us running and follows.

14

OUR HORSES SPRINT DOWN THE VALLEY'S SNAKing path. I follow Taha's example and contract my body in the rocking saddle. He nimbly directs his galloping colt around the bends in the path, but the frantic ride is endless. It feels like we aren't gaining any ground until we finally come upon a fork formed by a line of mountains. We hurtle on but don't change course. I lean forward to spy Taha's face. He is staring at the fork, and nothing is going on behind his eyes—no thoughts, no plans, no threat assessments of the various routes. Nothing. He has forgotten which way we need to go, or he can't think through his fear.

I shake his elbow. "Taha, which way?"

He blinks, pulls the reins, and takes us to the right. He addresses Reza over my shoulder. "Block it!"

The wiry man tugs his horse about and stops in the center of the path, his braid fluttering in the wind. Werehyenas scramble around the bend, long tongues lolling from their open jaws, dripping saliva. The sight of Reza ignites their bloodlust; they shriek and clumsily lunge on their misshapen limbs toward him. The young man's arms rise, palms open. Within seconds, the mountains begin to groan. The werehyenas pay this no mind; they are mere meters from Reza when he closes his fists and yanks his arms down. A monstrous crack sunders the air, and a huge chunk of stone slides off the mountainside and smashes over the path, burying the screeching werehyenas.

Taha slows us to a stop, giving me a chance to survey the incredible sight. "Well done, Cousin," he calls out.

"I could kiss you right now," Fey exclaims to Reza as he rides over. He is already flush with exertion, but he manages to steep an even deeper shade of red.

I can't help but be swept up in the relief of victory. "Thank you for saving us, Reza. Your affinity is truly impressive."

He actually acknowledges my compliment with a nod, and then, like the rest of us, studies the pile of rubble. "I think that's the biggest single hunk of earth I have ever manipulated."

"Easily," says Taha.

"Yes . . . it was really something," murmurs Fey, brushing a hand along the length of Reza's arm.

At that, Taha brusquely turns the horse and squeezes his heels. "Keep moving."

We ride on, slower now, and the conversation lapses and isn't picked up again. Night arrives like a thief, with a slow creep, stealing the day piece by piece. It is in this total quiet, mountain walls raised to enclose us, that the dire reality of our situation becomes clear.

"We should have followed my auntie's instructions," I say in Taha's ear.

He ignores me, though he cannot deny it is becoming difficult to see a few meters ahead, and even his skin is stippled with goose bumps from the cold. In many parts of the Sahir, it is hot in the day and freezing at night. For an unwary traveler, the conditions can quickly prove fatal.

I try again. "We must stop soon and make camp. Somewhere sheltered, or we will die of exposure before our lack of food has a chance to be a concern."

He stops to consult his map in the half-light. Worry etches his brow, setting me further on edge. I try to lean around him to check the map too, but he quickly replaces it in his saddlebag and leads us on. I am too weak to protest. I haven't had a chance to check the wound in my side, but it feels worse than a graze, and sticky blood has begun running down my torso. I want nothing more than somewhere to stop, and soon.

The route we follow takes us from the comparatively open riverbed to a narrow pass between granite walls. Hours slip past with us wading through the gloom, the rising, veering path vanishing, the shadows thickening, the air turning icy, unforgiving, and thin. Details are snatched from my vision; the world swims and shrinks. When we finally emerge from the mountain pass, the light of the crescent moon is only just enough to see what Taha has led us to.

The path ahead opens wide like lungs expanding for a full breath. On either side, it is crowded by cedar trees that are far too lush for a dead place. And there, at the end, towers a granite rock face with an extravagant carved façade and the words *Al-Medina-Al-Uwla*. Between the whittled pillars and delicate floral details below waits an entrance.

"What is this place?" Reza asks as we slowly ride toward it.

"Haven't we had enough ruins for one day?" laments Fey.

Pale moonlight reflects eerie slivers in Taha's eyes. "I took some wrong turns back there, and there was no way off this path but to pass through . . . whatever this place is."

"The First City." I read the name aloud, carefully studying the façade again. "It must have been created and inhabited by ancient tribes. We may be the first people in *centuries* to lay eyes upon it." For a moment, I forget my pain and grief. "My mother won't believe this when I tell her."

Fey waves an arm. "Great, interesting! I'd like to know if we must venture *inside*?"

"Yes, we've no choice," answers Taha. "But if the map is correct, going through the city should prove more efficient than the route we were taking anyway. Once we descend the mountain on the other side, we'll leave the Vale and be only a few days from the Sands. So we make camp inside and leave at dawn. We'll hunt for food tomorrow the first chance we get."

"Wonderful," Fey mutters. "A night spent in an ancient, abandoned city nobody has set foot in for an eternity."

The hairs on the nape of my neck stand up, and I am suddenly impatient for the comfort of light. I reach for my torch, but thankfully, Fey is of the same mind. She holds a hand over her unlit torch, and I sense the emanating heat she is drawing from our environment and her own body. The heat intensifies, there is a gasp and low roar, and the torch head ignites. With a flutter of her fingers, she tosses fire onto our torches too. Curiously, the flames only serve to emphasize the darkness.

Taha leads the way up the stairs and across the portico into the entrance. The clopping of our horses' hooves echoes down a very long tunnel. Red torchlight splashes on its walls and the detailed landscapes etched there—a dune sea, fertile plains, a pride of lions, a gathering of people on camels. I experience an intense, disorienting certainty that I have seen something like these artworks before, but I cannot remember where.

My eyes snag on an etching that infuses terror into my very bones. "Taha, slow down," I whisper.

He pulls the reins, stopping his colt. I raise my torch as high as I can without causing myself pain. The light fills the curving ribbons of engraved branches.

Taha quirks a brow. "It's a tree."

"No," I breathe, sweeping my gaze over the carving, "not just any tree. One identical to the misra tree in the Sanctuary. But why is it depicted here?"

He looks at me over his shoulder. "Hold on, you've seen the misra tree?"

"Once, before we left Qalia. My auntie showed it to me."

"Of course she did." He faces the carving again and shakes his head. "You're mistaken. The misra tree has only ever grown in the Sanctuary."

It is what every historical account states, but I cannot shake the feeling that there is something deeply special about the tree etched into this ancient wall. Something special about this place too. I recall the magnificent city I keep seeing in my dreams these last few weeks . . . Could it be this place? *How?*

Unconvinced, Taha continues on. Slowly my torchlight melts off the tips of the tree's branches, submerging it into darkness once again. A few moments later, we emerge from the hall onto a plaza, and we gasp in chorus.

The city has been constructed almost entirely in the same pale granite, and the previously weak light of the moon is being amplified by it, generating a diffuse glow. Misty mountains stand on the left and right, nestling between them a climbing maze of staircases and ramps linking dome-roofed buildings. Between the lattice of ramps are more cedar trees, and obelisks from which dangle silver lanterns. A roaring waterfall cascades over a mountain peak on the right; the crystal-clear water rushes into a channel that wends down through the city, across the plaza in front of us, over the edge of a platform dozens of meters to our left, and falls to somewhere below.

"Unbelievable," says Fey. "It's as if the city has been—"

"Untouched by time." Not a single stone is cracked or crumbling. The silver of the lanterns has taken no patina; the houses look as if they've only recently been constructed. Spirits' sakes, there is flowing water in what should be a land of death and despair.

"This is it," I murmur to myself. "This is the place."

"What is?" Taha asks, glancing over his shoulder at me.

I don't answer—how can I? Sensing no answer is forthcoming, Taha hops off his horse and ventures to the channel with that stubborn confidence he seems incapable of surrendering. We watch him, and I am certain the others are waiting for the same thing: a river serpent to surge out of the water and drag him under. Nothing of the sort happens. He fills his waterskins and drinks heartily.

"Freshest water I've ever tasted," he declares.

Fey extinguishes our torches, and I reluctantly join her and Reza in filling our waterskins. The channel's water is the coldest

I have felt in my life, so visibly pure, it must issue from under the watchful gaze of the Great Spirit itself.

"Where should we make camp?" Reza asks when we are finishing up.

"We could stay in a building," Taha suggests.

"Are you looking for trouble? We're not sleeping in a . . ." Fey pauses to look around. "How old is this place? Centuries? Millennia? You know something, it doesn't matter. We are not sleeping in an ancient house. I say we camp outside somewhere close to the city gates."

"Agreed," Reza says, rubbing a hand along Fey's shoulders.

"It will be warmer inside," says Taha. "The stone will insulate us, and we won't have to light a campfire that could attract attention. We're in a ruin, or what should be a ruin, remember? We don't know what dwells here."

We look at each other for answers. Taha turns to me. "What do you think?"

Is he really asking my opinion? Could it be he feels some *guilt* over what he did to Badr? Nonsense. Sooner a lion feels guilt over slaying a gazelle than Taha reflects on his behavior. Regardless, my bones are turning to ice, and the wound in my side is painfully stiff.

"Inside," I say through chattering teeth. "Nothing indicates we are safer out here. At least in one of the buildings, we'll be warm, and right now, exposure is our biggest threat."

Taha nods. "Fine. We'll find the gate leading out of the city and choose a building close by."

Reza sighs, but it is a compromise at least. We walk our horses across the bridge and up a ramp to the first level. The city is dreamlike in its magnificence, the stone of its fabrication lovingly capturing every glimmer of moonlight and sending it back one hundredfold. Every building we pass has doors of solid gold carved with geometric patterns, their entrances flanked by bronze urns brimful of iridescent purple flowers. On some levels, the land is spacious enough to sustain fenced fields, abounding with blooming fruit trees and rows of ripe vegetables. Reza and Fey creep between the fields, pilfering as much as they can stack in their arms for dinner. As we pass a meadow of fig trees, Taha hoists himself over the stone fence and pulls a few figs off the branches. He presses one to his nose.

"What's it like?" I whisper.

"Like real." He calls ahead to Reza and Fey. "We'll refill our food supplies before we leave at dawn."

They nod and we press on, along wide staircases and ramps meandering up the mountain and around the waterfall, the fine spray of which I feel on my heated face as a cool mist. But for all the clean water and thriving plant life, there isn't a single living creature to be seen or heard. No birds in the trees, no insects in the grass, no mice hidden in nook or garden. It is unnatural.

We have risen a substantial way up the mountain when we reach a long garden of cedar trees. At the other end is a rock face similar to the entrance, and a dark hall seems to lead to the city's exit.

"There it is," I say, tapping Taha's shoulder. "Let's stop here. We can pen the horses and find a house to stay in."

I take his silence as assent. Though I am hurting, I do my best to pretend I'm not. It is melancholic, helping unsaddle and feed

Taha's colt, watching him gently drape a cloth over the beast's back and call down Sinan, his amber-eyed falcon. He feeds strips of meat to Sinan and the smaller messenger falcons, then covers their cages with blankets too. The tenderness he shows to his animals surprises me, considering how remote his relationship with his father seems. It angers me too, inciting a profound sense of loss. It is his cruelty that left Badr to rot in the harsh sun and cold night, never to be found again, except perhaps by monsters who will devour her flesh, and if that has gone, gnaw her bones to dust.

Soon the emotional pain is too much for me to help him. I help Fey instead, winding rope around several trees to make an enclosure. But that is no better—I think of Baba back in Qalia, striding around the pen, clicking his tongue as he trains his horses, often helped by Atheer on his days off. We trained Badr together, Baba and I, preparing her to join me in the Shields. I miss Baba so much, although I am accustomed to being away from home for extended periods. I miss them all, and even the thought of reuniting my family with Atheer only chases away some of the ache. I dread what awaits me in Alqibah; I fear learning that my brother has perished as much as I fear discovering that my brother is a person I no longer recognize.

I try to concentrate on the task at hand, using my numb fingers to tie the makeshift warning charms to the ropes. When that's done, we collect our bags and descend the ramp in search of somewhere to stay. I am reduced to limping along at the back. Taha glances at me a few times but doesn't address it.

Each house we pass looks acceptable enough, but it seems we

are all afraid of making the decision, Taha included, and that is awfully unlike him. I impatiently point at a house perched on a rocky outcrop, shaped like a stocky minaret with a gold roof.

"How about that one?"

They give tentative nods. Taha climbs the front steps and feels around the ornate gold door for a grip he can push. The door groans open onto a dark room. I hold my breath, expecting a pall of dust, but the interior isn't musty at all. Like the rest of the First City, it is unspoiled by time.

We inch into a fully furnished entry hall.

"How . . ." Reza goes to a cedarwood console. A fringed rug hangs on the wall above it. "How is this possible?"

It shouldn't be. It can't be.

Fey lights a tall candelabra, allowing us to marvel at what is revealed: patterned engravings in the walls; a skylight above us overgrown with purple flowers and vines; traditional, ornate furnishings, including a silver shisha pipe by red floor seating. Everything is pristine, as if the inhabitants of the house stepped out mere minutes ago.

We drift from room to room, exploring in stunned, terrified silence. The house is even heated cozily, despite there not being any fire going. And though there are beds with beaded blankets and soft pillows, we choose to settle on the sitting room rug. Reza and Fey bunch their bedrolls together and feast on their small boon of fruits, away from me and Taha. He is still scrutinizing the locks on the windows and doors. I don't have much of an appetite, so I set up in the corner, kick off my boots, and, when the others aren't looking, carefully lift my tunic. A jagged, blood-encrusted gash stretches under my ribs, likely caused by one of the rocks I fell on. It isn't long or too wide, but it requires stitching if it is to heal properly and not get infected. Doing that will be painful, but I don't want to reveal any weakness in front of the others. I'll have to wait until they've fallen asleep to do it.

I gingerly lower my tunic and slide under my blanket. Fey and Reza curl on their sides too, Reza telling a joke, Fey giggling softly. The lulling ambience beckons my exhausted body to sleep, but at the sound of shuffling, I narrowly open my eyes. Taha has placed his bedroll near mine and is standing with his back to me. I watch him meticulously remove his riding cloak and unfasten his leather armor, stripping down to his sirwal and a flimsy beige tunic that clings across his muscular shoulders. He turns, and in the shifting candlelight, I detect the shadow of a bruise on his jaw from where I hit him earlier.

As he lies down with a sigh, I pretend to be asleep. I let a few moments pass before I peer at him through my lashes again. It is akin to safely studying a dangerous animal from outside an enclosure. He reclines with an arm folded behind his head, the top of his tunic opening on his chest. His other hand fingers a wooden falcon pendant hanging from a leather cord around his neck. With him quiet like that, not ordering anyone around or being ordered by his father, I begin to see something in his hard eyes I never thought I would. Free thoughts and emotions too, a tumultuous ocean churning. Worry, glinting between the roiling waves. Fear, perhaps even doubt. Or I think I do—I *want* to— so I don't quite feel I am placing my safety into the hands of a stranger with unknown intent.

Taha frowns at himself and releases the pendant, which resembles the figurines Atheer carved. He turns over toward me, and whatever meaningful thing was going on in there, it's finished.

I shut my eyes and sink into the silence. Then, when I am confident he has fallen asleep too, I sit up, drag my bag over, and remove from it a small medical kit. I work as quietly as humanly possible, uncorking an antibacterial tincture, but somehow I still manage to rouse Taha—or he was pretending to be asleep too.

"You're hurt," he whispers, sitting up.

Damn it, I think. "The fall. It's not a problem."

He casts a glance over his shoulder at Fey and Reza. Finding them asleep, he looks back at me. Now he is the young man I sparred with. Not hard-faced and arrogant, but a little vulnerable, that chink in his armor showing again. "Let me see it."

"I said it's not a problem." I pour a few drops of the clear tincture onto a dressing.

Taha lightly places his hand on my wrist. "Let me help you. I've stitched many wounds before, even bad ones."

"I don't need your help," I rasp as my heart pounds. "Why do you even care?"

He takes the dressing from me anyway. "Spirits, I'd heard you were more stubborn than a mountain, but I thought that was an exaggeration. Imani." He slides closer. "Do you want this done right or not?"

"Who says I'm stubborn?" I mutter.

He gazes at me expectantly. I hesitate, my ears shaking with the drum of my pulse. Taha, stitching me up. *Touching* me in a caring way. I don't know why the idea makes me tremble. Perhaps the last two years, I had only been lying to myself that I didn't care if he ignored me.

I reluctantly lift my tunic. "Fine."

He inches even closer and gently places his warm fingertips on my body, holding me still. "Is that all right?" he asks softly. A pale rose blush has begun flourishing across his jaw.

"Yes," I squeak, my heart crawling up my chest.

He nods and begins dabbing the gash. It stings something diabolic, like a thousand tiny daggers are stabbing me. I suck a breath through clenched teeth and direct my teary gaze at the ceiling. Taha clears his throat.

"I wanted to apologize for what happened to Badr. You were right, I pushed the horses too hard, and . . ." He swallows. "I didn't want to take her life. I only did because it had to be done. Your father is the greatest horselord in Qalia. You know most horses never recover from open fractures."

I nod wordlessly. My throat is tight, an ache pressing behind my eyes. I am at a loss for words over his unexpected confession, so much so that it has even distracted me from the pain.

"It's . . . it's all right," I find myself whispering back. "In some ways, it was a kindness. You spared me the burden of the act without a second thought."

Taha wipes his hands clean with tincture and expertly threads a needle. "This will hurt," he says, raising the needle to my torso and leaning in. "Try to think of something else."

"Like what?" I ask weakly, raising my eyes to the ceiling again.

"Something that makes you feel good."

I look back down at him, my heavy gaze tracing his dark, disheveled hair and bright eyes glistening in the candlelight. His lips, moist from where he keeps running his tongue over them in concentration. The needle pokes flesh. Fever finds me, and suddenly I am awfully jumbled inside, a river with all its muddy sediment stirred up. Is it the pain of being sutured, or how different from usual Taha is behaving? The confusion over how changeable he is, as unpredictable as the weather. Clear-skied, then stormy without warning, nimbly evading my attempts to understand him. I don't know, but I hurriedly seek a lighter avenue of conversation to divert attention from myself. I jut my chin at the falcon pendant hanging from his neck.

"I've never seen that pendant before. It's beautiful." Without thinking, I reach over and touch the wood, my fingers grazing his bare chest. I realize where my words are going after I've already said them. "It reminds me of the statuettes Atheer used to carve in his spare time at home. They were always so lifelike. Once something caught his interest, a person or animal, a curiously shaped tree, even if he had only glimpsed it for a moment during his travels, he never forgot its details . . ." The ache behind my eyes intensifies; a vise tightens around my temples. I pull my hand away, but not before I notice goose bumps racing across Taha's skin, despite the room's pleasant warmth.

"You are dedicated to your family," he says.

"Yes. I would lay down my life for theirs."

"Even if they've done something wrong?" he asks.

He means Atheer, and I don't know whether to feel hurt or indignant. "My brother is not the person you think he is," I say, even as a small part of me wonders if Atheer is still the person *I* think he is. "He is selfless, kindhearted. A man of honor." Taha doesn't respond or argue, only continues to look at me. I sigh.

"No matter what happens to me, my brother is returning home safely."

"I admire your devotion," he says, but his tone is sad. He drops his gaze, though I swear on the Spirits, the silver of tears laces his eyes. "Finished," he says after a few quiet moments, snipping the thread with a pair of scissors. "Just need to wrap it." I glance down at his handiwork; he wasn't lying when he said he had experience suturing wounds. This one is perfectly threaded. He ties a bandage around my torso and neatly replaces my things in my bag.

"Thank you, Taha." They are words I never thought I'd have cause to utter in my life. But I also once thought my brother was dead and I would never bind a djinni to myself. I suppose there is a first time for everything.

"Don't mention it." He tucks the pendant under his shirt and lies down on his other side, shielding his face from me.

I sit a little longer, watching the gentle rise and fall of his shoulder. I am unsure how to feel, but I feel it all at once. Sorrow, disquiet, and the worst of them: desire. For what, I don't ask myself. I lie down too and close my eyes.

15

FOR ONCE, SLEEP IS DREAMLESS, ALL-CONSUMING. When I rouse, I can't tell if I drifted off a minute ago, or an entire year has passed. It's unclear what has woken me, but the candelabra is halfway spent, meaning it is not yet morning. The house is soundless, as is the world outside. The First City. I am so accustomed to the night-calls of birds that this solid silence is earsplitting. I close my eyes, willing myself back to sleep before my worries can intrude. *Too late.* An idea occurs to me, an opportunity to resolve two problems at once without getting caught. Taha's letter, and Qayn.

Slowly, quietly, I sit up and look over the others. Fey and Reza are turned inward, and Taha is still lying on his opposite side. But by the way their shoulders are moving, the rhythm of their breathing—they are sound asleep.

I push my blanket aside and creep over to my bag. Once the letter is stuffed safely into my pocket, I take one of the tallest burning candles down the corridor to a bedroom and shut the door. I press my ear to it, listening, but no one has noticed my departure.

I fix the candle in a gold vessel by the door and unfold the crinkled page. Again, I am struck by the unsteady handwriting, the sense that the writer is unsure of himself but attempting to appear otherwise. The scribbled message reads:

Dear Father,

I write to assuage your concerns.

Though repeated attempts to force her return have failed, rest assured. Her presence will neither distract nor hinder me from fulfilling your will. I remain focused and dedicated to our cause, and should she present an obstacle, she will be summarily dealt with.

Our expedition is due to reach Alqibah on schedule. We have been traveling well each day.

The remainder of the letter gives painstaking details of our daily agenda, the times we rise, how long we ride for, when we rest. There is neither conclusion nor signature, so I assume Taha didn't have a chance to finish the letter before it was lost.

I read the message two, three, four times, growing more ill at ease with every pass. Tricky questions bite at me with pointed teeth. I've no doubt the *her* mentioned is me. I was right, then. Taha's harassment was a concerted attempt to turn me back to Qalia. But for what purpose, and what is Bayek's *will* that he writes of? What does *dealt with* mean? And why do I feel so crushingly disappointed by all of this? Taha behaves to his father and friends one way—with them, he is cold, arrogant, cruel. And with me, another, if only slightly—he is warmer, kinder, even a little playful. It is as if there are two sides of him and he cannot decide which one he wants to lead. Under his strength, armor, and deadly weapons, I suspect Taha is little more than a hollow boy yearning for direction.

I crush the letter in my fist and lean my head against the door. Why should I even care? This is Taha I am thinking of, and I am a fool who has allowed herself to be drawn in by his magical talent, his discipline, his apology, and his occasional acts of generosity. It is all a show. He is toying with me; he *must* be—yet I despise how I am still holding out hope that the face he puts on for his father and friends is the real pretense.

Sighing, I whisper, "Qayn, I command your presence."

The djinni materializes before me in a breath of wind that almost extinguishes the candle's flame. "Finally, you deign to consider me worthy of release," he drawls, sliding his black eyes around the room. They find me finally, and settle on the crushed letter in my fist. "What's that?"

I look at the sheet opening in my palm. I intended only to ask Qayn a few questions about Alqibah, but before I know it, I am pacing the room, heatedly whispering a condensed account, from Badr's slaughter to the contents of the letter. It is difficult, relating how Taha killed the filly, and I have to conceal my teary eyes with one hand.

"I am sorry for your loss, Slayer. It was an unjust death."

I peek at him between my fingers, but Qayn's expression is genuine. I hadn't thought him capable; it only strengthens my desire to talk. I shuffle over and slump onto the bed.

"I accept that Taha had to do it, truly, but after reading his letter . . . I don't know what to think of him, or what he means to do."

Qayn leans against the wall by the frosted-glass window, sighing as if the subject bores him. "Seems rather obvious to me. This is the boy who has been sent to capture your brother, after all. *Recover*—my apologies."

I arch a brow. "What are you implying?"

He strolls away from the window, sliding his hands into his pockets. "Oh, I don't know. Perhaps that he will arrest Atheer and merrily parade him through the Sahir like a fat, tethered goat going to slaughter."

My gut twists like a wet cloth being wrung of water. "If you've only distressing things to say, pack your forked tongue back into your mouth, snake. Taha can't arrest my brother on a whim. It is only if Atheer resists, which he won't."

Qayn raises a finger. "One, you don't know that about Atheer." He raises another. "Two, provided he *does* agree to return peacefully, Taha will provoke him, as he regularly does you, creating the ideal justification for an arrest." Seeing my horror, a savage smirk crosses Qayn's face. "You said it yourself. Taha, eldest son of the mighty Grand Zahim, both men with everything to lose and everything to gain. The pleasure of putting someone from the Beya clan in chains will last them a lifetime."

"And pressing this awful subject is little more than entertainment for you," I shoot back. "I still don't believe you've only come for a sightseeing tour or to check on my brother's welfare. You are hiding things from me."

"Am I?" he asks in the ambiguous lilt that invites no argument.

"At least answer me this, devil. Were you lying when you said Atheer had been stealing misra for years?"

"No, I was truthful about that," he says.

I fidget with a loose thread in my sleeve, thinking of the accusations Taha and the others leveled at me before we entered the Vale. "Did Atheer tell you why he started stealing it?"

"To smuggle it to the rebels in Alqibah."

"Not because he had become magically obsessed?" I ask.

Qayn shakes his head. "He enjoyed using magic, like any human would, but he was in control of himself."

Just as Amira said. Why did I ever doubt her? I attended Atheer's first Proving Trial at the Order of Sorcerers with my family. Atheer was the only sorcerer in his cohort able to fully exercise his affinity by that stage. He could only skin-change into a small lion for a minute, but that minute was one of total control for him—and one of overwhelming pride for our parents. Atheer didn't falter in and out of his lion form; he didn't have to stay totally still to maintain the transformation like other novice skin-changers do. There was no struggle maintaining the practice of "mind over magic." Spirits, he even mustered a roar that made the gathered families startle and laugh. As with Auntie Aziza, I always considered my brother the essence of magical discipline, and perhaps the only reason I began to believe otherwise was because I desperately needed an explanation for his baffling theft and disappearance. The thought of Mama's sister reminds me of something else. The most significant question I want to ask hangs on the tip of my tongue—*Did Atheer ever mention if my auntie was helping him?*—but for the life of me, I cannot eject it. It sits there, a short blade lodged in my throat.

"You seem troubled, Slayer," Qayn says.

"Have you ever felt you may not know someone as well as you once thought?" I ask quietly.

"Yes, and I paid a terrible price for my mistake." He stops at the window, where he is washed in the cold light of the moon. It makes him even more ethereal and impossibly beautiful; it somehow darkens the black of his eyes, intensifying the danger swimming in them. The same scent I perceived back in the Forbidden Wastes permeates the room: that of fire and ruin. "I was not always this way, you see," he says. "Powerless."

I know better than to entertain this conversation, no matter how much this monster intrigues me, but my curiosity to know more about him is ravenous. "You weren't?"

"No. I had magic once, like you. It was stolen by someone I held very dear, someone I thought I could trust. . . . They knew how important magic was to me, but wanting to hurt me, they took it away. I have been weak ever since, a pitiful shadow of my former self."

A sting with no physical source gouges me, and I think of Atheer and Auntie. People I love and trust. People who would never hide the truth from me . . . would they?

"Do you hate them for it?" I ask.

The opaque glass obscures the city, but Qayn looks to where the moon hangs in the sky. "I have hated them every day for a thousand years."

A thousand years. Qayn is not old; he is *ancient,* a being outside time. "How did they take your magic away?" I ask.

"If someone takes your misra away, you no longer have magic. Someone took my source," he answers.

"But isn't there any way you can get it back?"

Rage twists his delicate features. "Some things, once taken, can never be returned. Some things, once broken, are broken forever."

I feel a stab of guilt. I thought Qayn little more than a devil, roistering about spreading wickedness and cheap fun. But learning this about him . . . He has lived many lives before me; he has experienced loss and anguish. Are other djinn the same? I was taught in the Shields to never, under any circumstances, try to understand a monster. What if that was wrong?

"Why are you telling me any of this?" I ask.

"Consider it a gesture of goodwill." He peers at me sideways. "I may no longer have my own, but I know much about different magics. I could help you improve yours." He waits for me to respond, but I can hardly move my tongue, I am so conflicted by this conversation. Qayn leaves the window. "Your ability to transform your blade is impressive. But you could do more."

"How?" I ask thinly.

He stops barely a step away. "I could teach you ways to become the blade, to fuse your soul with it. Even to transform it into other things."

An excited shiver climbs my spine. He lightly brushes away a lock of hair that's fallen across my cheek. "Why settle for competing with that mediocre boy, Taha, for the title of best Shield?" he croons in a dark-honey voice, tracing a cold finger along my jaw. "I know the desire for magical power flows through the blood of the famed Beya clan. You are your ancestors' progeny, after all. But I could make you the greatest sorcerer to have ever lived, more accomplished than even them. Wouldn't you like that?"

Yes, I want to shout, with an intensity that startles me. *No,* cries another voice inside. *He is leading you astray, like he led Atheer astray.* I know it, yet dark desire is a maelstrom within me. I must use everything in my power to fight it, to fight *him* and his wicked temptations, and even then, I still feel weak.

"You are evil," I whisper.

Frustration flickers in his eyes. "And you are content to remain naïve." He drops his hand and returns to the window. "Where are we in the Sahir?"

I exhale a pent-up breath. Standing so close to him, feeling his deathly touch, it was like being submerged under water. "Al-Medina-Al-Uwla, in the Vale of Bones," I answer. "Do you know it? It isn't in any history books that I've read."

He halts by the window, his narrow shoulders constricting. "You should not have come here," he says in an oddly restrained voice.

"We didn't intend to, but as I was saying before, Taha led us along the wrong route. I may not have another chance to confer with you before we reach the Sands. I must know what to do once I am in Alqibah. You mentioned the city of Taeel-Sa, but can you give me more specific—"

"You should not have come here," he says again, clenching his fists. "This is a wretched place."

"I *know* that. We only came into the Vale to save time."

"Not the Vale, Slayer. *Here.* . . . The city of regret." He rests his hand on the glass. Icicles form around his fingers, creeping out in silver vines, creaking and cracking across the window.

I gawk at him. "You *know* this place?"

"Yes. Arrogance poisoned its people long ago. They exiled

their king and usurped his throne. But when tragedy found them, they begged for their scorned king's protection."

White breath curls from my trembling lips—the temperature in the room is rapidly plummeting. I edge closer. "Well . . . did he help them?"

Qayn's brows float up. "No," he whispers, shaking his head. "He favored watching them fall."

A chill sinks into my quaking muscles and starts crystallizing my blood. "Qayn, how do you know this?"

After a long, terrible silence, he whispers, "The king was me."

I blink at him, once, twice, half expecting him to fade in a tendril of smoke, and for the realization that I am dreaming to dawn upon me. It doesn't. I shake my head, exhaling a throttled chuckle, though the twitching muscles of my face don't know whether to grimace or lift in a derisive laugh. "Now is not the time for your tales, devil."

"It is the truth. I was exceedingly powerful when I possessed my magic. I built this city as a gift for the one I held dear, and your people flocked to its wonder. But then . . ." He swings his dead eyes over. "Have you heard the name Hubaal?"

Icy terror cleaves me. My mouth noiselessly opens and closes. I can only nod.

Qayn looks back to the window, to his fingers and the frost radiating from them. "Here Hubaal lies, under the First City . . . dreaming."

"H-here," I stammer, reeling. "You're saying . . . Hubaal is *here*?"

Outside the house, a girl screams.

16

THE SCREAM SHATTERS THE NIGHT, ROUSING THE others who drowsily demand answers of each other. Taha says my name; then he shouts it.

"Imani! Where are you?"

He must think *I'm* the one who screamed. Qayn's and my eyes meet. The worry in his rattles me to my core; I have a thousand questions about his confession that he was once king of this city, but I cannot deal with him right now, and I cannot have his existence discovered. I point the blade. "Go."

"You need me."

Footsteps patter down the hall toward the room. Taha, looking for me.

"No time," I hiss, glancing back at Qayn.

"Slayer, stop the noise—"

"Leave *now*!"

The door slams open, the force of the wind snuffing the candle.

"There you are." Taha's alarm morphs to confusion. "Who were you talking to?"

I look at where I still have the dagger pointed, but Qayn is gone. I exhale shakily, lowering my arm. "I wasn't."

Taha glances between me and the room. "I heard you. What were you doing?"

"Practicing my sparring stances." My breathing is short, and sweat thinly glosses my skin. The lie is a good one, but the quiver in my voice might still give it away.

"In the middle of the night? With your wound?"

"I couldn't sleep." I push past him, sheathing the dagger on my thigh. "Did you hear that scream?"

Fey and Reza are bunched at the end of the corridor. "I thought it was you," says Reza, rubbing his tired eyes.

"Someone else. We must investigate."

"No." Taha comes out of the bedroom. My skin crawls with the realization that he actually went in to check if I was lying.

"Why not?" I ask as he marches down the corridor.

"It's a trap. Monsters trying to lure us out."

"Yes, of course," says Fey. Something occurs to her and she stiffens. "They may get into the house."

Taha returns to the living room. "They shouldn't know where we are. We can keep it that way if we stay quiet—"

Another scream rings out, but this one is clearer than the first. And this time, the girl says, *"Help me, please!"*

"Oh, Spirits." Dizziness grips my skull and I stumble into Taha.

He holds me steady. "What's wrong with you?"

"That's her." I hobble over to my things, bundle up my bedroll, and shove it into my bag.

"What are you talking about?" he asks, rounding on me.

I crouch and pull my boots on, jump up and start fitting on my armor.

He snaps his fingers. "Imani? Explain, will you?"

"It's Amira out there," I say impatiently, slinging my cloak on and fastening it.

"Your sister? It can't be," says Fey.

I swallow three bitter gulps from a flask of cold misra tea and stash it. "I know my sister's voice. I have to help her." I hoist my bag onto my shoulders and start for the door.

Taha obstructs me. "You are not going out there."

He isn't stalk-slender like Qayn, relying on deceit and dark words to get his way. Taha was hewn from stone and given life. I try to sidestep him anyway. "Move."

He grabs my shoulder. "It's a trap."

"I don't care," I growl, struggling against him. It's as good as trying to walk through a wall. "Let. Me. *Go.*"

"You're not thinking. She's not thinking," he says to the others. "Amira is not really out there, Imani. She can't be."

Yes, she can. He doesn't know what my sister said the eve of our departure from Qalia: *I am coming with you tomorrow.*

"Imani, can you hear me?" she screams. "I need you!"

I push against Taha, but he only tightens his grip. How strange he is. He loathes me, yet he won't let me run into danger. "*Stop,*" he says. "Remember your training."

"Remember *yours!*" I yell. "Yes, some monsters can fool our minds into believing we are hearing or seeing the people we love, but if we are all hearing the same girl's screams, then this is not an illusion. I will not ignore that voice, whether it is my sister's or not. I am a Shield, sworn to protect and defend our people. You can abandon your duty, Taha, but I won't. Release me now or so help me, I will maim you."

I've strummed the right chord, but I don't know if it was by mentioning duty or my dagger.

"Fine, damn you. Gear up," he instructs Fey and Reza. They race past and gather their things. Taha jolts me. "We go as a *squad*. And if it really is your sister out there, you have some explaining to do."

He unhands me and gets to work. I pace in a tiny circle, urging them to hurry, but the Scouts are nothing if not fast. They are geared in half a minute, and by now, magic is surging readily through my veins.

Taha goes to the door first, me close behind. He opens it, and we both peer out. The moon is shining brightly on the veranda, but it is impossible to see beyond that. The mist that garlanded the mountains earlier has descended to blanket the city, concealing the other buildings. We exchange a glance before stealing down the front steps. I can't see where I am going, and we are so precariously high in the mountains that one wrong move will see me tumble over a railing to my death. I am forced to inch along, waving my hands to disperse the mist.

"Amira, can you hear me?"

"Keep your voice down," he orders.

"*Imani?* Yes, it's me!" Amira shouts from somewhere lower in the city. Her voice is strained; she seems to be under pressure, or in pain.

I lurch on with outstretched hands, desperately trying to find the railing of the ramp that will lead me to the lower level. "I'm coming to you, but I need to keep hearing your voice," I call out.

"*Agh* . . . I don't know if I can . . ." A second later, she utters a short scream and begins sobbing.

"Oh, Spirits," I rasp. *"Amira, please hold on!"*

I reach the end of the ramp and follow the awful sound of my sister's terror, keeping my hand hissing along the railing. I want to move faster, but I am trapped by the rational need to be cautious of where I step. I scan the mist as panic blooms in my chest.

"I don't know," I whisper to myself. "I don't know where . . ."

"Straight ahead, near the waterfall," Taha gruffly supplies.

We continue to the end of the railing and fan away the mist to reveal Amira, clinging by her fingers to the edge of the platform where the waterfall chutes down the mountain.

"I can't hold on!" she cries, her pleading eyes peering at me over the platform's edge.

I lunge forward, yanking my dagger off my thigh, and slam into the balustrade. In the same instant, Amira's fingers slip. She falls, unleashing a scream loud enough to rouse the dead.

"Grab on," I shout, swinging the blade over my head and sending magic rushing through my hand into the steel.

The blade glows vivid blue as it lengthens to a spear. It lowers just in time for Amira to grab hold, though she slips a few inches down the smooth length. The sudden weight on the spear tugs me forward, provoking a scream of protest from the wound in my side. I tilt into the wind and dizzying height, the dark, misty valley spinning beneath me.

Strong arms wrap around me. Taha drags me up and back, and the others help pull the spear over the balustrade. Fey catches my sobbing sister and collapses to the stone with her. I sink on my haunches, my heart thrashing perilously fast. The spear clatters on the ground beside me, shrinking to its original form.

"Thank you!" Amira sprints over and crashes into me, still sobbing. "Thank you, Imani. It was the mist. I—I couldn't see where I was walking . . ."

I am dazed, like I have suffered a thump across the face and had the thoughts knocked out of my ears. My mouth is dry, my wound is throbbing, and my mind is whirling so quickly that I cannot comfort Amira with words. I bundle her shivering body between my arms, hoping that is enough.

"What is going on, Imani? You had your sister shadow us?"

Taha stands over me, Fey and Reza forming up behind him. Somehow he has grown taller. Angrier. My tears dry, my arms slacken; Amira slips away, as quiet as a mouse.

I push up to my feet. "I did no such thing. She has come of her own accord." A belated wave of shock crashes over me. I plant my hands on my knees, panting, every muscle in my body still shaking. Taha isn't making me feel any better.

"That's horseshit and you know it," he says.

I try to straighten up again. "I did *not* ask her to follow us, do you hear? I ordered her to stay in Qalia while I brought Atheer home—and she disobeyed, as usual."

"Hey—" she peeps.

"Not now," I snap.

Taha's eyes are a savanna on fire. "If that is true, order her to go home."

I sigh. "Taha, please, don't be unreasonable. She has already journeyed too far on her own to return home safely."

He steps closer, tilting his head down to glare at me. "I don't care if it's not safe. This mission is already at risk with you here. I am not having another of Atheer's siblings interfering."

"Interfering in what?" I ask, thinking of the letter in my pocket. "Arresting my brother?"

His brows form a hard line. "Carrying out my orders. Send her home. Better yet, if you know what's good for you, take her home yourself and let us go on our way."

"I refuse—"

"Please, listen," Amira picks up again.

Taha isn't listening. He stands close enough that we would brush noses if we were the same height. "Who were you talking to in the house before?"

My gut transforms to a cartwheeling jester. "I wasn't talking to anyone. I already told you, I was practicing stances."

"I heard you." He narrows his vivid eyes; the green is bone-pale in the moonlight. "Speaking, stopping, speaking again. You were having a conversation."

I manage a clumsy shrug. "I don't know what to tell you. You'd just woken up; perhaps you were still shaking off a dream."

"No, you are lying to us and the Council," he fumes. "Spirits help you, Imani, if you've come to help your brother, to give him a resupply of misra or aid him in his plans against us—"

"That is ridiculous!" I exclaim. Yet fear scuttles up the length of me, amassing inexplicable strength. Taha has it set in his mind that Atheer is a traitor to our people, and now he is making space to assign me the role of co-conspirator. He is wrong on both counts, so why am I cowering before his scrutiny like this? It shouldn't matter. Spirits willing, I am bringing Atheer home, and once we are back in Qalia, surrounded by our family and friends, we will be safe from the outsiders and the Harrowland Empire, and from Taha's and Bayek's scheming.

Amira shakes my arm. *"Listen* to me, please! Something is happening!"

Taha reluctantly moves his glare off me. "What are you talking about, girl?"

"Look," she says, gesturing around.

We do, and I quickly realize she is right. Earlier the First City was swimming in mist. Now the mist is dispersing. Not drifting elsewhere on a gust of wind but vanishing entirely. In moments, houses and buildings emerge from the fog, and the mountains spear into the night sky. An invisible curtain drops, and as it does, a different city is revealed. A wretched one.

The glow of the stones fades, the moonlight wanes; the gleaming gold domes and doors dim, dull, and erode; cracks appear in the walls, fissuring out like slithering snakes; entire chunks of ground crumble away, leaving structures to precariously tilt into the valley's steep drop; the cedar trees shed their leaves, and their trunks blanch as the pleasant scent of resin twists and rots; purple flowers wilt, crops shrivel, the waterfall dries up, and over everything settles a layer of ancient decay. The ground trembles, and a deep sigh hums in the city's decrepit bones.

"What is going on?" Amira whispers.

Qayn's warning. It makes sense now.

"Hubaal," I say, slowly turning. "We've woken him."

17

TAHA NUDGES ME. "WHAT DID YOU SAY?"

"Hubaal. He dwells here, in the First City, slumbering . . ." I drift off, understanding at last why the city appeared to us as an impossibly beautiful mirage at first. "Somehow Al-Medina-Al-Uwla was his dream, and a giant's magic must be powerful enough that it tricked us. But now that he has woken . . . this, the way it appears to us now, *this* is the truth."

"How do you know that?"

Fey shakes her head. "You're wrong. It's impossible; this is not happening—"

"We were *in* Hubaal's dream?" Reza asks in that skeptical tone he employs so regularly with me.

I ignore their protests and search for Hubaal. But he cannot be *in* the city, surely not a giant such as him. This place isn't spacious enough to accommodate him. The ground trembles again, the mountains rumbling. Amira clutches my hand, wobbling on her feet.

"Imani, what do we do?"

"Do?" Fey points at a nearby ramp. "How about *run*?"

Taha fires her an irate look. "We don't know what we're dealing with to know where we can go for safety."

"Imani said it was Hubaal. She should know," says Fey, pointing accusingly at me.

"Well?" he demands. "Are you sure of what you speak, or is it another lie?"

I cast my eyes over the ruins pegged unevenly in the mountain. "Where? From where will you rise?"

Here Hubaal lies, under the First City . . . dreaming.

"That's it." I sprint to the balustrade and peer down the sheer drop into the sea of mist. The others join me.

"I don't see a damned . . . thing . . ." Taha's words die in his throat.

The mist swells upward for an age, the waves breaking and rolling off the dark mass rising from the valley floor. We back away from the balustrade as another deep rumble shakes the city. Amira holds on to me; a trembling Reza tries to comfort an increasingly panicked Fey. Taha is silent and still, staring at the ascending monster. The only thing about him that moves is the pulse in his sweaty neck.

Hubaal the Terrible finally stands in the moonlight, and he is as immense as the mountains themselves. Little is known about elusive giants, their magic or temperament, but I once read a short, ancient account of Hubaal in the Almanac. The words and accompanying sketch are seared in my memory.

Hubaal's face is the face of a lion, his gigantic body is armored in thorny scales, he possesses the claws of a vulture for feet, and from his mane appear the horns of a wild bull; his tail ends with the head of a snake.

The rest of the nightmarish passage spills from my lips. "His gaze is dread; his roar is deluge; his fists are devastation."

Hubaal opens his eyes, revealing the sick fusion of gold and crimson—and he sees us. I don't divert my gaze quickly enough. Existential dread seeds, sprouts, and flourishes in a single breath, its decayed vine wrapping around my heart and urging me to find solace over the balustrade.

"You dare disturb my slumber?" Hubaal booms. My rib cage shakes, my ears ache. *"You dare enter Al-Medina-Al-Uwla without my blessing? All who trespass in the sacred city must die."*

I grab Amira's clammy hand. "Run."

She doesn't move; none of them do. They are rooted to their spots, transfixed by Hubaal's terrible might, petrified by his gaze. I try to push her away.

"Run, find cover while you still can!"

"None who dare enter shall escape."

I have to physically turn Amira's face to break her eye contact with the giant, but it works. She reels at first, baffled, before turning and carefully traversing the clefts in the stone away from the balustrade. I do the same to Reza and Fey, who throws long ropes of fire from her hands at every dead cedar she passes. They ignite, transforming into lampposts blazing against the dusty darkness.

"We need to leave," I say, jogging over to Taha.

"Why?" He blinks dully at the giant. "There is nowhere to go. Look at the size of him."

His ready surrender shocks me. Taha isn't meant to be the one who gives up, even in the face of a giant. He is arrogant, proud, the Shield who thinks he is the best and seems to have enough evidence to convince people. But this person before me . . . Hubaal has scared Taha away and left only the shell.

I try to drag him from the balustrade. "We can hide, and if we can't hide, we can fight!"

"Fight?" He laughs, refusing to shift his weight. "You really do believe the world kneels before you."

"They have defied his will," Hubaal bellows. In my periphery, I see the giant swing his fist. It casts a huge shadow over the city—a shadow rapidly shrinking as it closes the gap to *us.*

I use my hands to tilt Taha's face down, forcing him to see me. "Would your father let you surrender so easily?"

He blinks, his brow furrows, and his hand finds mine. We turn and sprint after the others up a ramp to the next level, navigating the treacherous fractures by the light of the burning trees. Hubaal's scaly fist crashes into the balustrade, destroying the pathway we were standing on moments ago. Huge stones fling to the valley floor; some slingshot into the sky like motes of dust caught on a breeze. A quake rips through the city, throwing Taha and me off our feet. I tumble and tangle in my cloak, or is it his?

Hubaal's fist appears above us again. *"They have ill-used his bounty."*

I scramble up and drag Taha with me into a lane between two houses. "Get down!" I yell.

We drop to the ground. A solid shadow flattens the house before us; I am hit by the wall of air expelling around Hubaal's fist. I scream and wrap my arms over my head as large rocks pelt me. The shadow lifts, raining debris.

"Up here!" comes Amira's shout.

I search for the source of her voice and spot her on the front steps of a house one level up. I pull Taha with me through the rubble toward a ramp. I recognize the mortal quaking of the mountains before it occurs to me that Hubaal has roared. It is so loud, I almost don't hear it, but I feel it in my heart, which writhes and threatens to give up this very moment. We duck down a shadowed lane between more houses as something cracks in the mountains high above. Taha pulls me against the wall and presses his warm body over mine.

"Hold on." He places a firm hand under my collarbone. "Wait for Hubaal to focus elsewhere."

We stay still, enveloped in the shadows, my heart racing under Taha's palm. Boulders from the mountains crash onto the city's top level; I jump as our horses squeal and scream. Taha pats my chest, signaling me to stay calm. I shut my eyes, trying to breathe evenly while praying the horses are unharmed. Hubaal crushes a structure a few houses over.

"Now," Taha whispers.

We dash out of the lane and up the crumbling ramp. I leap over the fissures, catching glimpses through them of the level below, and the vertical drop to the valley.

"Hurry," Amira cries from the house ahead. She is holding the door open, gesturing us on.

"They must atone," Hubaal thunders behind us.

We fly up the narrow steps into the dark house, and Amira slams the door shut behind us. I slide to my knees across the cold stone floor, wheezing. Amira hugs me.

"Are you hurt?"

"No, no, I'm all right," I say, patting her arm. I sit back and paw the sweat off my forehead.

Taha has his back pressed against the door, eyes gilded as he shares his mind with Sinan. The others huddle in a tight circle around me.

"Is it wise to hide in a house?" Reza whispers, while Fey warily inspects the ceiling.

"Better than hiding in the open, isn't it?" says Amira.

Taha joins us. "The giant doesn't know where we are."

"But he will the moment we set foot out that door!" Fey jabs her finger at the entrance. "We can't escape him. As sure as the sun rises, we can't fight him either. Great Spirit forgive you, Taha. We should not have come here."

"We had no choice," he grumbles, lowering to one knee.

"You could have listened to me." I shouldn't be using this moment to prove a point, but I suppose I really am as stubborn as he is arrogant. "My auntie's route would not have brought us these woes. It would have been slower, yes, but safer."

To my astonishment, Fey agrees. "Imani is right. We wouldn't have encountered those werehyenas, and we wouldn't have been the ones to rouse bloody Hubaal after a millennium!"

"That's beside the matter at hand," Taha growls, raking his gaze across us. "We need a plan to fight that beast."

"*Fight* him?" Fey claps her hands to her forehead. "How? Do you think your arrows will pierce his hide? My fires will burn him? Face it. We are trapped here, and if we try to leave, we are dead."

The sound of Hubaal breathing outside fills the silence; it resembles the distant roar of waves.

"He was asleep before, wasn't he?" Amira says to me. "Perhaps we could wait for him to fall asleep again."

"How long will that take?" asks Fey. "It could be hours; it

could be days or weeks. He has been alive since the Desert's Bane. I doubt he perceives time the same way we do."

"You aren't being helpful," Taha mutters.

"And you are?" Reza counters.

But Fey *has* been helpful. She's reminded me of something Qayn said: *Time doesn't really work that way for individuals like me.* And something else. *You need me.* He must have meant in relation to Hubaal.

"Where do the rats hide?" shouts the giant.

Amira clamps her hands over her ears, Fey protects her head as if bracing for a blow; Taha, Reza, and I stare at the shuddering ceiling and the rivers of dust streaming down from it.

Reza wipes the fine powder off his sweaty forehead. "So long as Hubaal knows we are here, he isn't going to fall asleep."

Taha curses under his breath. "There must be a way. Imani, you seem to know a lot about Hubaal. All monsters have weaknesses. What are his?"

"I have no idea," I say, shrugging. "All I know I learned from the Almanac."

"The Almanac doesn't mention this city or the fact that Hubaal sleeps under it. How did you know that?"

Amira bows her head. She must have realized that my source of information is Qayn. The djinni must be able to help us, seeing as he proclaimed himself the king of this cursed city. I have trouble believing a word of that, but he certainly seems to know more about what is going on than we can, imprisoned in this filthy home. He could have an answer for how we can get past Hubaal—but I will need to summon him to ask, and I am not sure I can take that risk with Taha around.

I look over at Amira, who is anxiously picking her nails. She risked so much to follow me here. I don't approve of it, but she is my sister and my charge. I can't let anything happen to her. This is a risk I cannot avoid.

"I need time alone to think."

I head for the corridor under Taha's watchful gaze. Thankfully, he doesn't try to stop me. I find a room at the end of the corridor with its door still intact. I shut it and stand with my back against it. The last thing I need is Taha bursting in on me.

"Qayn, come out," I whisper.

The djinni appears and immediately appraises the dilapidated room. "It happened, didn't it? You roused Hubaal from his slumber."

"Are the rats . . . here?" A boom rattles the city as Hubaal crushes a house not far from this one. In the living room, Amira cries out, and Fey loudly curses.

"Is that answer enough?" I hiss. "I need your help. Tell me what Hubaal's weaknesses are."

Qayn's brows slowly rise. "Weaknesses? He has none. You cannot fight him."

"Then tell me how to get around him."

"There is no way around him." Qayn haughtily crosses his thin arms. "I appointed Hubaal to guard the First City and the Vale's cedar trees. He loved this place so dearly that only dreams of its former glory bring him peace. Nothing can evade his watchful eye."

"You *appointed* him? He's a giant; he's—"

"Evil?" Qayn finishes for me. "Not all of us are monsters, Slayer, merely painted that way by your Council's brush."

"Spirits, what folly have I found myself in?" I mutter, dragging my fingers through my tangled hair. "So that's it, then? We are destined to die here? Know this, devil: if I die, *you* die."

He fixes me with his vacant eyes. "Hubaal must return to his slumber. Then you may pass."

I exhale. "All right, good, that's what Amira suggested. How do I do that?"

"You can't."

"Some king you are!" I raise a clenched fist. "What good is your binding if you do not aid me?"

"*Well,* if you had let me finish my thought, Slayer, you would have learned that while *you* cannot achieve such a feat, *I* can."

My fist slowly drops. "How? You're powerless."

"Words are mightier than both the sword and the flask of tea."

"I don't understand," I say, wrinkling my face. "You're proposing *talking* to Hubaal?"

"Yes. As I am yours to command, he is mine. I shall command him to return to his slumber and grant us safe passage."

I draw my dagger and jam it against his neck. "On my ancestors, this is not the time for your jesting—"

"I tell no lie nor tale, Slayer. When will you understand that? I was the king of this city. Hubaal will listen to me."

A thin whine vibrates my chest. "How can it *be* that you ruled this city? And Hubaal was helping the Desert's Bane. Does that mean you were too?"

"*I will find you,*" Hubaal rages outside. An explosion rocks the city, closer this time. Another house destroyed. What if ours is next? In the living room, Taha impatiently calls my name. Any moment now, he will try to bust through the door, demanding answers.

"Must we *really* discuss this matter right now, Slayer?" says Qayn.

"Tell me. It's important—"

"Do you wish for me to save your life, or don't you?"

"Yes, I do!" I drag in air; my lungs are pinched, and I am dizzier than if I had been revolving on the spot for the last hour.

"Excellent. First I will need help reaching Hubaal, by way of a distraction perhaps? He is far too enraged and liable to crush me the moment I set foot outside this house."

"But then you will have to appear before the others," I say, aghast. "Taha will find out you are bound to me."

"Yes, the boy will know you broke the law and be beside himself with excitement. He may even bring out the shackles. Do you have a better idea? No? Well, I may have a solution of my own." He inches far too close for comfort. I don't want to look into his eyes, but they swim before me, consuming my vision. "You can leave the First City alone. Get me to Hubaal. On my request, the giant will spare you, but not Taha—"

I recoil against the door. "Absolutely not! How could you suggest such a wicked thing?"

His shrug is unsettlingly flippant. "Seems to me a better outcome than confronting the Grand Zahim for your lawbreaking."

"You are suggesting *murdering* an innocent person."

"Innocent, hmm." Qayn brings his face alongside mine, his soft lips skimming my ear. "Perhaps when this is done, Taha will pen another enlightening letter to his father. Do you think Bayek will keep our little indiscretion secret? Or is this something people throughout Qalia will soon be discussing over tea and *ka'ak*? Imani of the proud Beya clan, bound to a very wicked djinni—"

My shoulders heave; my breath whistles in my throat. "Just what are you, Qayn?"

He leans back, a smile snaking across his thin face. "A friend."

"No, you are not my friend! And I will speak reason into Taha; I will find a way." I turn to the door. If I stand here listening to his venom any longer, he will rot whatever resolve I have left.

"Silly girl," he croons, laughing. "Taha doesn't listen to reason; he listens to his father."

I pause with my hand on the knob as it twists from the other side. I close my fist, stopping Taha. He starts banging on the door.

"Imani, let me in right now."

Evil incarnate loiters at my elbow. "Word to the wise: make the hard choices today, Slayer. When you are enjoying victory tomorrow, you won't feel so bad about them."

"This is not over, Qayn." I open the door.

18

TAHA SCARCELY SEES ME BEFORE HE HAS LOCKED eyes with Qayn. All color drains from his face but a red band lashing the bridge of his nose. "You . . ."

I march past him, and Qayn ambles after me down the corridor.

"I can't *believe* you," Taha splutters.

Amira, Reza, and Fey rise from the floor as we enter the living room. My sister looks like she has swallowed a lemon.

"This is Qayn," I announce. "He is—"

"A djinni," Taha finishes for me.

I turn my head to him, treading into the room like a twitchy wolf. "You're the bloody Djinni Slayer, and you have one *bound* to you?"

The weight of their reproving gazes is crushing. "Yes," I confess on a strangled breath. "He is mine to command."

Fey and Reza curse; Taha starts closing the gap between us. "You broke the law, just like your brother. This treachery, it's in your family, isn't it? It flows like poison in your blood."

"Watch your tongue," I say, but I am asking myself what I

have done. Atheer stole misra; I have bound myself to an evil I don't understand. . . . Is Taha right about us?

"You've betrayed the Council, the Shields, the Great Spirit," he says. "The praise everyone heaps on you, and *this* is how you mastered your affinity? With the help of a filthy djinni?"

My brows snap together. "I resent that, Taha. This was only a recent binding—"

"Does your aunt know?" asks Fey, barely flinching as another house is destroyed nearby.

Amira steps between us, waving her arms. "Please, *stop*. We don't have time for this!"

"Do you think you'll get away with it?" Taha shakes his head. "Not this time, Imani. Your crime will not go unpunished."

"It will if you don't allow me to help," says Qayn.

They carefully crowd around him, like hens only now noticing the fox that has stolen into their house.

"How?" Taha growls.

"Qayn can stop Hubaal, if he can get close enough," I grudgingly explain. "He is our only way out of this city alive."

The djinni smiles. "Correct. So if I were you, *boy,* I would step away from the Slayer."

Taha rounds on him instead. "Are you threatening me, devil? Don't you know what Shields are sworn to do to your kind?"

Taha is a head taller and looks like he stole Qayn's food growing up, but Qayn actually *yawns.* "Yes, yes, eliminate the abominable enemies of the Great Spirit." He shrugs, but he is not in the least bit ambivalent. "I was around a long time before you. I will be around a long time after."

Shivers skate down my spine. I cannot fathom that he is

speaking the truth that he once ruled this city. A djinni ruling people? Perhaps he was also speaking the truth when he said he was not a djinni at all . . .

Taha clenches his teeth so hard, his jawbone is threatening to pop out of his skin. He makes to talk, but Amira interrupts him.

"Taha, *please,* deal with this later, when we're not all about to be crushed!"

I catch Qayn's eye and read the heinous proposal in it. I shake my head, but I do it more out of spite than disagreement. In fact, a dark, unfamiliar part of me has begun considering his offer of doing away with Taha once and for all, turning the idea over like a precious jewel, inspecting its facets, wondering if I can afford it. *What am I even thinking?* Nothing would bring Qayn greater pleasure than debasing me further, like he did to Atheer.

Taha exhales heavily. "What do you need?"

"We must create a distraction," I say. "Give Qayn enough time to reach the balustrade and be close enough for Hubaal to recognize him." I hold a hand up. "Don't ask why. You have to just trust me."

"Trust you," Taha mutters bitterly. He looks away from us, and gradually his dull gaze livens with a plan. At last he nods. "Fine, a distraction. Amira, stay here with me. Imani, you accompany the devil. Fey, Reza—get ready."

THE PLAN AGREED, the others solemnly drain two cold flasks of misra tea. Afterward we bunch at the door. Taha crouches beside it, and Amira kneels beside him.

"Wait for when Hubaal turns his attention away," he says.

The others nod, and Amira gives me a taut smile.

"Be safe," I say. "Both of you. And, Taha, . . . if Sinan is killed while you're sharing minds with him . . . some beastseers don't come back from that."

"Worry about yourself." He bows his head and his eyes flood gold.

I sigh and prize the door open a crack so we can peer out at Hubaal vigilantly looming over the city. I brace, tensing my muscles. For a few moments, nothing changes. Then Fey pats my shoulder, whispering, "Look there, from the upper part of the city."

I scour the skies and spot the lithe black falcon soaring toward Hubaal. As he gets closer, Sinan unleashes a piercing scream that reverbs throughout the city. Hubaal's head jerks, and his attention is drawn away from the houses—including us.

"Now," I whisper, yanking the door back.

Sinan makes for Hubaal's colossal eyes, screaming again.

What is the little moth doing?" booms the giant, jerking his head away.

We sprint down the fractured stone steps and split up. Fey runs to my left; Reza cuts to the right on the next level. Qayn lopes by my side, head turning as he takes stock of the city, or what is left of it. If he was king of Al-Medina-Al-Uwla, then it was *he* who watched it fall. He must have been one of the first djinn to enter the Sahir alongside the Desert's Bane, which means he was around when the Bane was later burning across the land, including the Vale. What was he doing in that time? The fact that I don't have an answer terrifies me.

Sinan attempts another attack on Hubaal's eye and then retreats, spiraling on the giant's left, keeping Hubaal's head turned that way.

"Agh! Begone, creature!" commands the irate giant, swiping an enormous fist.

My insides contract as he comes within a meter of crushing Sinan; the wind produced by Hubaal's momentum is enough to blow Sinan off course. The falcon dives as Taha attempts to regain control of his flight. In the lull, Hubaal glances over the city again and immediately notices Qayn and me sprinting between houses toward the balustrade.

"Aha! The rats!" His fist centers over our route and drops fast.

"This way!" I grab Qayn's hand and tug him to the right, across a narrow garden toward a stone fence. We throw ourselves over it as the house behind us is flattened. I drop to the ground and drag Qayn back against the fence. Debris crashes through the upper half of the fence, showering us in stone and almost taking our heads with it. We compress our bodies, Qayn shivering beside me.

"Some distraction, Slayer," he says hoarsely.

I clamber to my feet and drag him with me. Hand in hand, we leap over strewn chunks of brick and reach the corner of an undamaged house, where we pause, waiting in the shadows. The balustrade is less than two hundred meters away.

"Anytime now, Fey," I murmur.

A high-pitched shout rises from high on our left. An immense ball of fire sails through the air and hits Hubaal's arm, scorching him. He howls angrily, turning his attention from us to Fey, who has scaled the roof of a squat house and has her arms raised above her head.

"Incredible," I whisper before pulling Qayn down a long lane toward the balustrade. "Come on, this is our chance."

Hubaal has fully fixed his fury on Fey. In glimpses, I see her leap off the roof of the building and land in an agile tumble roll. She sprints for cover as Hubaal squashes the house to dust. But just as she moves fast, so too does the giant. He seeks her with both fists.

"Hurry, before he kills her," I urge Qayn, trying to gallop faster than my body will permit.

"Over here, big man!"

A mass of flying rock slams into the other side of Hubaal's head, knocking him off-balance.

"Reza," I gasp in relief, though I cannot see the Scout.

Hubaal relinquishes his hunt of Fey and begins a new search for the sorcerer with the earth affinity. At the same time, Taha has regained control of Sinan's flying and makes a daring assault on the giant's eyes. Hubaal stumbles back, flailing his arms and shaking the earth. I almost lose my footing and tumble headfirst through a crevasse in the path. Qayn yanks me back and pushes me on to the balustrade. The assault on Hubaal continues; orbs of fire and shards of earth bombard him from either side, and Sinan adroitly circles with a graceful yet murderous intent.

We are several meters from the balustrade when Qayn stops me. "Wait here," he puffs, pushing me toward another house. I hurry into the safety of the shadows and crouch down.

Qayn straightens his tunic and approaches the balustrade

with an unsettling, swaggering confidence. He stops calmly before it and shouts, "Hubaal!"

The frenzied attack on the giant suddenly ceases, with Sinan arcing and flying off. Hubaal, breathing heavily, peers straight down at Qayn. I clamp my hands over my mouth, preparing to stifle a scream. Qayn makes an open gesture with his arms and says something I don't catch. And incredibly, recognition sparks in the giant's eyes. In moments, he has lowered to one knee and brought his lion's face level with the city. Without any hint of fear, Qayn ambles to the edge of what remains of the platform, and the two begin conversing.

"Great Spirit have mercy," I whisper to myself.

They are actually talking in an exquisitely melodic language. It is almost like Sahiran, but not quite. Listening to it is akin to recalling a dream I have just woken from. The words are familiar, yet the closer I come to deciphering them, the more unfamiliar they feel. From the tone, the way Hubaal is nodding, I see that Qayn is pacifying him—and it's working. A few minutes pass, and the giant bows his head and lowers into the valley out of sight.

The city is a crypt. Still, quiet; even the dust does not stir. Slowly figures appear from the wreckage, gravitating toward Qayn at the balustrade. First Reza, then Fey, congratulating each other, then Taha and Amira, both safe. I emerge last, on unsteady feet. Qayn really must be the king, as he said. I am relieved to have been spared Hubaal's wrath, but only by a hair's width. Approaching Qayn now, I realize we are in more danger than ever.

The joyous air dissipates instantly as I reach the group and Taha turns to face me. "How did your djinni do that?"

The better question is, how can I have bound this monster to my blade? Whatever the dreadful answers, Taha cannot be involved.

"Not your concern." I shove past him to give Amira a hug. He shadows me.

"It is my concern, Imani. The safety of this group is my responsibility. What is going on here? Your sister shows up, you have a strange djinni bound to you—"

I turn to face him. "Is there sand in your ears? Again, my sister followed me here of her own accord, and I've yet to have a word with her about that. But she will not be interfering, if that is your concern." I toss a pointed glance her way; she stares back defiantly. *Some things never change.* We can share a hug one moment and be at each other's throats the next.

"And this devil?" Taha gestures at Qayn.

"Imani favors my company," he says. "Rather fortunate for you, I should think."

Taha pulls him in with one fist and draws a short curved dagger with the other. "You find this amusing?"

"Just you, boy," Qayn drawls, considering Taha through dancing eyes.

I edge forward. "Stop, don't harm him."

"It is my duty to eliminate him."

"Taha, *stop*! I don't want to do this." But seeing him not lift his lethal gaze from the djinni, I have no choice. I wield my dagger and point it at him. "Put it away."

Reza draws his sword. Fey's hands are engulfed with flames, primed for me too. "You first," she says.

Amira bounces on her heels. "Great Spirit, how are the four

of you Shields? Don't you see we need to leave before the giant rouses again?"

"You will not harm him, Taha," I say, steadying my grip on my hilt.

He peers at me. "You really do favor his company. What, are you . . . in love with him?"

Amira plants her hands on her hips. "*Excuse* me?"

"The whole Beya clan is sick," Reza mutters. Beside him, Fey gags on her disgust.

"What's wrong, Taha?" Qayn asks softly. "You're not jealous, are you?"

A hot flash hits my cheeks. "Shut your indecent mouths!"

Taha grabs Qayn by his hair and yanks his head back, exposing his slender neck. "I will have the last laugh," he growls, jamming the blade to Qayn's throat.

"No, we need his help," I shout, stopping him. "Qayn is the only one who knows where to find my brother! Without him, Atheer is lost to us!"

Taha breathes hard, droplets of sweat sliding down his face despite the chill. He flicks his confused eyes to me. "How is Atheer connected to this devil?"

Despite his precarious position, Qayn's smirk broadens. "He favored my company too. Seems I am rather popular with the Beya clan."

"Ignore him," I say, though my fingers itch with the desire to kill him. "He manipulated my brother in conversation and learned things about him, but Qayn refused to tell me Atheer's whereabouts unless I agreed to bind him to my dagger. Supposedly he wants to see beyond the Sands."

"Your kind truly are pathetic," Taha says to Qayn. "You bargained your liberty for a *holiday*?"

Though Qayn's grin slowly fades, his sharp canines stay bared. He looks primed to take a bite out of Taha's cheek. "I am a bird and my cage is the Sahir. What does a trapped bird yearn for most? Space to spread its wings, even if it is only in a bigger cage."

"You think yourself clever," Taha says.

"And you think yourself impenetrable," Qayn replies without missing a beat. "I see your weaknesses, boy, and my, how many you have."

Taha bares his teeth too, his hand trembling around the blade. I lower my dagger.

"*Please,* Taha, I am begging you. What I did was wrong, and I would never have broken the law if it weren't absolutely necessary. Without Qayn, we will never find Atheer; we will never stop my brother before he does something that impacts the Sahir. All of us." I look across at Fey and Reza. "Right now the lives of our families and friends depend on this djinni, monster or not. Binding him was the only way; you must see that. Once we have found Atheer, you have my word—I will kill this devil as I am sworn to do."

And I mean it. I knew Qayn was a liar, but I also thought he was a petty djinni. But too much has happened to make me now suspect that his appearance of insignificance has been a careful trick on his part—and I intend to find out what he's hiding. Still, I catch the djinni's eye, praying he believes I am only speaking these words to placate the others.

Taha digs the dagger in harder, drawing a drop of onyx blood.

"I could have him howling the information we need if you gave us a moment alone."

Qayn laughs low in his chest. "I'll never sing for you, unless . . ." His devilish eyes slide over to Fey and Reza. "Use this blade on one of your squadmates. Your choice who, I don't mind, but make it *hurt*. Then I will tell you everything you need to know about Atheer."

"Snake," Taha spits, shoving Qayn away in disgust. "I greatly anticipate watching your execution. You two—" He turns his attention to Fey and Reza. "Not a word of this is to be carried back to the Council. Understood? The mission is the priority." He looks at me. "Proceed carefully, Imani. If you try to pull the wool over our eyes once more, I am sending a letter back to my father, informing him that you've come under the influence of a djinni." He stashes his dagger, muttering, "Let's go. I've had enough of this Spirits-forsaken city."

The flames extinguish from Fey's hands, and Reza lowers his sword. We collect our belongings in exhausted silence, then trudge up a ramp leading to the field where we penned the horses. Though the beasts are restless, they're unharmed, and I feel a glimmer of hope noticing Raad trotting over to me. At least I will be able to reunite Atheer with his horse after all this time. I glance at Amira walking by my side; she returns a sheepish smile.

"He bore me here well, with no complaints." She squeezes my arm. "I'm sorry for Badr. I saw her on the trail when I was following your tracks."

I say nothing; I feel nothing but despair. While the others saddle their horses, I pull her behind Raad.

"Why? You promised you would stay home."

"I changed my mind," she says.

"You lied! You don't know what you've gotten yourself into, and Mama and Baba will be worried sick."

She waves a dismissive hand. "I left them a note, said I was going to the Zhofal oasis to clear my mind, and when I return, I will be a better student."

My jaw drops. "That's an extremely hurtful thing to do—"

"But leaving me behind isn't?" She peeks over Raad's flank, but the others are still distracted. "I had time to think during the journey, and I realized something. Atheer left Qalia and the Council behind on purpose. Imani, what if he doesn't *want* to come back?"

I narrow my eyes. "What in the Sahir are you on about? The whole purpose of this mission is to return Atheer to his family and people."

"But it is not your decision to make. Atheer has the right to choose where and how he wants to live. We should ensure he is safe, nothing else."

"Nothing else?" I shake my head. "Atheer isn't in the right mind to be deciding whether or not he will stay in the cursed lands and continue revealing our magic."

"And if he is in the right mind?" She shrugs a shoulder as if to say *Well?* "If he has made every decision deliberately, with full intention? Will you impose your will upon him then?"

After the day's events, I am tired, bloated, and sick under my armor, and the wound in my side is aching. I don't want to discuss a matter like this in my state; I don't want to envision a world where my brother is a changed person. Where he elects to stay in Alqibah, aiding outsiders rather than coming home to his family.

"He has been manipulated into sharing our magic, whether he knows it or not," I say, seizing her wrist. "Please, listen to me carefully, Amira. You got your way coming with us, but I meant what I said to Taha. You cannot interfere. Do you understand?"

"People have a right to think for themselves. Do you understand that?"

I tighten my grip, though my emotional grip on everything is only becoming more tenuous. "Do *not* interfere."

"Know your boundaries—they don't extend to others." She yanks her wrist out of my clutches and jogs across the field. "Hey, Fey, is it? Do you mind if I ride with you?"

I remember something Baba once said to her—*Running from a trial merely delays it*—and I am tempted to call it out. But it feels so futile. Ever since Atheer left, Amira and I have been at odds. He unknowingly erected this barrier between us and left without telling us how to dismantle it.

I sigh and try to focus on my saddlebags, but Qayn has silently sidled up alongside me.

"Given that the nature of our agreement is that I get to sight-see around Alqibah, and since everyone knows of my existence now and can't do a thing about it, there is no harm in me staying out, is there? And you've plenty of space on Raad for me." He smiles, brushing an elegant hand over the nickering stallion. "Hello, my fearless boy."

The devil's mere presence infuriates me. I pivot and grab his tunic, shoving him against a dead cedar. "You had better start giving me answers, Qayn, or there won't be an agreement between us for much longer. Admit you were lying about being king of this city. Admit it!"

He takes on that dark look again, like he is more jackal than boy. "I was not lying," he says, seething. "I told you, I created this city when I still had magic, and your people ventured from across the Sahir to marvel at it."

"Impossible! No djinni is that powerful."

"I was."

I push him harder. "And from your own tongue, you watched Hubaal destroy it under the Desert's Bane's instruction. Just how many were slaughtered here, Qayn?"

"Hundreds," he replies.

My hands quake around the bunched fabric. "*Hundreds*. And you did nothing to save them."

"I did not take kindly to their exploiting me." He sniffs coolly. "In any case, the Desert's Bane was not someone you talked down. If you had seen that monster's wrath, you would judge no error in my actions."

"You saw . . ." My breathing dips; my fingers relax from a sudden surge of frailty. This djinni who found my brother in the Forbidden Wastes, who found me too, once personally encountered the most significant figure of my people's history, the very impetus for the Great Spirit giving us magic. I suddenly want Qayn to stop talking. I feel as if I am coming to view the dark side of the moon, or brushing the moss off an ancient tablet and reading truths upon it I should not know if I wish to maintain my sanity. My world is changing in ways it shouldn't, but I am morbidly curious to hear a firsthand account of the tragedy that scarred the Sahir.

"What was the Bane like?" I whisper.

Qayn fixes me with his otherworldly eyes, the ones that do not belong to him, or anyone. The ones that seem less like eyes and more like hollows trying to engulf me. "That is a memory I do not wish to explore."

I feel like a burst bubble. "I command you—" I start, pulling my dagger on him.

"You cannot," he cuts me off.

"I will extract the answers from you," I say through clenched teeth, "if not now, then soon, Qayn. You have my word." I step away from him. "Leave. We are not in Alqibah yet."

He sighs, ambling off. With his back to me, he says, "It is a pity, Imani, how little of your people's history you truly know. The truth has been hidden from you, and you have welcomed the deception with open arms."

A question as to his meaning appears on my tongue. I swallow it, closing my fist around my dagger until my knuckles ache. Anger burns my chest; it is far preferable over the anxiety making my palms sweat.

"My mother is one of the most esteemed scholars in Qalia. I know my people's history."

A gentle gust teases his long hair and baggy tunic as he studies the annihilated city, wafting over to me the scent of destruction. "Your mother knows falsehoods, so you know falsehoods."

He vanishes on the breeze. A second later, I feel his displeasure heating my blade's hilt.

Heart thumping, I hoist myself into the saddle and follow the others to the city gates, the rock face now touched by pale morning light. I am the last to leave the First City, but I cannot go without casting a look back either. It is as pristine as we found it, the houses restored, the cedar trees thriving, the fields in full bloom, the early sun teasing diamonds in the waterfall rushing over the mountainside.

Hubaal dreams again—and somewhere underneath lies the bones of my people.

19

WE ESCAPE THE VALE BY LATE AFTERNOON AND descend upon a broad, calm countryside. The sight of the rolling green plains is a salve to my tender nerves. I can scarcely believe my fortunes to have escaped Hubaal the Terrible with my life. Skimming so close to death has only intensified my need to save Atheer one thousandfold—my impatience too.

After hours of nearly ceaseless riding, my stomach begins to grumble, and Fey has mentioned her hunger more than once, each time in a higher whine that isn't soothed even by Reza's crass attempts at humor. Taha takes mercy on us shortly before dusk, stopping our party by a patch of oak trees.

"Fey, set up camp; refill our flasks in the nearby stream. Reza and I will see what we can catch." He slides off his horse and unties his bow and quiver. I wait for him to give me an order too, but he has resumed acting as if I don't exist.

I catch Amira's eye as she descends from Fey's mare. Seeing the argument brewing in her gaze, I decide to help the hunting party, whether Taha has invited me or not. Right now, I would take his and Reza's company over my sister's.

I tether Raad to a tree, and once I've given him some water, I jog after Taha. He has crested a nearby hill with Reza, recurve bow slung over one shoulder, the brown, woven sack tossed across the other. They are in the middle of a quiet conversation about what quarry they may find.

"What do you want?" Taha asks when he notices my arrival.

"To help," I say, looking between them. "What can I do?"

"How about go away?" Reza suggests brightly.

I purse my lips. *Pleasant thoughts, Imani. When you see Atheer again, this will all be worth it.* "My food was lost too. I'd like to contribute."

"I thought your kind prefer to have others do things for them," Reza says.

If I were anyone else, I might perceive him as joking, as he usually does. But I know this is personal. He leans forward to look at me past Taha, squinting one eye.

"Anyway, do you even know how to hunt? Having your baba go down to the bazaar for food doesn't count, by the way."

I don't quite know how far pleasant thoughts will carry me, but I pray it is as far as the horizon. "I know as much as what we were taught in the Shields," I respond stiffly.

"It's fine," Taha mutters, sounding fed up. "You can join us."

Reza shrugs and faces front again, having said his part and seeming satisfied enough. I don't address his insults, lest Taha send me away for good, forcing me to confront Amira. I mutely hike alongside them over hills and through brush whispering dreamy songs around our calves. Every so often, Taha points at an inconspicuous rumple in the soil, and Reza places his fingers there, contemplating it before taking us in a new direction.

"Geomancy," Taha explains after the fifth time, evidently spotting my confusion.

I quickly mask it with a brusque nod. "I knew that. He is scrying the soil for any animals that have stepped on it recently."

"Yes." Reza dusts his hands on his knees. "And about five goldenhares headed toward those trees not long ago. I bet they have a burrow there."

"Good. Send them my way." Taha pulls the sack off his shoulder. While Reza picks a quiet path toward the trees, he shoves the sack into my hands. "This isn't a two-person job, but since you insisted on coming: Reza will chase the hares out. I'll catch them. You hold this while I bag them."

He arms himself with his bow and stalks in the opposite direction. I pursue as light-footedly as possible. I might not be an experienced hunter, but I know that the less I stomp and make noise, the better our dinner will be.

Taha locates a suitable spot and crouches in the underbrush. I mimic him and gaze over the plain singed red in the late light. After a while, I sneak a glance at him. He is like a falcon, unblinkingly scanning our surroundings, even though they have not changed and I've half a mind to query if Reza lost his way to the trees. I don't, and the vast silence between us widens, imploring to be filled with something. But *what*? For how much I have disliked Taha over the years, I don't know enough about him to strike up a conversation and dispel the tension.

"We'll reach the Swallowing Sands soon," I say eventually. "What are they like?"

He shrugs a shoulder, not lifting his eyes from the plain. "Difficult . . . like walking through mist. There is no ground and no sky, no forward or back, no past or future. Just sand everywhere." He glances over at me chewing my lip. "But don't worry. Keep by my side, and you'll traverse them safely."

Happiness bubbles in my chest. It shouldn't—he's doing it again, acting completely different around me now that we're alone. But I can't help enjoying his company when he is this way; it's like being given access to a secret garden.

"What about Alqibah?" I ask. "Is it as awful as Fey made it out to be?"

He chuckles softly. "No. I mean, yes, there is violence and poverty, but Alqibah is very ordinary. No magic, boring cities and towns. Just a place, really, and like all places, it has its ugly, bad parts."

"Qalia doesn't have any ugly, bad parts," I say with a faint smile.

He glances at me from under thorny lashes. "Not for you it doesn't, no."

Movement catches his eye before I can query him further. He stands, nocks an arrow, and fires in one seamless motion. I jump to my feet and observe the whistling arrow, but I can't tell what it's going for until it sticks the sprinting goldenhare. Reza emerges from the distant grove, raising a commotion that would make me run too. Taha is already moving. He hops onto a rock a few paces away and fires an arrow, deftly twists to the left, tracks his target for a few seconds, fires, then at once fires another to the right. Each hits a floppy-eared goldenhare as it comes bounding out of the brush.

"Too easy, Cousin!" Reza shouts across the plain. "That enough for now?"

"Yes, you can head back," Taha calls, waving. He replaces his bow on his shoulder and nods to me. "Let's pick them up."

I follow him toward the first hare, my ears already burning over the compliment I'm about to give. "You're an excellent archer," I choke out, then quickly add, "And you seem happy hunting. Why did you pursue the Shields instead?"

"Thank you." He yanks the arrow free of the hare. "My father wanted me to continue his tradition of being a Shield, and I was just as happy to carry his torch."

"Why? You have a far older tradition of being hunters."

"And my father rightly understands that the Al-Baz clan are more than hunters," he says, replacing the arrow in his quiver.

"My father says we are strongest where we are interested." I bag our quarry and follow him to the next hare. "I didn't want to be a scholar like my mother, or go to university like Auntie, and although I love horses, training them isn't what I want to do right now. I was interested in magic and combat since I was a girl, like Atheer. Joining the Shields was only natural. I think I've excelled in it because of that."

"Only natural, of course." Taha removes the bloodied arrow. "I bet the thought of being turned away from the Shields never crossed your mind."

"Not at all. I was confident in my prospects because I was trained by the very best—"

"I was trained by the Grand Commander, and I still worried I wouldn't be admitted," he says.

I hesitate. "Well, I can't think why—"

He dumps the limp hare into my hands. "For the same reason my father was overlooked for the position of Grand Zahim at first. In our society, hard work and aptitude never mean as much as your lineage."

"That's not true—"

"Isn't it?" he interrupts me. "How did you phrase it? My father had to *strong-arm* the Elders?"

My tongue twists and knots. "Well, perhaps I was wrong about that," I mumble. I slide the hare into the sack and hurry after him. "I do hope you're not suggesting I was initiated into the Shields on something other than merit."

"Why do you care?" he says over his shoulder. "You're in the Shields regardless of what I suggest."

"Regardless?" I crouch in front of him. "I care for more than being in the Shields, Taha. I care about being capable and respected for what I can do, separate from my clan's reputation." I pause, hearing my own hypocrisy. It is awfully loud, even in this immense space. "I suppose you feel the same way."

"Suppose I do," he says, looking up at me. The sunset finds his jeweled eyes, turning them to fiery emeralds framed by intense black lashes. In the right light, I realize, they can be rather disarming. So much so that I openly gaze at him, and he at me, and between us, time drifts. When I first encountered Taha in the barracks, he was being fawned over by a group of Shields. I waited for him to find me and seek a formal introduction; I thought it only right, given his father's position and my auntie's, but in two years, he never once did. Before I could dismiss Taha as someone with no clue as to how upper Qalian society worked, he dismissed me. Before I could decide that Taha was wrong in thinking his father's election to the Council placed his clan on par with one like mine, Taha decided I was not worth his time. He realized, before I did, that I could not see the importance of what his clan had achieved—that I did not *want* to. But how can I expect respect if I am not willing to give it?

"I'm sorry," I say softly. "Sometimes I act without thinking of how it will impact others."

His jaw flares as he pulls the arrow from the last hare. "Tell me something. Do you really believe your brother has done nothing wrong?" His tone is different now; neither restrained nor aggressive. It is intimate, like last night in the First City when he apologized. And like one of his precisely fired arrows, it slices past my guard to my core.

"I never said that. I think Atheer has not been himself—he was manipulated by the outsiders, and that devil, Qayn—but I don't agree with his actions in the least. I wouldn't have bound Qayn to my dagger if I did. I wouldn't be here dealing with a sister who stubbornly refuses to listen to me. I want to save Atheer, but I also want to *stop* him from making any more mistakes and upsetting our promise to the Great Spirit to keep our magic secret." I sigh, shaking my head. "Frankly, I think the Council was wrong to ever send Scouts into Alqibah, even if it was simply for the purpose of observation. We shouldn't be getting involved with the outsiders and their troubles. It only endangers our peace."

A faint strawberry blush graces Taha's face. The entire time

I was speaking, he was running his thumb along the tip of the arrowhead. Back and forth, back and forth, as if considering whether to draw blood. Now he replaces it in his quiver.

"That surprises me."

I frown. "What does?"

"We have finally agreed on something."

He bags the hare, slings the lumpy sack over his shoulder, and heads back to camp. I follow, wondering whether the island we once fleetingly shared is larger than I first thought.

After a minute of silent side-by-side trekking, Taha whistles a soft song. "Do you like music?" he asks me.

"Yes," I say, confused by the sudden shift in conversation, let alone the fact that he's chosen to continue one.

"Anybody in particular?" he asks.

"Well," I say slowly, "my mother once took Amira and me to see Sabah perform a concert at the Qalian Theater."

"Sabah," he murmurs, smiling to himself. "My mama would hum her songs while she worked around the house."

He extends a hand into the cool air as gold streaks swirl in his eyes. The color does not consume the usual green but rather melds with it—somehow Taha is occupying the space between magic and the mundane. To my astonishment, a tiny, blue-chested ney-bird flutters across the sky and lands in his open palm. Gently he shifts it to his shoulder while humming a familiar tune. The bird gladly perches and sings the same melody back with its own delightful embellishments—but Sabah's most famous song, "My Heart and My Love," is still recognizable. I burst into delighted laughter, the happy bubble in my chest expanding so much, I think I could lift one foot off the grass and float away.

"Very impressive, but I already agreed you were the best beastseer I know of. There's no need to boast."

"Little trick I've been working on." He flashes me a handsome sideways grin, then softly adds, "Thought you might like it."

My eyes widen. I bow my head. "I do, yes, thank you."

He nods, and that seems to seal it. Taha's bird continues to sing as we make our way back to camp, a place where I've no doubt the music will cease and he will forget I exist once more. Questions clamor at me, desperate to be asked, here and right now. I must know why he is kind to me when we are alone yet so mean in company. I must know how he can behave warmly and coldly and still manage to function. I want to know who the *real* Taha is—and how does he feel about me? Does he resent me for my clan and my brother's actions? Am I little more than entertainment for him during boring moments? Or perhaps he feels a little of what I feel toward *him* . . .

But asking would only ruin the pleasant moment, and they are so rare between us that this feels too precious to chase away. So I stay silent and let the music ring out across the plain. Above us, stars intensify in the purple sky, and the day, at last, resigns to night.

20

THE YELLOW DUNES OF THE SWALLOWING SANDS rise from the grit without warning and undulate as far as the eye can see—waves that all look exactly the same.

We stop before them and kneel in the shade of a large boulder for a tea ceremony. The familiarity of the act helps soothe some of my anxiety; it reminds me of home, and family—it reminds me of everything I am fighting to save.

Taha creates a small fire and places upon it a full teapot. While that boils, he grinds the misra with mortar and pestle, unleashing its enigmatic scent. I expect to catch a hint of bitterness, but a part of me hopes to inhale that pleasing scent from the day he and I sparred. Instead I smell apple shisha, sand, and wood. Atheer.

Startled, I look away from Taha into the hazy distance. Whatever comfort I felt from that unique fragrance is transitory; as Taha pours tea for each of us, the smell intensifies, and my anxiety returns tenfold. This time, it is inextricably mingled with unpleasant thoughts. Might I be too late to save Atheer and our people? Perhaps this fight will have been in vain. And if it isn't, why did Atheer torment us, and for so long? The brother I know and love shouldn't have been capable of doing that. But he did.

I drink the tea with shaking hands, finding it as bitter as ever. Strangely, I am relieved about that. At least it is one thing in my world that has not changed.

After the tea ceremony, Taha meditates away from our group. Reza uses the time to pen a letter informing the Council of our progress, which he will send using one of the messenger falcons we've brought along. Amira hovers at his elbow like a mosquito, keenly inspecting his dancing quill.

"Don't tell them I'm here, please? My parents think I've gone on a trip to the Zhofal oasis."

Reza twists away with a grunt. "Away with you, kid."

She casts a pleading look my way, but I am not in the mood to defend her delinquency, and I don't want to annoy Reza—he and Taha seem close, as cousins would be, but I don't want to give him any incentive to vengefully report my binding to Qayn.

I shift my indifferent gaze to Taha instead. He cuts a stark figure between his white colt and black falcon perched on a nearby boulder. It is no small task guiding our group across the Sands, and I wish I could help somehow. I loathe that only the Scouts have the knowledge of the way, though I am not so proud that I cannot recognize the irony: this must be how they felt about me hiding Atheer's whereabouts, before they understood that I didn't actually know it myself.

Thinking of that, I turn to Qayn. The djinni is cross-legged on a nearby rock, eating the last plum Amira brought with her. "Where do we go first in Alqibah?" I ask him.

He pops the pit into his mouth, juice dribbling down his

pointed chin. "You will need to pass through Bashtal to the city of Taeel-Sa," he mumbles around it. "Atheer met an intermediary from the rebellion there, a fisherman who introduced him to Farida. We will meet him too."

I pace on the spot. "I need more details. How did Atheer meet this fisherman? When—"

"Gather round," Taha interrupts.

Qayn tosses the pit over his shoulder with a wink, sliding his tongue along the juice on his lower lip. "Just follow me, Slayer. I will not lead you astray."

I clench my fists. *Yes, of course, follow a wicked djinni who is entirely invested in his own sightseeing tour around Alqibah.* What can one say in the face of such shameless dishonesty? Nothing, other than to command him to spare me his accursed company. When he has returned to the blade, I join the others assembling around Taha. A long rope is coiled between his scarred hands.

"One can learn how to cross the Sands by traversing it. In my training to be a Scout, my father led me." He looks in my direction. "Now I will lead you. We will move single file and trail this rope along the line of horses to reduce the risk of someone deviating from the path. If one of you does, the rest of you are not to follow. Do I make myself clear? Either let them go or doom yourself as well." He waits for each of us to give a grim nod. "Good. Follow my steps precisely, Imani, Amira. Keep hold of the rope, and do not stop. The journey made in one attempt is safest. Do not talk, or you will get distracted from your sole focus which must, at all times, be this—" He holds up the rope. "And do not, under any circumstances, heed the illusions of the Sands, regardless of how real they look or feel or sound. They are only illusions, but they are unkind and they *will* attempt to lead you off course."

His sobering speech finished, we disperse to our horses. Taha tosses the rope back to me; I catch and toss its end to Fey, and a dour-faced Amira in the saddle; she throws it to Reza bringing up the rear. Taha tilts his face to the sky.

"Great Spirit guide me."

He squeezes his heels, and his horse steps onto the sand.

WHERE HAS THE TIME GONE?

We climb one dune, we slide down the next, and still, an ocean of gold ripples to the unreachable horizon. Sand clutches Raad's hooves, it sighs at our intrusion, it tumbles and sprays and piles in small mounds. The sky offers no respite. It poses, blue, flat, and oblivious, strangely surreal and lacking dimension. I look to the sun for aid; it is on the right of me now, when it was left before, behind before that. I don't think we are turning, but we must be for any of this to make sense.

Truthfully, I can't be sure if we are walking straight or circling like aimless moths around the sun's flame. Taha said I would learn the way by following him, but I cannot remember the last step Raad took, let alone the first. Even Taha's silhouette has not changed in—how long has it been? A minute, an hour, a *year*? He remains the same, a young man on a white colt, head bent against the occasional gusts of sand. Hateful sand, everywhere. I must stop and drink water to flush it from my airways; I must wipe it off every inch of my flustered skin. The heat is insufferable. My eyes have been replaced by shriveled plum pits; my lips crack in the dry air. The sun beats down on us with monstrous cruelty, and the air is heavy, unreasonably still. How I yearn to escape this place; I am desperate for it. I consider throwing the rope and fleeing simply for the desire of seeing anything but sand. The impulse is shockingly strong, and I've already lifted one sweaty hand off the rope. Quickly I direct it toward my dagger. To Qayn. Yes, that is better. I can find cool solace in the devil's black eyes, and he will remind me to keep hold of the rope if I am to have any hope of seeing Atheer again.

I plant my hand on the hilt, only to find it thrumming with a terrifying frenzy.

"Qayn?" I rasp, but my voice scarcely leaves my parched throat.

Suddenly a cool breath wafts over the dunes on my right. I revel in the touch of it on my skin as the heat is prized away. I love it even when the wind rises to a squall; I laugh and cheer as it tosses my damp braid and flaps my cloak. A second, stronger gust almost knocks me out of the saddle, and this one is laden with sand that lashes my bare skin. I cry out as it scrapes, claws, and draws blood, obscuring everything but Raad under me.

Raad.

I yank the reins and direct the stallion in the opposite direction of the attack. The wind worsens, gaining speed and strength, possessing no limit to its fury. I fold over and wrap my hands around my head, shrieking, *"Stop!"* Within the storm's howling maw are voices, dwindling. My sister, screaming my name. Taha too, barking something back. Taha, who said to never let go of the rope. But I have let go, and my horse has not stopped moving.

I jolt upright, all the air leaving my lungs. The day has turned to night and the sandstorm has vanished. How is it *night*? I stare up at a solid black sky, mind spinning. No moon, no stars. No time; it is not possible for the time to have passed so quickly.

I twist in the saddle, searching the darkness. "Amira? Taha? Can anyone hear me?"

My ears suck up the silence; my eyes drink the night. No, of course they can't hear me. They didn't leave the path; *I* did. The Sands have swallowed me and Raad, as they were avowed to do a millennium ago.

"Oh, Spirits," I gasp.

Bile riots in my chest; my head floats above my shoulders. Dizzy, I drop out of my saddle into sand that is deeper than expected. I can't regain my footing in time. Arms reaching, a yelp in my throat, I crash down the dune, shoulder over shoulder, rolling for an eternity—yet simultaneously, for not long at all. As I spin, I realize I cannot grasp the moments passing; they are water between my fingers, or I am water between the fingers of time. Suddenly I am slumped at the foot of the dune, crying out from pain twinging in my neck.

I pinch the muscle and only relent when the pain fades to a bearable throb. Then, gingerly, I try to stand. It is hard in a way I cannot fathom. I don't know where I am; I don't know *how* I am, don't know which way is north or south, east or west. Like Taha described, *no ground and no sky, no forward or back, no past or future.*

I turn in circles, tossing sand around my calves, but that flawless obsidian sheet above me doesn't move, doesn't yield a thing. It is a grave—like looking into Qayn's eyes.

"That's it," I whisper.

He must be able to help me; he must have some guidance he can pull from his ancient well of knowledge. I reach for my hilt to summon him, but the moment my fingers skim the steel, the ground shifts. I can't see it happen, but I hear the menacing rustle. I *feel* it: a pit opening in the sand under my feet.

"No, no, no—"

I tilt and totter; my feet struggle for purchase. I fall forward and desperately claw at the ground, trying to stop from being dragged down. My sore neck protests every movement; the wound in my side shrills murder. The sand rises around my thighs, reaching for my chest and entombing me in cold, whispering darkness. My screaming mouth fills with sand; I cough and splutter, but with every rasping breath, more chokes me. I thrash my arms over my head in an attempt to stay aboveground; sweat sheets off me, and my muscles shake. None of it makes any difference. I am moments from being buried, far from home, far from everyone I love. I will die without ever seeing Atheer again. I will never hug him one last time, never hear a silly joke or practice a new sparring technique or go horse-riding together. I will never know his truth.

"Imani!"

It can't be. It shouldn't be. I am hearing things, so why are warm hands grasping for mine? A few moments later, they pull. My head pops free of the sand, then my shoulders, my chest.

"Come ON!" Amira cries.

The tomb relents and spits me free. My sister grunts and stumbles, our fingers slipping from each other. I fall onto my heaving chest, coughing out sand and drawing in cool, clean air. Amira scrambles over to me.

"Are you all right?" Her voice is piercingly clear against the quiet. It doesn't belong here. "Imani? Oh, please say something."

I roll onto my back, sobbing. "Why did you come after me? Why didn't you listen to Taha's orders?"

"What?" she breathes. "I couldn't—"

I sit up and feel around for her face. I find it, damp, muscles tense.

"Don't you understand? We left the path, Amira. We are lost to the Sands, doomed to wander and die!" Mama's anguished face flashes in my mind. How will she fare when she finds out only one of her children is returning home? Or perhaps none will return because Atheer has long departed this realm. She will be devastated, left with an empty, darkened home, a corridor upstairs with nothing but closed doors. A row of tombs, frozen in time while she gets older and sadder. I crumple to my hands and knees. "You shouldn't have come after me! Why can't you ever just do what you're told?"

"I couldn't leave you," she cries.

I press my face to the cold sand. "You should have. You've killed yourself."

"So I have!" She shoves me upright. "I would rather die by my sister's side than lead a dismal existence knowing I abandoned you here. I would rather die in Alqibah with you and Atheer, and I would not shed a tear because at least we would be together. That is all I want, Imani, all I've ever wanted. For us to be *together*."

My tears hush, and in the total dark, I finally see my sister. I see her soul, who she really is under that hard, argumentative exterior. The girl who defied the Sahir to be with me and

Atheer. The girl who knew leaving the path would doom her to the Sands but did it anyway. Perhaps this unshakable courage has not been hiding under her exterior at all—I have only refused to recognize the person she has become, even though she has been right in front of me. I took her independence and strong will for disobedience, her desire to think freely for contrariness. I entirely overlooked her love for our family, a love she has proven she will serve till her dying breath. Atheer I have long recognized as my best friend. But what of my sister, who only wants to be *my* friend? Why did I ignore her for so long?

"Oh, I am a fool." I reach up and brush her lank hair. "Can you forgive me? When you told me I might need you out here, and I said I wouldn't . . . I was wrong. I did need you; I *do*. They are empty words to utter, but I wish . . ." My voice cracks. "Spirits, I wish I had gotten to know you more when I had the chance."

She holds me firmly. "There is time yet, Sister."

"No," I whisper, "not enough. Not a lifetime's worth."

"Yes, there *is*. We are not perishing here."

We part and I shake my head, even though she can't see it. "Nobody has ever escaped the Swallowing Sands."

"And you are not anybody! There must be some way out, a magical solution, surely?"

I smile sadly. There is another thing I never appreciated about my sister until now: she is full of hope. She is woven from it; she shines as bright as the sun with it. For her, the end is never the end; it is the door to a new and better beginning. She never gave up hope that Atheer is alive; she never stopped believing things could improve for our family. And I let her down, as I let Atheer down. I turned away from them when they needed me most, because I feared the change I would recognize in them. I did not want to accept that the people I love will evolve with time, and perhaps that is all right, in the same way it is all right for trees to flourish in the forms and directions they please, for rivers to forge their own course, bringing life with them, for the colors of the sunset to delight differently from one day to the next.

"Imani, are you even listening to me?"

I have my hands pressed to my face, silently sobbing. Amira starts pacing in front of me; the sand crushes under her boots; the gentle breeze fans over as she passes me.

"There must be a way, there must." She snaps her fingers. "What about Qayn? He could help us."

"No," I croak. "I've tried summoning him, but it angers the Sands. Perhaps the enchantment senses I am smuggling a monster across that should be confined to the Sahir." I sigh, reaching for her in the dark. I get ahold of her silk hem and pull her over. "Please, Amira, let's not make this any harder. So many must spend their last desperate moments in the Sands searching for escape, never realizing they are walking in circles. I don't want to do that."

"Ugh, would you *think*? We're not even a quarter of the way to dead, and you've given up!" She crouches in front of me. "I remember in the tale of the Scholar Queen and her sparrow, Queen Nuha says to approach a difficult problem one equation at a time, else one will be overwhelmed and unable to see their way through. *Aha!* Speaking of seeing, the first thing that would help us is some light. Do you have a torch in your saddlebag? Raad? Here, boy." She goes off, whistling for the horse.

"Light," I murmur. The creaky loom of strategy spins in my mind, taking disparate threads and weaving them into something cohesive, something I can use. A memory of Auntie. *I do not know what awaits you on this journey, but a lamppost in the dark is often all one needs to find one's way.* The crystal vial.

"Imani, Raad is refusing to come to me. Can you try calling him?"

I jump to my feet. "Hold on. You and Queen Nuha have given me an idea."

"We have?" She rushes over as I pat my sirwal pockets. My hand falls on a hard lump, and relief washes down the length of me. Tentatively I reach inside and pull out a leather pouch. I need only untie the drawstring to release the pure light.

Amira gasps. "Is that an explorer's globe?"

"Something better. Undying light. Auntie created it using a thread of her soul." I lift the vial. Though small, the light within illuminates an endless dune sea radiating away from us in every direction. And my clever, courageous sister, without whom I would assuredly be lost. She gazes at the light, transfixed; I gaze at her as if this is the first time I ever have.

"Auntie's soul," she breathes. "It is beautiful. And it is more than a globe."

"Yes. She said, 'If ever you are lost, release the light. It will guide you true.'" I pull the stopper free. With a soft, swirling hum, the light escapes the vial and floats high above our heads. Even the infinite black sky is not enough of a canvas to contain its brilliance. It is not simply a light; Auntie's soul exudes from every beam. Sentience, goodness. *Hope.* A moment later, the light serenely drifts across the sky.

"It's moving."

I take Amira's hand. "Yes, it must be leading us out of the Sands. Hurry."

We jog up the dune to Raad and clamber into the saddle. Somehow the stallion knows salvation when he sees it. He trots after the guiding light with no direction from me. Amira weeps as we journey across the ridges of the dunes, but she laughs too. She laughs, she hugs me, and I hug her back.

And little by little, we leave the all-consuming darkness behind.

21

W E ESCAPE THE SWALLOWING SANDS AS SUD-
denly as we entered them, and it is an act more re-
storative than returning home after an eternity lost.
The last dune tapers to a low bed of sand, and the night turns
to afternoon in a blink. The haze that was draped over my mind
lifts; even the heat attacks less intensely. I utter a silent prayer of
thanks to the Spirits, and to Auntie's ingenuity.

"She led us to Alqibah instead of back home," Amira says as
we emerge on an unfamiliar plain framed by stony hills.

"She guided us true," I say, my eyes scouring the scrubby land.
"This is where our destiny lies." In the Kingdom of Alqibah, a
place I did not even know existed a couple of months ago. It isn't
much different from the Sahir, not yet at least, but it is enough
for me to realize I am trekking on the same ground where my
brother might be this very moment.

A falcon's call sounds above us. Sinan, soaring behind Auntie's undying light. Which means . . . I look back at the three
figures sprinting across the grit toward us, Taha at the fore. I
descend from the saddle and help Amira down as he reaches us.

"You made it out," he puffs, staggering to a stop. He is flush from the heat, skin beaded with sweat, worry evident in the lines crowding his eyes. I stare at him disbelievingly when he pats my arm. "You made it out," he repeats, nodding, as if he still doesn't believe we aren't a mirage. "I'm glad."

I try not to make my shock obvious. Reza and Fey pile up behind him, rounded eyes gawking out from between smudges of dirt.

"How?" Reza croaks. "I watched you ride off, Imani."

"I watched you run after her," Fey says to Amira.

"I shouted at you both to stop," Taha murmurs distantly, as if speaking from within a terrible memory. I recognize the look on his face. . . . As leader of the group, the fear and helplessness he must have experienced, witnessing us venture off the path to our certain dooms, would have been paralyzing. It is the same fear and helplessness I felt watching Amira plunge from the balustrade in the First City. Watching the door to Atheer's room close for the final time.

"It wasn't your fault." I show him the vial. "I would have perished if it weren't for my sister. She saved me as I was being buried alive by the Sands, and she reminded me that I possessed this—" Slowly the light descends from the sky and returns to its crystal housing, where it swirls gladly. I push the stopper back in. "A gift of undying light, woven with a piece of our auntie's soul. It guided us out of the Sands." I slide the vial into its leather pouch and put that in my pocket.

Taha's eyes dance over me. "Aziza Zahim has mastered *animancy*?"

I can't help but laugh. "Auntie believes *mastered* is a strong word, but I am inclined to say yes, she has. You all seem surprised. Why? Did you think she was elected Master of the Misra for reasons other than her magical genius?"

"Oh, Imani," Amira groans, clapping her forehead. "You can't enjoy one moment in peace, can you?"

Fey's face burns brighter than the ball of orange above us, and Reza is unable to look at either of us. Taha, meanwhile, continues to stare at me. I grin.

"I am enjoying this moment," I say.

I tug Raad over to the horses gathered in the shade of some pines. And somehow, despite having endured the trip through the Sands in a blur, upon recollection, I am curiously certain I could return through them if I concentrated hard enough.

Under the trees, I feed Raad, and Amira drains an entire flask of water. Taha, Fey, and Reza stand a little to the side, sharing loaded looks. They are waiting for directions only I can provide. Or rather, only Qayn.

I pull the dagger off my thigh. "Qayn, come out."

The djinni appears in a gust of hot air, as striking as ever, loose hair aflutter. But rather than wearing his usual smirk, he is troubled, shaking his head. "That was very close, Slayer. *Too* close. Your auntie is a bright woman, gifting you that light. You would be dead without it."

I sheathe the dagger and cross the thin grass. "You should be apologizing to me."

"For what?" he asks, following.

"I was only pushed off the path when I tried summoning you. The second time, I was almost buried alive. The Sands were furious about you being there."

"Naturally," he says. "They would sense you were sneaking a djinni across. The enchantment was not only created to keep strangers out, but me *in*."

I half turn, obstructing his path. "Correct. I risked my life getting you here. So, *king without a crown,* repay the favor and lead me to my brother."

His gaze darkens. "I resent that epithet, Slayer."

"Oh, do you?" I stop again, almost knocking into him. "Why? It's true, isn't it?" I wait for a retort; he keeps silent, his temple pulsing. I inch closer. "Perhaps it was better for everyone that your magic was stolen, Qayn. I wonder, was it taken away by the one you held dear before or after you watched your city be massacred?"

He stares at me, but I don't think he is really seeing me. "The matter is complicated."

"Uncomplicate it for me, king without a crown."

The air tightens with the pluming, bitter scent of ash. "You will know the truth when you deserve it," he snarls. "But the ignorant deserve *nothing.*"

A chill races up my spine. Somewhere along the road of this conversation, we took a wrong turn. I am in that dark place again, learning things I should not, involving myself in matters I am not equipped to understand. Or I am being lied to with great aplomb—I'm surprised to find I actually *hope* he is lying.

Qayn's long lashes flutter, and he blinks several times, as if he is returning from that dark place too. He leans back and looks away, the tension easing from his jaw, the sneer being replaced with a relaxed, laughing smile. "Forgive me, Slayer; that was unkind. But I find that name very hurtful, and I implore you not to use it again."

And *that* is how he responded to the insult. Is it any wonder this monster let hundreds of people be destroyed because he perceived them as taking advantage of him?

"Spirits," I mutter, turning away. "Keep silent if you refuse to give me straight answers about who you are and what you are doing here." I hurry off, eager to put distance between us. I don't trust Qayn or his intentions. The sightseeing trip can't be the sum of it, and him wanting to check up on Atheer is even less believable. As I join the others, I resolve to find out the truth, and soon.

"You are now in the Kingdom of Alqibah," Taha announces, tearing his hostile gaze from Qayn. "We have fulfilled our end, Imani. It's your turn to lead us to Atheer."

And I have to look to Qayn for an answer. The djinni is busy inspecting the world around him. I tap my foot. "Hello?"

He smiles. "Look at you all, standing outside the Sahir. Think of how few Sahirans can make that claim."

"Nobody is claiming anything," Taha growls. "We are sworn to secrecy. Now give us directions."

Qayn stuffs his hands into his pockets and rocks on his heels. "Mm, no, I don't know if I will. As I recall, I am not bound to you, boy. I am under no obligation to help."

I grab his elbow. "But you are to *me*. Tell us or I will take your head for a pretty souvenir."

He laughs, dark eyes twinkling. The waywardness is only emphasized by his appearance, with his bare feet and beaded anklet, tousled hair gleaming in the afternoon sunlight. He doesn't look like a king who oversaw a massacre at the hands of a giant; he looks like a young man inviting you out for a romantic afternoon stroll along the riverbank. The sort your parents warn you about, who will whisper sweet poetry in your ear and leave you devastated in his wake. A jackal.

He bows his head. "Of course, Slayer. A map, if you please."

Taha begrudgingly unfurls the scroll on the ground between us. We squat around it, and Qayn points at a city.

"This is Bashtal. As I understand, it is the closest major city this end of the Spice Road. Passing through it will be the most efficient way to reach Taeel-Sa, once the seat of the king of Al-qibah. There we will find a fellow named Zakariya, a fisherman and something of a mediator for the rebellion Atheer is aiding."

I exhale a pent-up breath. For a moment, I feared Qayn had led us all this way only to strand us. I wouldn't put it past him.

"Why do we need Zakariya?" Taha asks.

Qayn makes a show of sighing. "A stranger does not simply approach a paranoid rebellion and expect a warm welcome, boy."

"We need a familiar face," I say, and Qayn nods. I look over the map again. "So the plan is to find Zakariya and ask him to take us to Farida, the rebellion leader. Atheer should be with her."

"He will be," Amira murmurs, pointedly catching my eye. I recall what she said to me that day in the Forbidden Wastes: *Just this time, hold on to hope. Please? We are bankrupt without it.*

Qayn, meanwhile, studies an ant he has given a ride on his finger. "Yes, Atheer described to me the whereabouts of Zak's home in Taeel-Sa."

"What if Zak doesn't agree to help us?" Reza asks, voicing my own concern.

Qayn holds his hand level with his face so we can all see the ant tumbling along his smooth brown skin. "I don't see why he wouldn't. Atheer said he was a most amenable fellow."

"But if—" I start.

"I am certain you lot can find ways to convince him," Qayn says, cutting me off with a smirk.

I purse my lips. "Did Atheer say anything else about the rebellion? What sort of people we're dealing with?"

"Not much. By Atheer's telling, they are upstanding people who are angry that their homeland has been stolen. Farida is a capable young woman of great integrity, the daughter of a ship captain. Atheer spoke *very* highly of her." He shrugs, letting the ant safely disembark into the dirt. "I am afraid I don't know more than that."

Taha rolls the map. "Good enough. Let's change into less conspicuous outfits and head out."

The group disperses, and Qayn slinks off after Amira. I take my bag behind some rocks and swap my dirty clothes for a green belted tunic and dark brown sirwal. I use the opportunity to check that the stitches haven't split open on my wound. Thankfully, Taha's handiwork has held up. As I am pulling on a pair of embroidered slippers, I notice him several meters away, half-hidden between the trees. Pulling his dirty tunic over his head.

I glance around to make sure no one is watching me, but Amira is brushing Raad, Qayn is hunting through her bags, probably for more plums, and Fey and Reza are concealed somewhere, changing. I look back at Taha's bare, sweaty torso; it gleams under the hot sun, his defined muscles rippling whenever he moves his strong arms. I look and look, and Spirits help me, it still doesn't feel like enough. He bears a noticeable number of scars, bruises, and old welts on his body. I know he is a Shield and a Scout. He traverses dangerous territory, he battles monsters, but still . . . he has far more injuries than he should. They tell a story using his skin as parchment, and I am so wrapped up decoding it that I am embarrassingly slow to react when he notices me staring. But rather than ducking into the cover of the trees, Taha straightens up, still bare-chested, and stands there as if inviting me to keep watching. A furious skipping erupts in my chest. I veer my eyes to my slippers and pretend I am enthusiastically interested in them, though I am certain he can hear my drumming pulse from over there, or at least see how flushed my face is. At last, he moves out of sight, and I can breathe freely.

"Fool," I mutter to myself, pulling on my other slipper. "You are a flaming fool."

I dawdle behind the rocks as the others gather around their horses. I intend to stay hidden for far longer, but Amira is on her tiptoes, looking for me, and to loiter would only make things obvious. I gather my things and stride across the grass.

"There you are," she says. "I gave Raad a good brush. He was so *dusty*—"

"Excellent, thank you." Qayn shoos her toward Fey. "Unfortunately, I shall be traveling with the Slayer, so you must find a ride elsewhere."

They start bickering as I hook my bag to the saddle. The air shifts behind me, and a shadow slants across Raad's flank.

"Next time you desire a look, ask first." Taha's breath tickles my ear. "Spying is unbecoming to someone of your station."

My head jerks up, but he is already sauntering off to his horse. I drag my flustered gaze back to my bag buckle, but my fingers are lettuce, and I can't get the damned thing secure. Was he joking or serious? And was that smugness I detected in his tone? All this time he has coolly ignored me, and now he catches me slack-jawed, gawking like every other infatuated Shield. If I was going to pretend I wasn't interested in him, I've obliterated that chance, and I think he knows it.

"Damn it," I mutter under my breath. Why couldn't I have kept my gaze to myself?

"What was that about?" Qayn asks, startling me.

I flop against Raad, planting my hand over my racing heart. "Spirits, don't *do* that. Announce yourself, please. And nothing," I grumble. "It was about nothing."

I finish buckling my bag and join the others when they are lined up on their horses, chatting amongst themselves. Somehow Taha and I end up riding alongside each other minutes later anyway. Predictably, he doesn't look at me. In fact, he seems to be actively avoiding it, and that is perfectly fine by me. I came here to save my brother, not concern myself with Taha and his opinion of me.

Gradually the grit gives way to rugged grassland sizzling in the early afternoon heat. As if a figment, a town much like one I could find in the Sahir crops up on the horizon, and a wide path cuts through the plain toward it.

"Wow, is this—"

"The Spice Road, yes," Qayn answers.

We follow it in the opposite direction of the town. I squint back, marveling that there would be people there who are not Sahiran. Outsiders who don't know who we are, and we don't know who they are. Outsiders who think we went extinct in the desert a thousand years ago. And here I am on the Spice Road, just like Atheer, riding the real-life ribbon I traced along the map back in the Forbidden Wastes.

Farther up the road, we find a squat sandstone building with a wide arched gate. Outside it, men in white robes and red keffiyehs smoke pipes and converse.

"It's a caravanserai," Taha explains, glancing at me. "A wayfarer's inn, stocked with supplies for beasts of burden and their weary travelers."

"Yes, we have some back home."

And that is what discomforts me. The structures are so similar-looking, and those outsiders—the tones of their brown skin, their features, attire, manners of speaking, the way they gesture expressively using their hands—they are uncannily like people across the Sahir. *But they can't be,* I tell myself. There will be something about them that is different and wrong, something that sets them apart as outsiders from the cursed lands.

Yet the journey that I envisioned would be a nightmare through a barbaric wasteland is a surprisingly mild dream instead. Ordinary, as Taha described it. That is, until the road vibrates with the pound of hooves, and a convoy of horses in military regalia appears over the hill ahead, cantering toward us. Then the dream decays around the edges.

Poised with straight backs in the saddles are haughty men unlike any I have ever seen before. Their skin is ghostly white but singed raw where it has been insulted by the sun; their eyes are cold in tone, unfriendly in air; their tall frames are protected by a mixture of fine leather and plate armor, and deadly longswords hang from their belts. The pair of men at the back of the convoy bear long poles flying brown banners, stamped in a white symbol of a stag.

"Is that them?" I ask Taha. "The Harrowlanders."

The invaders who so traumatized Atheer that he turned his back on everything he knew and everyone he loved.

"Yes. Keep your manner unchanged, and they may let us pass."

I do my best, but I am struggling to stay upright from the force of my pounding heart. A soldier at the front holds up a gloved fist and whistles. The convoy slows to a trot.

"Taha," I say, my pitch rising.

"Be easy. Let me deal with them."

Our convoys meet. The Harrowlanders stop, and the soldier at the fore says a word in Harrowtongue I recognize: "Halt."

Taha signals us to stop. The soldier begins addressing him in his harsh, curt language, and a phrase Taha went to great lengths to teach me crops up: "State your business."

Taha responds in kind, and although I only understand the word *hunters,* I am impressed by his fluency and self-assurance. He points at his bow and the animal pelts slung over the back of his horse, which he crafted during our journey here. The soldier impassively listens while studying us, and I cannot resist peering into his eyes. They are blue of a kind I have never encountered. Many Sahirans have light eyes—Taha is one of them—but this man's eyes are different. Their blue evokes a cold, stark land scarcely unveiled by a reticent sun. What impulse would compel him to venture to a land like Alqibah, one so distinct from what he must know, and seek to exercise his dominion over it?

The soldier says something, and by his tone alone, I understand we are permitted to move on. Taha responds with a phrase he described to me as "vital" for surviving our mission here: "Long live King Glaedric."

The soldiers repeat the refrain and ride off in a dusty shroud. I exhale a long breath and move closer to Taha. "What did he say?"

Taha stares after them. "He wanted to know our business. I told him we're hunters. He stressed that we must pay our dues to the king when we reach the next market and sell our meat and fur. I promised we would."

"I thought the Harrowlanders would have deposed the king when they assumed control," says Amira, in an astute manner that reminds me so much of Mama.

"They did," Taha says. "It is *their* king who sits on Alqibah's throne now."

We exchange a confused glance. "That's wrong," Amira says.

Taha tugs the reins. "Much is wrong in the world beyond the Sahir, girl. *Yah.*"

22

B Y LATE AFTERNOON, WE ARE AMIDST GRASSY HILLS coated in a dark, dense scrub and scattered with carob. We passed several carriages in the hours preceding, and two spice trading caravans that fanned behind them the deliciously hot and heady aromas of sumac, cumin, peppers, and saffron. Most of the travelers are Alqibahis who don't look at us twice. I look at them twice, thrice, as many times as I can manage before they have ridden out of sight. I am searching for our differences yet finding only similarities in the ways we look, speak, dress, live. Apart from those soldiers, nobody has tried to ambush or attack us—there is no hint of the deadly wilds I was taught about as a child. This could simply be an extension of the Sahir, and if I had never been told it wasn't, I would never know. In fact, I am aghast realizing it is not the Alqibahi people who stand out to me as outsiders, but the Harrowlanders. They are the unwelcome splinters in this land's flesh.

"How did the colonizers arrive here?" I ask as we ride along the border of a vast cumin farm. The green rows are dotted with kneeling Alqibahi workers, the perimeter guarded by Harrow-lander soldiers who monitor their picking of the seeds.

Taha looks like he wants to answer my question, but Qayn beats him to it. "Where is *here*? In Taeel-Sa, they loaned a stu-pendous quantity of gold to the king to dress up his city, with interest, of course."

"It's called *usury*," Taha supplies in a mutter.

Qayn points at him. "Quite right, boy. Well, when this re-markably inflated debt came due, the king realized he couldn't repay it. 'Not to worry,' said the Harrowlanders. 'We will control Alqibah to administer repayment of the debt.' The king was hav-ing none of that, so they chopped off his head."

"Great Spirit, that is unjust," I say. "It was different else-where?"

"Yes, in—" Taha starts, but he is cut off again by Qayn.

"You see, Slayer, *Kingdom of Alqibah* is something of a mis-nomer, I've learned," he declares in an erudite tone that has us all watching him. "There is a king, yes, but Alqibah is far from what you would consider unified. It is divided by ancient argu-ments over land, wealth, religion, honor. Bashtal, for example, is ruled by a powerful spice merchant whom Atheer once described as a corrupt traitor. Supposedly he surrendered his city to the Harrowlanders on the promise that he will be granted a signifi-cant portion of territory and trade lines once the debt is paid and they have left."

"Will they really leave?" Amira asks.

Qayn chuckles. "No, my dear girl. With the effort they've put into getting here, I doubt they will. Now, in the east of Alqibah, you have the major city of Brooma, ruled by a warlord, and Ghazali, ruled by a holy woman. Once they learned of the debt, they roundly pulled support from their king and refused to entertain negotiations with the Harrowlanders. In a rather dramatic turn of events, foreign merchants on the Spice Road began complaining of being ambushed by mercenaries sent at the behest of Brooma's and Ghazali's rulers. The Harrowlanders attacked the cities on the grounds that their rulers are a threat to the Empire's civil order. The Harrowlanders promised to leave once things are stable again."

"They're plainly lying," I say. "Has their wickedness no bounds?"

"With magic comes monsters in the Sahir. Here, with riches come thieves," Qayn answers.

WE EMERGE FROM THE HILLS to Bashtal sitting on a lush plain below, the Azurite River flowing through it. And though it is a walled city, like Qalia, it is small and lacking in grandeur.

"I'm starving," says Fey, rubbing her stomach. "Let's replenish our food inside before we move on for Taeel-Sa."

"We could stay the night at an inn," Qayn suggests, leaning his head over my shoulder. "Far more comfortable than sleeping in the wilds, and there would be food, drink, card games." He lowers his voice. "Dancing, perhaps."

"Dancing?" I twist in my saddle, hoping Taha didn't hear that comment, lest he get the wrong idea about Qayn and me. "You may have lived as a king once, but no longer," I hiss in a similarly low voice.

"We can't do either," says Taha over me, riding past us down the hill. "Our coin pouches fell out of Imani's bags when her horse went down in the Vale."

Fey's jaw drops. "And you're only *now* telling us we don't have money for food or supplies?"

"We have one pouch, but it's reserved for tolls and other dues soldiers may demand of us." Taha reluctantly sighs. "Yes, we have no money for supplies."

Fey throws her hands up. "Magnificent, well done! Yet another instance of your brilliant leadership skills."

I sink my teeth into my bottom lip, expecting Taha to lash out at her for daring to insult the eldest son of the Grand Zahim. Reza leans over and tries to soothe Fey with a squeeze of her hand, but he looks to his cousin riding ahead of us.

"We've no choice," he says to Taha. "We will have to dip into that pouch—"

"Out of the question." Taha twists his colt sideways, blocking the road. "This is not a problem. We can hunt for food like we've been doing."

"Oh, no we won't." Fey wags a finger. "You two might be used to surviving on hares and bugs and dirt, but I am *not*. My family may not be wealthy, but my baba provides. At every breakfast, there is always fresh bread, olives, *labneh,* eggs, tea—"

The gaze shared by the cousins clouds over. Taha cocks his head in Fey's direction, and over her blathering, I hear him quietly say to Reza, "Will you stand for that? She called you poor."

Reza shakes his head. "Don't start this, Taha, please."

"Honor comes first," Taha says in a warning tone.

I watch their interaction through wide eyes. Where only

harmony existed between the cousins before, there is now tangible friction generating an uncomfortable heat. Perhaps they aren't as close as I previously thought, or perhaps Reza is trying to be amicable but Taha's affinity for alienating everyone around him is too powerful.

"We could collect leftovers," Amira chimes in. Her suggestion interrupts Fey's incessant prattling and the argument festering between Taha and Reza.

"How do you mean?" Fey asks with unmistakable hope.

Amira confidently sweeps her gaze over her newfound audience. "In Qalia, bakers close up earlier than anybody else, and they always have leftovers. Because they can't sell them the next day, they throw the stuff out. The better bakers distribute it to people in need. I doubt they would be different here."

Fey nods enthusiastically. "Finally, someone is using their head! Thank you, Amira. That's a great idea."

The world has gone mad—Taha and Reza arguing, Fey complimenting my sister. Right now only the devil is consistent, considering our commotion with a smirk that tells how amusingly foolish he finds us all.

"Didn't take your family for the type to know about leftovers," Taha mutters, turning back toward Bashtal. "Fine. We stock up on food and water and continue to Taeel-Sa. We'll make camp somewhere along the way."

As we ride for the city, I pull closer to Fey and Amira. "How *did* you know about the leftovers?" I quietly ask my sister.

"From a few friends of mine. You don't know them," she adds.

I want to ask if these are the same friends involved in her thievery, but I would sooner perish than voice that question with the others in earshot. I have to settle for the uncomfortable realization that while I was pouring myself into the Shields, my sister was leading a life I know nothing about. A life I never asked to be involved in.

Frowning, I focus on studying the city guards as we approach. Most are Bashtali, several flanking the open wooden gates, a few bowmen dotting the ramparts. But the most senior of them are Harrowlander, and they militantly watch over the others. The man standing on the ramparts above the gates must be an officer—he is the only one in a silver helmet, the crown of which is shaped into twisting metal horns. The menacing, inhuman visage monitors us entering through the gates, stag horns framed bleakly against the blue sky.

Inside awaits a cramped, cluttered city of lime-plastered walls painted a fading emerald. The sun-bathed street we trot along is choked with carriages and daring people dashing between them, tight cobbled laneways branching off it like veins in a leaf. There seems to be no rhyme or reason to Bashtal. Short buildings sit beside tall buildings which sit beside long buildings, like uneven rows of green-stained teeth. The people hurry about the day's business with bent heads, and though their robes, dresses, and cloaks are cheerily colorful, their demeanors are not. Harrowlander soldiers pepper the crowds; the armored men patrol, regularly stopping people to search their bags or question them; they perch at checkpoints along the main roads, slowing traffic to inspect carriages, forcing the anxious occupants to wait in the dirt; they ride around on tall horses, seemingly for the pleasure of intimidation.

There are other Harrowlanders apart from the soldiers: officious men in straight-cut robes and cloaks, bearing scrolls, books, and quills, and puffed-up women in big hats and heavy brocaded dresses, sweeping about spinning lacy parasols. On one prominent wall, someone has painted *The Empire brings peace and unity* in Alqibahi. Nearby reads a similar statement: *Look to our king—fighting is death.* They must harken back to when the invaders first arrived. Given the few signs of long-standing conflict, it is evident Bashtal surrendered rather than be gradually decimated by such an organized military force.

"I don't know how anyone makes their way around here," I remark a few moments later, to which Amira holds her hands out and shrugs.

The city is seemingly arranged by whim rather than reason; a moment ago, we were navigating crisscrossing laneways. Now we've been ejected onto a vast public square bustling with people. I clutch the reins, bracing myself for even more sights, smells, and sounds, although I am already overwhelmed. No matter how fiercely I fight the thought, one in particular keeps returning, stronger every time: save for the lack of magic, Bashtal and her people could be lifted from Alqibah and seamlessly placed in the Sahir. The very same people the Great Spirit warned us of and commanded us to hide our magic and prosperity from. But why? They seem so *normal.* How could the outsiders lead lives almost identical to ours for centuries upon centuries while we did the same in the Sahir, completely unaware? But we were only unaware because of the Council's teachings. We were *deceived* about Alqibah's existence. What if we've been deceived about other things, like what the Great Spirit commanded us to do? What if Atheer was right, and the Council *does* lie to us about many things?

I squeeze my eyes shut in an attempt to block everything out and stop these wicked thoughts. The mere existence of this world is angering me; how can I return to Qalia and forget what I've seen? I wanted to go home with Atheer and Amira and have everything return to normal, but nothing will ever be the same after this, and I don't know who to be mad at. My brother? The Council? Myself? I am fast untethering from my body, my life, my history—all that has composed me until this moment. I have operated under the misconception that my foundation is sturdy stone, when I fear it might in fact be sand, and the tide has finally come in.

"The marketplace isn't far." Taha's voice cuts through the fog of my anxiety. "We'll leave our horses ahead and go on foot."

I shadow him to the public stables, fearing a repeat of what happened in the Sands. Amira must feel the same, for as we venture into the square, she takes my hand and doesn't let go.

As with the rest of the city, the square is a regular hub we could find in Qalia. It is bordered by shops, and there is even a sandstone correspondence tower at one corner. Columns of fragrant burning spices billow from its peak, and its many balconies receive falcon after falcon clutching scrolls in their talons. But in the very heart of this normalcy stands a broken statue that must have once depicted the former king of Alqibah. Now it is little more than the lower half of a robed, sandaled man on a throne clutching the nub of a staff, his name plaque scratched out. And beside this sad symbol of surrender is a scaffold of nooses from which hang *people*.

I slow behind the crowd gathered at the execution. Some of the hanging people seem to have been dead for some time. Their bodies are sallow and drooping, their flesh yearning to slide off their bones. Their faces disturb me most: contorted in misery, mouths ajar, cheekbones poking the leathered skin. And their eyes, void, their very souls stolen. A placard hangs from each of their necks, the Alqibahi words *insurgent, agitator, incendiary,* and *rebel* painted on the wooden boards in red. That last word ricochets around in my head. Rebel, like those Atheer risked his life to help.

A skinny handcuffed girl is pushed onto the scaffold by a burly foreign man in a black hood, holes cut out for his eyes. Their sudden movement startles into flight the vultures gathered along the top of the scaffold.

"What is this cruelty?" I ask Taha, who has joined me at my side. I am well aware of executions from history books, the punishment having been outlawed by the Council centuries ago. But it is one heinous act to kill a person, and another to commit the act publicly and leave the rotting dead as a threat to the living.

"It is not safe to linger," he mutters.

But I could not move even if I wanted to. Another Harrowlander, this one in a dark purple, patterned robe, reads from a scroll through a pair of slim spectacles pinched between his thumb and forefinger. Beside him, a meek Alqibahi man translates.

"Layla Al-Din, for the treacherous act of cursing and inciting others to curse His Majesty King Glaedric and the Great Harrowland Empire, you are found guilty and sentenced to hang by the neck until dead. Have you any final words?"

"This is unbelievable," I say on a low breath. "Hung for uttering a curse?"

"Quiet," Taha growls, surveying the nervous crowd.

The executioner fits a noose around Layla's neck. My own neck tightens, the air scraping in my throat. Layla struggles against him but it is woefully futile, and once the noose closes, she resigns to sadly gazing at the crowd. At me.

Amira's fingers interlock with mine as I stare up at this girl who is no older than my own sister. What if it really were Amira up on that scaffold? And so what if it isn't? Should I not be angered equally for a stranger as for my own family, as I would want a stranger to do if it were Amira up there? Can one expect mercy for their own while refusing it to others?

She is an outsider, I say in my mind. *Her plight is not my concern.* The fingers of my right hand graze the hilt of my dagger. *She is an outsider.* I dart my eyes between the rope and the crowds—*her plight is not my concern*—counting the soldiers, searching for the closest exit to the square—*she is an outsider*—flushing the magic from this morning's tea ceremony through my veins. Suddenly Taha grabs my hand and steers me away from the execution. I don't hear Layla's last words; I hear the trapdoor open, the rope pull taut, and the crowd gasp.

"Spirits," Amira whimpers, burying her face in my shoulder.

"It's all right," I say, but I don't believe my own assurance. Nothing here is right.

Taha leads us away from the square to a marketplace; the contrast between murder and mundane is jarring, loosening another parcel of sand from the foundation holding me up. Why would Atheer come to this wretched place and decide to stay? It is the only thing I can think of, over and over. *Why?*

The marketplace is an open-air maze of stalls and jostling crowds moving through like giant flocks of colorful birds, ignorant to the savagery happening a few laneways over. There are more wares here than one can imagine, but the most popular stall is the one selling spices from large coarse sacks. The wonderfully tangy, sharp, biting aromas fill the entire market like a lure. People throng the stall, shouting their offers and elbowing to the counter to pay with silver coins. The hubbub takes place under the vigilant eye of Harrowlander soldiers. They observe the other stalls too, but not with the same intensity. With this stall, they are as interested in the people purchasing from it as the people operating it. Whenever a sale is made, the soldiers scrutinize the shopkeepers recording the details in a thick book and placing the coins into a chest.

"Remember what that soldier said on the road outside Bashtal?" Amira whispers in my ear as we pass.

I nod. "They're ensuring the spice merchants aren't withholding their dues to King Glaedric."

"Quite right," says Qayn from my other side. "Imagine that. The shopkeepers' hard-earned coin, brazenly pilfered and placed in the coffers of a foreign king while the people of Bashtal languish."

The thought angers me more than it should, but when Taha

glances over at me, I am careful to appear disinterested. I don't know how convinced he is, and I don't know how he could describe what's going on here as *ordinary* or *boring*.

After a short walk, he stops us near a bakery on a quiet lane. "There are your leftovers," he says to Amira.

I follow his gaze to a stout baker carrying his display tables back inside the shop—and some still have bags of *khobz* and pastries on them.

"Yes. Wait here for us." Amira takes my hand and leads me to the bakery.

"Hold on," I whisper. "What if this doesn't work?"

"Then we move on to the next plan. Pardon me, sir," she calls sweetly to the baker. "Are you throwing that bread out?"

"Go away, urchins." He picks up another table and bustles into the bakery.

Amira and I exchange glances. I shake my head, but she hasn't surrendered yet. She shadows the man inside. "It is wrong to waste good food, sir."

He sets the table down with a grunt. "Who said I was wasting it? I'm taking it home and eating it."

We look at his belly straining his white button-up shirt. He notices and stuffily closes his black vest. "This is a place of business, not a charity. Get out. I don't allow beggars in my shop."

"One bag, please. We can pay you back," I offer. "We don't have our coin pouch with us right now, but—"

"That, then."

"Huh?"

He nods at my dagger strapped under the hem of my tunic.

"Trade me that, and I will let you take as much bread as you want for the rest of the week."

"Rest of the *week*?" I forget the plan in an instant and trail after him outside. "Are you a fool or merely playing at one? This dagger is worth more than your entire building—"

He shoves me aside with another table. "No dagger, no food."

He disappears inside the shop, leaving my stomach to churn with every whiff of delicious bread.

"Bloody fool," I grumble, "who does he think he is, asking for my dagger? It's probably older than Bashtal itself." I turn to Amira; over her shoulder, I notice Taha, arms crossed, watching us. I sigh. "We'd probably have to go through fifty bakeries before we find someone feeling generous, and there isn't enough time left in the day to do that."

"You're right." Amira pulls me around the corner. "Which is why we need a distraction."

"I don't follow—"

She clicks her tongue. "The *baker*. You distract him; I'll steal some of the bread when he's not looking."

"I don't know, Amira," I say, shifting on my feet. "What would Mama say if she knew I approved of your thieving?"

"I wouldn't suggest it if he didn't look like he could use a break from bread."

"You don't know his circumstances—"

"I know *ours*." Her brown eyes flash. "Sometimes you have to do things you don't like, in order to survive. We need to eat, yes? This is how we do it."

I recall the proverb Auntie said when we were walking to the barracks that day: *The tree who heeds the typhoon endures the longest.* Perhaps there was another reason why she accepted Taha becoming a Scout, why she didn't resist Bayek during the briefing—she recognized the Grand Zahim as a typhoon in that moment and decided it was wiser not to battle him. Not yet.

"Fine," I huff. "But be honest, do you do this regularly back in Qalia?"

"Yes. But most of the time, I don't do it for me." She heads to the street corner. "Come, we must be quick. You go round first, call him over, and try to barter with your dagger. Make sure his back is to the tables. Once you see me—"

"Yes, yes," I mutter, straightening my tunic. "I can't believe I'm doing this." I round the corner, pass the front of the bakery, and stop a few paces away on the footpath. "Sir," I call when the baker comes slapping along the sidewalk in his old leather slippers. I unstrap my dagger from my thigh. "I have reconsidered your offer."

"Oh, have you now?" He drops the table and comes over, greedily eyeing his prize.

I glance at Amira. She's crept up behind him, quieter than a ghost, and begun stuffing bags of khobz and pastries down her tunic. At the far end of the street, Fey is waving her arms in some deranged form of encouragement. I clear my throat.

"Yes, but this is a very fine dagger. Ancient, in fact." I hold it up so the steel can gleam in the afternoon light.

The baker rubs his stubby, flour-dusted hands. "How ancient?"

"A thousand years."

He heaves a sigh that quivers his belly. "A *thousand*? You weren't satisfied with a less fanciful number?"

I pull it half-free of the scabbard. "I'm not lying. Look at the watered steel blade. The quality speaks for itself. This dagger has seen battle against foes the likes of which you cannot even imagine."

Amira flashes me a thumbs-up and scurries around the street corner.

"All right, I've had enough of the tall tales," says the baker. "What are you asking?"

"A month's worth of bread, as much as I want."

"A *month*?" He plucks at his shirt. "What, do you want to *bankrupt* me?"

"You're right." I snap the dagger back into its scabbard. "What is a month compared to a millennium?" I secure it to my thigh and walk away, shrugging. Out of the corner of my eye, I notice a smile flit across Taha's face—and that makes me grin.

"Two weeks, that is my final offer," the baker calls after me.

I wave a hand. "A good day to you, sir."

"Yes, yes, a good day to you too, *scoundrel*."

23

AMIRA IS WAITING FOR ME DOWN THE SIDE street, pulling bags of khobz and pastry from her tunic.

"Impressive haul," I compliment, joining her.

She winks. "We make quite the team."

Footsteps sound at the head of the street. I glance over my shoulder at Taha and the others. They'll be here in less than a minute, and I will lose my chance to broach the subject.

"Amira, when you said earlier that you didn't do this for you in Qalia, what did you mean?"

She leans against the sun-warmed wall, chewing the inside of her cheek. "Those friends I mentioned . . . they don't always have food to eat or decent clothes to wear."

I frown. "You steal things for them? But everyone is looked after in Qalia."

"No, they aren't. You only think they are because *we* are." She pauses as a disheveled, barefoot woman shuffles past us. I think of Taha disagreeing with me when I said there are no ugly or bad parts to Qalia.

"And it's relative," Amira goes on. "We are far more blessed in the Sahir than the people here."

"Yes, I'm beginning to see that," I murmur. "But why do *you* steal for your friends?"

"Unlike them, if I get caught, I won't be in any trouble," she answers.

Again, just like what Taha said about Atheer not having to face the same punishment as others for stealing misra. The sandy foundation under me loosens some more.

I shake my head. "How did you go from reading fantasy tales to stealing for the poor?"

"Easily. Those tales speak of people who protect and care for others, even at great cost to themselves. I tired of reading about people like that—"

"You wanted to become one instead," I realize aloud.

She smiles warmly at me, then holds up the bags as the others arrive. "Is this enough?"

"Mmm." Fey presses a bag of *sfiha* to her nose, inhaling the scent of spiced meat and pastry within. "Delicious. Thank you so much, Amira. Guess I was wrong calling you a *mean* thief. You're a rather generous one, actually."

Amira rolls her eyes, chuckling along with Reza. If I wasn't disjointed enough before I heard Fey earnestly thank my sister, I have been entirely fragmented now. Everything I thought I once knew is being pulled apart before my very eyes.

Taha solemnly bags the food and directs us to a public well, where we fill our water flasks. He spares us the scaffolds on the return journey, leading us to the stables through quieter lanes soaking up the last of the sun's rays.

"I warned you to watch yourself," he says to me. We are walking side by side at the front of the group while Reza, Fey, and Amira chat away amicably.

"You can't say and do what you want here. Spies listen in the crowds for dissenters to take away and torture for information. Before the Harrowlanders, they worked for the merchant ruler your devil spoke about. Now they are paid by the colonizers to do the same."

His warning only reminds me of Layla's terror as the noose was placed around her neck. The cold hand of death come to claim its dues too. I think of the people in the marketplace I considered ignorant at first. But they are doing what they can, carrying on their lives as well as possible under the invader's iron fist. What if it isn't *they* who are ignorant of the injustices going on, but *us*?

"Has it ever bothered you that this society exists, but our people don't know about it?" I ask.

"No. You know about it, and see how it's affected you," he replies. "You were about to do something reckless back there."

"I wasn't," I lie. How did he even know? "So you judge it fair, what happened to that girl?"

He cuts me a hard look. "*No.* But we shouldn't be involving ourselves in the troubles here. You said so yourself. The Great Spirit charged us with the Sahir, not Alqibah, and it is our duty to protect the Sahir and our people from this brutality. Your brother either failed to understand that lesson or ignored it."

"Are the Alqibahis and the Sahirans so different, Taha?" I should shut my mouth. I am teetering dangerously close to saying something improper, but the words flow, undammed. "We were taught that the outsiders are to be feared and shunned, yet they appear almost indistinguishable from our own people. Yes, they do not possess magic, but how can we determine what they would do with it, if we have never given it to them?"

"It is not our responsibility to determine what the Great Spirit has already," he says, his cheeks reddening.

"So we were told by the Council of old. The Great Spirit spoke to them directly when bestowing upon them the misra tree."

"Yes, and the Great Spirit commanded them to protect the misra and the Sahir from monsters and outsiders alike," he says rigidly as if reciting from a tome.

"But what if they *lied* to us about that exchange and what was said?" I press. "It would be easy. No one would be able to ask any questions. The Council could've said anything that suited them at the time."

"But they *didn't*." He stops me with a hand on my arm. "Listen to me closely, Imani. You are in shock from what you've seen today, and it is deceiving your senses. But you know our history and our beliefs; you spoke with total conviction back in the Sahir about how you disagreed with your brother's actions."

"I didn't know then what I know now," I mumble, but he cuts me off.

"There is *nothing* beyond our borders for us. Cities or not, societies or not, this is not our world. We don't belong in it; you shouldn't want to. We have our place and our magic in the Sahir. And as Shields, we have our duties."

Duty, always about duty and rules with him. It should be the same with me. We continue walking; I numbly stare ahead at an elderly beggar, kneeling with his wrinkled hands held above his head. Taha sounds like I used to, before I came here and saw this destitution and violence. How can he witness the execution and not be moved? If anything, it has only entrenched his devotion to the Council's teachings. It is threatening to do the opposite to me. Is this what happened to Atheer? Perhaps Amira was right and our brother was never manipulated—perhaps this is the truth he saw and could not, in good conscience, turn away from. But I cannot believe that or else I am lost. I swore an oath to the Great Spirit, to the Shields and my people; my emotions must not get the better of me.

"Whether or not you believe me, I am saying these things for your own good." Taha considers me seriously. "You must not intervene here in any way, not for anything. It is the foremost rule of being a Scout. You have been across the Sands, and it was your auntie's idea to create the Scouts in the first place. You may as well start acting like one. We are invisible observers on a mission, do you understand?"

"Yes," I say, nodding, even as a strong emotion I cannot place fights for control of me. But Taha is right. I must be reasonable. Whatever the nature of the outsiders, I could not have stopped the execution, just as I cannot stop the Harrowland Empire. What I *can* do is ensure that the threat of it never reaches my people. I can find my brother and bring him home from this vile place; I can make sure he never does anything that will endanger our relationship with the Great Spirit, nor the peace and safety we have fought to protect for so long.

"Good," says Taha as we round the corner. There a Harrowlander soldier and a Bashtali woman are pressed against a wall.

The soldier is gripping her fearful face with one hand, his other hand sliding up her thigh. I don't need to know his language to know what I am seeing. The soldier's head twitches to us, and his glare goads us to interfere. The woman has a plea in her eyes.

Taha glances between them. For how adamant he just was that the outsiders' problems aren't ours, the agonizing decision plays out on his furrowed brow and in the hard line of his jaw, the hesitation in his stiff shoulders. He clears his throat, though doing so seems to pain him.

"Long live King Glaedric," he says in stilted Harrowtongue.

The soldier's glare eases. He waits for Taha to walk past with Fey and Reza. Amira and I haven't moved. Qayn's arm brushes mine, startling me. I forgot he was with us.

"Well, Slayer?" he whispers into my ear. "All this talk of the Great Spirit's mercies. What of your mercy? Will you deny justice its day?"

Magic throbs in my blood. The soldier immediately notices something is wrong and speaks at me in Harrowtongue.

"Imani," Taha warns.

I stare at him across the lane, my heart thudding. I try to force myself to comply; I repeat his earlier speech in my mind, but it lacks the strength it once possessed. Angered by my defiance, the soldier pushes the woman aside and marches toward me, one fist raised and ready to strike.

Suddenly Taha has jogged over and stepped between us, accidentally knocking the soldier away from me. The Harrowlander stumbles, his sunburned face twisting. Taha raises his open hands, hurriedly apologizing. It only sets the riled soldier off. He punches Taha in the face. Amira and I hop out of the way; Qayn takes a step back. Reza and Fey rigidly watch from the other side of the lane.

Taha lurches, one hand catching the blood fountaining from his lip, the other raised as he makes another attempt at appeasement. But the Harrowlander does not want to be appeased; he wants to *fight*. He strikes again, knocking Taha to his knees.

"Stop it!" Amira cries.

"Come on!" the Harrowlander barks, rounding on Taha with his long arms open and inviting. He *wants* Taha to react so he has a good reason to throw him up on the scaffold alongside Layla. And Taha is refusing to give in and participate in a world he does not acknowledge.

The soldier kicks him in the ribs, throwing him onto his side. Something in me snaps. I cannot stand by and let this soldier's violence go unchecked, not toward Taha, not toward that woman or anyone else, be they one of mine or someone from a foreign land ten thousand deserts away. We are all people, deserving of humanity.

The soldier swings his boot at Taha's head. My blade flies into my hand.

"Here!" I shout in Harrowtongue.

He freezes, looking up as I arc my shoulder and lob the dagger. Magic surges through my hand into the throw. The dagger spins, thrumming menacingly. Bright white-blue light licks its length, transforming it to a sword that drives through the man's shoulder. The tip of the blade bursts out of his back, and his blood hisses on the cobblestone. He exclaims and falls, slamming his head, and suddenly he is a cloth doll, limp and sprawling.

"Gods, protect us!" The Bashtali woman staggers away, screaming at the top of her lungs.

"Why did you—" Fey starts.

I run over, yank the sword from the soldier, and sheathe it as a dagger. My stomach jumps at the sight of crimson pooling around him; the wound in his shoulder is worse than I intended it to be, and he is unconscious from hitting his head. He might be dead. I have killed many creatures that took the guises of people, but never a real person. I turn and throw up in the gutter.

"Why did you do that?" Taha comes up behind me. "I warned you not to get involved. I *told* you, damn it! You used magic in front of them! What were you thinking?"

I wipe the sick off my chin and straighten up, though I am secured by jitters and nothing else. "I was thinking of saving your life." It is only half a truth. I was acting on an impulse I could not control, an impulse I understand but dread confronting.

Taha shoves me against the wall. "I didn't *ask* you to save my life, Imani. I've endured far worse beatings than that. Heed me well: if you know what is good for you, you will *never* do something like that again. Ever. Are we clear?"

We stare into each other's eyes. A deadly promise lurks in his, one I dare not test, though I fear I may come to anyway. Has he been right about me? He is pledged to our people's welfare at the expense of his own, the way I thought I was. But I fear I may have been mistaken. The proof is the man bleeding on the ground at our feet. And now I have shown another dangerous man that he and I may very well be striving at odds—that regardless of the words coming from my mouth, my hand will act independently. The blade follows the heart.

Low thunder rolls behind us. Horses' hooves, coming this way.

"Bloody *soldiers*," Taha growls, pushing off me. "Run, all of you, before we end up on those scaffolds."

24

T IS HARD TO MOVE; MY FEET ARE VINES WORKED INTO the gaps between the cobblestones. Taha barks orders at the others.

"Split up. Amira, go on your own, left up here, back through the square. The soldiers won't be looking for an unarmed girl. Reza, Fey, straight along, try to curve round. I'll take Imani." He grabs my wrist. "Get back to the stables, and when it's safe, *leave*. If you make it out of Bashtal, wait off the Spice Road and keep a lookout for the rest of us. Go." He shakes me. *"Move."*

I blink out of my trance, only because Amira hugs me. "I'll see you soon," she says. "Go safely." She pivots and sprints around the bend out of sight, bravely gone to endure a fate I don't know and cannot control.

I point my dagger at Qayn, but he's vanished before I've even uttered the command. Men shout at us from the other end of the lane. I catch a glimpse of the soldiers on horseback before Taha hauls me into the next lane over. He whistles as we run; a piercing call responds, and a moment later, Sinan is soaring high above us. We race around the next corner and topple into some women bearing bags of fabric.

"*Ugh,* watch where you're going," says one from under a pile of white linen.

"Forgive me."

Taha jumps to his feet and drags me up with him. It's like being pulled by a runaway carriage. He is about six-foot-two and built like a stallion, but I possess a trained stamina. The same day Atheer learned I wanted to join the Shields, he began training me to be a warrior, teaching me how to spar, running laps with me around the city. I tuck my chin into my chest and pump my legs, breathing long and evenly. Taha sees I'm keeping up and releases my hand, and now we are two spears piercing the world. People leap out of our way, some curse us, a few even bemusedly laugh. Sinan calls from where he glides on our right.

"This way." Taha directs me left. We bounce around the alley's tight corners, and lunge out of it into a sluggish crowd. We shove through and sprint across a busy street, narrowly dodging an oncoming wagon. My cloak whips around me; the panicked driver hollers at us. Behind us, men shout "Halt!" in Harrowtongue.

We dive into a lane where workers are lifting a sheet of wood crossways. They see us coming and freeze like hares at the end of a hunter's arrow, blocking the lane.

"Don't stop," Taha puffs.

We vault over the sheet in tandem, slide along it, and land on the other side, picking up again. Sinan gives another warning cry from our left. We cut right, up a long, narrow staircase and straight into more soldiers.

I can't see them yet, but I hear them speeding at us from the other end of the street. We're boxed in. On our left are private terraces, the windows and doors shut. On our right, a few shops in short buildings, except for one. A narrow, three-level sandstone building—a smoking lounge, from the sign—its shutters open on narrow windows that reveal fluttering silk curtains, the sound of laughter, and the alluring, heavy aroma of black coffee. The footpath outside is crowded with tables, all occupied by silent, staring Harrowlanders.

I skate to a stop in front of them. "What now, Taha?"

He stares at them, sweat dripping down his face. Eyes two glassy green buttons—full of vacant fear, like back in the Vale. Soldiers' shouts sunder the air at the base of the stairs behind us.

"Damn it, we need to get off the street," I say. I grab his hot hand and barge through the door of the lounge. Patrons exclaim; chairs scrape floorboards; coffee cups tinkle on trays; the bubble of water in shisha pipes ceases. A Bashtali server in silk sirwal and vest appears, making shooing motions with his hands.

"You can't be in here!"

"Out of the way!" I shove past him to the carpeted staircase. We hustle up, two at a time, surprising a server, who drops his tray of coffee on the rugs, and knocking aside a Harrowlander woman dawdling on the stairs to the third floor. We burst in on a private function taking place in a long room. White faces glower at us, men in stuffy suits rising from their chairs, trying to drive us away in Harrowtongue. Behind them, a keyhole-shaped window frames Bashtal's disordered silhouette—including the roof of the next building. Downstairs, soldiers mob the lounge and thunder up the stairs.

Taha and I exchange a knowing nod. We sprint past the babbling Harrowlanders; they shout; a few hop onto their chairs as if we are rats come to nibble their ugly shoes. We launch at the window. It explodes in a magnificent crash, and glass shards suspend around us, colorfully catching the sun like a shower of jewels. I sail through the rushing wind and land roughly, crumbling to my knees. The people in the lounge point at us from the shattered window but quickly disappear from view and are replaced by soldiers.

"Come on!" I tow Taha along the roof.

Men fly through the broken window behind us like birds of prey, *thud* after *thud* sounding as they land. One shouts at us; the imminence of his voice almost makes me stumble. I clumsily lunge onto the next roof, this one built lower on the slope. I manage to regain my stride and clamber over a short wall where a woman hangs out her washing.

"Watch out," I yell.

She skips back, giving us room to scuttle between the hanging sheets for the next roof. But it is impossible to judge the distance of the jump or whether I'll make it. My knees threaten to buckle, and fear stubbornly courses through me. Like a lifeline, I remember when Atheer taught me how to climb a tree when we were children. He stood at the base, laughing and calling up, "Are you sure you can't skin-change into a monkey? You're a natural!" The memory of my brother is like Auntie's undying light, guiding me through the darkness to salvation. To a better future, a happier world. It gives me enough hope to jump.

I soar over the yawning gap and stumble. The terrace meets my knees; pain howls in my thighs. Taha helps me up and we press on. Terrace after terrace, balcony after balcony, I repeat Atheer's encouragement and leap, dodging clay urns, outdoor lounges, a man in prayer. The buildings descend the hill to a main part of the city where the sound of hawking fills the humid air.

"Fresh fish!"

"Half-price watermelons!"

"It's a bazaar," I tell Taha. "We can hide between the customers."

We race across the roof; the bazaar emerges on our right, teeming with people. We need to get down to ground level, but without access to this building's interior stairwell, we can only climb down its exterior walls. I hear a soldier shout below us and turn my head. I spot them on horseback, galloping down the street alongside the building. They're trying to cut us off ahead.

We vault to the terrace of the next building. I move in a blind panic, lose my footing, and skate off the edge.

"No, no, no—"

I hook my fingers onto the bricks and slam into the side of the building, legs flailing. Horses shake the lane below, still more charging past on the street.

"I've got you." Taha appears over the roof's edge and hauls me up. The momentum sends him falling back and me landing on his heaving chest. A soldier says something in the lane below. Taha's eyes widen.

"They're going up the stairs inside to corner us."

"We need to beat them." I stand despite the throb under my ribs and the glass cutting me through my clothes. This is no place to rest, no place to die.

We run past the roof door as a soldier bursts through it.

Reaching fingers brush the back of my cloak. I career left out of his grip and push on with Taha, but there is nothing beyond this building except the glittering Azurite River, two, perhaps three, floors below.

Hands appear on the tiled edge of the roof before us, followed by a soldier's head. We hurtle right; he climbs onto the roof and gives chase. I dodge empty washing lines, only to crash into a wicker chair. I fall; the soldier dives to the ground and grabs me, digging his nails into my flesh.

"No!" I shriek, kicking him anywhere I can. The other soldier is closing in, longsword drawn.

Taha kicks this one off me. The man's grip loosens, allowing me space to roll out of his clutches. I scramble to the roof's edge; he lurches after me, ordering us to stop. But if I stop, I will meet cuffs and a noose. My sister will be lost and alone, my brother too, and my people will be in danger. It is a fate I am not willing to accept, for the hope is not yet spent, the better world not yet out of reach. There is still a chance to open the door and let the light in.

I reach my hand out, only to find Taha's already waiting. Our fingers interlock and we jump.

The roar of the wind steals the scream from my lungs. I drop like a stone, toes pointed, and break the surface. I plunge deep into warm, rushing waters. My thoughts hush, my body relaxes. Heavy peace sweeps over me, trailed swiftly by an irresistible need to rest. I am shutting my eyes when something flashes in the murk. A fish. Nothing else. I need to sleep.

Another thought prods my fatigued brain. *Crocodile,* it whispers.

I snap my eyes open, searching for the glint of arrowhead teeth ready to sink into me. But there is no attacking predator, only threads of color and light woven together by the hand of a cosmic seamstress. They unite to produce an image of younger Baba, floating, ghostly, before me. He is waist-deep in a pond at the woody Zhofal oasis we visited when I was seven. Mama is behind him, sitting in the shade of a tree, reading a fantasy story to Amira while Atheer pokes between some rocks with a stick. My own voice, small and frightened, calls from somewhere.

"I'm afraid to put my head under the water, Baba."

His dark eyes are gentle, and Mama is smiling at me over his shoulder. "Never fear, Imani. We are right here with you. I promise, we won't let you sink."

A bubble of air escapes my lips; I writhe, chest fevered, throat craving air. The gasp is coming. I am about to *drown*.

I cock my head to the sunlight illuminating the surface of the water and kick my legs, fighting the pain and fatigue doing a deadly dance in my limbs. I focus on nothing but that sunlight— the same sunlight that's falling on everyone I love. I cannot fail them.

I break the surface and gulp a lungful of sweet air between spluttering coughs. The dumbfounded soldiers are still on the rooftop, but they don't notice that I have survived, or that the river is carrying me safely out of reach.

THE RIVER NARROWS around a bend where the edge of a drain protrudes into the water. I climb out, thankful some sunlight remains to warm my shivering body. I toss my sopping cloak aside and work my hair free of my tangled braid before collapsing onto the stone.

Slowly it occurs to me what happened, and my relief over surviving the drop is so intense, I start to sob. And I don't know where Taha is; I didn't see him after we jumped. My tears flow harder, my body shaking with a sudden, unexpected eruption of grief. My training was meant to have conditioned me to the risks of being a Shield, but the lived experience of a fellow warrior succumbing is so starkly different—no amount of talking or reading about death could have prepared me for the chest-gouging shock I feel. I desperately search for solace, telling myself it's Taha I am weeping over—loathsome, conceited Taha who deserves none of my sympathies, but it doesn't make things any better or easier. It makes things worse, in fact, because now I realize that despite all his flaws, I actually *care* for Taha and his welfare. It would be my fault if he drowned. I disobeyed his order not to get involved; I forced him to disobey his own order and stop the soldier from attacking me. That one act sparked this trouble.

I press my hands to my face, shielding my crying eyes from the sunlight. What could I have done differently? Taha would have had me walk on and leave that woman to whatever fate the soldier had in mind, but I am no longer confident I am capable of doing that. Even if I could travel back in time, with what I know would ensue, the dagger would still be thrown. I would still try to intervene, because in my heart and soul, I feel it is the right thing to do; it is what my parents and Auntie would encourage me to do. That is the truth, and as difficult as it may be, the truth must always prevail, regardless of the rules it defies and the false history it rewrites. Atheer was right, the truth is the thorn, not the rose. And perhaps Bayek was too—if the correct constitution is apathy, I think I lack it.

The sound of coughing makes me sit up. A young man is climbing out of the water, drenched tunic and sirwal clinging to the hard lines of his powerful body.

"Taha!" I exclaim, scrambling to my feet. "Thank the Spirits, you survived! I was so worried."

My relief is too strong for me to care about revealing to Taha how I truly feel. I run over and, without thinking, throw my arms around him. And instead of shoving me away, he pulls me closer and kisses me.

My mind empties, yet I do not recoil. I lean into him, letting him cradle my face and caress my cheeks with his thumbs, sweeping away the cool drops of water left by his spiked hair. And how I enjoy it, as if my world lacked color all this time and now it is vibrantly exploding with it. Taha's kiss is not what I expect, not brash and boastful. It is ever so shy and tentative, afraid of me, more afraid of himself. Tender, withdrawn, but with a tempting hint of something more, like a dawn sun glancing over the horizon, not quite ready to light up the world. And it's ended too quickly.

He steps back, huskily stammering, "Forgive me. I—I didn't mean to do that."

"You didn't?" I freeze, cringing over how horribly disappointed I sound. But I *am* disappointed, and hurt, and confused. I'm convinced there is more to Taha than he is letting on. And I am so full of longing too, this sickening desire to repeat the kiss and more. I wish I could excise that yearning from myself and go back to how I was before this mission, when I didn't know Taha at all and I was confident I didn't care whether he acknowledged me. I didn't care that this talented, dedicated warrior couldn't even remember my name.

He shakes his head, gesturing at the river. "No. The fall, the shock of it, almost drowning . . ." He squeezes his eyes shut and draws a short breath. "Let's just focus on the mission."

I recall the letter he penned to his father: *Her presence will neither distract nor hinder me.* So he wasn't lying. *But why?* I want to demand. *Why do you toy with me, then?* And how can I stop myself from caring? I must convince myself that the real Taha is this one: cruel, arrogant, unfeeling. Not the one who stitched me up, or summoned a songbird to thrill me. Not the one who kissed me. Ugly thoughts swarm my head like buzzing bees, stingers primed: *He* should be grateful to even be in my company. *He* should be desperate for my approval. *He* is the nobody from a petty clan with the disgraceful bully of a father, and I am Imani of the Beya clan, descended from an illustrious lineage that shall endure for another thousand glorious years while his falls into disrepute and dust.

"Imani," he says quietly.

I turn away, blinking the angry tears from my eyes. "Right," I mutter. "Let's return to the stables."

He nods, wringing the water out of his clothes while considering the mouth of the tunnel behind me. "If we move through the drains, we can stay out of sight of the soldiers. Give me a minute."

He kneels on the embankment, and his eyes turn gold. I spot Sinan in the sky, the falcon's head turning left and right as he appraises the city. I look back down at Taha, and in spite of everything, I steal long looks at him. His lip has been split, and his cheekbone is shadowed by a bruise; little baubles of water are clinging bravely to his sopping ebony hair. He is attractive, but not in the same way as Qayn, wickedly showy. Taha is different. Uncomplicated, serious, reserved. I hate that I experience nostalgic comfort in his presence. He reminds me of the familiar: he stands for the Sahir, family, and the Shields; for well-accepted, oft-repeated teachings; for everything that is dutiful and ordered. He embodies the life I knew, the one my brother is upending. He represents a terrible choice.

His eyes return to pale green, and he stands. "I have a good sense of the way. Follow me."

We walk the tunnels under Bashtal in stormy silence. At one point, he has the gall to ask if I'd like to practice some more Harrowtongue, but I am so livid, my tongue is knotted and I can only shake my head.

It is dusk when we climb out of the grate on the street opposite the stables. We wait for the street to be clear of soldiers before we cross over. Taha enters and returns with only his white colt and Fey's horse. My relief over Raad being gone is cut short by an awful realization: Fey didn't collect her horse.

It is a melancholic ride back through the defeated city. I tremble with the cold as dusk surrenders to night, but my anguish is too great for me to care. Mercifully, there is no excessive guard force around the gates as we leave Bashtal. Perhaps the soldiers are convinced Taha and I died falling into the river. A part of me certainly died coming out of it.

We get back onto the wide Spice Road, and some ways down,

figures I recognize jog out from the tree-line to meet us. I jump out of the saddle and race across the grass to Amira, and lift her in an embrace.

"Thank the Spirits, I'm so glad to see you! Are you all right?"

"Yes, I had no trouble leaving," she says, glancing apologetically at Reza beside her.

The young man is shaking Taha's hand, his eyes bloodshot and glazed with the mist of fresh tears. "Fey fell when we were fleeing," he explains. "The soldiers took her away. We need to save her."

Taha grimaces, holding out the reins to her horse. "Sorry, Cousin. The mission has priority."

"But . . . it's Fey," says Reza, frowning. "We have to help her."

"Not while a mission is still active. She knows that, and she knew the risks."

"I didn't *ask* for this, Taha!" Reza gestures around us: to Bashtal, twinkling in the gloom; the lone carriage creaking along the Spice Road, a glimmering oil lamp swinging off its perch. "I wanted to be a Shield, man."

"Serving the Council as a Scout is the kind of honor our clan could only dream of until now," Taha replies coldly. "Respect what we have achieved and adjust to your duties. Is that understood?"

Tears well in Reza's eyes. "What if they hang her like they did that girl? We have to do something quickly, *please.*"

"Is it understood?" Taha repeats in a hard voice.

Reza's shoulders heave. "Yes," he whispers after a long moment. "It's understood."

"Good." Taha directs his horse toward a tree. "We make camp and set out for Taeel-Sa at first light."

Reza stares after him, silent tears sliding down his cheeks. I wonder if, like me, he is finally realizing Taha's true nature: a young man who cares for nothing but what he is told to care about by the Council. By his father. Someone who will sacrifice everything, everyone, even himself, in service of his father's goals.

I step closer to Reza. "I'm sorry," I say. "After we find Atheer, I will help you get Fey back."

"Just—just do what you're told," he mutters, angrily swiping the tears off his face.

I flinch as he marches away with Fey's horse in tow. But for once, I don't resent his unkindness. He is hurting deeply and raising defensive walls to stop anyone from touching that open wound. He wants to focus on our work, not on his loss, not on the person he loves whom he may never see again. It is a pain I understand too well, so I silently let him leave. Behind him, Taha is gathering wood from between the trees. I am tempted to call out and ask why he is bothering. Not even the warmth of a thousand campfires would be enough to thaw his heart.

25

THE COASTAL CITY OF TAEEL-SA IS MAJESTIC DESPITE the indelible marks war has left upon it. Its defensive sandstone walls have taken a battering; in some areas, the ramparts have been destroyed by trebuchet fire, and blocks of stone have been left like grave markers in the outer fields. Erected in a grid around the rubble are hundreds of tents, their rows interspersed with campfires, carriages, horses, and Harrowlander soldiers. The camp is a display of military might unlike any I have seen before, and it makes the Sahiran armed forces look pitiful in comparison. We have magic, yes; we are trained; but we haven't seen true war in a thousand years. These men breathe it.

The sight of these vultures gathered on the city's carcass dampens my already low spirits. We have finally arrived at the city where Atheer should be hiding with the rebels, yet rather than feeling relief and excitement, I am anxious. What awaits me within those scarred walls? News of Atheer's death, perhaps, or a brother I will not recognize? *Have hope,* I tell myself. *Without it, you have nothing.*

"Where will we find Zakariya?" Taha asks Qayn, who is

riding along with me again. The djinni was very pleased when I summoned him and he saw that I was alive; he even gave me a hug. Taha, on the other hand, has not spoken to me since our kiss. I sense he is trying to bury the memory and pretend it never happened.

"He lives in a house off the Field of Memories," Qayn answers.

Taha inspects his map and nods. "I see it. Follow me."

Taeel-Sa is busy on a scale that rivals Qalia, but its atmosphere is intimidating. There are even more soldiers inside than out, and each is armed with a glinting longsword and a meaner glint in his eyes. Despite its war wounds, the city underneath is undeniably breathtaking. Sun-loved and sand-yellow, its soaring minarets and ornate arcades contrast in white marble; its glittering domes are tooled in solid gold. It is sprinkled with date palms; long walls of intact, intricate tile work; meandering laneways skirted by almond-colored doors and blooming flower beds; even mossy ponds with mallard ducks gliding along their emerald surfaces. Tangles of grapevines droop over the streets declining gently to the sea; the corners are marked by decorative wrought-iron lampposts. It is altogether hazy and dreamlike, a city built during a balmy, drowsy afternoon that never ended.

Our route takes us through the Grand Bazaar, so we leave our horses at some stables and go on foot. We are not spared the sight of a scaffold on our way. It is the same as in Bashtal; the blue dead swing with signs around their necks proclaiming their crimes against the Empire. But there is one difference. Here the scaffolds are accompanied by a raised platform on which another punishment is exacted: floggings. Few gather to watch the savagery; many do not spare a glance as they pass. This time, I am not ignorant enough to blame them.

I am only too glad to exchange the sickening sights and sounds for the Grand Bazaar's lanes. They are crammed with shops and their shouting keepers, some in Harrowtongue. That disturbs me, the number of Taeel-Sani people I hear speaking the foreign language. An uncomfortable-looking few are even dressed like the invaders too.

"There is so much to look at," Amira says in my ear.

I toss her a bewildered nod. Some sections of the bazaar have been reduced to rubble or blackened by fire, but in every undamaged alcove, someone hawks something that makes me want to stop and stare: glass blown into the shape of birds, woven baskets, beaded cushions, silk rugs with intricate floral motifs, fine leather shoes and bags, heady perfumes, pouches of incense, bejeweled hand mirrors, silver and gold jewelry inlaid with precious stones, figurines of animal-headed and winged deities, bags of rich-smelling coffee, even colorful birds in gilded cages.

But the farther we walk through the bazaar, the more I realize that the only people who are affording these items are the invaders. And for all the stately city's apparent wealth, there is a staggering amount of poverty tucked just out of sight. I spy an entire family in tattered tunics asleep on the ground in a rubble-strewn alley behind a fabric shop. On the next corner, a man holds up his young son.

"Someone, please, take him," he calls out. "I cannot afford to feed my children. Please, show mercy. He is only a boy!"

I bow my head as we pass, Amira's fingers curling tighter around my hand. Taha glances over his shoulder at us, but this time, I don't bother to hide how much the man's desperate pleas have upset me. Further along, an elderly woman prostrates in an alcove, imploring us for aid. I turn my head away, only to catch a glimpse down a quieter, shadowed lane on our right. Outside a curtained den, a pair of young people in bright silks dance and call out to the foreign soldiers walking past. But their flirtatious smiles do not touch their eyes.

Everywhere I look, I am confronted by destitution: small, scruffy children labor in shops and trades rather than being in school; the poor wear malnutrition and ailments unseen in the Sahir, like cloudy eyes and bowed legs. Soldiers watch over the deprivation without a care in the world. More than a few grin, shifting easily between bullying innocent people and joking with their fellow soldiers. They are intoxicated on the unfettered power, and I am sickened by it.

Unlike in Bashtal, where the presence of the foreigners was mostly limited to soldiers and officials, Taeel-Sa has a large civilian population of Harrowlanders proudly gallivanting about the place as if it is rightfully theirs. Everywhere I expect to see a Taeel-Sani, there is a colonizer instead. They crowd the lounges, restaurants, and gardens; they indolently laze on the balconies of beautiful houses that must have been owned by Taeel-Sani families who had lived and died there for countless generations. The people who created these very establishments are nowhere to be seen. Either they cannot afford to participate or they are forbidden. Many buildings have been or are in the process of being repurposed—a resplendent marble temple that must have once been dedicated to local gods now sports a statue of an ashen half man, half stag bearing a golden scepter. A Harrowlander official oversees several Taeel-Sani men nailing signs written in Harrow-tongue to the walls. The city is a stone being smothered by moss.

I come to recognize the shops that sell spices not only from their aromas but from their red doors and constant streams of customers, most of whom are colonists or visitors from other lands. Each sports a heavy presence of soldiers: the red-faced men stand outside, angrily ordering and sometimes kicking beggars away like they are little more than pests. And from what I can tell of the people I sight through the windows, none of the spice shops are operating without a Harrowlander behind the counter, keeping watch of all coin being exchanged. Safeguarding their ill-gotten dues.

We reach the bazaar's sprawling produce quarter and follow Taha's example, dodging needy children clutching at our hems, begging for coin; and teens carrying crates of pomegranate and fig for Harrowlander customers. Enormous crowds of foreigners dawdle here, haggling over fish from the nearby Bay of Glass, the salty, fresh breeze of which curtains every corridor. We pass so many food vendors selling something delicious that my belly protests. Amira nudges me and points at the stalls we pass.

"How similar their food is to ours," she marvels.

I wish I could deny it, but I am familiar with every item. The sticky, golden squares of pistachio-filled baklawa, the diced lamb drizzled with garlic-infused sauce, the flat khobz fresh from the furnace topped in melted goat's cheese or za'atar spice.

"We grew up eating this food," I say, my gut churning. Though I am famished, I am guiltier still. So many hunger here, and I have gone so long with a full belly and ignorant heart.

I emerge from the bazaar an unsettled, barely threaded

collection of exposed nerves. I don't notice the colonist barging toward us until the obnoxious breadth of her skirt has knocked me and Amira off the sidewalk into a smelly puddle of mysterious origin. Insulted as I am, I don't want to attract attention like I did in Bashtal.

"Keep walking," I mutter, guiding Amira onward, to which Taha nods approvingly.

Past the Grand Bazaar, the city loses its luster and somehow becomes even more crowded. The buildings here are nothing like those I saw when we first entered Taeel-Sa, though certainly not for lack of effort. The careful tile work is chipped, fragments broken off entirely in places. The lime plaster on the walls has not been maintained, and some parts are cracked and exposing the bricks within, like flesh peeled back over weary bones. Even the pleasing fragrances of the bazaar cannot contend with the waste and rubbish. Homeless people gather in alleyways, coughing and commiserating; the weary impoverished hunch on the stoops of homes and flagging shops, smoking pipes, handling prayer beads, whiling the day away for lack of a viable alternative. Their eyes are sad, their mouths downturned, their clothes faded and tatty. Disappointment and defeat prowl everywhere. And on at least one wall in every street hangs a scroll, written in both Alqibahi and Harrowtongue, encouraging people to report treasonous behavior against the Empire for reward.

"You see it, don't you?" Amira whispers to me. "The same thing Atheer did."

I find it impossibly difficult to summon use of my voice, so I only nod. Back in Qalia, I wondered what could have changed Atheer so drastically. I was convinced he was suffering from magical obsession or being manipulated. Witnessing this place, living it, experiencing the desperation soaking my flesh and staining my very gristle—I am beginning to understand the truth he spoke of. And the terror I experience at this realization is consummate.

Qayn interrupts my thoughts, pointing ahead. "That is the Field of Memories."

It is a beautiful but neglected garden enclosed by a vine-choked stone fence. Black obelisks spear from open wounds in the grass, each etched with Alqibahi names. Aside from an elderly man leaning on his cane, dutifully pulling weeds from the base of an obelisk, the garden is empty.

"And this"—Qayn stops us outside a shabby terraced house next to the garden—"must be Zakariya's home."

I scarcely believe we have reached our destination. I take a deep breath and make to knock on the front door, when I notice the sheet of paper nailed to it.

"What's this?" I murmur, pulling it free. The others crowd around me to read along.

I am not home.

Should you need to see me, please go to the boat shed.

Z.

"An address is listed," says Taha, taking the sheet from me and inspecting it.

"Damn it," I whisper, going to the shuttered windows. One

of them hasn't been secured and swings open with little effort. I peer through into a sitting room. To say the house is simply furnished is kind. The room hosts two worn sofas and a broken-legged coffee table littered with empty bottles. Not content to have stayed there, the bottles have spilled over onto the tattered rug too. They must have once contained arak; I can smell the pungent licorice of the liquor from here. It has practically steeped into the walls.

"So the man likes to indulge," Qayn says from beside me.

"*Indulge* is an understatement," I mutter, running my eyes over the thick layer of dust and the pile of clothes tossed onto one sofa. "What sort of man did you say Zakariya was again?"

"A decent one, apparently."

"I know where the boat shed is," Taha says behind us, packing away his map.

I close the shutter and nod. "Take us there."

TAHA GUIDES US PAST THE WHARVES, where the Bay of Glass lies as flat and calm as a splash of sapphire dye, flecked with white sails. The smell of salt and fish permeates the still air, seagulls hovering on it as if suspended by strings, indistinct sailors' shouts carrying like a half-remembered dream. Light winks in the polished wood of several Harrowlander warships dominating the water. They surround a long, lithe ship, three-masted and flying the Empire's brown flag.

"What is that?" I ask the others. Fishing boats carefully weave around the ship like mice creeping past a guard dog.

"That must be King Glaedric's ship," Qayn answers. "Atheer told me about it. The Harrowlanders deem it unsafe to have the king onshore for extended periods."

After that, we pass several merchant ships being loaded with crates. The tangy scent gives their contents away, but I would know these are spice ships simply from the exhausted workers surrounded by soldiers and being ordered by Harrowlander officials.

"Look, Imani," Amira whispers.

She points at a long stretch of rubble where some buildings must've once stood. I acknowledge it with a grim nod. The war is echoed everywhere here, in the collapsed fences; the half walls mulishly resisting fate's cruel nudge; the unfilled trenches in place of sidewalks, their furrows littered with scraps of bloodstained clothes, glass, and wood; the patches of scorched earth; the stray arrows and snapped hilts discarded in rubbish-strewn gutters. A fine two-horse carriage with brass fittings is jarringly out of place. It rolls along the potholed street, window open; a Harrowlander man reclines inside with a Taeel-Sani who leans out as they pass us.

"You, young man," he calls, nodding when Taha looks over. "Yes, you. My Lord Osgar is sponsoring new gladiators for the Grounds on a very generous seventy-thirty split of winnings, and you look like you've a mighty fighting chance. Equipment and training are included—"

Taha bows at the carriage. "I am not interested, but please, convey my thanks to Lord Osgar for his most kind offer."

"What was that?" I ask when the carriage has gone.

"He is seeking combatants for the Valor Grounds," Taha answers. "The people here call them the Death Pits."

"Death Pits? What happens in them?"

"Use your imagination, Slayer," Qayn says from my left. "Strapping young men like Taha here fighting each other and wild animals to the death for coin. Pardon me, a thirty percent share of the coin. How very generous indeed."

Amira gasps. "That's barbaric."

"Surely you jest," I scoff. "Why would anyone willingly participate?"

"A desperate individual will do just about anything, and vile individuals are always standing by, ready to take advantage for their own gratification."

I glance over at Qayn. He is ambling with his head tipped, wavy black hair concealing his eyes, hands dug deep in his pockets. I sense a personal edge buried in his answer, and I can't help but think of how he described the people of the First City exploiting him. *But in what way?* I wonder.

"We're here," Taha announces.

We pause at the top of a dirt path. On the bank of the Bay below is a blue boat shed. And standing under the deck lantern outside the closed door are two Harrowlander soldiers, their horses tethered nearby.

We crouch in the shadow of some trees and watch one of the Harrowlanders enter the boat shed; the other shuts the door behind him.

"What's going on?" Amira whispers.

I chew the inside of my cheek. "Nothing good. If Zak is in there with them . . ."

"They might be interrogating him," Taha finishes.

"Could we wait for them to leave?" Amira asks.

A pained shout emerges from within the boat shed, making us flinch.

"Sounds like torture," Taha mutters.

My gut churns as my imagination visits possibilities I wish it wouldn't. "We must reach Zak before they hurt him *permanently*."

"But if you go in there now, you'll have to deal with those soldiers," Amira says, tugging my elbow.

"So we lure them away first. A small earthquake that spooks their horses, perhaps? With any luck, that will give us enough time to reach Zak." I look over at Taha, then Reza, who is staring down at the boat shed. Since Fey was taken, he has been withdrawn and avoiding everyone's gaze, including Taha's.

"Well?" Taha prods softly.

Reza wordlessly nods and shuffles over to the edge of the small hill we are perched upon. He digs his hand into the sandy soil and retrieves a fistful of it. With eyes intently fixed on the horses, he slowly rocks his fist back and forth, shaking the soil in his palm. The ground under the horses responds in kind. A low rumble builds and the earth begins to quake. The horses shuffle on the spot, snorting and huffing, their anxiety rising with the tremors.

Fair face furrowing, the Harrowlander soldier pushes off the wall he was leaning against. He calls something at the horses, palms up in an attempt to pacify them until the earthquake passes. Reza shakes his fist roughly; the rumble grows to a roar and the soil hums under my slippers. Fine fissures begin forming in the ground around the horses. Gaping at it, the soldier sways in his boots before tottering back to the boat shed, arms held aloft. Behind him, the horses whinny and pull their tethers free, then bolt up the hill past us a moment later.

"Well done. A little more," Taha whispers, patting his cousin on the back.

Sweat dots Reza's upper lip, and the muscles of his face tighten, but his focus doesn't waver; he doesn't even blink. The soldier bangs on the door, fumbles with the handle and gets it open. The other is already waiting there. They exchange harried words, the first soldier pointing up the hill. The second one casts an irate glance at the boat shed's interior before they both jog up the hill. We shrink into the underbrush as they pass us. When they've gone, Reza ceases the earthquake. Nobody speaks for a full minute, until we are certain the soldiers are not coming back.

"That was excellent," I tell Reza.

He doesn't acknowledge me as he mops his sweaty face with the front of his tunic; nor does he respond when Taha directs him to stay and keep watch for the soldiers. The rest of us hurry down the hill to the boat shed. I am only a few meters from it when a silhouetted figure within shuts the door.

"Zak?" I call, jogging over. I knock on the front door. "Zakariya?"

"Who's asking?" comes a gruff voice.

"Not the soldiers."

The door cracks open, and a bloodshot brown eye peers out. "What do you want?"

"My name is Imani. I am looking for someone you may know. His name is Atheer."

Zak makes to close the door, but Taha shoves his heft against it. "Not so fast."

"Get off the bloody door," Zak growls, pushing from the other side. "I don't know anyone by that name."

Qayn leans around Taha to get a look at the man inside the boat shed. He is still little more than a silhouette.

"Come now, yes you do. You introduced him to Farida."

With a grunt, a balled fist emerges from the gap and boxes Taha on the ear. In the moment Taha relinquishes his grasp, the door has bolted shut again.

"Leave me alone."

"We only have a few questions," I say. "Please, won't you help us?"

If Zak heard my plea, he has chosen to ignore it. I slump against the boat shed's wall and gaze out miserably across the placid water. Taha, meanwhile, has begun pacing the deck like a caged beast while rubbing his reddened ear. Except he is not as desperate to get out as he is to get *in*.

"There must be a way," he mutters.

I follow his example and look around the boat shed. There is only one window I can see, and it is firmly shuttered. The door is constructed from sturdy wood, and I am not keen on transforming my dagger to an axe and destroying Zak's property, so that isn't a possibility either. But the shed is the kind with a door that hovers over the water where boats can enter. I pull Taha to the edge of the bank and point it out.

"Fancy a swim?"

With a resigned sigh, he slips into the water first. I tell Amira and Qayn to wait for us here; then I suck in a sharp breath and join Taha in the water, puckering my lips to stop from calling out. The water is cool and up to my shoulders in an instant, my tunic comically inflating around me. It isn't cold, but I am so accustomed to the warm waters of the oases in the Sahir that this almost feels like ice. I grit my teeth and follow Taha to the large door. Side by side, we fix a hand on its bottom edge, pinch our nostrils, and submerge; we glide under the door and surface inside the shed like a pair of crocodiles.

A man with a mop of chin-length hair has his back to us; he rifles through a crate of items on a countertop, muttering curses. The boat shed is empty aside from Zak, and like his home, it is cluttered with bottles of arak and mess. But Zak does not look like the sort of man who is ordinarily messy or careless. The moored boat that Taha and I float past is handsome, and the boat shed would be too, if it were clean. And with a makeshift cot pushed up against one wall, Zak seems to spend enough time here to keep it tidy. But why would he choose to sleep here, rather than back home?

Taha and I reach the edge of the stone platform, the sound of our approach disguised by the lap of the water. He gestures at me with his fingers, counting us down. At zero, we hoist out of the water in a lunge, water droplets flying off us and splashing onto the ground.

"What the hells?" Zak grunts, twisting round. He is in his late twenties, bearded, with the shadow of bruises around both eyes and the swollen lip of someone who has recently suffered a beating. And apart from the scent of liquor and blood that clings to him, I smell sadness.

"What do you think you're doing?" he slurs, clumsily reaching for a wooden rod on the counter.

I hold my hands up. "Please, Zak, we do not mean any trouble. We only want to talk."

"You don't have to mean it to cause it."

"I am just looking for my brother," I insist.

He falters, lips silently moving. "Brother?" he murmurs after a moment. "You . . . You're from the magical land across the Sands?"

"You know about where we come from," Taha says in a tight voice as he unlatches the boat shed door, allowing Amira and Qayn to enter.

"I must get in touch with my brother," I say quickly. I need to keep the conversation focused on Atheer, before Taha lashes out. I can already feel the rage exuding from him.

"I don't know where he is," says Zak. "I don't work with them anymore."

I have begun feeling breathless, even though the swim would hardly constitute an exertion. "You mean the rebellion," I say, and Zak nods. "When was the last time you saw my brother?"

"Months ago. Maybe nine or ten months."

My heart sinks. "That long? And you don't know what's happened to him since?"

Zak shakes his head. "Couldn't tell you."

I don't know whether to be relieved or not. As of ten months ago, my brother was alive. But ten months is a long time, and tragedy can happen in a heartbeat.

"But Farida can tell us," Qayn interrupts, strolling past me. "Atheer will be with her, so take us to her."

Zak bares clenched teeth. "I will say it one more time: I am *not* involved with them anymore."

Qayn continues his approach, radiating regal impatience. Zak shuffles back, glancing warily at the djinni's bare feet, then his fine linen clothes. My own outfit is by no means cheap, but Qayn's exudes wealth even in its simplicity. And though he is lean, more boy than man, he can be intimidating at will.

"We are not requesting that you assassinate King Glaedric on their behalf, my dear boy," he says. "We are merely requesting that you take us to Farida. We cannot make contact with her rebels on our own; we need a face they know and trust. Once we are in, we will take care of the rest, all right?"

"No, I won't do it." Zak steps away, shaking his head. "I've lost too much to those idealistic fools. I am not risking my life getting involved again."

Out of the corner of my eye, I notice items on the countertop that are out of place: a fine hair comb; a neatly folded rose floral scarf; a small, thriving yellow flower in a clay pot. They are the only things in this boat shed that are not coated in dust.

"Why did you leave the rebellion?" I ask. "What did you lose?"

"Not what," he mutters. *"Who."*

Of course. It is not merely sadness weeping off this man but *grief.* Something I understand all too well.

"Someone you loved," I supply.

His gaze wanders over to the scarf and the potted flower. "My sister. Rima."

Her name was mentioned in one of Atheer's letters. "She was caught by the soldiers, wasn't she?" I say.

"Worked to death in their prison." Zak's face contorts, tears welling in his eyes. He turns away. "It's Farida's fault. She filled Rima's head with ridiculous ideas of retaking our city from the Harrowlanders. Rima was only twenty-one."

"I'm so sorry, Zak. But I need your help—I must know my brother's fate."

He grabs the rod off the counter and points it at me. "Get out. I can't help you."

"Please," I say desperately, approaching him. "Can you at least direct us to someone else who can help—"

He swings the rod, halting my advance. "No! And if you don't leave, I'll call for the soldiers!"

"Are you mad?" Qayn laughs in his face. "Haven't you had enough of their punishment? Oh, you think they'll spare you in exchange for us? *Tsk, tsk.* You'll be swinging on the scaffolds alongside us for your long, treasonous history, boy."

Zak stops swinging but holds the rod out to keep us at bay. "I will take my chances. I can't help you. Please, just leave."

I sigh, lowering my hands. He cannot be convinced; his pain is so great that he cannot see anything beyond it. He certainly won't for a bunch of strangers. I don't know where that leaves me, but Zak's boat shed is not the place to figure that out.

I've turned to go to the door when Taha strides across the room. "You're giving up that easily, Imani?" He points at Zak. "We don't have time for your horseshit."

Zak wields the stick again. Taha nimbly sidesteps it, grabs the man's neck and shoves him against the counter, almost knocking over the potted flower. "You've two options, Zak. Choose wisely: do what we ask or die refusing."

"I won't," Zak chokes out, banging his fists on Taha's shoulders. "I won't—"

"I *will.*" Taha squeezes his neck. Zak gurgles and tries to kick his legs, fluttering hands working uselessly at Taha's wrists.

"Don't do that," Amira cries, but Taha ignores her.

I run over to him. "Taha, stop, you're hurting him!"

"So I am," he grunts, pinning Zak against the counter. The man's face is mottled purple, almost green around his bruised eyes, and he has become too weak to thrash his legs anymore.

"*Please!* There are other ways—"

"There aren't!" he barks. "We need him to find Atheer!"

Zak finally makes a sound that vaguely sounds like the word *yes,* and Taha drops him onto the dank stone floor. Zak doubles over, coughing violently.

"Fine, you bastard," he croaks, massaging his raw neck. "I will take you to Farida. Just don't kill me."

"You have two minutes to be ready outside." Taha catches my eye on his way to the door, then glances at the look of horror painting Amira's face.

"This is no place for you, girl," he says, pushing past her.

I storm after him out of the boat shed. "Hey, hold on."

"Not you too," he mutters.

"Not me too?" I drag him into the shade of a sycamore growing over the water. "What was that? You almost killed the man."

He folds his arms across his chest. "I was following orders."

The will of his father, I realize uneasily. "We are *Shields,* Taha, not executioners. At what cost will these orders come?"

He narrows his eyes. "Any, so long as the mission is completed."

A chill crawls across my skin. "Would you sacrifice your soul for it?" When he doesn't answer, I quietly ask him, "What happened to your dog, Rashiq, in the end? You never finished your story."

He looks past me, his temple ticking. "I had to put him down."

"*You* did? What cruelty," I breathe. "Why didn't your father do it to spare you the distress, the same way you did for me with Badr?"

He blinks and breathes slowly; he remains silent for such a long time, I begin thinking he won't answer. Then, quietly, he says, "Some of us had to learn hard lessons to survive."

I feel as if I am standing at an angle, witnessing an unbearably crooked world. Taha doesn't look at me as he speaks. He gazes at the water, but he is seeing nothing; perhaps he is lost in the same memory I am imagining. That of a small, sad boy with a knife forced into his hand by a heartless father. A boy forced to kill what he loves.

Zak trudges across the grit behind us. "Ready," he grunts dejectedly.

"Good." Taha steps past me. "Lead the way."

26

ZAK LEADS US TO THE END OF THE WHARVES AND nods at the dock. "There it is. I think."

I squint against the late sun at a lonely two-masted sailing ship moored ahead. It is handsome, its curved prow rising into a lion's head, its stern similarly carved with vines. A single, smoking sailor judges us from the end of the dock.

"You think?" I ask.

Zak gives a thick, wet cough into the elbow of his tunic. "Well, Farida's rebels largely quarter themselves on vessels," he explains, patting his chest. "Most of her ranks are like me, fishermen, sailors, dockworkers who fought alongside our king's army against the Harrowlanders, and now want to retake the city from the invaders. This ship belonged to Farida's late father—he was killed in the war when the Harrowlanders stormed Taeel-Sa—"

"But?" I say impatiently, sensing Zak is dithering in his speech.

"But there used to be more than one ship and one sailor . . ."

It is too late to enquire further. We've reached the ship, and the lanky sailor is stalking over.

"Long time, Zak," he says without a lick of friendliness. He has a deep scar across his right cheek, thinly veiled by black stubble.

Zak merely budges his thick brows. "Where is everyone, Makeen?"

"Where?" Makeen huffs. "Gone the way of your sister or abandoned the cause after the latest raids. Cowards, like you."

"Is it really so?" murmurs Zak, glancing over the ship. He seems more upset by the revelation than Makeen's insult.

"Rebellion's fallen apart, brother. We're the only ones left." Makeen nods at the ship. "You here to join back up?"

"No," Zak says firmly. "These people need to see the captain, if she's here."

"She is." Makeen looks us over. "You think you can bring new faces without telling us first?"

Zak touches his neck gingerly; it is ringed in red welts shaped like Taha's fingers. "I wasn't given much warning." He steps aside, motioning at me. "This is Atheer's sister, Imani, and others from . . . their land."

"Atheer?" Makeen's mocking leer is replaced with shock. "You look like him," he says, and nods at Zak. "Come aboard."

Zak elbows through us, away from the ship. "Thanks, but I've done my part. Happy? I wish to never see any of you again."

He hurries down the pier, coughing; Taha watches after him like the man is a goldenhare, and Makeen spits into the water and mutters, "Coward."

I take Amira's hand and totter after the sailor across the creaky ramp to the ship. The upper deck is in a state of dishevelment, cluttered with crates, nets, half-unwound rope, open bags of supplies. At one end, a group of sailors—none of them Atheer—smoke, drink, and play dice, though they cease the game to observe us. Even the sailor in the crow's nest watches us rather than our surrounds. I gullibly imagined this rebellion would be so much more than a disorderly ship and a bunch of sweaty gamblers, and I am both sorely disappointed and intensely worried about the failed cause Atheer traded his safety to help. And I am frantic to see him at last; my tears are lined up behind my eyes. I haven't prepared what I am going to say or do, but I think it will not matter if I had.

We follow Makeen to one end of the deck, up some stairs to a closed door. He knocks and pauses with his hand on the knob. By now, my heart has taken residence in my throat, and Amira's limp hand is trembling in mine. A husky voice returns. Makeen opens the door and motions us inside.

The stuffy cabin smells of sea and old frankincense. It is walled in dark wood, cheered marginally by a scruffy red rug underfoot that matches the curtains in the curving window opposite. A desk stands there, littered in scrolls, inkpots, bronze seafaring instruments, and a wooden lion figurine—one of Atheer's creations. Seated behind the desk is a young woman looking over a map. One woman, alone.

I slow to a stop, my hand tightening around Amira's. This must be Farida, the woman Atheer supposedly loves. The woman he described as someone of "great integrity." I only see the person who stole my brother away.

The rebel leader is perhaps twenty-three; she has russet skin and a full pout that seems accustomed to giving orders. One kohl-lined eye is the color of wet clay and exudes hard judgment; the other is concealed by a black patch. Under a loosely slung scarf, her curly brown hair falls to her shoulders. She dresses informally, almost shabbily, in black sirwal and a loose, stained white tunic with the sleeves rolled up, under a short, black vest.

Makeen taps two fingers to his forehead in a salute. "Captain, Zak brought them. This girl says she is Atheer's sister." He gestures me forward, takes his leave, and shuts the cabin door behind him.

Farida's eye glides over my face, brows crooking in the center. "Atheer's sister . . . from Qalia?"

It takes me a moment to answer, I am so anxious to finally speak to the person at the other end of Atheer's letters. This ghost made real, this end finally met. This outsider who speaks Qalia's name with unnerving familiarity.

"Yes," I choke out. "My name is Imani, and this is Amira, also Atheer's sister. This is Taha and Reza, mutual friends from Qalia, and Qayn. You are Farida, the woman my brother left home to meet over a year ago." I cannot disguise the resentment in my voice.

Farida limps round the desk, cutting a tall, commanding figure. "I am."

My breathing shallows. *This is it.* After all this time and journeying, I can ask the one question that has been burning on my tongue since Atheer left Qalia's gilded gates.

"Where is our brother? Is he . . . alive? We must speak with him; it is a matter of great urgency."

Farida falters by the desk, tracing a finger along the carved lion.

"Imani, Amira," she says, not looking at us. "It pains me to tell you this, but . . . your brother, Atheer . . . He is in prison."

27

ARIDA SWALLOWS; TEARS GATHER IN HER EYE BUT
don't fall. Amira sobs into my shoulder. I am still as the
world collapses around me, and I struggle to know whether
to experience an ounce of relief over her answer.

"He was arrested a few months ago, trying to stop a group
of soldiers beating a man," Farida explains. "I found out he was
only spared execution because of his strength. They placed him
in their hard-labor prison, and I haven't seen him since. I'm sorry.
I wish I had better news for you both. I love your brother and I
miss him every day."

A thousand questions shoot through my mind, but I am incapable of catching any to ask them. Amira falls into my arms,
weeping, saying no again and again. I stare over her shoulder at
Farida, my life pulsing in my ears. It's trying to remind me that
I am here, I can do something, my brother is still alive. But it
feels vain, about as good as firing arrows at the sun on a hot day.
The joyous relief I should have felt in this moment, knowing my
brother is alive, is absent. Farida has stolen him from me again.

"You love and you miss him," I echo.

She nods. "He means the world to me. It was Zak who introduced us. During the war for Taeel-Sa, Atheer helped my people evade certain death. Zak approached and told him of our cause, and Atheer was adamant that he wanted to help, at first to fight off the invaders, and later as a rebel. The moment we met . . ." She shakes her head, looking off to the side. "He showed me, *us,* incredible things, like your people's magic—he offered us a real chance at victory when all hope felt lost. He had a plan to take back not only Taeel-Sa but Alqibah . . . and then he was arrested."

Taha clears his throat; he is dying to voice his disapproval of Atheer's actions, and if he dares, I will drive this dagger through his eye.

I surrender to the contempt that has risen in my breast, and sneer. "How romantic of you. At least you knew he was alive. We spent a year believing he was dead. Can you imagine what that was like for us, for our parents? We held a funeral. My father etched his name onto our ancestors' wall; we prayed to the Great Spirit to ferry his soul to the afterlife. I cried for weeks trying to accept that our big brother and best friend was gone forever."

My voice cracks. Amira is weakly slung over me, pouring her soul into her tears. I hug her, but I continue glaring at Farida. I don't know why I am telling her these things, but I don't stop. I want her to hurt the way we did, the way *she* hurt us.

"We grieved him, Farida. We tried our best to move on, but we couldn't. His disappearance took *everything* from us; it almost destroyed us. And now—" I clench my teeth through a wave of tears. "We journey *so* far, we lose one of our party, we face death and despair, and you tell me he is in prison? What does that mean? Is he safe? Are they working him to death like they did Rima?"

Farida gasps, pressing a hand to her neck. "How do you know about—"

"Well, are *they*?" I exclaim.

"I—I don't know," she stammers. "I lost my contact at the City Guard, so I can't tell you what's going on in the prison, but I hope—"

"You *hope*?" I laugh harshly. "Your hope means nothing."

"I thought we'd find him here with you!" Amira erupts. "We were meant to; he was meant to be here. *You took him from us!*"

For her, this is Atheer's second death. First he was taken by the Council, now by this shambles of a rebellion. Our sweet brother, only trying to do the right thing, being pushed from one corner into another, taking on suffering that doesn't belong to him.

"I'm sorry," Farida musters faintly.

I extend a questioning hand. "That's it, then? That's the answer you have for us? Our brother sacrificed his happy, safe life for you, and the most you can do is shrug and say he is in prison and you don't know the state of him. I thought you were part of a rebellion."

Her gaze hardens. "I am."

Molten wrath spews up from my depths, shooting out into my fissures, finding my heart and blackening it to ash. "Oh? Where? Is this it, a leaky tub and some drunken sailors? Why didn't you rally to save our brother, Farida? You have enough experience in battle to have done *something* at least. Why did you abandon him in his time of need when you *know* he wouldn't do that to you?"

"It's not that simple—"

"Isn't it?" I guide Amira to a chair in the corner. "You eagerly accepted his magic. I've no doubt you knew the consequences that would have for him, the whole nation he was putting at risk, the laws he was violating. But you encouraged him to steal it and leave his family and people behind. You convinced him to betray us for you—"

"That is *not* what happened—"

"And now it's too difficult to save him?" I yell over her, my voice humming in the wooden walls. "After everything he endured for you?"

Crimson circles splotch her cheeks. "You don't know what you're talking about. I know you're hurting—"

"You don't know *anything*!"

She purses her lips, then sighs a moment later. "Please. I know you are hurting, and I do not blame you one grain of sand. But you must understand, your brother's arrest was one of many. Without him, something happened to us. Our operations . . . I don't know, we made mistakes, *I* made mistakes. . . . We suffered several raids; we ran out of misra because we didn't know how to use it properly; many of us were killed. Our numbers were whittled down, and the ones who survived, well." She thrusts a shaking hand at the door. "Have a look out there for the miserable proof you seek. They drink themselves blind and gamble with coin they don't have. I have to fight to get them to do any bloody work to keep us afloat. They've lost all faith in me, and I don't know if I should condemn them or join them."

"I didn't trek this far to hear tales of your woes," I mutter.

She swills from a brown bottle on the desk. It's wine; I smell the acrimony from here. "Then why did you?"

"To bring Atheer back."

"Back?" She considers me coldly over her shoulder. "You mean home to Qalia?" It's her turn to laugh. "You really don't know what you're talking about, then."

"Tell us about the prison," Taha interjects.

I forgot he was in the room with us, listening to my tirade. I feel exposed suddenly, a fresh wound open to the cold wind. He comes over to the desk as Farida slumps into the chair behind it.

"Must we do this—"

"Why didn't you get Atheer out?" he demands. I feel a small swell of relief that he hasn't left me alone to press the matter.

Farida manually lifts her right leg and props her scuffed boots on the desk. "I cannot walk for long before I am in pain. The others out there fare no better. What did you expect me to do? Order them into battle with the dozens of soldiers stationed up at the prison? With what weapons? Our dull scimitars and fishing daggers against their bows and longswords?"

"Battle is not necessary," he says. "One of you could have disguised yourself as a prison guard and snuck inside."

She claps a hand to her cheek. "Oh, of course, why didn't *I* think of that?" She gulps wine and winces. "There isn't a single soldier there who isn't Harrowlander. You may be fair, but among those asses, you'd still stand out like a horse."

"There must be other workers, then," I say, taking up his clever train of thought. "Alqibahi people who service the prison's lower functions, cooking, cleaning—"

"What does it matter?"

I slam my fist onto the desk. "It *matters*. Great Spirit damn you to Alard, it matters! Answer our questions; it is the least you can do after you got my brother into this mess."

"You really think you're going to break him out," she says, shaking her head.

I cannot believe *this* is the woman Atheer fell in love with. "With your help, it is possible," I say through clenched teeth.

"It's *not*. Why won't you listen to me?" She pushes her feet off the desk and sits up. "It is the prisoners themselves who do the menial tasks. The Harrowlanders do everything else. They drive the prisoner and supply wagons, their swordsmen guard the gates, their archers patrol the walls. Forgive me, Imani, *truly,* but this breakout is impossible. I have thought of everything you are right now. I have followed every avenue; I have pursued every silver palmfish down every worthless burrow and still come up wanting. There is no way into that prison."

"Except as a prisoner," Qayn appends from the back of the cabin.

We crane our necks to look at him. He wears a wide, charming smile, his arms held out like a circus performer expecting applause. He sighs, letting them float down by his sides.

"Come now, don't tell me *none* of you thought of that. It's so *easy,* though I suppose the cunning *is* in the simplicity—"

"Who is this again?" Farida asks me.

Taha and I speak simultaneously.

"A friend—"

"A djinni whose time is nearly up."

Farida soundlessly mouths the word *djinni* while gawking at Qayn. Meanwhile, Amira has wiped the tears from her cheeks and hastened over to me.

"It could work, couldn't it?"

"No." Farida presses the wine bottle to her sweaty forehead.

"You're welcome to get yourselves imprisoned there, but you won't escape, certainly not with Atheer in tow. The only prisoners who get out of that place are the dead ones."

"I should think so, if the Harrowlanders are to live up to their reputation. But with magic?" Qayn's smirk stretches. "We have in our midst some of the best and brightest sorcerers Qalia has to offer."

Taha half shrugs, looking at me. "It could work. My falcon can see into areas we can't; he can do what we can't—"

"You're a skin-changer like Atheer?" Farida interrupts.

Taha doesn't hide his distaste, either to being likened to Atheer or to having to discuss our magic with an outsider. Both, probably, and given my own feelings toward Farida, I don't blame him.

"No, I am a beastseer. They're completely different classes of affinity. I share minds with falcons. I don't change into one."

"Impressive. My affinity is for water. Unsurprising, given—" She gestures at the ship.

Taha ignores her and looks to his cousin, but Reza is addressing Farida. "People captured in Bashtal . . . is there any chance they could end up at this labor prison too?"

My eyes widen. *Of course.* Fey. Taha's jaw flares, but thankfully he doesn't object. We shouldn't pass up an opportunity to save Atheer and Fey at the same time.

"Yes, suitable prisoners are brought in from other cities," Farida answers. "Why?"

"Curiosity." He nods to Taha with more energy in his recently dull eyes. "I could make an escape tunnel for us."

"There's no way I could smuggle my blade in," I think aloud.

"Is it possible to ferry anything into the prison using a falcon?" I ask Farida.

The captain cuts the air with her hands. "Impossible. The archers recognize their few messenger falcons. Any others are shot out of the sky to prevent people from smuggling items in."

"Damn it," I whisper, clenching my fist.

"It won't matter," Taha says. "Reza's and my affinities are invisible. We won't need anything else."

"Easy for you to say," I mutter. He won't be helpless without magic, relying on others he doesn't trust for safety.

"Pity," Qayn says into my ear. "If only you knew someone who could teach you how to use your magic in new, inventive ways."

Our eyes meet. I give a minute shake of my head and mouth, *Not now,* but his tempting offer has already burrowed deep into my mind.

"We still need to get *in*to the prison," Taha says, pacing the cabin. "Is being arrested the only way?"

"It's risky," Farida says, resting against the desk. "Some people are beaten during arrest, at times ruthlessly. If that happens, it'll be impossible to know whether you'll be judged fit for labor or execution."

Reza curses and turns away from us, undoubtedly thinking of Fey's horrible fate. I wish to comfort him, but I am certain he would rebuke the gesture.

"There's no guarantee of how long it will take to process us into the prison either," I say, turning my attention to Taha.

He runs his thumb along his lower lip. "The magic. We need

to get in and out the same day we drink the tea. If it runs out before we get out, we'll be stuck in prison."

We fall silent; in the gap, the sea laps the ship, gulls squawk; out on deck, the sailors jeer and heckle each other. I snap my fingers.

"There might be another way. We *pose* as prisoners."

"Ambush a prisoner wagon," Taha says, his eyes lighting up.

Farida nods slowly. "It's possible. One of my sailors knows their routes to the prison."

I pace faster as the flicker of hope in my chest becomes a fire. "If we can stop one of those wagons without alerting the soldiers on board or anyone else, we can swap places with the prisoners inside and be on our way."

"That's a lot of *if*s," Amira says between biting her nails.

"And we can do it," Taha says gruffly.

I gaze at him, realizing that I have finally learned something substantial about who Taha is—the maxim he lives by: find a way or make one. I've never really had to do that in my life, have I? There was always a way for me, paved, well-lit, secure. My becoming a Shield and being initiated into the Order of Sorcerers was assumed, like he implied when we were hunting in the Sahir. My parents were pleased and proud of me, as was the rest of our clan, but never was anyone surprised. They didn't throw a huge party for me that involved the neighborhood, the way Taha's family did, because it wasn't unexpected for us. And perhaps that is what separates Taha and me. Adversity has carved away the parts that would make him waver and left only hard determination.

"We'll need a good distraction to keep the soldiers off the perch while we make the swap," he is saying.

Qayn tucks a wavy lock behind his ear, smirking. "You're in luck there, boy. I am exceptional at being the center of attention."

"Savor it while you can," Taha replies, much to Farida's confusion.

"What about finding Atheer?" Amira asks.

Farida pulls her gaze from Taha. "Your guess is as good as mine. You'll have to find him once you're inside. Perhaps ask the other prisoners."

I stifle a curse. Atheer is always the one factor in the equation that cannot be determined with any certainty. He is the elusive oasis on the horizon, the reprieve just out of reach. I try to not let the thought drag me down. He is alive, and we have more than enough to work with here to get him out; we have the beginnings of a strong plan.

Farida looks across us wistfully. "You are really doing this. You're going to save Atheer."

"Or die trying," I say. "It's settled. We need details of the prisoner wagon's routes."

Farida starts for the door. "Speak with Muhab out there. You can't miss him; he's the mean, bearded bastard with the wooden leg. And you're welcome to stay aboard in the crew quarters." Farida gives a grimacing smile. "They're not much and they stink gods-awful, but they're free and among friends."

I can't help but glance at Taha as I leave the cabin, curious to see if he is looking at me. He is; of course he is. *Friends.* If only Farida knew the bitter truth.

28

A FEW DAYS LATER, I ROUSE FROM A NIGHTMARE about the burning garden with an idea.

We have spent the past week sneaking into the city with Muhab to watch the prisoner wagons. Taha has been using his falcon to monitor them from angles we can't, and we've learned the route the wagons use, and the times they arrive. What we haven't deciphered is a way to conceal our swap with the prisoners inside the wagon—but I might have a solution.

I swing my legs out and hop down to the cool, creaky wood. It is before dawn, and stone-blue light is filtering through the port window across Reza, Amira, and the sailors, fast asleep. Taha's bunk is empty, but I expected as much. Since we left Qalia, he has risen earlier than everyone else to train. I pull on my boots, thinking of my initial response to his habit. I was convinced he only did it to prove how supremely dedicated he is to his duties, but he never once mentioned it to me. I only discovered it when I woke early once and secretly observed him doing push-ups in a clearing near camp. Then it made sense why, on the day we sparred, I'd found his bedroll empty. Bayek probably instilled the routine in him from a young age, and now I am convinced Taha would rise early to train even if he were the last person alive and there was no one left to impress.

I get dressed, pad up the narrow stairwell, and emerge on deck. Before me is a picture of peace. Apart from the dozing sailor in the crow's nest, the deck is empty, the door to Farida's cabin closed. Out on the Bay's flat waters, the warships bob quietly; even the gulls hover in silence. I turn slowly, yawning and rubbing my eyes, searching for Taha. I notice him, but not where I expected: he is walking along the pier *away* from the ship.

A dozen theories spring to mind. He is going to buy breakfast with coin Farida lent him, or he needs to conduct another investigation for the prison breakout. The answer will be innocuous, but something about the way Taha is behaving has me scurrying across the ramp to the dock. And although he admonished me for spying once already, I don't announce my presence. I sneak behind him, carefully maintaining a buffer of distance between us. Occasionally, when he seems about to glance over his shoulder, I even duck behind a wall or a parked carriage and wait him out.

I stalk him away from the pier, and soon the same city war scars that Amira pointed out on the way to Zak's boat shed make an appearance. My suspicions are confirmed when the black obelisks of the Field of Memories sprout into view. Taha passes the front of Zak's home, enters the Field, and takes position behind an obelisk—then he settles to watch the line of terraces.

I creep into a nearby shadowed alcove. Taha intersperses his observation of Zak's home with glances at the sky, seeming to measure the time that is passing.

"What are you doing?" I murmur.

The front door to Zak's terrace swings open. I shrink against the wall as Zak emerges, a cloth bag hanging from his shoulder. The gruff, uneasy man appraises the street, likely looking for soldiers, then shuts the door behind him and hurries away in the direction of the bazaar. Taha watches him go without a hint of surprise at this development. A moment later, he rises to his feet and follows.

I wait for them to disappear from view before I skulk out of the alcove and, with my hood pulled low, shadow the pair. Around us, the day proclaims itself in pale pink sheets that cloak the fractured walls. From the intensifying sound of merchants echoing down to me, I know that we are headed for the bazaar. Within minutes, an archway appears with a sign reading AL-BAZAAR AL-KABIR, and I am enveloped between early shoppers.

"Pardon me," I say softly, pushing past child beggars clutching my cloak. I keep my eyes on Taha's back; several meters ahead of him, Zak walks, oblivious to the menace hunting him. And that is what's happening here—Taha is *hunting* this man. But for what purpose?

We enter the produce quarter. People are already thronging the area, come to buy warm khobz, freshly caught fish, and the ripest fruits and vegetables. Taha is closing the gap with Zak, and we are coming upon a choke point where the bazaar narrows to a tight corridor and people are crammed shoulder to shoulder. I pick up the pace, dodging hagglers at a dates-and-nuts store, a man pushing a baklawa cart, a pair of Harrowlander soldiers on muscular horses. I strain to keep my head above the chaos, but I am reduced to mere glimpses of Taha, and I have lost Zak entirely.

I sidestep a toy seller surrounded by a gaggle of gawking children, only to brush into a Harrowlander woman wearing a feathered wide-brim hat.

"Mind yourself, girl," she says through a petulant, red-painted scowl. It is a phrase Taha taught me that the colonizers are fond of using. Not "pardon *me*," but "mind *yourself*."

"Please, forgive me," I reply in clunky Harrowtongue, bowing, though it vexes me to do so. But a soldier is watching me from his posting at a nearby spice shop, and I don't have time to be questioned.

My apology appeases the woman enough and I am allowed to hurry on. I push my way through the crowd, uttering yet more apologies in Alqibahi and Harrowtongue, and finally catch sight of Taha pulling his hood over his head. I cut into a small pocket between two men, right behind Taha as we reach the choke point. My stomach shrivels when I realize Zak is part of the row directly in front—and a slender dagger is sliding from Taha's sleeve into his hand.

I shove aside the young woman walking next to Taha and step into the space, grabbing his elbow. "Whatever it is you think you are doing, I caution you to reconsider."

He doesn't react how I imagined he would—he doesn't react at all—and that chills me to the bone. *He is a river, remember?* Even if a mountain rose before him, he would be confident that his current would destroy it eventually. He will find a way, or he will forge his own.

We exit the choke point. Zak continues along, but I direct Taha to the left. I don't surrender my hold of him until we have left the stir of the arterial lanes and I can speak without being overheard. I pull him into an empty alley and corner him against the wall.

"What are you *doing*?"

The green of his eyes is dull this morning; less savanna and more moss budding in a shadowed grove, some lonely place no one ever visits.

"You shouldn't be following me," he says.

"You were following Zak and pulling a dagger. Why?"

He stares at me, lips pressed together. I thrust my forearm across his chest, forcing him against the clammy stone. "You are one unanswered question away from having my dagger pulled on *you*."

He exhales through his nose. "I have orders to deal with any outsider who knows of the misra."

"Orders to *assassinate* them?" When he nods, I release him and stand back. "Spirits have mercy, you cannot be speaking the truth."

"I am." He straightens the creases I've left in his white tunic. "And owing to you, I missed my only opportunity today."

"Your opportunity to *murder*." I pace a short, frantic line in front of him. "Zak isn't the only one who knows of the misra. Farida does, Makeen too, Muhab, all the sailors on that ship." I freeze, staring at him. "You intend to eliminate them. *Why*, Taha? These orders weren't in our mission brief."

"They were in my mission brief."

The letter to Bayek, the mysterious words inked in Taha's unsure hand: *Her presence will neither distract nor hinder me from fulfilling your will. I remain focused and dedicated to our cause.*

"The mission brief from your father," I realize aloud.

He visibly bristles at that, like he's trodden on a bed of quills. "Your orders are to guide us to Atheer. I will deal with the rest."

"No!" I exclaim. "You are a Scout, not an assassin. Killing others is not what we do; it's not what *any* of us in the Sahir do. It's wrong!"

He begins walking to the alley's end. I jog after him and seize his arm. "Taha, listen to me. You cannot do this, not tomorrow or ever, no matter what your father says."

His temple pulses. "Eliminating any trace of the magic here is the only way to protect our people, like the Great Spirit wanted."

"It isn't." I drag him to a stop. "Please, I am asking not only for Zak's sake or Farida's but *yours* too."

He slows then and studies me. I seize my opportunity. "Killing another person is not something you can easily return from. It will cost you terribly, Taha—it will damage your *soul.*"

He exhales a shaky breath, forlornly looking about the alley as if this place is a prison he is trapped in. "How have you still not understood this? I don't have the luxury of doing whatever I want, like you do. If I am given an order, I must obey it. I have no choice."

"We always have a choice, as difficult as it may be." I hold his hand, noticing his blush deepen. Longing shades his gaze too, like on the afternoon he kissed me. The kiss he said was a mistake, the one I wished wasn't. Perhaps I was wrong and he only said that to avoid being embarrassed by his true feelings and true self. Perhaps he really did mean it.

I tighten my grip. "Don't do this. We can swear Farida and the others to secrecy. There are other ways to protect our nation besides killing them."

"The world you live in is not the same as mine," he says quietly, hopelessly.

I am struck by a potent desire to pull him against me and comfort him. "Please," I whisper, stepping closer.

He shuts his eyes, seeming to try to compose himself; then he utters a soft, irate growl and pulls his hand away. "I will not repeat myself, Imani. Do *not* interrupt or distract me from my orders ever again. I do not care how strongly opposed to them you are. I am acting according to the Council's will."

"The Council would never—"

"I don't care!" he hollers, the tendons of his neck straining. "Get in my way one more time, and you will regret it."

"I thought we had something, Taha," I blurt out angrily, my heart thundering against my ribs.

"Like what?" he mutters without looking at me, his blush intensifying to a bright red.

"You're the one who acts like a completely different person when it's only us two. You tell me."

He hesitates, and I sense a fierce battle raging in his depths. A battle he has lost.

"We have nothing," he says finally, his words palpably laced with despair.

He marches down the alley, clenching and unclenching his fists, his cloak fluttering in the wind. Against the morning's new light, his retreating silhouette is unyielding black. My skin crawls with shadows and goose bumps; my heart aches. I revealed my weakness for him yet again in some naïve hope that my feelings would be reciprocated, but all he gave in return was that impenetrable defensive wall. I am wrong about Taha; I have been from the first moment I thought he was showing kindness during our language lessons. It wasn't kindness or a budding mutual attraction—it was deception so he could get to my brother and the rebels, all to fulfil his father's wishes. Before he killed Badr, I asked Taha what he was doing and he said, "What must be done." Perhaps he killed my filly not out of an eagerness to spare me the pain but because he is accustomed to the act. He can murder if he must, beast and man both. Bayek has made sure of that. I have hardened my heart to steel, but Taha? He has discarded his heart altogether, and I don't know whether to pity him for having been raised by a man like Bayek or hate him for passively accepting this fate. But if he can tolerate being callous to me and his own cousin, if he has orders to deal death to the outsiders who know of the misra, how will he treat my brother, a person he openly despises and is ideologically opposed to? Will he let Atheer accompany us home peacefully, or will he insist on dragging Atheer home in chains, mistreating him every step of the way?

Or worse, whispers a voice from the murky depths. *Or worse.*

29

THE NEXT FEW DAYS GO BY QUICKLY, ONCE I COM-
mit to focusing on nothing but bringing my brother home.
When we are assured of a plan to hijack a prisoner
wagon, we study the prison itself. Taha can't bring Sinan too
close before an archer takes aim, but he is able to sketch us a
rough layout of the prison, and it is a surprising one. I imagined
a single, impenetrable fortress, but the prison is a collection of
buildings encircled by two concentric defensive walls and situated
on a mound overlooking the sea. Prisoners roam freely inside the
compound during the very early mornings and evenings, though
they are constantly observed by archers on the ramparts. During
the day, they are ushered into the various buildings, presumably
to work; meals are taken in a separate building at dawn and dusk;
at night, the prisoners are shepherded inside long, squat dormitories, and soldiers patrol the grounds to ensure nobody is out past
curfew. I assume that if anyone is caught, they are flogged on the
platform in the center of the prison yard.

After much debate, our plan for getting around and out
of the prison is settled. On the day before the breakout, I sit

at a creaky table belowdecks and study the layout of the prison by bobbing lantern light. At first, Amira joins me to help—without looking at the map, I describe a certain aspect of it, and she tells me if I'm right or wrong—but eventually I study the sketch in silence, and she curls up on the opposite bench to nap.

"You've been looking at that thing for hours," says Farida, leaning against the doorway.

"And I will look for hours more until I have committed every area and building to memory." I wait for the captain to leave so I can concentrate, but she lingers, watching me. Sighing, I sit back in my chair. "Did you want something?"

"Yes, to speak with you." She enters the room and closes the door behind her. "About Atheer."

Now she has my full attention. "What do you mean?"

"Why you're here," she says, limping to the bench where Amira is now sitting up. "What you think you're going to do if you break him out of prison tomorrow."

"I already told you, we are taking him home to Qalia," I say.

She sits beside Amira. "That's just it, Imani. Your brother is not going back with you."

"Enough," I mutter at the table. I cannot look at the person who brazenly stole Atheer from me once and is trying to do it again. My eyes land on the map, sketched in Taha's hand. The same hand that cradled my cheek one day and readied to kill Zak on another. Curse my fortune that has put me in the company of people who only want the things I don't.

"I understand that Atheer is your brother, and you know him better than most—" Farida starts.

"Everyone." I crush the edge of the map. "Better than everyone, including you."

"No, Imani. I knew the man he was *here*." She looks between me and Amira. "I know you don't like me, but you both must understand: the things Atheer saw and participated in, the war . . ."

Amira rubs her puffy eyes. "He fought in it?"

"Yes. He was involved in several skirmishes during the war for Taeel-Sa. He fought beside us with sword and bow and magic, which he later shared with us, on the condition that we would use it cautiously."

I roll my eyes. "Oh, you really didn't go about using it as you pleased?"

"No. I tried to explain to you, none of this is what you think. Atheer warned us about using the magic and the consequences that could have for us and your people. He taught us to use it discreetly, and we did. He was a good leader." Her voice wavers. "He was even there when my father was killed by a Harrowlander's arrow. He promised Baba he would save us, and Baba believed him. But Atheer had to return to Qalia. Taeel-Sa fell, the king was executed, the casualties were significant . . ."

I keep my gaze down, not wanting to reveal my tears in front of Farida. Brave Atheer, he wasn't making bad choices due to an unsound mind or being manipulated. Yes, he revealed our magic, but not out of malice or ill will. He was acting out of generosity and care, to a fault perhaps. He has always been possessed of a lion's loyalty to his pride, but I realize now that Atheer's pride is everyone, not only our family, or the people in Qalia, or the people in Alqibah, or Farida. All of us. He didn't distinguish between "us" and the "outsiders."

"I've no doubt those experiences changed him," Farida goes on. "He will not come back to Qalia with you, and if he does, it will not be permanent. Before he was arrested, he told me he had been working on a plan to save Alqibah. He didn't explain what it was, but I know he intends to finish it. He can do anything he sets his mind to—"

"And he is stubborn." Amira flashes a lopsided smile. "It's a Beya clan thing."

Farida returns the smile and reaches across the table for my hand. I refuse to give it to her.

"I only wanted to warn you ahead of time, Imani," she says. "I don't know about you, but Taha and Reza seem intent on bringing Atheer home as soon as possible. There isn't any chance it'll be by force, will it?"

"No," I lie. What else can I say? If I tell her the truth that Atheer is returning to the Sahir whether he likes it or not, she may thwart the prison breakout. But what about Taha? What will he say when he realizes Atheer is returning with us, but only temporarily? When he figures out Atheer is dedicated to this cause, against the will of the Council—against Bayek's own cause? It won't be good, and I don't know if I have what it takes to stop Taha, when and if the time comes. I must take control of this situation now, before it spirals away from me any further.

"In any case," I say, folding my arms, "my brother will listen to me. I will convince him to come home."

Farida pushes up to standing. "I thought you might say that. Come with me, both of you. I have something I want you to see."

She disappears through the door. Amira and I exchange a quizzical glance and hurry after her onto the deck. Taha is at the other end, sparring with Reza, though his cold eyes track me as we take the ramp down to the pier.

"Where are we going?" I ask Farida.

She draws her scarf over her forehead. "You'll see."

IN LONG, STIFF STRIDES, Farida leads us from the wharves to a busy square. I cannot fathom what she intends when we arrive at a grand, circular amphitheater with an arcaded exterior. She pays the few silver coins for our entrance, and we join a mass of patrons walking through a dim tunnel that reeks of body odor and metal. We hustle after her up a dank stairwell and emerge in blinding sunlight, being shoved and pushed by a crowd of foreigners and Taeel-Sanis. She pulls us to an empty spot against the wall. We are standing on one of the amphitheater's tiered terraces, overlooking an empty grit oval. A Harrowlander passes in front of us; I sense he is calling for bets, given the coin and slips of paper being exchanged.

"Why have you brought us to watch athletics?" I ask.

Farida wordlessly slings the tail of her scarf over the lower half of her face. Someone bellows an announcement in Harrowtongue, and the crowd roars as a tall, young, white man strides across the oval. Wearing chain mail and gripping a saber, he is a barrel of a man with legs as thick as tree trunks—he almost makes Taha look delicate.

"What are the rules of this game?" I ask nervously.

A reedy Taeel-Sani boy, no older than seventeen, tentatively shuffles across the oval from the other side. He is armored and geared too, but nothing of his looks as expensive or durable as the other's.

"Farida, what are the—"

"The winner is the one who survives," she says.

A chill vaults up my spine. I gaze around at the sea of excited foreign and local faces. "These are the Valor Grounds," I realize, thinking of the carriage from days ago. "The Death Pits."

A horn trumpets and the audience begins baying. Farida nods at the oval.

"Most of the time, the gladiators are Alqibahi, but foreigners are increasingly participating. They are always better geared and trained; they always win. Behind the transactions are the people who sponsor the gladiators, and many Harrowlanders are making the Death Pits their business. They seek out people from across Alqibah, luring them off streets, from schools, bazaars, farms, orphanages. Many don't care if their gladiators win or lose; they are paid a flat fee for every person they supply for the show. Merchants, lords, even officials are bringing their own gladiators, trained by the best, protected by the best armor and armed with the best weapons. But don't be fooled. Their gladiators are often people from poor families who see very little of the profits. Every other contender, when they are despairing enough, enters with nothing and is given the most basic equipment to fight in. The disparity is considered part of the show's fun."

"Fun," Amira echoes hollowly.

The gladiators begin to circle each other. The boy's eyes are so wide and unblinking, it is as if someone has stitched them open. He is terrified—and I am shaking.

"The surviving gladiator's sponsor is paid, as are the gamblers who bet on the victor," Farida explains, "but there are other winning conditions for the gamblers: correctly guessing, for example, how long it takes the loser to die, in what manner, if they have their limbs by the end. Many gladiators volunteer hoping to escape destitution, but it is here, where they hoped for redemption, that they meet their end."

The foreigner lunges, swinging his saber. The boy leaps out of the way, but the very tip of the blade slices him on the shoulder. Blood sheets down, and the audience jeers.

Nausea crashes over me. "I don't want to see this," I say.

Farida grips my hand with surprising strength. "Your brother saw it."

The foreigner charges again; the boy stumbles in his attempt at escape. He falls to the grit and scrambles as the big man advances. He is bellowing laughter, the foreigner, spinning his saber so fast that it is scarcely a snatch of steel. The boy manages to get back up and swing. His opponent dodges, flicking his blade across the boy's thigh. This wound is far worse than the first. The gash is deep, the flesh lips parting in a ghoulish grin spewing blood. My stomach heaves. I battle Farida's hand, but she has me locked in place.

"The Harrowlanders pride themselves on their dignified

civility, yet they encourage violence against us under the guise of entertainment."

The boy staggers back, panting as blood rolls freely down his leg. Instead of attacking, the foreigner faces the deafening crowd, waving his hand and inciting their fervor. He is *toying* with the boy, drawing out the butchery like a cat playing with a mouse. He won't kill the boy with a swift blow. He will undo him, bit by bit, inflicting enough pain and gore to satisfy the ghouls in the audience, but not enough to end the show too quickly.

"I can't watch." I drag my hand from Farida's and shove Amira to the stairs. We tear down them into the tunnel, leaping over puddles of spilled wine. The ceiling shakes with delighted screams. Sickness shoots up my chest as I finally recognize the metal scent in here. Blood.

I burst out of the amphitheater and drag Amira down a side alley with me. I collapse against the wall, gasping at the sky while she sobs into her hands. The vision of the boy is burned on my mind. I even imagine Taha down there, lured to a gruesome, pitiless death by Lord Osgar in his extravagant carriage.

"Imani."

I whirl around and shove Farida. "Why did you bring us here?" I double over, pressing the base of my palms to my forehead. "It's not fair. That boy was being slaughtered in front of hundreds of people, and *nobody* stopped it! They cheered it on!"

Farida steers us deeper into the alley. "Take what you witnessed, multiply it many times over, and you will have the war Atheer and I fought in."

I feel a pinch of guilt over how fiercely I have disliked the captain. Until now, I spared no thought to the terrible experiences

Farida endured, like witnessing the death of her father and being helpless to stop it. I paid no mind to how desperate for aid she would have been, nor the mettle it takes to foment a rebellion in a kingdom where a mere curse can see you hanged. To stand tall in the face of violence worse than that of the Death Pits would take the kind of courage I don't think I possess. I can't yet trust her, nor forgive her for dragging Atheer into such a mess, but I am beginning to feel a small respect for her—perhaps even seeing in her what Atheer did.

"Do you understand now?" she asks me. "Your brother will not turn his back on what is happening here, even if you try to force him; you know this truth in your soul. He is too good a person to ignore the suffering of others. And so are you."

I lower my hands. "What do you mean by that?"

"Save your brother and stay here with us. We need people if we are to take our land back, people like *you*."

I slump against the mossy wall, scoffing. "You mean sorcerers who can give you more misra."

"Skillful warriors who will fight injustice."

A flock of cooing pigeons startles into flight on a roof above us. "I'll think about it," I say weakly, watching them scatter into the glary sky.

Farida squeezes my shoulders, dragging my gaze back down. "Imani, this land is yours too. Qalia and the Sahir . . . they are part of Alqibah. We are not neighbors; we are *sisters*."

"And sisters fight for each other." Amira joins my side and says to me, "You fear our land will come under attack if we involve ourselves? It already is."

"I said I'll think about it," I repeat.

Amira looks crestfallen, as does Farida, but too much is changing too fast, and I feel out of control. It is one thing to fight Taha and Reza for my brother's freedom, another entirely for me to abandon my family and people to stay here with the rebellion, no matter if I agree with their cause.

"But," I say, looking between them, "I will break Atheer out of prison. Beyond that, his decisions are his own. I will respect whatever he chooses. It's the right thing to do."

Amira's eyes flood with relieved tears. "Thank you," she whispers, hugging me while Farida runs a hand along my arm.

"It will mean a lot to him," the captain says.

Amira nods at the head of the alleyway. "Come, let's go back. We can fit in a little more study before tomorrow."

I follow them back to the ship, happy enough with thoughts of what it will be like to finally reunite with Atheer. But then my mind turns to the relentless shadow that stalks my brother—Taha. He said if Atheer resists returning, he will put Atheer in chains. But Atheer isn't the sort of man one easily subdues. He can transform into a lion the size of a small carriage, and once he believes in something, he is dedicated to it. He will put up a fight tomorrow—one that could end dangerously for Taha. But Taha—no, *Bayek*—is nothing if not a dispassionate strategist. If either of them have already deduced the possible threat to Taha's life, Taha may not risk attempting to arrest Atheer at all—he may simply kill my brother the moment he lays eyes on him.

That's folly, I tell myself, yet nothing feels closer to the truth. I witnessed Taha readying to kill Zak; I read in his letter that he is dedicated to his father's cause. He is capable of it, and he has the right motivation—hatred of my clan. But I need him and Reza if I have any hope of getting in and out of the prison tomorrow. I am as trapped as Atheer right now.

Amira brushes my arm. "Are you okay? You don't look well."

"I—I'm fine," I stammer. I am anything but, for I have realized that it is not the Harrowlanders I must ultimately save my brother from tomorrow—it is one of ours.

Taha, the assassin.

30

WE RETURN TO THE SHIP A LITTLE BEFORE DUSK. Amira invites me to resume studying the map, but I decline the offer and gently send her away. I must prepare for tomorrow in a different way; thankfully, Farida has graciously offered me the captain's cabin for privacy.

As soon as Amira shuts the door to the cabin, I pull my dagger free. "Qayn, come out."

The djinni appears before me, one straight brow raised. "How may I help, Slayer?"

Despite my conviction, my tongue feels weighted with rocks. I pace the cabin to the grimy window and pause to gaze at the beleaguered city.

"I have decided to accept your offer of magical training." I reluctantly look over my shoulder at Qayn. "I fear what Taha might do tomorrow. I need to be ready, even if I am without my blade." I place it firmly on Farida's desk and stand back.

Qayn considers it, his lips curling at the corners. The smirk is quickly subdued. "As you wish, Slayer. I am pleased to offer my knowledge to ensure your brother's safety."

"Good." I nod brusquely, though my pulse has hiked in anticipation of what this lesson could involve. "I won't have my dagger tomorrow, but I was hoping there is a way I can still use my magic."

"There is." Qayn approaches the desk and, after a tentative glance my way, collects both the dagger and one of Farida's small knives lodged in the wood. He holds them up. "These weapons are fabricated from steel, itself created from iron."

"My affinity," I say, coming to perch on the edge of the desk.

"Yes. Thus, for your purposes, these weapons can be considered one and the same."

I frown. "But my affinity applies specifically to my blade."

"No. The *scope* of your affinity is narrowed to your blade, in the same way a beastseer such as Taha may only control one individual falcon, despite him possessing the magic to enter the mind of any falcon."

"Actually, Taha can control his falcon *and* songbirds, at the very least," I glumly correct.

"So the mediocre boy is less mediocre than I thought," Qayn concedes through a sharp sneer. "Regardless, this narrowing of an affinity is common in fledgling sorcerers who are still learning how to master one aspect of their magic. Most sorcerers never advance beyond this stage, even if they become very good within that narrowed scope. Water sorcerers who can summon a stream but not a storm, for example. There is, however, a fundamental difference between you and such sorcerers. You have the Beya clan ambition. Like your auntie, studying animancy and combining it with her sun affinity to create that vial."

"Thank you, I guess," I mumble, my cheeks heating up. "But what does that mean for me?"

Qayn sighs and places the weapons on the desk. "You are thinking too *narrowly* about your magic. Speaking of your auntie, didn't she teach you anything?"

"Tread lightly," I warn.

He ignores that and fixes his hands on my shoulders. "Heed this lesson, Slayer. It will take you further than anyone else. Misra is a *key*. That is all there is to it."

"A key," I echo, turning the new concept over in my mind.

"Yes. A key that unlocks access to the building blocks of the world. Misra allows you to see and manipulate the world as the Great Spirit does. It is not magic itself—it is the bridge to magic. And your affinity is for *iron*, not for your blade alone."

I study Qayn carefully. "I've never heard anyone speak about the misra in those terms. How could you know so much about a magic that isn't yours?"

He drops his arms, shrugging. "I have encountered enough of your people to have generated my own theories."

"Theories, hmm," I say, sniffing. "So you aren't sure of what you speak."

"Sure enough that I could have you wielding any blade as intuitively as your own," he retorts.

I collect Farida's knife and inspect it. "I don't see how. I don't feel any connection to this blade, despite it being made of the same material."

"Try," he says.

I shut my eyes and summon the magic that's been swimming

in my veins since this morning's tea ceremony. I direct it down to the hand holding the knife, but it seems to reach the tips of my fingers and stop, as if blocked by an invisible wall.

"I can't," I say, opening my eyes.

Qayn has been watching me. "Try again," he urges.

I glance at the window. The sun has all but set, casting long shadows through the cabin. It's getting late, and this exercise seems futile. I should be using the little time I have left to study the map of the prison, not taking phony lessons from a powerless djinni.

"Slayer," he says impatiently. "Try again."

I reluctantly draw a deep breath and, on the exhale, flood the magic to my hand. It tingles in my palm, up my fingers—and crashes to a stop.

"This is useless," I mutter, tossing the knife onto the desk.

"You're quitting?"

"I can't even *sense* the damned thing," I exclaim. "My dagger is an extension of myself. I feel it as readily as my own hands. But this—you'd think I wasn't even holding it. This whole thing has been a waste of time, yet another of your deceptions."

Qayn watches me pace for a moment; the shadows around him mature, crowding in to cloak him. "You're afraid," he says in that dark honeyed voice.

I scoff. "Afraid of what?"

"Stepping outside what you know. Trying new things. Discovering that the ideals you've always clung to might not be the whole of it."

I roll my eyes, but Qayn nods.

"You'll say you aren't. You'll tell yourself you are determined to be the best, the strongest, the brightest, the bravest. But the pitiable truth, Imani, is that you don't possess what it takes to go the distance. You are far too rigid for your own good."

"Oh, am I?" I halt my pacing. "I bound you to my dagger, didn't I? Rigid, my behind."

"The tiny steps of a timid babe," he taunts, sinking back into the shadows. Only his eyes stand out, despite them being darker than darkness itself. "I've a proposal for you—a way for you to really grasp this lesson and use it—but you will immediately reject it out of fear and an unreasonable concern for 'the rules.'"

I glare at him sideways. "Try me, devil."

He emerges from the pool of shadow as if rising from a black, depthless ocean. "Bind me to your soul. I will be able to communicate this lesson to you directly, and I guarantee, you will be able to wield another weapon as you do your own."

"B-bind you to my soul," I stammer, my insides pitching and rolling. Binding a monster to an object is perilous enough. Binding a djinni's soul to *your own* is fraught with unthinkable danger; it means Qayn could experience everything through me, every thought, every feeling, every action—and the same in reverse. It is not a partnership but a joining to become one.

"If only for a moment," he says softly, coming toward me. "A minute at most, and I agree to return to the dagger afterward."

He stops before me; we're too close, but I am petrified solid and can't step away. Qayn is a vortex, some kind of salt flat, and you need but set a single toe in his midst for him to pull you down and smother you.

"Give it a try," he says, brushing his fingers against mine. "I won't harm you, I promise."

"Your promises mean nothing," I rasp, moving my hand from his.

He sighs and steps away, releasing the tension that had been simmering between us. "I knew you would say no. Suppose you really are content to be helpless tomorrow. Taha will learn to summon an entire aviary while you stubbornly cling to that dagger."

I curse under my breath. "*Fine.* One minute, nothing more, for the sole purpose of communicating this lesson." I point a warning finger. "If you try *anything* else, I will release you from your binding and kill you before the enchantment of the Sands even has a chance to drag you back to the Wastes. Understood?"

He raises his hands in surrender, smiling. "Understood. Repeat these words after me."

I recite them back to him. "Qayn, to my soul I will bind you for one minute, after which you will return to your original binding in my dagger. Do you accept?"

"I accept," he says instantly.

He vanishes; the shadows in the cabin rise. I feel him entwine with my soul, like we are two threads twisting, spiraling, coiling, rapidly becoming impossible to disentangle. It is a sensation I have never experienced before and can't quite grasp. That of being alone and not—the lines that separate me and *not* me blurring like paint left to dribble and run in a sun shower. The intuitive understanding that something foreign flows alongside the blood in my veins.

And though I am as still as a statue in this empty captain's cabin, I am elsewhere too. I only have to shut my eyes to be transported there: a cold, never-ending corridor of closed doors. All of them belonging to Qayn. Parts of him, memories, thoughts, *secrets.* This is his palace, and I am standing in it, free to do as I wish.

I sense him going to my doors too; his hand snakes along the doorknob to one, the temptation to venture inside and discover what he wants about me rising to an unbearable crescendo. I tense, readying to unbind and kill him, but he releases the doorknob and leaves the corridor. He has kept his word not to pry—but he never made me promise the same.

I feel him elsewhere, whispering indistinct words in his mysterious language, words that will soon become a lesson I won't forget. I should patiently wait for him to finish, but the hourglass is almost empty. Soon I will lose my only opportunity to finally get the answers he refuses to give.

"The First City," I whisper, and my request wends, lonely, down the corridor. "Show me what happened there."

An invisible hand shunts me along and drops me before a towering wooden door. Many of the surrounding doors are coated in dust, but this one? Immaculate—it has seen regular visits. I twist the doorknob and shove into the memory. Elsewhere, I sense Qayn's alarm as he realizes what I am doing.

He is too late. I stand in an opulent granite-floored room. Silent, blue-shaded with dawn light that creeps through a window on my right; so too does a mild breeze, carrying birdsong and frankincense. It billows open the white linen curtains to reveal a lush, walled garden—the garden of my nightmares. No, not mine. *Qayn's.*

The rest of the place is familiar architecturally, from the patterned engravings in the walls to the glass roof enveloped in purple flowering vines. I am somewhere in the First City. To my left, a large bed is piled high with beaded silk cushions—and resting upon them, a young sleeping man, his burnished, chin-length black hair snugly adorned with an ethereal triple-jeweled crown that is woven in gold, silver, and light itself.

"It's you," I breathe.

His eyes flutter open. The Qayn I know possesses a dead gaze, but this one's eyes are fiercely, defiantly alive. Somehow he is even more beautiful than now, so unworldly, like a star. I shrink against a rug on the wall as he sits up, the mosaic-pattern blanket falling from his skinny bare chest. But Qayn doesn't see me. He looks at the empty bed beside him, crumpled from where someone was lying. He touches a loving hand to the wrinkles in the fabric, brows slowly knitting.

"Nahla," he murmurs. He pushes the blanket aside and pads around the bed. "Nahla," he calls, looking around the vast room. "Where are you?"

Something catches his eye. A door in the opposite wall leading to the garden. It's been left open, the sheer curtain rising and curling ominously. A dark look—a familiar one—crosses Qayn's face. He makes his way toward the door.

"Nahla," he says again, but harder now, his glowing crown bleeding a strong, angered light. "Are you out there?"

I stalk after him as he pushes the curtain aside and steps into the garden. He inhales sharply and utters the word *no* on a low breath. "No, *please,* no."

But before I can see the source of his shock, present Qayn frantically drags me back. I struggle against him, desperate to peer through the door into the garden and finally learn the truth of what turns Qayn's joy to bitter rage in every nightmare I have, but it is impossible to fight his steely strength. The vision ebbs like shisha smoke in a draft—the last thing I hear is past Qayn hoarsely shouting into the crisp morning air:

"NAHLA! How could you do this to me? *How could you?*"

I am ejected from the memory, or rather, Qayn is ejected from my soul. I snap my eyes open, breathing hard. He stands in front of me, his shoulders rising and falling rapidly. The sight of him, the captain's cabin, the salty, stuffy scent of the real world, it spins my brain in my skull. I collapse against the desk.

"Who is Nahla?" I pant, pressing a hand to my pounding head. "Is she the one who stole your magic? Is that what was happening?"

"You violated my privacy, Imani."

My heart skips. "What? I thought—"

"You thought it would be fine to deceive me when I avoided doing the same to you?" he demands. "You thought you were entitled to my past simply because I am in your company, or rather, I am at your mercy?"

My throat tightens; the walls seem to rush in. "No, but I didn't think it would bother you this much—"

"Why would it? It's only one of my most painful memories." Anguish twists his fine features; tears glisten in his eyes. "You didn't care if it would hurt me because you see me as little more than a means to an end. You are nothing like Atheer. He respected me; he treated me with *dignity*. But you only use others to get what you want, and you are outraged when they refuse. You're like the rest of your kind. *Selfish.*"

"Qayn." I gather his cold hands. "You're right, it was wrong of me to view your memory without your consent. My curiosity got the better of me. Your past is your own, and you only need to share it with me if you feel comfortable."

He drops his gaze as a single tear falls, as pure and precious as a crystal. I reel from it—I had thought Qayn would get angry at me before he ever got upset or hurt, and I was prepared to deal with it. But I didn't expect this; I didn't expect the pain I witnessed in that memory, nor how guilty I feel right now.

He removes his hands from mine. "I left the lesson somewhere you would find it," he says flatly. "Sleep on it. It will come to you when you need it. If there is nothing else . . ."

He returns to the dagger on the desk, leaving me truly alone in the murky dark. Shame twists my insides like a wet rag, wringing me of every defensive excuse I thought I had. All this time, I was operating under the belief that Qayn is malicious— yet he has done nothing but fulfil his end of our bargain. He has brought me this far, and on the eve of saving my brother, I took advantage of his help. Spirits forgive me, I feel like I've hurt a *friend*. Qayn is yet another person in my life I have thoughtlessly misjudged and upset.

I barely hear the knock on the door, and the creaking as it opens.

"Imani?" Amira shuffles in, peering about the darkened cabin. "I hope I'm not interrupting you. I wanted to wish you good fortunes tomorrow. Also, I put together some dinner below-decks."

My own tears fall. I go to my sweet sister and pull her into a hug. "I'm so sorry for the times I hurt you," I sob.

Frowning, she rubs my back. "Imani, you don't need to apologize. I know you've always meant well."

But that is the problem. It is not enough to mean well, not anymore—I must also *do* well. Otherwise, are Taha and I so different? Both of us alienate others in pursuit of our own ideals, meaning well along the way, only to find ourselves alone at the end. No family, no friends. Victors of a path littered with hurt people and apologies never uttered.

Amira pats my hand, startling me from my dark thoughts. "You are doing your best, do you hear? It is all anyone can ask of you. Come, let's eat. It'll make you feel better."

Still sobbing, I follow her out of the cabin, but I am not convinced I have found redemption just yet.

31

THE RHYTHMIC THUD OF HORSES' HOOVES SOUNDS long before the prisoner wagon comes around the bend. Right on schedule. If there is one thing I am learning, it is that the Harrowlanders are orderly; in all things, they seem to be on time, organized, and efficient, perhaps overly so. That works in our favor. From our tea ceremony this morning, we have roughly until sundown to get Atheer out. Any later than that, our magic will be exhausted—and the prison will become our home.

I push off the alley wall I've been leaning against for almost half an hour, immersed in my troubled thoughts. In the dirt by my slipper crawls a black scarab, the first reaches of morning sun shimmering on its curved back. Startled, it emits a high-pitched squeak and flails its rayed legs. I step over it and out into Taeel-Sa's fashion district, shadowed by Taha and Reza.

The choking, foul odor of rotting raw animal skins, pigeon droppings, salt, and limestone wafts over to me from the tannery up the road. My eyes water and I wrinkle my nose as I scan my surroundings. Brown imperial banners, staid despite their gold fringes, hang between the buildings, fluttering in the hot breeze. Under them, seamstresses, tailors, and shoemakers open their shops for the day. And though the people of Taeel-Sa still dress like their ancestors, the front windows of the shops are dominated by what I imagine are the silhouettes of King Glaedric's homeland: cinched waists and voluminous skirts for the women, tight trousers, doublets, and long tunics for the men. I wonder if the colonizers believe they can change the arid weather of Alqibah simply by dressing for it.

In an alleyway further up the road idles a wagon driven by Qayn. Our distraction, who barely spoke to me this morning. I lift my eyes to the stone façade of the shop opposite me, where one end of the banners is knotted to a metal hook in the wall. Perched on the flat roof between potted palms is Amira, with my dagger, and Farida, both their scarves pulled down over their foreheads. My sister smiles encouragingly, but Farida continues pensively gazing up the road at the prison. The monstrous fort hulks over the yellow city like a beast, sunlight fanning in blades around its ramparts and watchtowers. And somewhere inside its belly is Atheer.

I reach into the pocket of my sirwal for my lockpick, then I turn and squint down the road while running my fingers over the cool steel. Distantly I note the sweat forming on my forehead, the heavy thud of my heart, the magic jittering in my muscles. I have done harder things than this; I have fought a sand serpent as long as three carriages; I have faced a cemetery of ghouls; I have evaded Hubaal the Terrible. But that doesn't stop the nerves. This isn't like any of those missions. This is about my brother.

The wagon thunders around the corner, its two bay horses

cantering briskly. I begin a slow, casual amble along the sidewalk, Taha and Reza following. The wagon trundles alongside; in a heartbeat, everything changes. The horses squeal and pull to one side of the road; wheels creak, axles groan in protest, angry shouts erupt, and the few pedestrians on the street stop and stare at Qayn's wagon, now cut across the other's path. The two soldiers spit words at him that can only be curses, but he refuses to move. Instead he exclaims,

"Watch where you're going, you *donkeys*!"

The soldiers must know some Alqibahi. They disembark the wagon's perch and march over with their hands on their sword hilts, giving us a narrow window, and the only one we have.

We sidle alongside the wagon as Farida severs the rope suspending the banners over the street. The rope snaps; the banners fold in a flutter and blanket the wagon, cloaking us with it. That part was my idea. Ahead the soldiers curse again, and there is a small swell of cries from onlookers.

"Never mind the banners. You fools almost hit my wagon," says Qayn. He adds a few choice words in Harrowtongue that draw the soldiers' ire back to him.

Taha hops onto the wagon's back step and briefly peers at the prisoners through the small bronze window, then Reza lifts the wooden bar locking the door and opens it. Six manacled prisoners stare back at us, their grimy, worried faces slick with sweat.

"You three get your freedom," Taha whispers, pointing at two young men and a woman. "The rest of you, keep quiet and still. If any one of you even thinks of alerting the soldiers, you will die before the words are in your throat."

And now I know he means his threats. I sense that the other

prisoners want to ask us questions, perhaps plead with us to let them go too, but their fear of Taha cows them. I don't simply understand their silence in that respect; I am counting on it.

Outside, the soldiers are still arguing with Qayn, but their voices are climbing. Any moment now, they may tire of the quarrel and draw swords on him. We take our lockpicks and hurriedly free the three prisoners of their manacles.

"Now your clothes," I say, setting the manacles on the bench.

"Why are you doing this?" asks one as she pulls her tunic over her head. "No one wants to go to prison."

"Some do. Here, put these on."

We swap clothes, and I don the bristly, beige prison-issue tunic and sirwal. New prisoners are searched on arrival, so Reza and Taha toss their lockpicks out the door before they sit on the opposite bench and close the manacles on their wrists. I finish pulling my slippers on but halt as banners rustle over the roof. The distraction is over. We have to move fast, before the carriage is exposed.

"Lock the door with the bar and walk away like you've broken no law," I tell the prisoners, flicking my lockpick out too.

The carriage shifts and rocks. The prisoners thank us, stealing one last, bewildered look before scurrying out and shutting the door. I press my ear to it, waiting for someone to notice the swap and warn the soldiers of their escaped commodity. The bar slides back into place, and the prisoners land in the grit. The banners lift off the carriage with a final pull, followed by a shout. I suck in a sharp breath.

"It's all right," Taha whispers. "He said they're ready to go."

The wagon dips as the soldiers climb back onto the perch.

The wheels squeak and we begin rolling up the road, past Qayn on his wagon now pulled to the side. He gives me a curt nod, but it is loaded with a warning. I think of what he offered me back in the First City—a chance to do away with Taha, once and for all. A chance I've lost.

I take the empty space on the bench, closing the manacles on my wrists and trying to ignore the sudden climb in my anxiety. The wagon gathers speed, and within moments, it is roaring up the long, winding road to the prison. We lurch and sway in the humid quiet, the horses galloping to make up for the lost time. Minutes crawl by in the sweltering heat, the manacles on my wrists growing heavier every second. The weight of Taha's furtive glances is heavier. I shut my eyes and tilt my head against the wall, breathing deeply. There is no turning back now. Whatever he may have planned for Atheer, it is in motion.

Shouts outside slow the wagon's approach. Wooden doors groan, heralding our entrance into the prison. The others shift in their spots, their manacles whispering sadly on their wrists. The wagon stops, the bar is lifted, and the doors swing open. Cool, salty sea air floods in, and we all take big gulps.

"Out," says a soldier, knocking his fist against the door.

I follow the others jumping down to the dirt. We are in a small yard enclosed by towering walls, their ramparts patrolled by archers, some of whom impassively gaze down at us. A waiting official greets one of the soldiers; they exchange words and what looks like a passenger manifest. The official inspects the paperwork as more soldiers approach. A stony-faced one removes my manacles. He says words I don't understand, but he mimics holding my arms out, so I do. He runs his freckled hands along them, patting the baggy parts of my sleeves, then down my torso, up and down my legs, even checking inside my shoes. Without warning, he prizes my mouth open and uses a finger to search under my tongue and the back of my teeth. I almost retch, but he seems not to care. Satisfied I am not attempting to smuggle anything inside the prison, he goes to help check the other prisoners.

Shivering, I stand to the side and watch Taha move up to the front of the line. The soldier barking at him is far more aggressive. Following the man's orders, Taha lifts his tunic on his scored chest and turns out his pockets. The soldier pats him down, even sliding a finger between the waistband of Taha's sirwal and his hips. He pulls the waistband back and casts a shameless, lingering look down. Taha endures the abuse with a clenched jaw. The soldier roughly checks his mouth before shoving him forward and moving on to the others.

At the end of the inspection, we are handed thin leather necklaces. Each has a square wooden pendant with a symbol—likely a number—etched into it. The official, flanked by soldiers, leads us through a covered passageway. To my surprise, the ginger-haired man speaks Alqibahi fluently.

"You are to wear your necklaces at all times to aid in identification. Anyone who loses or refuses to wear their necklace will be flogged. Men sleep in the red dormitory; women sleep in the blue dormitory. Your day begins before dawn; you will be fed in the dining hall and escorted to your tasks. The workday ends late afternoon, no earlier. This is followed by a meal and one hour in the yard for exercise. At the sound of the bell, you are to punctually return to your dormitories and remain there until the following morning. Anyone caught outside after the bell will be flogged without exception. Work hard and follow the rules; that is what is expected of you."

We pass through an iron gate onto a bleak dirt yard hedged by buildings. The official stops us outside a long one; shouts of soldiers emanate from within, together with the cries of what can only be prisoners.

"Men, you will work the treadmill."

A soldier opens the door. I am not at an angle where I can see inside, but the sour smell of sweat billows out, and I hear the pulsing, incessant grind of some kind of machine. The other prisoners shuffle inside; Taha casts a glance back at me, and I nod. We agreed earlier that if we were split up, we would meet again by the dead tree in the yard at break time.

The official continues on. "You will work in the oakum-picking room," he says to me.

We stop outside a building, and a soldier opens a door on a long room. It is lined with rows of benches; the people seated upon them have their heads bent as they unravel ropes. They are up to their ankles in loose rope fibers, and the length of the room reeks of tar. Soldiers watch over the work from the front, the back, and the sides. As I shuffle in and get closer, I see that many of the prisoners have bloody nails and bruised fingers from the rough, repetitive work. They chance fearful glances at the official; I scour the faces I can see, hoping beyond hope that one will belong to my brother or Fey. The official snaps his fingers at a girl about my age on the end of a nearby bench. She is alarmingly thin, richly brown-skinned with large amber eyes, though there is something lackluster in their glaze. She scurries over.

"Explain the task to this prisoner," says the official. "No time wasting."

She bows and nods at me. I follow her to the bench and sit down. The official watches for a moment, turns on his heel, and marches out; the soldiers shut the door again and trap us in the heat. And like that, the prisoners' heads bend and their work is resumed.

"What's your name?" whispers the girl in Alqibahi.

I flick my eyes at the soldier watching us from the front. "Imani. What about you?"

"I'm Safiya." She barely smiles before placing a mound of coiled ropes on the bench between us. "Oakum is a tarred fiber that the Harrowlanders use in their ships to seal planks and joints. It can be recycled from old ropes. Our job is to unravel the ropes down to their fibers, like this." She begins picking at the rope with deft fingers and untangling it. I try to follow along, mimicking her movements.

"It's hard," I say, wincing. "And it hurts my fingers."

"Yes, but it must be done. Each person must pick at least half a kilogram a day or face punishment."

"Flogging, you mean."

"Yes, or worse, but it's all right. You are shown lenience on your first day. And your fingers get used to it after a while."

I pray I will only ever have a first day in this Spirits-forsaken place. But what of everyone else trapped here? I have a plan to escape; they have nothing but this torment, day in and day out.

"What is the treadmill?" I ask, thinking of Taha and Reza.

Safiya glances at me. "Why? Have you been tasked to it?"

"No, my friends."

She frowns at the rope between her fingers. I keep working too; I don't want to give the soldiers any reason to come over here.

"It's a kind of wheel with paddles. The prisoners have to step on the paddles to turn the wheel and grind wheat under it. We call it the eternal staircase." She pulls a strand of fiber free and tosses it into the pile at her bony ankles. "I hope your friends are strong. The soldiers who oversee it keep whips at the ready."

I can imagine Taha enduring the torture in determined silence. In Bashtal, he said he'd "endured far worse beatings than that." I wonder at whose hands he meant. I wonder why I even care.

I lean over to Safiya. "Do you mind if I ask why you're in here?"

"Girl," a soldier at the front says loudly. I look up and find him staring at me. He places a finger over his lips. I hastily lower my gaze to my ropes.

"We're not allowed to talk," Safiya whispers.

Evidently. I work like that for some time, until the soldier shifts his attention off me. Then I surreptitiously glance at the faces around me. All kinds of people are imprisoned here, old and young, strong and some on the frailer side, as the work has clearly taken its toll. All Alqibahi, none Atheer.

Time meanders on; eventually I become convinced it has gotten lost somewhere along the way to day's end. The sun has risen higher in the sky, cultivating the heat inside the workroom to an unbearable intensity. Sweat sheets from me and sticks my tunic to my body. My mouth may as well be sealed by fibers too, how thick and dry it feels. I yearn for a splash of cold water, a mere breath of fresh air. The soldiers patrolling the workroom regularly duck out, presumably for a break, and always return refreshed. The prisoners are not allowed to even move. My fingers chafe and bleed, my back aches from sitting in this one position, and my backside is numb. I am desperate to ask Safiya about Atheer, but one of the soldiers has been watching me, likely to make sure I am settling in and following the rules. I keep my mouth shut and my fingers moving.

At midmorning, the woman in front of me collapses face-first into her pile of oakum. The girl beside her startles, but incredibly, doesn't stop working. I slide my eyes sideways at Safiya; she has her head down, fingers efficiently picking, even though I know she has seen the woman collapse too. But everyone is ignoring it.

I set aside my rope and slide forward on the bench. "Are you all right?" I whisper.

The woman doesn't respond; she is curled up in her bristly pile of unraveled fibers. A soldier at the front has noticed me, and his blond brows are lowering over his cold, gray eyes. I leave my bench and reach over the one in front of me.

"Imani," Safiya hisses. "Leave this alone."

I put my hand on the woman's shoulder and shake her. She still doesn't respond. Terrible intuition spikes in me. I press my fingers to her clammy neck.

"She has no pulse," I cry. "She needs help!"

A soldier arrives and shoves me off. I stumble, knocking my head on the bench behind me. Woozily I push myself onto it and hunch, rubbing the sore spot at the back of my head.

"Start working," Safiya urges.

I know she is trying to protect me, but I am irrationally

angered by the order. I take up the rope as more soldiers crowd the woman. One turns her over, revealing a pallid, slack face and lost gaze. He checks her pulse, says something clipped to the others. They leave and return with a cart. The woman is thrown into it and wheeled off. The soldier who shoved me gives me a threatening look before returning to his post at the front of the room.

"Where are they taking her?" I whisper.

Safiya speaks at her rope. "She's dead. They will take her into the small building at the end of the prison and dump her body down into the sea. It's the only way out of here."

Like Farida said. "The only prisoners who get out of that place are the dead ones."

"Great Spirit," I mutter. "What nightmare is this?"

Safiya doesn't answer.

32

AT MIDAFTERNOON WE ARE PERMITTED A SHORT break in the yard. We line up at a well and are given two mugs of water and a minute to relieve ourselves in the filthy washroom, though it is not a room with walls or doors, nor is it located inside. After the humiliating experience, I find Safiya dutifully waiting against the outer wall of the workroom.

"I'm sorry," she says when I join her. "This place is tough. The sooner you are used to the way things work, the better it will be for you."

I look across the yard at the building Taha and Reza went into. They haven't been allowed on break yet, but I believe it's so the soldiers are not overwhelmed by too many prisoners at once.

"Why?" I ask, scouring the faces of some walking past. "Will you be freed if you behave?"

"I hope so." She sidles closer. "Earlier you asked why I am here. I was caught stealing food from a soldiers' station about six months ago. I shouldn't have done it, but I was starving, and they keep so much of it. Before the Harrowlanders, my parents operated a caravan that traded goods all along the Spice Road, mostly spices in exchange for silks from the Jade Kingdom. The Harrowlanders raised the dues we owed to their king, and soon, more than half our income was going to the crown. It became so much, the caravan was no longer profitable. My family ran out of money."

"I'm sorry," I say, wishing I could do something more for her. "I don't understand why they would make it onerous to the extent where it drove your parents out of business."

"They don't want anyone profiting off the spice trade but them."

"Then why not ban everyone from trading it immediately?" I ask.

Her eyes are glassy, skinny arms crossing her stained tunic. "The slower they do it, the less likely people are to fight back. They tell us they are only here to run our cities and take taxes for the debt, and people accept it, thinking they will be safe. But then they expel us from our ancestral homes, they steal our businesses, they take control of our most lucrative trades, they dedicate our temples to their gods, they speak their tongue in the streets, and they have the nerve to tell us things are better and more peaceful this way. Before you know it, there will be nothing left for us."

The Sahir is left, glorious Qalia, untouched and unharmed. But instead of being happy about that, I am ashamed. I have been peering at the world through a cracked lens my entire life.

Our conversation is interrupted by a soldier wheeling a cart before us. A limp brown arm dangles over the side, its curled, bloody fingers encrusted with dirt.

"Another one," I say, watching the soldier trundle toward the squat building overlooking the sea. A lighthouse tower rises from it, swamped by frenzied seagulls.

"A couple go every day, but our numbers are always replenished."

We share a sad glance. The soldier stops at the gate, exchanging easy words with the two men standing guard. They check the body in the cart before allowing him through with his macabre delivery. He takes it inside the building and slams the door shut behind him.

"Why are you here?" Safiya asks.

"My brother, and a friend of mine," I say, still staring at the lighthouse. "They're both here."

"You were arrested on purpose to join them?"

"Something like that," I mutter. "Do you know anyone named Atheer or Feyrouz?"

"Sorry, no. I only know the girls I sleep beside in the dorm. But—"

She is cut off by a soldier ringing a bell, signaling the end of break. Our line starts moving to the workroom door.

"But what?" I press, shuffling along.

She shakes her head. "Not now."

I take my spot on the bench inside and start unraveling rope again, but I can't concentrate. Whatever answer Safiya has, I need it now. Regardless of what happens, we need to break out of the prison tonight, before our magic is exhausted and Reza can no longer forge us a tunnel to freedom. But I cannot leave this prison without Atheer. To think my long-lost brother is so close to me, somewhere in one of these buildings, and not only would I be forced to leave without him, but I would not even get to glimpse his wonderful face . . . it makes me want to scream.

I work hard, foolishly believing it will make time go faster, but the opposite happens. Time limps along, the brutal heat ridicules us, the pile of coarse fiber sprouts around my ankles, the skin around my nails bleeds. I work until I am sick with impatience and that scream has erected a ladder up my chest and is readying to climb out. I glance at the soldiers; the pair at the front are close together, talking.

"Safiya," I whisper. "I must know what you were going to say."

She frowns at a droplet of sweat splashing onto the rope between her fingers. "Not *now*."

"Please, it's really important. Just tell me—"

"Is there a problem here?"

A soldier is striding down the side of the room, one hand on the hilt of his longsword. Safiya's frown evaporates as the man steps between the benches and glares down at us.

"N-no, sir, no problem," she stammers in Harrowtongue. She holds up her rope. "Please."

He reluctantly leaves us. I wait for him to go back to his post at the front of the room. Instead he takes position against the nearby wall and watches us. Safiya brings her rope close to her face and bunches her shoulders, as if occupying less space may appease him. I try to focus on my rope too, but I can feel the soldier's shameless leer creeping over my skin. I glance over. He stares back at me while sliding his tongue over his lips. Furious magic suddenly sparks in my veins, and I am overwhelmed by a strong pull to the sword hanging from his belt. Startled, I drop my rope under the bench. He straightens off the wall. I crane over and hurriedly paw for it. When I sit back up, I find him towering over me.

I only understand the word *stop* before he has cuffed me across the face. My head jolts; my cheek smarts, red-hot; my fist opens and the rope falls again. Safiya flinches and stoops even lower over her rope. The attack only makes my affinity rage harder, Qayn's lesson finding me with crystal clarity. I turn my head front again, and without meaning to, I look at his sword. And like my own blade but fainter, the steel *calls* for me. My fingers tingle, my muscles tense; I plot the things I will do with that sword and how many I could kill before I am stopped.

The soldier thrusts the rope into my face. "Work."

I start picking again. Satisfied, he returns to the front, and my magic settles. Whatever that was, it has never happened to me before—but thanks to Qayn, I may not be as powerless in here as I first thought.

THE REMAINDER OF THE DAY is endured in tedious silence. I pick fibers until my eyes swim with the cursed things and my fingers are numb. At late afternoon, a bell tolls. We shuffle to the front with the oakum bundled in our arms. Each pile is weighed on scales and the amount written in a thick book. Thankfully, I have gathered enough not to warrant being singled out, and I can leave the workroom with Safiya. A few soldiers stand outside, shepherding us toward the dining hall. The winds have come in and cooled the prison down, but it is hardly a mercy. They've also wafted in a rotten, sour stench that adheres to the entire site like resin. I don't even want to imagine what it might be stemming from.

"I'm sorry," says Safiya. "That soldier needs no excuse to mistreat women."

"I'm the one who's sorry. I was behaving selfishly." I realized it about an hour after the soldier hit me. My outrage abated, the sharp sting in my jaw muted to a dull ache, and I remembered Qayn accusing me of using others for my own needs. I would be escaping tonight, but Safiya wouldn't. I was jeopardizing her safety in pursuit of my brother, and I think if Atheer found that out, he wouldn't want to be saved by me.

"Well, we're allowed to talk a little now, so I can give you your answer," she says.

I look up at her hopefully. She pulls me close, and we walk pressed together.

"There is a prisoner here named Zahir, a big, tall man with a burn on his neck. He has been here longer than anyone else, and even the soldiers have taken a liking to him for how tough he is and how hard he works. I've heard he knows everyone who comes into the prison. He should know the people you're looking for."

I marvel at her. "I would hug you, but I don't want to land either of us in trouble."

She actually laughs at that, but the cheery sound contrasts so severely with the prison that I am upset hearing it.

We shuffle into the fusty dining hall. It is a long, dour room lined with tables, watched over by soldiers stationed in the corners and at the doors on either end. Behind the table on the right wall are more prisoners waiting to serve us food. We collect our trays and join the long line. I continue to inspect the faces of all the people I can, but I don't see Atheer or Fey. I watch for them amidst the prisoners still streaming in from the doors and notice a young, sweaty man with bright, pistachio-green eyes. *Taha.* He looks exhausted, but at least he is in one piece. Reza tails him to the end of the line.

"Those are my friends," I tell Safiya. "Let's try to sit on the same table and you can tell them about Zahir."

She considers them curiously. "I don't understand. . . . They're *also* here for your brother and friend?"

"Yes," I blurt out before I can think of what that implies. It is too late to correct myself now that I've reached the food table. The prisoner behind it scoops chunky brown slop onto my tray, a few small oval vegetables, rough bread, an apple, and a mug of water. I step out of line, casting a glance over my shoulder. Taha notices me, and his expression opens. Is that relief? Even if it was, it's gone and he is as stoic as ever. We exchange nods, and I take a seat at an empty table.

Safiya joins me a moment later. "Imani, what do you mean you're 'here' for Atheer and Feyrouz?"

I pensively push my spoon around in the brown slop, catching a hint of beef. I could get Safiya out of here; I could take her with us when we escape. I am tempted to tell her the truth, but instinct cautions against it. Though she detests the Harrowlanders, she is still trying to leave this prison. What if she thinks snitching on us and winning the soldiers' favor is a better bet?

"I mean I want to see them both," I say. She probably doesn't believe me, but it is the best lie I have right now.

Taha and Reza sit opposite us, though we don't speak right away so that we don't appear to be colluding. I cautiously try the slosh on my tray; it is edible enough, and I am so ravenous that once I start eating, I can't stop. The vegetables, which Safiya calls "potatoes," are comforting in their plain mushiness, the bread is as expected, and the apple has a flat crunch. The dining hall quickly fills with prisoners, and a low hum of conversation provides a level of concealment that Taha finds acceptable. He leans forward.

"Well?"

I look to Safiya. "Tell them what you told me."

Under Taha's critical gaze, she turns the color of a peach and relates her information in a squeak.

"Zahir, I know him." Taha looks up and down the row of tables. "*Big guy* is an understatement. He walked the treadmill like he enjoyed it. There."

He nods at a few tables down, where an enormous, greasy-haired man hunches over his tray. He has double the quantity of food piled on it than everyone else. Safiya is right: the soldiers must like him.

"Yes, that's him," she says. "He will know if Atheer and Feyrouz are in the prison. But I've heard you need to offer him something first before he will answer questions."

"Like what?" Reza asks, leaning in. "We don't have anything."

Safiya points at the apple on Reza's tray. He immediately places it on the table, then takes Taha's and does the same. Safiya nods, smiling.

"That should do it."

With our next steps known, we return to our food. Taha has

already finished his meal and taken to impatiently tapping his finger against his tray. I know he is worrying about the same thing I am feeling: the magic leaving my veins. If we don't find Atheer before curfew, we have no choice but to escape the prison without him. I cannot let that happen.

As soon as a soldier rings a bell to signal the end of mealtime, I hurry to the door, losing Taha, Reza, and Safiya in the throng of prisoners. I dump my tray into a tub and exit the hall, searching the people streaming around me. Strong hands pull me behind a nearby wall. I throw my arms up and brace for an attack; I stay braced even when I see it's Taha.

"What are you doing?" I demand warily. He has trapped me in a tight corner partially hidden from view of the yard.

"You didn't disclose our plan to that Safiya girl, did you?"

I scowl, lowering my hands from my chest. "Absolutely not. I know the risks. You really do think so little of me."

"As if you don't think far less of me," he retorts.

I am oddly offended by his remark. "What does that mean?"

"Come now, you know perfectly well. What was it you called me back in the Vale? 'Cruel, ignoble monster.'"

My ears burn. I can't believe he remembers my insult; I'd forgotten all about it.

He plants his hand on the wall beside my head. "The *cruel monster* part I understand. It's the *ignoble* I'm wondering about," he says in a slinking voice. "So which is it? Am I contemptible, or am I of low birth? Both, perhaps."

My chest tightens; I sense the danger lurking around the edges of this encounter. "I was upset when I spoke. I didn't mean it."

"Yes, you did. Say it. You've always thought you're better than me."

I don't want to engage in this, whatever *this* is. He is reminding me of that Harrowlander soldier back in Bashtal, hunting for a fight. I won't give him one. I try to duck past him, but he takes my arm and pushes me against the wall.

"I am not done, Imani. You can go once you say the truth of how you feel about me."

The truth. What do I tell him? That I couldn't sleep last night, so I curled up on my side and gazed at him sleeping in the opposite bunk, admiring how the moonlight shone on his smooth skin and dark hair? That I watched him and agonized over how to deal with him once Atheer is safely out; I watched him and wrestled the gnarled part of me that wanted to go over and hold him instead?

I look up at his wild eyes, the fresh bruise forming on the peak of his cheekbone. "I wasn't only upset when I spoke. I was ignorant. I didn't know a thing about you then." I lightly stroke his face. "A soldier hurt you, didn't they? Are you all right?"

My gesture doesn't merely startle; it terrifies. Taha's brows float up; ruby red splashes across his jaw. Suddenly his hand cups my cheek and I am in his grip, my heart pounding. I should stop this—he said we have nothing between us—but when we lock eyes, it feels like we have everything. I cannot look away, even as dark, familiar hunger dowses his curiously sad gaze. I desire his lips on mine again; I need to confirm that our last kiss wasn't an accident like he so callously declared. I hate him, but how I like him too, more than his handsome face, those jeweled eyes, that powerful body—it's his unshakable determination and discipline, his spontaneous magical genius, his fearlessness, even his maddening confidence. It's him.

He tilts my chin up, nudging noses. "You still don't know a thing about me, Imani."

Our lips touch; the ephemeral contact blazes the fires of temptation in me. I take a fistful of his tunic and pull him closer. His breathing climbs and skips; his grasp on me trembles. He makes a frustrated sound low in his throat.

"Damn it," he whispers angrily. And then he kisses me.

When I stole his letter, I was trying to find the weakness he claimed he didn't have—now I realize his weakness is *me*. This kiss is not like before. No shyness, no reserve. It is a spark become an explosion, and the fear is more intense than ever; he frantically gathers me against his body, running his hands along me, as if I am sand he must stop from slipping between his fingers. But I sense time is running out for us and he knows; he is kissing me harder, fervently, seeking absolution before the hourglass empties. And it has.

"You'd better stop that before one of the soldiers spots you."

We are a mountain cleaved. A prisoner has found our nook, evidently *her* nook, and she's shooing us out. Taha exhales unsteadily, as if this woman has yanked him back from the edge of a dangerous precipice. As if this was another mistake. He straightens his tunic and marches off without looking at me.

"Don't fool around with other prisoners," she says as I duck past. "It'll make you hopeful about things, but there is no hope here."

What was I thinking? I was an impulsive fool wanting him to kiss me again, and I feel no better nor happier having had my wish granted. Our encounter was wrong; there is and always has been poison in the well. That hostile ocean still churns between us.

I weave after him between groups of prisoners bunched on the ground, others napping, some staring off into space. I search for my brother's face amongst them; I search for stability in the one person I can trust—the one person who can restore order to this chaotic world. But I have no luck finding him, and I begin wondering if I ever will. Perhaps Atheer was never more than a mirage, and I will perish in this desert chasing after him.

As agreed, Reza is waiting for us by the dead tree. "What took you so long? And why are you so out of breath?" he asks, considering Taha suspiciously.

Taha shakes his head. "Where's Zahir?"

Reza thumbs over his shoulder. I don't have to look long to spot the giant of a man smoking a pipe against the wall of a building. As we make our way to him, a soldier hops onto the nearby flogging platform, along with a prisoner who translates his announcement.

"Fighters, line up! Tonight's prize is a pouch of tobacco."

Several teen boys rush to the platform. They are met by soldiers who begin sorting between them.

"Pardon me, are you Zahir?"

I look back at Taha approaching the man seated on the ground. Zahir raises his small brown eyes.

"I am. You're the new prisoners." He has a deep, gravelly voice, the kind I imagine would belong to a cave if it could speak.

Taha crouches in front of him and pulls the two apples from

his pocket. He holds them out. "My name is Taha. This is Reza and Imani."

Zahir studies each of us carefully and takes the apples. "Welcome."

"Thank you." I kneel beside Taha. "Zahir, I was told you know all the prisoners who arrive here. Is that true?"

"It is," he says, smoke trickling around his words.

My hands have begun trembling, and Taha has noticed. I clench my fists. "I am looking for my older brother. He was arrested and placed here several months ago. I was hoping you could tell me where to find him. His name is Atheer."

"Atheer?" Frowning, Zahir pulls the pipe from his lips. "Yes, I know him. But Atheer is gone."

33

THE BIG MAN IS FAST DISAPPEARING BEHIND A WALL of tears. "Gone?" I choke out.

"Yes. He is not here anymore."

Carts of bodies rattle through my mind and vanish inside the lighthouse. I keel over, sobbing. "They worked him to death, didn't they?"

"Oh, they tried to, but he left before they could," says Zahir. "He was only in the prison a few weeks."

"Left? Do you mean he was taken away?" asks Taha.

I raise my head. Zahir pulls on his pipe, his eyes wistful. "Taken away, yes. It happened in the night. I am permitted to walk after curfew, you see, and I was smoking, like this, when the soldiers came. They were dressed differently from the ones here, more formally, in brown uniforms and cloaks. They even carried golden swords."

I wipe the tears off my face. "Did they say what they wanted with him?"

Zahir puffs a smoky plume. "Oh, yes. One said King Glaedric

wanted to see him. The other asked if he had ever been on a ship before. They took him away after that."

The Harrowlander king? I collapse on my haunches, my mind reeling.

"He was a good worker, your brother, very strong," rumbles Zahir. "I'm sorry you missed him."

Reza kneels down too. "We need information about another potential prisoner. A young woman named Feyrouz. She would have only arrived very recently."

Zahir contemplates for a long moment, then shakes his head. "The only Feyrouz has been here for six months."

Reza's eyes rim with tears, his fist clenching. "She was arrested in Bashtal two weeks ago."

"It can take time for prisoners from other cities to make it here, *if* she is assigned to this prison," answers Zahir.

A sad sigh escapes me. Both Reza and I came to this prison hoping to find someone we care about. Both of us will leave heartbroken, having been too late, or too early, to catch them.

"I'm sorry," Taha says quietly.

Reza nods jerkily. "Thanks, Zahir."

Dejected, we leave the smoking man with his apples. Nearby, jeering soldiers have formed a circle around two boys locked in a bare-fisted battle. We cluster by a wall away from the other prisoners, not that anyone could hear us, the soldiers are making such a racket.

"So much for a straightforward mission," mutters Taha.

"Does this make sense to either of you?" I ask. "Why would the king want to see my brother?"

"It doesn't matter why; we just need to find him," says Taha. "And I'd wager a whole bloody bag of misra that the ship Zahir mentioned is the same one we saw in the Bay."

"Yes, I remember it." Three-masted, flying an enormous Empire flag, surrounded by *warships*. I press my hands to my forehead. "Spirits, how are we going to reach it?"

"We'll figure it out," Taha says in that stubborn way as he absently watches the fight. It ends with one of the boys knocked out cold. The laughing soldiers exchange coins, and a pouch of tobacco is thrust between the victor's bloodied fists. Further up the yard, a bell tolls.

"That's curfew," says Taha, nudging Reza with his elbow. His cousin reluctantly trudges off toward the red dormitory.

"We're meeting past the north gate after first patrol, yes?" I ask.

Taha starts walking away too. "Yes. Don't be late, or we'll be forced to leave you behind. We're cutting it fine as it is with the magic we have left."

I nod and leave them, joining a trail of prisoners toward the blue dorm. My brother should have been here too, readying to escape the prison with us. But at least he isn't dead, not worked or flogged to death, or met some other unjust fate within these forsaken walls. He is alive, and I can still save him. I have to hold on to that truth, that hope; it is the undying light that will guide me out of this darkness.

THE BLUE DORM is a long room of bunks stacked with wafer-thin mattresses that reek of sweat and urine. A soldier checks off our numbers at the door, and once we are inside, closes the door behind him. Safiya takes me along, explaining the clusters of bunks like she is showing me around her neighborhood.

"The older women who repair soldiers' shoes sleep here. These ones belong to seven girls from the *same family,* which is, I know, rather remarkable. And this is mine." She pauses proudly at a bunk as wretched as the others. She points to an empty one near hers. "You can take that one. It belonged to the woman from today . . ."

The woman who was discarded into the sea. "Thanks, Safiya, but I think I may stay up awhile."

She hoists herself onto the top bunk, smiling at the girl settling on the lower one. "Take my word on this, Imani. You'll want as much rest as you can get. The nights go faster than you think."

"And the days go slower," adds the girl, and a few others nearby agree.

Lanterns begin snuffing around me. Shadows creep in, weary bodies settle into beds, a quiet blanket descends over the prison. Sighing, I perch on the lumpy lower bunk, though it feels wrong even touching it, let alone laying my head where that poor woman would have done just this morning.

"So that's it?" I ask Safiya. "One person leaves, another arrives."

"Life in here is the true treadmill. Say—" She curls on her side. "Did you speak to Zahir?"

That one question rubs me down to the bone. I miss Atheer and I fear for him, but at least I am leaving this place to look for him. What of Safiya? She isn't leaving to rejoin her parents, good behavior or not. Zahir is all the proof I need—he works hard enough that the soldiers give him tobacco and let him walk around after curfew. He is still imprisoned.

"I did. Hey, come down here a moment. I want to talk to you about something."

Only a couple of lanterns still flicker, enough light for me to see Safiya's frown. She swings her legs over the bunk and slides down, the tendons straining in her feet. She is too thin to last much longer here. I guide her to the end of the dorm where there is a gap between the bunks and the door. Moonlight sieves through the window beside us, illuminating her worried face.

"What is it?"

I hesitate as the last few claws of hesitation sink deeper into me. What if she refuses, or raises the alarm? And Taha will be furious when he sees her. Surely I can reason with him. Helping Safiya doesn't interrupt the mission, and it is the right thing to do, risk or not. I glance out the window at a soldier making his circuit. Any moment now, the first patrol will be over and I will need to be out of here.

"Imani?"

I look back at her. "Do you want to leave this prison?" I don't think she understands me. Her lips part but she doesn't speak. I try again. "I am escaping tonight, and I can get you out with me."

"You're . . . but . . . what about your brother, and Feyrouz?"

I glance at the patrolling soldier. I have a minute at best. "We only came here to break them out, but Fey isn't here, and my brother is already gone."

She covers her mouth. "He's *dead*?"

"No, no, he was taken away by some soldiers."

"How?" She screws her face. "Nobody is ever taken from the prison."

"I know, and I have to find out why. What do you say? I can break you out, but we have to leave right now."

"Yes," she says, nodding fervently. "Of course. I would do anything to leave this place and see my parents again."

A burden lifts off me; another replaces it instantly. My magic stores are low; when I call upon the misra, I receive a weaker response than I am comfortable with. And if that is happening to me, it's happening to Taha and Reza too. We have to move.

"All right, follow me and do exactly as I do."

I lead her to the double doors and carefully push down on the handle, opening it slightly. Cool, foul air wafts through the crevice. I peer out, and when I don't see any soldiers, I open it a little more and steal out with Safiya on my heels. I gently shut it behind me and pause to get my bearings. The view of these doors is sheltered from the ramparts by a large tree—I don't have to worry about archers spotting us right now, only soldiers. One patrols with his back to us several meters away on my right. I creep to the corner and check left, past the dorm. Two soldiers are chatting there. The line of sight for the one facing us is blocked by the other's head, but if he shifted on his feet, he'd only need to glance over the other's shoulder to see us. I wait as long as I can stand, but neither alters their position. We have to chance it.

"Light and fast," I whisper, tugging Safiya forward.

We break from cover and scamper across the yard to the next building. I brace for the shout of someone alerted to us, but all remains quiet. We reach the dense shadow hugging the building's back wall, and I bring Safiya down to a crouch with me. She is panting, studying her surroundings through short flutters of her eyelids. I slink to the corner and freeze. Something is moving in the darkness in front of me.

A soldier.

I twist and clamp a hand over Safiya's lips. She stiffens; I hold my breath. The whistling soldier ambles along not even two meters from us. I stare at his silhouette as my chest inflates, but I don't move until he and his cheery tune are well out of earshot. I lift my hand and simultaneously exhale a heavy breath.

"That was too close," Safiya gasps.

I point ahead to where the land slopes down to the shorter, inner defensive wall. "See that bunch of trees down there? We're going to run to them."

I check the ramparts and confirm that the archers are focused on threats outside the walls; then I glance left and right. I can't see any soldiers looking this way. Now is as good a time as any. I take Safiya's hand.

"Go," I whisper.

We trade the protective shadows for harsh moonlight. The land gamely unmasks around us, naked and exposed; I feel like an ant crossing a crowded dinner table, about to be noticed any second and squashed. And the slope is aiding my speed too much. My concentrated dash mangles to a clumsy sprint, every step laden with the risk of lost footing. I am forced to concentrate on dodging ruts, rocks, and rumples rather than keeping watch for soldiers.

We navigate the steepest part of the slope and cross a pathway, our slippers loudly scratching the grit. Back onto the grass crunching just as loudly under us. My lungs begin to burn; my eyes are getting blurry. Safiya's breath whistles in her chest, her clammy hand tensing in mine as she struggles to keep up. The thicket bounces around in my vision as a dark green blot. I dig my chin down and throw everything I have into the sprint. The shadow of the trees falls over us; the moonlight cuts in half. Seconds later, we are safely in the thicket's shrouding arms. Safiya skates to a wheezing stop. I slow a few steps ahead and strain my ears, but nothing indicates that we have been spotted.

"What now?" Safiya asks.

I wipe the sweat off my upper lip, scanning the grounds. "Now we follow the fence past that gate to another cluster of trees like this one. My friends will be waiting inside."

I check the area around us while Safiya catches her breath. The thicket is growing against the inner defensive wall of the prison. On the other side of the wall is a private area for the soldiers, housing their barracks and armory. One man is coming down the slope on our left now, along that path we crossed over. I wait for him to continue past the thicket; then I guide Safiya along in the shadow of the wall. The little-used north gate comes into view.

"We're close," I whisper.

I slow on one side of the gate and steal a glance through the bars at the private area. I spy a cut of a building with dark windows, closed doors, and no soldiers on the front steps or meandering along the footway. I nod to Safiya. We hurry past the gate and down to the next thicket.

Inside she leans against a trunk, hugging her shaking body. I thread between the trees, impatiently searching for Taha and Reza, who should be waiting here. But they aren't.

There is no sign of them.

34

WE AGREED TO MEET IN THIS GROVE, AND they're not here.

I reach the end of the trees and stare at the prison grounds, my pulse gibbering in my ears. Safiya creeps up behind me.

"Weren't your friends meant to be here?"

"Yes. They were."

But they're not. *Why* not? They are late, they must be, and I would accept that explanation if Taha hadn't impressed upon me the significance of *not* being late. Another dreadful possibility surfaces from the shadows. What if they *tricked* me? They told me to come here, but they've gone elsewhere to escape without me. I squeeze my eyes shut. They have no reason to betray me; this is paranoia. But what do I do now? I can't escape without Reza creating a tunnel under the walls, and I've brought Safiya with me on the promise I would get her out. Her life is in my hands. If we are caught, her punishment is my fault too. I feel the pressure of her looking to me for a solution, but I can't think of one. My brain is chained to the problems, and I have so many—

I am trapped here, my magic is fast fading, my brother is gone. My brother . . . I turn to Safiya.

"You said nobody is ever taken from the prison. My brother was, by King Glaedric's men. Is that unusual?"

"Extremely," she says. "Do you know why they took him?"

I shake my head, though the answer swims in the murky depths of my mind, a slippery eel of a thing. Why indeed? A gilt thread connects everything to Atheer: the Council, the rebels, now King Glaedric. What is it?

Safiya nudges me. "Your friends are here."

I peer incredulously between the trees. Sure enough, Taha and Reza are jogging up the opposite end of the fence line toward us. Relief and unease wash over me in equal turns. They didn't deceive me after all. Taha kept his word. I feel it then, the world slowly spinning out from under me. Every time I think Taha will do one thing, he does the opposite. And every time I think I will find Atheer, I find more puzzles to solve instead. Nobody and nothing is making sense.

The pair enter the thicket to meet us, Reza bearing a lantern. Taha notices Safiya half-hidden behind me, and his sweaty face contorts.

"What is this? I thought I made myself clear."

"Don't take that tone with me," I snap. "She can escape with us. No harm will come of it."

He drags me behind a tree. "She will see the magic," he hisses. "What is *wrong* with you?"

"Me?" I push his hand off. "What about you? We can't leave her behind. We wouldn't have known to ask Zahir without her. She deserves to leave this place."

He looks distressed, like he is trying to negotiate with a brush fire. "It is not about what she *deserves;* it is about how much risk we can feasibly shoulder before things start going wrong. We should be minimizing risk wherever we can, not increasing it. Don't you know anything from our Shields training, or are you truly as useless as I've always suspected?"

"How dare you!" I clench my fists to stop from strangling him. "There is a juncture where the minimization of risk and our duty to protect others meets, Taha. That was also in our training, but you probably skipped it. I judged this an acceptable risk outweighed by its benefit. She won't see the magic; she can look away."

"Look away?" He covers his eyes. "You can't be serious. Why can't you follow the orders I give you? You have no idea how much harder you've made things."

I suddenly feel like Amira when I used to scold her. I fold my arms. "I don't follow your orders because I don't agree with them—"

"No, you don't *respect* me, Imani," he says, seething and pointing in my face. "There is a difference."

"I respect you when you're not being like *this,*" I argue.

"Whatever," he mutters, staggering back. "As for our duty to protect others? Safiya would have been safer without you."

He stomps off. I take a moment to compose myself and round the tree too. Reza is patting him on the shoulder, muttering something into his ear, the both of them glaring at me. I ignore them and go to Safiya.

"This is a strange request, but I need you to turn around, shut your eyes, and cover your ears."

"Why—"

I physically turn her. "Please, Safiya. I can't let you see this."

She does as instructed, albeit uneasily. "Happy?" I whisper to Taha.

If looks had power, I would be eviscerated by his. I'm certain I am about to be, but thankfully, his eyes stain gold. Sinan appears above us, high out of the archers' range, a soaring smudge framed against the starry night sky. Taha returns from his trance and nods to Reza.

"Do it."

Reza kneels in front of the wall, swallowing breath after deep breath. Taha glances at Safiya, but she is still turned away, oblivious to what's going on. Reza thrusts his hands into the soil. A cavern yawns at his fingertips and drops, extending deep under the wall, the soil moving as if Hubaal is on the other side sucking it away through a straw. The muscles of his face and neck strain; he bares clenched teeth, groaning as he manipulates his affinity. A minute later, he doubles over, gasping.

"It's done. The tunnel will take us far beyond the outer wall."

Taha hands him the lantern. "Good. You go first."

I gently prod Safiya. She turns and gawps at the newly forged tunnel. "Is that . . . ?"

"Our way out."

Reza drops into the trench and disappears down the tunnel. Taha goes next. I follow, leading Safiya; she marvels at the red-lit walls.

"How did you make this?"

Taha's head twitches. I clear my throat.

"We dug it over several weeks."

I hope she will accept the answer, but I know I wouldn't. Weeks or not, the tunnel is a feat: tall and wide enough for us to comfortably walk without stooping, sturdy though nothing props it up, running all the way under two defensive walls and ejecting us outside the prison. It would take months of back-breaking work, if it were possible to do at all without the soldiers noticing. But Safiya has the good sense not to press the matter when freedom is so close.

We walk for about a hundred meters before I spy pale moonlight falling through an opening ahead. Taha abruptly stops, blocking us behind him. Reza reaches the end of the tunnel and signals for us to wait, then he scrambles up the dirt wall and pops his head out. A moment later, he bends back down into the tunnel and flashes a thumbs-up.

"All right," Taha says softly, as if to himself. "All right. Be ready on my mark."

Reza gives him a peculiar look before hoisting himself out. Taha turns to me. His face is submerged in shadow, but for his eyes—they stand out like a pair of cat's eyes in the night. Before I can ask him what is going on, he says,

"When I first heard you were joining this mission, I tried to make it as unpleasant for you as possible. I wanted to make you turn back and go home, for both our sakes, but you persevered. So I began hoping you would make the right choices. You would see your brother for the traitor and threat he is, and you would not pose a problem to my mission. I tried, yet time and time again, you proved you are incapable of serving your duty. You and Atheer are too similar."

Confused, I glance at the way out of the tunnel. It is so close,

I can taste the rot on the night air, but Taha is stopping me from reaching it. "Taha . . . why are you saying these things?" I ask.

"I know you intend to help Atheer escape arrest," he answers. "I know what you told Farida."

My heart jolts. Suddenly I am back in the alley outside the Death Pits, hearing the sound of pigeons startling into flight, gazing up at them scattering into the glary sky. It was Sinan, frightening them as he landed. "Spirits, you had your falcon follow me?"

"Yes. And now I have no doubt; you have become too much of a risk to my mission."

A cold, ghostly hand settles on my neck. "And what is your mission?" I rasp.

"To stop your brother from ever returning to the Sahir and spreading his corrupt ideology." Taha's fist finds my tunic; his fingers curl into the coarse fabric. "To punish him for his betrayals the way he deserves—with an arrow to the chest."

The ground seems to peel back under my feet; my stomach plummets, and suddenly I am falling with no end in sight. My suspicions of Taha barely grazed the horrifying truth. He hasn't decided to kill Atheer as a precaution—he was planning on doing this from the very beginning. *This* is the cause he spoke about in his letter to his father. *This* is why Bayek didn't want me joining the mission.

"Listen to me," I say breathlessly, "my brother is a good person who has never meant to hurt anyone. He is only trying to do the right thing. He doesn't deserve to be killed."

"Come now, this is the justice you are always prattling on about." Taha's fingers snap closed, locking me in place. "We both know that if Atheer returned to Qalia, he would be forgiven with a slap on the wrist. But if it were one of *my* brothers who stole and shared misra with outsiders? He would be imprisoned for life, my clan barred from every respectable establishment in the city." Taha glances over his shoulder. "Reza, on my mark."

"*No*, please!" I try to loosen his iron grip. "Killing my brother is not the will of the Council; it's your father's!"

He breathes a derisive laugh. "Are you so blinded by arrogance that you can't see it? My father *is* the Council. He controls the armed forces and commands the loyalty of all the Sahir. Whatever he decides, he will have the support of the people—people like *him* and *me*, the ignoble mob you detest. Even the Council will come round eventually because that is the true nature of you elitists. *Parasites.*" He spits the word. "The Zahim and Elders will do whatever they must to save their own hides and preserve their positions at the top, even if it means kneeling before my father, that lowborn, loathsome man. And down on their knees they will go."

I am distantly aware of my body shaking, the tears tracing paths down my face. "On my ancestors, you will never get away with this crime, Taha. Everyone will learn of what you and your wicked father have done when I return to Qalia."

I wonder why he does not argue with that, until I notice that he is gazing at me pityingly. Then I know I lack a crucial piece of information. I haven't realized that the last rungs of the ladder to salvation have been removed. Numbness blankets my face as I recall his letter's scribbled promise. *Should she present an obstacle, she will be summarily dealt with.* Killed, like Atheer.

"No," I sob. Then I scream it at his face. "NO! This is wrong, you know it is!" I push against his wrists; when that proves futile, I bang on his shoulders, though I am feeble with fright. "If you've been plotting to kill me and my brother since we left, why did you ever show me kindness? Why did you kiss me and make me think there was something between us?"

A flustered twitch rips across his face. He glances over his shoulder at where Reza must be perched above ground, listening. "Silly mistakes. They meant nothing."

"But I wanted them to mean something," I whimper, shaking my heavy head. "I wanted you to *like* me."

He frowns. "You did?"

He is taken aback by my admission, and that shocks me. Did he really think I was never interested in him? Perhaps everything he's ever said to me—that I consider him beneath me, that I don't respect him—perhaps he truly believes it.

"Yes, all along!" I press my palm to his chest; his heart drums frenetically under his shifting ribs. "Your heart is trying to tell you something, Taha. Why won't you listen to it? Please, listen to it and not your father."

His wide eyes grind back and forth over me; he has traded triumph for sublime terror. "D-don't you understand?" he stammers in a whisper only I can hear. He brings his face close to mine, and our noses brush. "I *can't,* even if I wanted to. I *have* to do this."

But understanding eludes me. What could a Shield fear more than the taking of innocent life?

"Please," I try through thick tears. "Taha, I am begging you—"

Reza's impatient voice floats down the tunnel. "Hurry up,

man! The mission has priority, remember? Or does that only apply when it's not the girl you're interested in?"

Taha's face flushes bright red. His expression hardens again, but this time, there is neither anger nor resentment in his eyes. They are emeralds, appearing as lifeless as my heart feels.

"Forgive me, Imani," he whispers. "I cannot let you ruin everything I have suffered for."

He shoves me, hard. Safiya scampers out of the way as I am thrown onto my back. My head slams into the ground; plumes of unreal gnats swarm my vision in swirling clumps. Taha moves faster than I can hope to, scaling the cavern wall and vanishing from the tunnel in one motion. I dizzily climb to my feet and lurch for the exit. The earth groans; the tunnel quakes under my feet. I press a steadying hand to the wall. Tremors kiss my palm from deep within the soil, but they are getting stronger, coming closer. The truth hits like a blade to the chest.

"It's going to collapse." I turn to Safiya. "Run, before we're buried!"

35

FIND SAFIYA'S HAND AND PULL HER BACK DOWN THE tunnel toward the prison yard. The exit caves; the closest walls sag before they give entirely and smother the light. Destruction roars after us like a monster. We run for the tunnel's entrance, but no moonlight falls through it, and I can't see in front of me. I move with a hand sweeping the pulsing wall; the floor swells the moment I lift my foot and launch into another stride. Rocks are driven from the avalanche; they ricochet off the roof and walls and strike me. Dust fills the air; it coats my skin and throat; specks of it land in my eyes and make them water. With agonizing slowness, the faint hint of fresh air ahead evolves into a beckoning draft. We are close, and then Safiya slips, falls, and I go tumbling over her.

We catch and roll in a tangle of thrashing limbs, like old rope that is impossible to pick apart. I slam to a stop, coughing, my eyes streaming. The earth groans and gripes around me, a jaw snapping shut. Cold soil falls onto my chest, my face, into my nostrils, burying my hands. I want to scream, but if I open my mouth, I will choke. My body rapidly drains of sensation, and rather than kicking free of the soil, I ask myself if I should spend my last moments struggling in vain. Death waits to meet me; death is free outside these walls too, hunting my brother—

"Come on," Safiya shrieks, pulling me to my feet.

My body reflexively moves, and I stagger into a sprint. It's the only thing I seem to be doing anymore, running from problems, running into worse ones. I slam against the wall at the mouth of the tunnel and drop to my knees with my hands interlocked. Safiya places her foot into them; I heave my arms and push her over the lip. I waste no time clawing the walls and throwing myself over too. As I land on my back, the cavern disintegrates at my feet. And just like that, the rumbling ceases, the prison is quiet, and we are trapped.

I stare at the sky peeking between the branches, my tears arriving in an unstoppable deluge. I clap my hands to my eyes and weep, and the grief is an anchor like no other, pulling me into the earth. Why didn't I surrender to the soil like I should have? What good is there in going on? I cannot save Atheer, my people, or the people of Alqibah. I cannot save Safiya or the rebels; I cannot even save myself. I will keep suffering defeat until there is nothing and nobody left but me, the last to witness my world crumble in the shadow of time.

"The soldiers are coming," Safiya wails. "If they find us—" The possibility is too terrifying to articulate. She shakes my shoulder. "Imani, what do we do?"

"How should I know?" I mumble. "This is over."

It is an awful sound she makes. She tries to drag me upright, but I am heavy and limp, flopping out of her hands. She balls them to fists and beats me, though I hardly feel it. "You're giving up? You promised! I wouldn't have come if I'd known! I shouldn't have. Gods, I'm a fool—"

You're giving up? Baba said something like that to me once, that evening in the courtyard when we were playing his favorite board game, Table, after our many lessons. My red stones were surrounded by his black ones, and I wanted to forfeit. But Baba forbade it. "Before you decide to give up, tell me why you sat down to play in the first place."

"Because I want to win," I answered gloomily. I thought Baba would scold me for that, but he reached across the board and took my hand.

"Then why do you not want to win anymore? If you forfeit now, you will assuredly lose. But if you press on while you can, you may find yourself a victor. The future is not final until we reach it." He picked up a red piece, placed it in my palm, and closed my fingers around it. "There is one lesson that comes above the rest, Imani, and it is this: if you decide to play, play until the end."

If Baba were here, wouldn't he demand I keep going? He would tell me I have struggled and come too far to give up now, not when I've life in my bones and a beat in my heart. Not when Atheer is hours from dying by Taha's arrow. There is an end to this game, and I intend to see it, no matter how bitter or bloody.

"Imani, *please*—"

I sit up and peer between the trees at the prison grounds. Safiya is right—the soldiers heard the commotion. Three are jogging this way from separate directions, and I am certain more are coming.

Safiya palms the sweat off her skinny face, replacing it with streaks of dirt. "We need to leave."

"I have an idea," I say, glancing up at the lighthouse at the other end of the prison. "We can still escape."

"No, it's too dangerous. We need to return to the dorm before any soldiers see our faces."

"I am not staying here, Safiya." I reach for her hand. "We can escape the same way the bodies do."

She pushes me away. "Are you *mad*? It's a cliff, a sheer drop. I wanted to escape this prison *alive*."

"There's no time for this. We'll make it; trust me—"

"I don't *trust* you," she hisses. "I don't even know who you are or where you've come from. I've traveled to many places along the Spice Road with my family, and I've never once heard of Qalia! Please, I must return to the dorm."

"You'll never leave here otherwise."

She swipes a tear from her eye. "Neither of us is leaving, Imani, but I am choosing to live a little longer."

Agony scalds my chest. I want to scream to feel some sort of relief, I want to rage at this unfair, unjust world, but I have no time, and nothing I can say to Safiya will make her listen to me. I can only ensure that she returns to the dorm without being seen. I glance at the approaching soldiers while hunting my veins for magic. *Come on, even a scrap,* I pray. A spark answers my probe, but it is tiny. There is no other choice. I must work with what I have left.

"I'm going to cause a distraction," I say, rising to my feet. "As soon as the soldiers come after me, you make a break for the dorm."

She shakes her head, chin crumpled. "Don't do this, please."

"It is my duty. Good luck, Safiya, and thank you."

She shakes my hand quickly, then hunches down while I stalk to the edge of the thicket. Still only three soldiers heading this way, and none from the direction of the lighthouse. I inhale and exhale, I ready my muscles, I tamp down on the swirling sandstorm of panic howling in my head. When it's quiet, I sprint out of the thicket.

"Halt!" shouts a soldier.

I glance over my shoulder and feel a spasm of relief seeing them pick up the chase. Safiya will have the distraction she needs. Now I have to survive it.

I sprint up the slope in the shadow of the defensive wall. If I stick close to it, I can avoid the archers' direct line of sight, which is one less problem to worry about. Another is rapidly approaching. A soldier who heard the commotion has cut down the corridor between two buildings on my left and is hurtling toward me. I race to think of a strategy, but my body is faster than my mind. His and my paths intersect, him missing me by an arm's length.

"Stop running!" He skids on the grass, pivots, and chases after me.

That makes four in pursuit, four who will be on top of me the moment I slip, or slow, or confront a barrier I cannot negotiate. It is too late now. I must keep pressing the way to the end of the prison. I must get past the soldiers at the gates and into the lighthouse, and from there, well, I suppose I will follow the smell.

A wooden fence crops into view on my left. I recall the prison map I studied with Amira. If I vault the fence and cut left again, I might make it to the dormitory. I can sneak back in, pretend to be asleep in my bunk, act like this never happened. I can resign to imprisonment or attempt a foolhardy escape another day. These men haven't properly seen my face, and I doubt they could identify me amidst the hundreds of other prisoners. But is it the right decision? Even if I make it out of here another time, I will be too late to save Atheer and the others.

Panic suffuses me. It throbs in my thigh muscles; it eats away at my lungs; it sprouts legs and goes walking around, kicking my ribs. The right decision. This entire journey from Qalia to here has been a cascade of decisions, one knocking into another, nudging me along a path, the end of which I cannot know. Who is to say what is right if wrong has not yet had its day? If only I had the clear orders I used to receive in the barracks; I yearn for those simple answers. But there are no simple answers anymore. What remains is to make a choice and strive for it relentlessly. Taha will not wait around in his hunt for my brother. I must escape *tonight* or die trying.

I continue past the fence, leaving behind my last chance of returning to the dorm. I trade the grass for the grit path winding its way between the buildings clustered at the head of the prison. The group of soldiers behind me has swelled to five, and they are making such a racket, it will be ten in little time.

A long set of stone steps rises before me. I vault them, two at a time. Something snaps by my ear; the air lashes my loose hair. I stumble, slamming my knee into a step and giving an unearthly growl. I manage to push on, and I've done so for several meters before I realize what it was back there. An arrow.

One bounces on the stone paver behind me; another wedges into a wooden pole with a dull, vibrating hum; a third dives over my right shoulder, and that one I felt searing across my neck. Warm blood gushes out from the wound; it seeps into my tunic; it slides down my right arm. Gasping, I clamp a hand over my neck. The sight of the lighthouse looming over the roofs ahead subdues some of my fear, and I am able to discern that the injury isn't severe. I am close to my destination, though close without a plan. I still can't stop, and I need to lose or confuse the soldiers coming after me.

I cut left down a corridor, take a sharp right, another left; then I hurtle straight ahead while fighting the growing sense of being detached from my own legs. I vault a low fence and burst out of the maze, then slide to a stop before the lighthouse gate. The two men who stand guard are ready and waiting for me— and one is the soldier who cuffed me back in the workroom.

Sadistic delight paints bright red splotches across his cheeks and glistens in his eyes.

"You," he says, pulling his longsword from his belt. He slides his tongue over his bloodless lips as he swaggers toward me. The other soldier brandishes his sword too. But I am unarmed in appearance alone, for I have finally, totally grasped Qayn's lesson. Magic roars in my veins and floods to my hands, violently eager, and all around me, *iron* sings my name. I feel and hear it in the earth, through the walls, in the sky above me. For the first time in my life, I glimpse an inkling of the world beyond the veil that Qayn impressed upon me. I don't fully understand it yet, but I begin to perceive how the Great Spirit may view existence, as little more than clay to be worked. And rather than cowering before this immensity, I dive into it headfirst.

"Give it to me," I order, flexing my hand.

To both my sheer terror and my wild delight, the sword rips from the soldier's grip, flies across the gap, and lands in my fist. Magic surges through my fingers into the hilt and along the blade. I don't pause to ask questions. I raise my other hand and point it at the second man.

"Be gone."

The sword flies from him, cartwheels through the air, and spears the soil several meters away. Both men stand there, blinking stupidly at me. Despite the fact that I feel as astounded as they look, there is no time to contemplate what's just happened. I seize the lull and dash forward, swinging the sword over my head. The first soldier ducks out of my sword's drop and backs away. I tighten my shoulders and turn into the momentum. The magic pitches, the sword glows blue, casting bright, shimmering wiggles on the surrounding walls that look like a reflection on water. The steel elongates and takes the form of a short spear. I readjust my hands, finish my rotation, and lob it. The spear splits the air and skewers the soldier through the chest. He spits blood, falling to the ground in a limp heap. My magic exhales and does not take another breath. That's it. I have exhausted my stores.

The other soldier runs for his sword, and the rest of them now emerge from between the buildings behind me. I pull the bloody spear free and sprint for the lighthouse. Arrows shower me. I slam the clanging gate shut; arrows spike the soil around my feet; one caroms off the gate. Gasping, I hustle up the ramp and pull open one of the double doors, spear at the ready, but I am confronted by an austere, empty room. I close the door and slide the spear through the handles. As I lift my hands off it, the door shudders in the frame from the other side. But the spear holds.

Exhaling, I turn to the room and flinch. A soldier has emerged from the corner by some stairs that must lead up into the lighthouse. A skinny young man, no older than me, with a fresh face of mellow blue eyes under a scrub of blond hair. He has a sword on his belt, but he hasn't drawn it.

"No afraid." He speaks in awkward Alqibahi and approaches me slowly.

"Step any closer, and I'll kill you," I say, though I've no idea how I can make good on the threat.

The door thuds behind me; the spear knells against the handle. A soldier pounds on it from the other side, shouting.

This one puts his hands up. "Me no hurt. You want go." He gestures at something in the wall—a square metal hatch. I notice an empty cart in the corner, partly hidden by the shadows. This must be it, the chute down which the bodies are dumped.

"Open." He pulls a key on a chain from his pocket and goes to the hatch.

I warily follow him, trying to detect the trap here. Perhaps Safiya was right and the drop from the chute isn't survivable. But why doesn't he cut me down instead? He may be even more pitiless than that; he will draw greater pleasure watching me hopelessly fall to my death. I glance at the stairs leading up to the lighthouse again, but there is no answer there. I certainly can't go back out the front door. I have cornered myself here with no egress but that chute.

The soldier unlocks the hatch and pulls it open. The scent

of death blooms from the bodies that have gone in before. I can only imagine how awful it is inside.

"Go. Fall . . ." He stops, frowning at himself as he thinks. Then, "*Big*. Fall big, but." He holds up a finger. "You will land, yes. You will live."

I fix a hand on the corner of the hatch, staring up at him. "Why are you doing this?"

The door bangs. He quails, glancing at it. "Me, farmer son . . . no want come here, Alqibah." He swallows, putting his hands to his chest. "But if me no help them, they will—" He points at the door, then makes the gesture of a noose around his neck. "Kill me."

"You were forced to come here on threat of execution," I say, frowning.

He nods emphatically. "Yes, yes. Forgive me. Go, please, now."

I cannot fathom what I have been told, nor stomach how far-reaching the spread of this pestilence is. I swing a leg over the edge of the hatch into the chute. "Throw your sword away; pretend I disarmed you. They'll believe it."

He nods and gestures for me to leave. I gaze down into the pitch-black, steadying myself. Then I swing my other leg over and let go.

36

ARKNESS SWALLOWS ME.

I unleash a wild scream and free-fall into decay, waving my arms, searching for purchase on the smooth walls of the chute and finding none. I fall and fall, and I wonder if I have been tricked into believing I could survive this drop. The rotten smell mushrooms under me, dense enough that I half expect to float upon it. Light blinds me, brighter than ever before. It is glancing off something—the sea, I realize, sweeping out in an eternal indigo mantle, moonlight tiptoeing across its sawtooth peaks and jinking off the yellow sand of a beach. I gaze at it, and as the wind howls in my ears and my tunic billows around my face, I listlessly try to understand. Then I slam into the ground.

Irate birds shriek in my ears as I topple over like a wheel sprung off its axle after a carriage accident. A mess of textures presses against my face and arms, my back and chest. Feathers, coarse cloth, supple clay, strands of straw, pockets of mud, something like hard wood poking me, and from this all effuses the worst smell I have ever encountered in my life. Rotten meat left to spoil in the sun, human waste, wet rags, decayed fish. Great

Spirit, I don't know. It is a mystery until I finally slump at the base of this mountain piled high against the cliff. This mountain of *bodies*.

I cower before the nightmarish sight; it almost eludes comprehension in the magnitude of its horror. Hundreds of dead prisoners have built a pyramid on the beach toward the chute's exit, skeletons at the base, bloated bodies with flesh still attached at the top, swarmed by greedy vultures and seagulls who nigh blot them out. That is what broke my fall—the dead saved me.

I vomit in the sand, and the moment I stop heaving, I push up to my feet and run at the foaming water. I am not a person anymore, not a collection of thoughts, feelings, and memories. I am something undone and left to flounder in the open air. I have only a vague idea of where I am, and I cannot stop to figure it out. One impulse guides me: get off this beach.

The sea takes me gladly. The water is shockingly cold, turbulent with a rancorous wind. I sink, I swallow water, I thrash my legs, I smash my arms into it, I tilt my neck and burst out of it, gasping. I am spun around by the inexorable current; I bob up and down, glimpsing slivers of the beach and its monument to death.

"*Mama!*" I shriek at the sky. "*Baba!* Help me, please! Help me!"

They cannot hear me. I scream until I cannot hear me either. Untold time passes; the current eventually shows mercy and nudges me round the black headland. Taeel-Sa's lights appear, a few coy eyes winking in the distance, and that shakes straight something askew in me. I remember what I am doing, what I need to do.

I thrash my limbs, barely making any ground, until the face of the person who put me here rises from my mental gloom like smoke off embers. Taha—the boy who kissed me and tried to kill me. My thrashing becomes an efficient paddle. I swing my arms and kick my legs; I divide the freezing night sea like an arrow with one objective: to save my brother and kill his assassin.

The thought alone carries me to safety. My sopping body runs aground on some rocks. An embankment is to my left, easily scalable any other time—the street, just in reach. But I am exhausted, and before I can decide to do anything, I am out cold with the sea licking my bare feet.

IT IS STILL THE PIT of night when I come to. I bolt upright and don't have to fight to remember where I am and what is happening.

I tear a strip of fabric from the hem of my tunic and tie it around my bloody neck. Carefully I climb over the slippery rocks to the street, where I stand, looking up and down. Nobody comes or goes; I may as well be the only soul in Taeel-Sa. But I know Taha is out there, and if I were thinking like him, I would return to Farida's ship so I could reach Atheer on the king's ship. The question is, would I kill Farida now, or after the job is done?

"Spirits, I have to hurry," I whisper to myself.

I launch into a sprint down the street. My sore feet slap the sidewalk; water flies off me and splats onto the stone. I don't know where I am exactly, but the pier curves in a gentle crescent, and if I am at one end, Farida's ship should be at the other.

A few minutes of frantic running leads me to a busy section of the docks where the Harrowlanders load their spice ships.

Even at this desolate hour, at least a dozen soldiers patrol in pairs, vigilantly ensuring no thief sneaks onto the ships and steals their ill-gotten bounty. I duck out of their sights into a back alley and continue in the tarry shadows, keeping off the main streets. I cross from alley to alley, stealing glimpses of the docks and the sea, but I keep my bearings.

I reach the end of the pier and scurry along the sea-eaten boardwalk, searching the docks for the two-masted silhouette of Farida's sailing ship. But it's not here. I slow to a stop and press my hands to my forehead, gasping. My sister is on board that ship, and if I am a target along with Atheer, she may be one too.

"What do I do?" I turn on the spot. "Think, Imani; you must *think*."

My mind refuses to cooperate. I don't have a weapon or misra, or any supplies, not even something as simple as drinking water, which I desperately need. I certainly don't have a vessel to pursue Taha. My feverish panic returns, worse than before, burning along my body and threatening to whittle me down to ash. Footsteps patter up behind me. I whirl around, fists raised. My lips part.

"Amira?"

"Oh, thank the Spirits!" She envelops me in a hug. I shut my eyes and soak up the warmth, falling happily into a well of relief because she has not been harmed. She gasps, pulling away. "You're bleeding."

"I'm fine," I croak. "An arrow grazed me." I sheepishly look over her shoulder at Qayn. The raven-haired djinni is laden with my bag. "What happened?"

"Taha and Reza returned about two hours ago," he says,

offering a solemn nod. "Taha claimed you didn't survive the prison. He told us Atheer is being held captive on the king's ship and asked Farida to sail them over to it with the intention of breaking him out. Of course, she said yes."

"But Qayn saw through their lies," Amira explains. "He convinced me, and we snuck off the ship as it was setting sail."

Yet another act of kindness I am in debt to him for. I clear my throat. "Thank you, Qayn. You saved my sister's life."

"What happened to you?" she asks.

I shake my head. "Taha and Reza collapsed the escape tunnel before I could get out. It almost killed me. And Taha admitted his father sent him here to assassinate Atheer."

"Those *devils,*" she hisses, clenching her fists. "How could they have done that?"

I don't answer—I don't *know.* Right before Taha escaped the tunnel, I sensed something in his frightened gaze. A connection, a flicker of regret. But he managed to douse it and continue his mission. Whatever feelings he held for me were not enough to steer him off the path his father has set him on. If I did not feel so numb already, I would be devoured by disappointment.

"How did you escape?" Amira asks.

"Don't ask. I just did." I swallow my nausea and glance back at Qayn. "You were right about Taha all along. I should've listened to you and been more prepared for his treachery."

"What matters is that you escaped with your life. But your brother's is still under threat. Here." He places my bag on the ground and pulls a spyglass from it. "I stole this off the ship before we left."

"Cunning of you," I murmur, feeling that guilty gratitude

again. I press the telescope to my eye. The mighty wind has swept clouds over the moon, and I am only able to discern the king's ship by the lantern lights speckling its long deck. I scan the water. Three warships are moored in a loose triangle around it, but there is a sizeable distance between them. If an alarm was raised that something untoward was afoot, it would take the soldiers a bit of time to reach the king's ship. I look back at it.

"I think I see some anchoring lines I could use to climb aboard, but I don't know how I will find Atheer, and I cannot save him without a boat."

"We saw some four-oars moored at the end of the pier," Amira suggests.

"Surely we need something bigger than that."

Qayn considers the sea. "On the contrary, Slayer. Being unobtrusive is your best hope of getting near those warships. Night can only cover so much."

"And from there, I'll need to swim," I say, chewing my lip.

"Yes. To the anchor line, which you'll use to climb onto the ship."

"Find Atheer and bring him back," Amira finishes.

"Spirits, it's not much of a plan."

Qayn takes the spyglass from me and peers across the Bay. "You've no time to devise another. See for yourself."

Frowning, I look through the glass. Gliding into a beam of moonlight escaping the clouds is a black falcon. Sinan.

"Damn it," I say, scouring the rest of the Bay. I don't see Farida's ship, but it must be out there, concealed by the darkness, waiting like a snake in the grass. And Taha is on the hunt.

I snap shut the spyglass. "We need to go."

WE HURRY TO THE END of the boardwalk and stop in some shadows. Amira and Qayn keep lookout while I retrieve a flask of cold misra tea from my bag. Holding it steady in one fist, I imagine myself in a safe, comfortable tea room in Qalia's barracks, about to begin a ceremony. I try to slow my breathing; I pretend to feel the warmth of the blazing firepit and hear the soft bubble of boiling water in the teapot. I uncork the flask and breathe the escaping scent.

Apple shisha. Sand. Wood. Light, and hope, and home.

I inhale the billow of memories deeply; I drink the sweet nectar and use it to patch the cracks that have formed in my courage. Slowly the magic streams through me, sparking energy in its wake. The invigoration is a deception, I know. Underneath it, my bones are weary, my heart all the more, and the misra is only masking it. Drinking too much for too long is hazardous to a sorcerer's health, as our bodies cannot tolerate an excess of magic, but I breeze through the entire flask. I am saving Atheer, and nothing—nobody—will stop me.

We move to a nearby alcove that gives us a good view of a gated fence at the end of the pier. Several small boats are moored behind it. I've seen them before, being used to ferry goods and passengers to and from ships in the Bay. The gate is being watched over by a single soldier who is more interested in filling his smoking pipe. Beside him, a two-story building bears a sign that reads TAEEL-SA FERRY SERVICE. A lantern is on inside; likely there are workers on duty for the duration of the night hours, should there be any need for them.

"We could swim around the fence and steal one of the boats," Amira whispers.

"We could kill him," Qayn suggests.

"Bloodshed is unnecessary," I say sharply, thinking of that young soldier back in the prison. "Sneaking past it is."

I take a moment to tighten the strip of fabric around my neck. Amira produces my dagger and holds it out with a small, encouraging smile. I've never been so glad to hold it, but it also reminds me of what I achieved earlier tonight.

"I did it, you know," I say to Qayn as I strap the blade to my thigh. "I exercised my affinity over a soldier's sword in the prison. Your lesson worked."

He shifts his straight brows. "I knew it would. It helps that magical genius runs in your family."

"You mean Atheer," I say, hoisting my bag onto my shoulders.

"Yes, him too," he murmurs.

We leave the alcove and head for a ramp sunken in the water. I consider Qayn out of the corner of my eye. "This hasn't been much of a sightseeing trip for you."

"Hm." He smiles to himself. "To be perfectly honest, Imani, I did not really come to Alqibah to visit. I came for the sole purpose of seeing Atheer saved, even if I have found it refreshing being outside the Sahir."

Amira looks up at the djinni with raised brows. "You really care about our brother, don't you?"

We stop at the ramp, and Qayn shrugs. "I told you both several times. Atheer is my friend, and I believe in his cause. I should quite like him to see it through."

"That's very compassionate of you," I say carefully. "Though, to be perfectly honest myself, it's something of a jarring contrast to your historical indifference, isn't it?"

In fact, everything about Qayn, his behavior, even his appearance, is in contrast to that cold king of old—he took the initiative to save my sister from Taha, he got us out of the First City unscathed, he guided me to Atheer. For all his lies, he continues to fulfil his promises and exceed them.

"What can I tell you, Slayer? Not all who are bad are bad the whole way through."

He ambles past me and wades into the sea without a moment's hesitation, despite the water's chill. Under the moon like this, the black sea lapping the ends of his wavy tresses, the same black sea I find in his eyes, Qayn is something else. The Qayn of memory. Otherworldly; regal. Impossible to truly know, as beguiling as a bountiful but treacherous land. We are coming upon the end of our own journey, he and I. If fate is on my side, I will free Atheer from the king's ship, and Qayn will have served his purpose. Yet now that it has come, I am unsure if I still wish to kill the mystifying devil, as I am ordered to do, or let him—let *us*—linger a while longer.

I am the last to immerse myself in the cold water. As it touches my skin, the prison's silver beach flashes behind my eyes. Amira and Qayn begin to paddle, but I sink. I muffle a cry, telling myself this is temporary. I move my arms and kick my legs, but for some damned reason, nothing happens. The water swallows me, invading my eyes, nostrils, and throat. I am going to drown three meters from the ramp, and somehow I know with certainty that my sodden corpse will wash up on that beach to join the others.

Someone pulls me out. I break the surface, spewing water and gasping for air. Qayn confronts me, dark eyes ablaze, black strands of wet hair dangling over them. "Quiet," he whispers, clamping my thrashing arms. "What is the matter with you?"

"N-nothing," I stammer. "I'm fine now."

He releases me but swims within arm's reach. We make our way alongside the dock in as gentle a glide as we can manage against the sea's push. The soldier's head dips into view on our left. He is puffing on his pipe, taking long drags and blowing streams of smoke. We round the rusty metal fence protruding a few meters across the water. Amira reaches a four-oar and secures a hand on the boat's rim. I edge up beside her, Qayn on my left.

"I'll untether it; you both push it away," I whisper.

I leave them and thread between the other boats nodding on the swell. It is an easy swim until it abruptly isn't. The water around the ramp is peppered with submerged rocks: slimy, protruding, and uneven, some jagged, and the current incessantly shoves me against them. I clinch my lips to stop from cursing every time I knock a knee or scrape an elbow.

I carefully navigate the rocks and emerge on the ramp one giant, sopping bruise. The soldier's head jerks. I crouch in the shadows and watch him between the bars of the gate. Frowning, he turns fully and stares in my direction, then right at me. I stop breathing; I don't dare move, not even to avert my gaze, lest he somehow hear the motion. But he shrugs and ambles in an arc, pulling on his pipe again. On the exhale, he launches into a loud coughing fit. Perhaps my luck has not yet run out tonight.

I use his hacking to conceal my unwinding of the rope

tethering the boat to this rotted wooden post. I sling the rope over my shoulder and slip back into the water, following Amira and Qayn, who are pushing the boat further out.

We stop over a dozen meters from the jetty, and I help Amira climb in. Water spits and splashes off her soaking clothes, and I thank the Great Spirit we are out of that soldier's hearing range. Qayn and I hoist ourselves in next; he and Amira sit on the bench and unhook their oars. I drop my bag into the bottom of the boat, lift the small sail on the mast, and take an oar to the bow.

We start rowing. The playful waves lift and toss us at the Bay; the boat slides and smacks the surface, provoking sheer spray that arcs about us and stings my eyes. I do my best to stay upright, rowing one side then the other, back and forth toward the warships and the king's ship anchored between them. Very quickly, my arms resemble dry branches bent at odd angles, my gasps scratch my hot throat, and the wound in my side throbs. I struggle to see ahead of us. The farther out on the vast Bay we go, the darker it is becoming. The sky and the sea have fused into a black sheet interrupted occasionally by moonbeams and fitfully flickering lanterns. I am beset by the certain fear that we are moments from sailing into the broad side of Farida's ship. They could be anywhere, moored and waiting. Taha's falcon may have even spotted us. I don't see the mindbeast anywhere, but he possesses far keener eyesight in the dark than I could hope to have. The mere prospect of that falcon haunting these skies burdens me like a blade resting on my neck.

We reach the perimeter of the triangle formed by the warships. Qayn drops anchor, I lower the sail, and we hunch together.

"It's a long swim," he says, eyeing the king's ship.

The insinuation isn't lost on me, but I am not prepared to address what happened at the ramp. "I'll make it. Our brother perishes if I don't."

"To think," Amira murmurs, "we saw this ship days ago and had no idea Atheer was inside all along."

"Seems there are prisoners everywhere in this city." I confirm that the straps holding my blade to my thigh are secure, and stand up. "Stay anchored here. I'll bring Atheer back."

"I want to help," she starts.

"You will be, by looking after this boat. It's our only way out, remember?" I fix my foot on the rim. Qayn stands too.

"Let me come with you, Slayer. You might need my help."

His random generosity has me tongue-tied again. Amira lurches over and hugs me.

"Look after yourself, please."

I kiss her forehead. "You too. I'll see you on the other side, Sister."

Qayn and I exchange a nod; then I grit my teeth and drop into the chilly sea.

37

WATER RISES TO MY JAW. THE SILVER BEACH haunts my mind's eye. Ashen skeletons, the touch of soft-sprawling, cloudy flesh. Panic riots in my head, but I knew it was coming and force my breathing to steady. I kick against the current, counting a rhythm and focusing on my body in the here and now—though I dare not dwell on what may lurk deep under my feet.

I swim for the king's ship, Qayn keeping pace by my side. Warships hulk on our flanks. I listen for sailors' voices that don't come. Save for the sea slapping the creaking hulls, the Bay is silent, and if I shut my eyes, I could convince myself I had been swallowed by a leviathan.

We inch between the warships. The cold stops me from feeling my limbs, and I am reduced to an anxious head bobbing along. Abruptly I hear a Harrowlander and oars splashing to my left. Qayn and I squint into the dark. He deciphers the form of the small boat bearing down on us first.

"Hold your breath," he says, and pulls me under.

I clamp my mouth as we dive. Our surroundings are an abyss;

I hold Qayn for comfort, and his fingers interlock with mine. The boat passes above us invisibly, but a cold billow curtains over us, and oars cleave the water. We float back up and softly, slowly break the surface, despite my lungs threatening to burst. I exhale and suck air, blinking the water from my eyes. The patrolling boat has gone on, and I cannot decipher our boat or my sister from the insatiable night either.

We continue swimming. As we near our target, Taha's falcon reveals himself above. Startled, I twist my head, half expecting Taha to be swimming beside me, murder in those gilded eyes. But it is only Qayn, hair hanging in vines around his pointed face—and again, I am enormously comforted by his company.

We reach the anchoring line of the king's ship. I expect to see a sign of sailors, but no one is looking overboard, and only the faint, eerie trill of a bird interrupts the quiet. The light song does little to soothe my nerves. I study the long chain reaching from sea to ship, cursing my luck of being bound to a powerless djinni.

"If you had your magic, you could whisk us up there," I whisper.

Qayn points his brows. "My, what a shrewd observation. Perhaps when this is over, you can help me get it back, and then I can whisk you to and fro as much as pleases you." He places my hand on the chain. "Time to climb, Slayer."

I hesitate. Back in the First City, he implied that his magic was permanently lost to him, stolen by whoever it was that betrayed him—Nahla, I am certain. But was that another lie, or is he merely joking now? I have to stow the problem away for another time; it won't *be* a problem if I don't survive this night first.

I grab the chain and pinch my thighs and ankles around it.

Predictably, the climb is easy for three hoists; then it is expo-
nentially more difficult. The chain is both slippery and abrasive,
and my hands are already weathered from oakum picking. My
heavy, soaked clothes make things harder. About halfway up,
my shoulders demand respite, and I have to hug the chain while
waiting for my head to stop spinning. *How wretched is this situation?* I wonder. And how unlikely is it that I'll escape it alive? We
began this journey with plans, schedules, maps. I am ending it
like an insect trying to escape a bathtub without the foggiest idea
of what awaits me if and once I do.

Qayn touches my ankle, prodding me on. A few minutes
later, I reach the top with gritted teeth almost shattered, but I
cannot flop onto the deck and catch my breath like I crave. I halt
in place and peer between the bars of the taffrail at the stern.
Because the ship is anchored, there is no helmsman by the ship
wheel, though I do hear people further down. I pull myself onto
the deck and help Qayn over too. We crouch, waiting, but it
seems no one has discovered our arrival. We creep past the helm.
The voices rise from below.

I inch my eyes over the edge of the deck and look directly
down at the captain's cabin, or in the case of this ship, the king's
cabin. Several men stand outside, speaking to someone out of
sight. I spy a military officer in a black uniform with a matching cape, hat held under his arm. He is flanked by subordinates
clutching scrolls. Further along is a deck like nothing I imagined,
more a stately abode than a ship. Gold lanterns are fixed to hooks
driven into the wood anywhere they can be securely placed; the
hand-carved rails are ornate and painted rich wine red. Below the

forecastle at the bow is a cabin with stained-glass windows and a carved door. At a wooden table in the center of the main deck sits a young Harrowlander woman drowning in a flouncy mauve dress. She reads a book by lantern light while a mousy servant girl pours her tea from a ceramic pot. The woman must be royalty; she wears a dainty diadem in her curled auburn hair and pearls around her swanlike neck. There is even a small dog on board, snoring on a poufy, frilled cushion by her slippered feet.

The woman is not the only sign that this ship is a home. Potted fruit trees, other plants, and flowers crowd the spare corners of the deck. Amidst their foliage, a colorful oasis bird in a gold cage sings its haunting melody. Further down, a reclining lounge shelters under a trellis draped with transparent curtains. And there are only two soldiers that I can see; both are on the forecastle, smoking pipes. No one else, certainly no Taha. Nothing but an air of smug, nonchalant luxury.

I catch a glimpse of Sinan circling high above us. If Taha is sharing minds with the falcon, there is a good chance he has seen us crouched here. But there is no way of knowing that, or anything, really. At least in the prison, it was easy to see what was happening, with all the soldiers marching about barking orders. Here, with that falcon in the sky and soldiers possibly concealed in every nook of this ship, it is impossible to fabricate a solid plan. I must improvise, and quickly.

The officer below salutes whomever he was speaking to, turns, and troops down the stairs with his juniors. They climb down the ship's rigging and out of sight, presumably to a waiting boat. Another fellow, a soldier with moss-green eyes, emerges from below deck and jogs up the stairs to the king's cabin, a bronze key in hand. And at last, the person out of view comes over and leans on the taffrail.

I only know that the man in the black cape is King Glaedric by the gold stag-horn wreath crowning him. Startling in presentation, he is not at all who I expected to be leading the colonizers. He is somewhere in his late twenties, all cold angles and lean, domineering height, the very personification of frost. His silken silver-blond hair is swept back, his haughty face possessed of striking blue eyes and a critical, down-turned mouth. It opens now as the soldier with the key bows before him. Green Eyes hands him the key, and I hear the word *prisoner* from Glaedric. The soldier speaks in the affirmative, bowing again. A nod later, the king has languidly strolled into his cabin and shut the ornamented red door behind him. Green Eyes waits a moment to be sure he is no longer needed, then crosses the deck and joins the other two on the forecastle.

"Glaedric said the word *prisoner*," I whisper to Qayn. "Atheer must be here."

"Somewhere belowdecks, most likely," he says.

"Agreed. Follow me."

Dagger in hand, I creep down the right side stairs, past the king's cabin, onto the main deck. Another door leads to a set of descending stairs, and without a map, exploring is my only way around this ship. I pause by the door and glance down. A sconce clarifies the salt-infused darkness, revealing no one coming or going. I steal down the stairs. With every step, the knot in my gut tightens and birds flutter inside my rib cage. I try to convince myself that this is it, but I simply cannot fathom actually coming face to face with my brother after so much hardship.

I reach the first landing. Though the stairs continue down to another deck, I shuffle into this room with my dagger held aloft. The combined storage-armory is empty. Barrels, crates, and trunks are pushed against one wall; swords, bows, and arrows are organized on the other. In the center, an iron drum is fixed to the decking, used to raise and lower the anchor. And at the very back, there is a door with a small barred window in its top half.

A prison cell.

I sheathe my dagger, collect a nearby lantern, and float across the room, though it fast falls away from me and I walk on air. I reach the door but I don't look through the window. I cannot confront what lies within.

I hunch down and press my hands to the door, followed by my forehead, and try to breathe. It could be him inside, it could be someone else, it could be nobody but a ghost. There is no telling if my brother survived this long, or if he was executed the day after he arrived on this ship, and this journey has been nothing but an exercise in the relentless lengths grief will drive us to if we let it. There is no telling, and yet, somehow, I know it in my soul. I feel him behind this door, my big brother and best friend, just . . . just waiting.

"Atheer," I say softly. "Are you in there?"

An engulfing silence endures, greater than the sum of all nights. Someone moves inside the cell. Fabric shifts, footsteps pad across the wood, hands wrap around the bars. An inhalation.

"Imani?"

38

THE STRENGTH LEAVES ME. I SAG ONTO THE FLOOR-boards, weeping silently.

"Imani," he whispers. "You're here."

I jump to my feet and reach through the bars, frantic to touch him and know, once and for all, that this is not a mirage conjured by a shattered mind. His warm fingers brush mine, his face hovers in the circle of lantern light, and at last, I see him.

My brother, Atheer.

Worn and thin, his usually strong body swims in his dirty tunic, and his mop of caramel curls hangs limply over his eyes. They are still so wonderfully warm but shadowed purple, a color matching the bright red cuts streaking his face and the sick bruised vine climbing his neck. My tortured, beaten brother.

Our fingers interlace, more securely than the best knot Baba ever taught us, one that can never be broken once it is tied. I struggle to stand under the weight of my bliss, but Atheer holds me up; he touches my face, he pushes back my wet hair, he laughs and honors my name in his lyrical voice. And I have no doubt now that true magic exists in this world, but it was never the misra. It is family, the people we love. With them, their support, their faith, their friendship, we can become and accomplish anything. And everyone in all the lands deserves this magic; everyone deserves to be safe with their loved ones.

"Won't you speak, my Bright Blade?" he whispers.

"We thought you were dead," I say.

A soft sob sounds low in his throat. He kisses my forehead through the bars. "Forgive me, Imani. I thought it was the best thing to do. But once I was captured, I realized you would never know what became of me, and I saw my error. It was wrong to lie and assume you would not understand. I should have told you the truth, all of you, and taken what consequences came. Forgive me, please."

"I do," I weep. "I forgive you, Atheer. I love you and I've missed you so, so much."

"*Shh,* it's all right," he soothes. "We're together again now. Tell me, what of our family?"

"They grieve you dreadfully but they are well. Amira never stopped searching for you; she always believed you were alive. She insisted on coming with me here; she's on a boat close by."

His brows rise, and his rounded lips turn into a smile. "As stubborn and brave as ever. And Mama?"

"Good, yes, but she worries too much now," I answer. "She wants me to leave the Shields."

"*Leave?* Never, not Bright Blade. The institution would crumble without you."

I laugh through my tears. After everything Atheer has endured, he is still making jokes. But he is as optimistic as the sun is radiant; he always has been. I think it is what draws people to him. He can make any problem conquerable, any mountain little more than a pleasant hill.

"And Baba?" he asks. "Is he still fighting that willful filly, Almas, or has he finally surrendered and sold her?"

I snort. "Has Baba ever surrendered to anyone? Rather it was Almas who declared defeat a few months ago. Now she is perfectly well-behaved."

Atheer grins; it is brilliant, dimpled and singing in his eyes. "I should have known."

"Oh, and Raad is stabled nearby," I say. "He's in good health, though he misses you as terribly as we do."

"Is that so?" A nostalgic smile touches Atheer's lips. "I hope the beast's not been too much of a handful. I suspected he might give you trouble with me leaving him behind in Qalia. Say, what about our silver steed, Badr?"

A lump forms in my throat. "No, she—she perished on the journey here." I've barely said the words before the tears flow again and I sink against the door. "We lost her as well as one of our party. Truthfully, I have lost so much since you left."

"I am sorry, Sister. You did not deserve the pain I put you through." Atheer cups my face between his hands, like Baba would do, and he has that intent look I haven't seen for so long. It calls me to attention immediately. "But you must tell me, how did you know to come here?"

In the shadows behind me, a foot falls. Is there any better answer? I step back as the smiling djinni comes into the light.

Atheer's jaw drops. *"Qayn."*

My brother reaches through the bars. The djinni approaches, and Atheer actually palms Qayn's cheek with one hand and mischievously ruffles his hair with the other. Like they are old friends. Good ones. Qayn told me so, but seeing it now, with my own eyes . . . it dims my happiness a little, and I am not sure why.

"I can't believe you came back, man," Atheer says.

Back? The word rattles ominously around in my head like I am a soothsayer's bone bag.

"Come now, I gave you my word," says Qayn. "As soon as I returned—"

"Returned," I repeat on a low breath, turning to him. "You mean . . . you were bound to my brother before me?"

They exchange a glance, and Qayn clears his throat. "Yes, for quite some time. After Atheer was arrested and it became clear the circumstances were not going to change, he released me from the binding, and the enchantment returned me to the Sahir. Better that we both didn't languish in prison. I'm sure you would agree."

Although I can see the floor, I can't feel it under me. I am free-falling like I did back in the prison, but I don't think even a mountain of bodies will be here to catch me this time.

"You—you lied to me—"

"Imani, it was not his idea," Atheer starts.

"This whole time, you *knew* Atheer was in prison and you didn't say anything!"

Another terrible thought occurs to me. If my brother released Qayn from *within* the prison, a place where nothing can be smuggled in, it means the djinni wasn't bound to an object of Atheer's—he was bound to Atheer *himself.* Bound to his soul, he must've been. That's why Farida didn't recognize Qayn—my brother had no need to summon Qayn the way I do, not when

Qayn was in his head and entwined with his soul. They could speak and share ideas without my brother ever opening his mouth—they were one. I've only done it for a minute, and I understand how intimate that is, how *dangerous* to be so close to Qayn. Atheer had Qayn bound to him for much longer than a minute. Who knows what they've shared?

"Imani, this is difficult, I know, but you must believe me," Atheer says. "I ordered Qayn to lie to you. If he had told you the whole truth right away, about our binding and Alqibah and the rebels, the rest—it would have been too much, and your confusion would have led you to distrust him, perhaps even me. But I needed you to help me—you, specifically, with your skills from the Shields and your magic. I knew you would come to the conclusion on your own about me and Alqibah, and you have." Atheer speaks with such ease, I begin wondering if I am overreacting. He taps Qayn's shoulder. "What then?"

Qayn returns his excited attention to my brother. "I immediately began working to alert your siblings to your presence here in Alqibah—"

"It was Raad who led us to you in the Forbidden Wastes," I interrupt.

"Yes, I called him to me at one of my old abodes, and you both followed."

I stare at Qayn, thinking of the day we met. The day now being placed in a new, glaring light and given new meaning. We were lured to the Wastes for the very purpose of saving Atheer. And Raad answered to Qayn better than he answers to me. Is it the same for my brother?

"Your sister informed the Council, and they dispatched a

group to retrieve you," Qayn explains. "But we recently learned that the leader of the expedition has secret orders to assassinate you for your supposedly traitorous acts."

Atheer's brows twitch, and his sunny mirth swaps with something battle-hardened and intimidating. "Where is this assassin now?"

I have the answer, but I cannot utter it. I am outside this conversation, this alliance between my brother and Qayn. I am trapped in the cold dark, viewing their bond through a foggy window. Desperate to join them, simultaneously afraid to.

"Close," Qayn answers. "We must free you from this cell now."

"It's not possible. The door is locked, and Glaedric keeps the key with him."

"Why?" I ask, louder than I should, given our situation. "What does Glaedric want with you, Atheer?"

He swallows. "The king knows. The magic, the Sahir, *us*. Everything."

"Ev-everything?" I stammer. "How?"

He turns from the bars and pulls his fingers through his curls. "Months ago, I was out in Taeel-Sa, late at night. In an alley behind a shisha lounge, I came across a group of soldiers viciously beating a man. There were so many of them, I was outnumbered, but the anger I experienced seeing their wanton violence . . . it was uncontrollable—"

My stomach plummets. "You used your magic in front of them."

"Yes, I'd done it before with no problem. I changed skins and attacked. I thought I had killed them all. When I was arrested a street away, I was convinced they'd hang me for the crime. They threw me in prison instead and worked me to the bone. A few weeks later, soldiers of the king arrived and pulled me out."

"You didn't kill all of them," Qayn says.

"No." Atheer draws a shaky breath. "One by one, they recovered the strength to talk, and they all told the same story. The person who'd attacked them was a young man who had transformed into a lion."

I feel so hot suddenly, like I've been set on fire. "But surely nobody here would believe such an outrageous allegation," I reason.

Atheer points at the ceiling. "*He* believed it, and that was enough. He'd heard earlier reports of fortuitous events that had occurred during the war, like the seas and winds miraculously changing against them, carriages being set alight with nobody nearby—"

"The magic you gave Farida and the others," I mumble thickly.

"Yes. He suspected there was more than luck involved in those incidents. Once he had his hands on me, he tortured the truth out of me and then some. He's *mad*." Atheer grips the bars, knuckles bulging. "I had a cache of misra stashed in the city. Glaedric discovered that and forced me to show him the magic. He even made me lead him across the Sands, Imani. Ever since, he has been having triple the number of meetings with his military heads. I've heard snippets of conversation. . . . They're talking about *invading* the Sahir."

My knees threaten to buckle. I wobble on the spot and have to grip the cell bars to stay steady. "He knows how to cross into the Sahir. . . . He could reach our people with his army. . . . He could reach Qalia. . . ."

And our family, Mama, Baba, Teta, Auntie . . .

"All the more reason why we must get you out," Qayn says impatiently.

"You *can't*," Atheer says. "The first sign of trouble and—"

Glass smashes on the deck above us. The Harrowlander woman's dog starts barking. We freeze, staring at the creaking ceiling.

"What was that?" Atheer asks.

A wall of violent red shoots up across the Bay. I hurry to the port window and gawk at the warship rapidly being swallowed by fire. Its deck swarms with sailors, their despairing cries carrying over the water.

"How did that happen?" Qayn murmurs at my shoulder.

A gold lantern floats past the window. I step back, startled. How was that lantern carried so high up? Fragile moments pass; something else shatters on the deck.

A bell begins tolling, and a man at the bow bellows, "Fire!"

39

DOORS OPEN; HARRIED FOOTSTEPS THUD ACROSS the deck. People shout at each other, more rising from below.

"Hide," Atheer hisses.

We duck into the shadows as several sailors hustle up the stairwell carrying barrels sloshing with water. No one so much as glances at the prison cell, or us.

"They can put it out, can't they?" Qayn asks.

"This is a wooden sailing ship; everything is flammable." Atheer presses his face to the bars. "Imani, use the commotion to escape before the soldiers arrive."

I stare at him, hearing but not listening. "This is Taha's doing," I say slowly. "His falcon . . . Sinan is shattering the lanterns on the ships, setting them on fire."

My brother's eyes bulge. "Hold on, did you say *Taha*? The Grand Zahim's eldest son?"

The commotion above rises into a squall. Glass shatters, and a woman shrieks as the low roar of flames becomes discernable.

More anxious sailors rush up the stairs from below. We retreat to the shadows and wait for them to pass.

"Yes, he's the Scout who replaced you," I say when they're gone. "And the assassin sent to kill you. He is trying to sink the ship."

"Taha," my brother repeats softly, his gaze unfocused. He shakes his head. "No, Imani, you don't understand. The soldiers won't *let* me die. I am too important to the king."

"Yes, and Taha is counting on that." I have no doubt he has identified the thread that connects my brother to the Council, the rebels, and now the king—misra.

Qayn pulls a face. "I hardly think that boy and his bird can contend with the king's men—"

"You don't know Taha," I say, peering out the porthole. The sinking warship is overcome, and the flames hungrily consuming ours are reflecting like devil's laughter on the murky sea. Above, a man repeats a hollered announcement.

"What is he saying?" I ask Atheer.

His wide eyes find mine. "Save the king. Abandon ship."

A loud crack is followed by something enormous crashing on deck. Screams ring out. A slim moment later, a tremor rips through the ship, its groan sounding in the wood like the rumbling of a monster—and then the ship begins to list. My stomach floats into my chest. Through the opposite porthole, I see that the sea level has risen toward us.

"We're sinking," Atheer says, but his voice doesn't sound attached to him.

I turn and place my hands over his. "Do not be afraid. I will keep you safe, I promise."

Me, keeping my brave brother safe. How? I am already drowning in a cacophony of terror—the dying groans of the ship, the frantic cries of the souls on board, the thought of our sister out there on the choppy waters, helplessly watching this madness unfold.

Up on the main deck, someone shouts about "the prisoner." The soldiers must be on their way to secure Atheer. I anxiously study the cell window, thinking about how, back in the prison, I was able to sense iron beyond that of the soldiers' swords. But even if it were possible to use my affinity so broadly, and even if I were practiced enough that I could magically manipulate the bars, it is still too small a gap for Atheer to escape through. I doubt I could efficiently pick the door's lock open either; it appears too well constructed. I need another plan, and fast. I force myself to speak through the panic grabbing my lungs.

"Qayn, we must stay here and protect my brother. Atheer, when the soldiers arrive, tell them Qayn and I are both your siblings and we came to break you out. *Insist* we are just as valuable to the king as you are. We have knowledge of the misra and where the king can get more of it, so they must protect us as well."

Atheer bangs his fist against the door. "Get *out* of here, Imani, please!"

"No." I pull my dagger off my thigh. "I am never abandoning you again."

I rinse magic through my veins and flush it to my hands. They heat up and tingle, the magic dancing in my nerves like stars are shooting through them.

"What are you doing?" Qayn asks.

"Now or never," I say to myself.

Either this journey ends here, with me sunken in the Bay or speared through the chest by a Harrowlander soldier, or I save my brother. Either we escape or these waters become our final resting place, and grief destroys my parents long before the Harrowlanders can. I move my hand over my dagger; it glows bright blue and begins to curve.

"Imani," Qayn says, trying to get my attention.

I ignore him and concentrate my willpower and intent on the act; with my affinity, I reach through the veil and bend my dagger to my purposes. After all, why should I be limited to only fashioning it into other weapons? If Qayn is right about the nature of my affinity, then my dominion over this blade should allow me to transform it into whatever iron object I wish. My magic exhales as the blade's edge loses its fatal sharpness, the steel thinning and shrinking. A few moments later, the magic dips in my veins, but I am done. I pull my hand away to reveal an inconspicuous ring that I slide onto my finger. Now the dagger resembles something the soldiers will not readily seize from me.

"Spirits, I didn't know you were capable of that," says Atheer.

"Neither did I," murmurs Qayn.

I catch his eye as I lower to my knees. He is entranced, if not mildly wary of what he has witnessed.

Four sweaty men burst onto the deck. The green-eyed man at the front is the one who was talking to Glaedric earlier. He squints at us and draws his sword. Qayn joins me on the floor.

"Very impressive indeed, Slayer," he says, raising his hands over his head.

"Please," Atheer shouts in Harrowtongue as the men advance.

He launches into a protest I don't fully understand, but it makes Green Eyes pause. The soldier considers us, spits a curse, and turns to bark orders at his subordinates. While he unlocks the prison cell door, two soldiers pat us down for weapons and drag us to our feet by the backs of our tunics. Atheer is freed, and the three of us are pushed to the stairs.

I scramble onto the main deck and raise my hands to shield my face. Columns of fire whip in the wind; the heat of it sears my eyes, licks my cheeks, scorches my lungs. It has taken the masts; two lay broken and sprawled across the deck like snapped twigs; one is a stubbornly standing, smoldering matchstick. The deck is littered with the glass of shattered lanterns, their hooks in the walls empty. Sailors run past us carrying crates, trunks, and bundles of scrolls, which they stack on the deck; others throw them overboard, presumably to waiting boats. On my right, more sailors are between the rigging or hurriedly helping the woman in the mauve dress onto a boat hoisted to the ship's side. She is weeping, her barking dog clutched to her chest. Holding a rope for support behind her is King Glaedric.

"Your Majesty," says Green Eyes.

The king turns and appraises us in an encompassing sweep, as cold and aloof as the moon itself. The soldier explains to him who we are. The king's sharp jaw flexes, his gilded brows lowering.

"Glaedric, *hurry*," cries the hysterical woman over the wind.

His pale fist closes on the rope. He stares at Atheer, Qayn, then me, where he lingers. Understanding flares in his gaze. He *knows* something sinister is stirring, but he cannot do anything about it. His floating home is minutes from sinking away like little more than the dreaming Bay's figment, and he is not prepared to kill potential sorcerers who could give him more of what he wants. As I stare up at his vile face, so reminiscent of alabaster, I twist the ring on my finger and wonder if I can do something about *him*. He knows the way through the Swallowing Sands— a secret he could not divulge to others with a dagger lodged in his ashen throat. I slide the ring down my finger.

"You won't achieve anything but getting us killed," Atheer mutters into my ear, breaking the spell. I close my hand around my ring finger, my heart leaping in my chest.

Glaedric points at Green Eyes and seems to threaten him, because the soldier bobs his head with great enthusiasm. The king climbs into the boat, together with the woman and six soldiers, and the sailors lower it to the water.

Green Eyes shoves us to another boat being hoisted up. We clamber on, and are joined by five soldiers crowding on with us. Slowly we are lowered to the sea. The waters around the ship are thick with boats come from the warships to lend aid. A few are pulled frightfully close to the ship, the occupying men catching items being tossed overboard. Several more are rowing in to surround and escort the king's boat away from the carnage.

Ours hits the water roughly; Atheer holds me steady. The soldiers scramble for the oars and begin rowing us away. Green Eyes belts, "Heave-ho! Heave-ho!" presumably to keep the others sculling to a regular rhythm and to warn nearby boats of our proximity. He is drowned out by the colossal groan rising from the burning ship. Those still on board scream as it lists toward us; crates and buckets slide across the deck, bounce off the handrails, and rain into the Bay. Barrels hit the soldiers whose boats are pulled too close to the ship; their limp forms are knocked overboard, one after the other, and sunk. The wind howls, driving flaming embers across the water toward us. Our soldiers row harder; sweat and soot lacquers them; fear mists their pale eyes. I try to get my bearings in relation to Amira by pinpointing the remaining warships. I see only a fragment of one off to the left; archers dot its deck, aiming skyward, but other soldiers are extinguishing the last of its lanterns. Then it's snuffed, vanished in the murk as if it never were.

"Why?" Qayn asks on Atheer's right.

A chill slithers down my spine. "They fear meeting the same fate as the king's ship."

But without those lanterns, the Bay is at the mercy of dense darkness, and we are rowing away from the only source of diminishing light. We are also rowing with nothing to guide us after the others. Their voices are being swallowed by the night in all directions, as if a ghoul is slowly picking them off. Minutes of seemingly aimless rowing pass, and by some widespread unspoken agreement, the strangest silence descends on the Bay. Even Green Eyes halts his refrain, and the soldiers cease rowing. We drift, bodies twisted to look across the water. The king's ship finally capsizes, and the last flames sink beneath the surface, tinging it the reddish brown of congealed blood. Green Eyes says something with the tone used in prayer; then he begins belting "Heave-ho" again, and the solemn men row.

"Seems Taha failed," Qayn says to Atheer and me.

It appears that way, yet I cannot shake the sense that whatever he had planned, it isn't over. Too much has happened to his advantage. The warships dousing their lanterns, rendering the soldiers useless and no longer a threat; the boats of survivors scattering across the unlit Bay like petals on a wayward breeze—it can't be over, can it?

Wind whispers overhead. I lift my gaze and strain my ears. Nothing. No, it's there again, behind now, a sharp *whoosh* of the air being diced. I jump in my seat as a bird screeches. A falcon's call.

Qayn curses. The soldiers flinch too. Green Eyes stubbornly raises the pitch and tempo of his chant. The men row faster, with greater urgency. I slide my ring down my finger.

"Careful," says Atheer in my ear. "You'll attract their attention."

I know, but it is a risk I must take. I have to work fast. I must get free before—

"Do you see that?" Qayn asks.

An eerie light floats toward us through the dark. For a moment, we are captivated by the red warmth gliding across the turbulent sea. Slowly I realize what it is: a lantern borne in a falcon's talons. And behind it, white, frothy waves being driven by the probing hull of a sailing ship, one with a curved prow fashioned like a roaring lion's head. Farida's ship, sails hoisted, bearing down on us.

"Watch out!" Atheer shouts.

Green Eyes bellows something; the soldiers on our left row in an attempt to turn us away. Sinan circles out of reach above us with the lantern, exposing our position. The air snaps, and a soldier grunts and collapses over the side of the boat, an arrow sticking out of his chest. Atheer pulls me protectively against him. I stare at the soldier swiftly being claimed by the water. Shouts rise from Farida's ship, lantern lights bloom, canvas flutters, ropes rustle. A soldier is hit in the chest with an arrow, a third in the head. The fourth takes an arrow through the neck. He staggers before us, rocking the boat as he gurgles, blood staining his teeth, bubbling down his chin. And then he's gone, toppled over the side in a splash.

Farida's ship sails past, lifting us on the swell. Finally I see him behind the handrail, armored and wielding a nocked bow pointed down at us. Taha. Powerful, determined, angry.

Green Eyes watches Taha as the ship comes about. I expect the soldier to beg or menace, but he does neither. He stands there, oar limply in hand, staring at Taha releasing the bowstring. The arrow whistles across the water and hits Green Eyes in the forehead. The man silently tilts and drops headfirst into the water, oar still clutched in his fist.

40

FARIDA'S SHIP SLOWS BESIDE US. TAHA NOCKS AN-other arrow and trains it on me, and he looks both enraged and unsettled. "I can't seem to rid myself of you, can I?"

Such cold words from someone who once tenderly stitched me up. I clench my shaking fists. "Not so easily, no."

"Hello, Atheer," he calls, moving the arrow's target over. "I've come a long way to find you."

"Hope I don't disappoint," my brother replies.

"I had low expectations." Taha gestures at the rope ladder fixed to the side of the ship. "Climb aboard before any more soldiers arrive. Imani, you first. Try anything clever, and I promise, you will regret it."

That was the threat I uttered to him back in Qalia, when he provoked me in front of Auntie and the Council. Has he been taking note of every word I have ever directed at him? I jump into the freezing water, swim over to the ship, and climb the rope. Taha stands over me with his bow, only stepping back when I climb over the handrail, though he keeps the arrow trained on my heart. I'm tempted to tell him not to bother—he's already broken it into many pieces. Something animalistic lives in his gaze now; he seems unhinged, as if the violence he committed at the prison shattered the remaining human part of him.

"Here, on your knees," he says.

I shuffle over. The rebels are working the rigging by lantern light, glancing at us nervously. I see Makeen, Muhab . . . and on the balcony outside the captain's cabin, Amira and Farida, kneeling, wrists bound, mouths gagged, Reza standing behind them with a dagger, poised to strike at the slightest hint of mutiny. Amira sees us and cries; Farida stares at me as if I am a ghost.

"You *bastard*," I seethe, twisting on my heel.

Taha pulls the bowstring taut. "Not so fast."

I shake with rage, but I must hold myself together. If I die now, my brother and sister do too. Atheer and Qayn climb on, and the three of us kneel on the deck.

"Makeen, check them for weapons."

The lanky sailor lopes over and pats us down. "Sorry. We had no choice," he whispers to me before standing up. "Nothing."

Taha eyes me. "Where is your blade?"

"At the bottom of the Bay, where you belong," I say through gritted teeth.

His jaw flashes, but he seems to accept the lie. "Take us back," he tells Makeen. "And remember: anyone tries anything, your captain dies. You have my word; don't test it."

The sailors dutifully get to work on the rigging; moments later, the ship picks up speed. Taha replaces the arrow in the quiver on his back.

"Atheer, you are probably aware by now that the Council sent us after you for your betrayal of our people."

"You mean your father sent you to kill me," Atheer replies without a hint of fear. He stares impassively at Taha, his posture solid.

Taha slides the bow over his shoulder. "He judged you a threat to our nation. I am here to see you do no more harm."

"And you believe you will achieve that by killing me," Atheer says.

"Your fate is sealed, as is Imani's, who has openly declared her support for the outsiders. But your youngest sister . . ." He squats in front of Atheer, elbows balanced on his knees. "If you answer my questions, the Great Spirit is my witness, I will spare her life. How many outsiders know of the magic?"

I ball my fists behind my back. The brutality and injustice Taha witnessed in this land had no impact on him. Or it did, but he cannot allow his reputation as an obedient warrior and dutiful son to be tainted. Bayek's orders will always come before everything else, before reason, compassion, friendship, before *love,* and he will not abandon those orders, even if their pursuit will certainly kill him.

"You intend to punish them too?" Atheer asks.

"Either them or your beloved." He nods to Reza, who holds the dagger to Farida's neck. She concedes nothing, not even a peep, but stares defiantly ahead. I use the distraction to pull the ring off my finger. Taha looks back at Atheer with a raised brow.

"Well?"

"It's not so straightforward—"

"I want names and where I can find them," he says over Atheer.

I inhale, and on the exhale, push my magic through my hands into the ring.

"Do you have a quill and sheet of paper handy?" Atheer retorts. "It's a long list."

Taha's nostrils flare. He looks back at the balcony. Reza smacks Farida with his free hand, knocking her onto her side. Amira whines behind her gag; the sound cuts into my bones like a saw. In my fist, the steel takes weight, the hilt lengthening. Taha faces Atheer again.

"Names, now. I have a good memory."

"Everybody on this ship, to start."

He nods. "I have already factored them in."

I grit my teeth, breathing every ounce of intent into my magic. The hilt completes, and the blade begins to reforge its lethal edge.

"Of course you have, sixteen souls by my last count," says my brother. "But what of your soul, Taha? Has your father assured you of its integrity after this exercise is complete? I would caution against relying on the promise of a man who doesn't possess one."

Taha's gaze darkens. "You speak ill of my father."

"With enthusiasm. Well, has he? No, he made you blood your blade long before this, hoping it would inoculate you against guilt. Quite the roster of roles you've racked up in your short life: Shield, Scout, . . . the Grand Zahim's Personal Assassin."

"What are you talking about?" I demand.

"Go on," Atheer goads him, "tell Imani the names of the people who've met death at your hands before today."

Taha draws a dagger and rests it against Atheer's neck before I can even blink. "Say another word and I'll—"

"You'll what?" Atheer growls, staring brazenly into his eyes.

"Kill me without first hearing the valuable information I have? Imagine what Bayek would do to you then."

The blade jabs Atheer's skin; a crimson dome swells under it and skids down his neck. My dagger completes. I close my fist around the cool hilt and lunge, slamming into Taha and driving him across the deck. He shouts and lands on his back, his dagger sliding away. I clamber onto his chest and stick my blade to his neck. He freezes, chest heaving.

"How did you escape the prison?" he gasps.

"With the dead." I lean into him. "Stand up calmly, or I will bleed the life from you." I climb off him, dagger held out, and address Reza. "Release Amira and Farida. If you refuse, I will drive this blade through Taha's heart." I glance back at Taha. "But take comfort. You have little use for it anyway."

He actually *laughs* at me, drunk on a callousness that is extreme even for him. "You still don't know anything about me, even after what we've been through together. Why am I surprised? You thought you were too good for me the very first day you saw me in the barracks, expecting me to come over and grovel at your feet. Nothing has changed since."

It destabilizes me, how earnestly hurt he sounds, how vividly he remembers our interactions. And if I have understood Atheer's monstrous implication, Taha has killed others while acting as assassin for his father back in Qalia. Shadows cling to him that I never perceived, deeper and far darker than I thought possible.

He turns to Reza on the balcony. "Don't release them."

I dig in the dagger. "I mean it, Reza—"

"So do I," Taha says, laughing harder, the thick vein in his neck recklessly taunting my blade. "Under no circumstance are you to release them. That is an order."

"Understood," Reza replies coldly.

Taha leers at me over the blade. "I suspect my cousin doesn't like me much after what happened with Fey, so he'd enjoy watching me bleed out. And after I'm gone? He still won't release Amira. No, given it's your fault Fey was captured, he would gladly trade his own life for the opportunity to steal your sister from you." Taha grins, but his eyes are intensely sad. "You see, Imani? As terrible as they are, our fates are sealed. You and I—we never had a chance."

A furious shout vibrates my chest. "You can surrender to your father's oppression if you wish, but I refuse!" I shove him aside and thrust my hand up at the balcony, roaring, *"Give it to me!"*

The dagger rips from Reza's fingers and flies through the rail like an arrow. The hilt lands in my waiting fist. Amira leaps to her feet and runs down the stairs. Farida twists onto her back and kicks Reza in the knee, folding him to the ground. Makeen hurries up to his captain; Atheer sprints over to Amira and wraps her in his arms while Qayn backs off to the side of the deck, looking like he doesn't want any part in this.

I discard Reza's dagger in the dark sea and turn back to Taha. He has already nocked his bow and targeted Atheer and Amira. I point my blade as I walk over to him.

"Put it down."

"I can't do that, Imani," he says. "You know I have a mission to complete."

I hold the dagger to his neck. "You will die before your arrow flees the bow."

But he doesn't lift his gaze from Atheer. "I'll chance it."

Atheer positions his body in front of Amira. "The mission is over, Taha. Killing me will not change what's coming; it will only make matters worse."

"King Glaedric knows of our magic and the way across the Sands," I say.

"What?" Taha blinks the sweat from his eyes. "Great Spirit, you traitor!"

"The king tortured him," I exclaim hoarsely.

"It doesn't matter! You shouldn't have told him, Atheer; you should've taken the secret to your grave if you had to!"

Atheer raises his hands and steadily approaches. "You are absolutely right, but I couldn't do it. Perhaps you could, but I am not so trained to withstand cruelty as you are."

Taha falters. "I don't know what you're talking about."

Atheer nods at his chest. "I see you're still wearing the pendant I gave you."

The *wooden falcon?* Taha glances down at it peeking over the neckline of his tunic. He shrugs a shoulder. "So?"

"I bet when your father asked how you got it, you told him it was a gift from a friend. Didn't tell him *which* friend, though, did you?"

"You were Taha's friend?" I ask my brother incredulously.

"Mentor, privately," Atheer corrects, not shifting his eyes from Taha. "Couldn't have Bayek knowing about our friendship, could we, with how much he despises the 'privileged,' and especially the Beya clan?"

"My father wouldn't care if you gave me this pendant," Taha says defensively.

"No? I was the Council's Scout, man. I was around the Sanctuary in the early mornings and late evenings, during the hours when it isn't busy, when conversations echo through closed doors and down corridors. . . . The times when it was only you and *him*."

Taha's breath audibly shakes. "Stop talking."

"I heard things. . . . I saw how he treats you—"

"Shut up or I will put this arrow through your eye!" he yells.

Atheer stops inches from the arrowhead and somehow finds it in him to speak with brotherly kindness. "You don't want to upset your father. I understand that. But what do you think would please him more? If you kill me, you will be returning to Qalia with no valuable information the Council can use to protect our people. Or you can adapt. You can prove you are capable of thinking on your feet without someone always having to be there, telling you what to do." Atheer reaches for the bow. "Look what you did tonight. You single-handedly brought a small fleet to its knees. See what you can accomplish on your own direction?" He pushes the arrow aside. "Our people are facing the biggest threat in a millennium, and if we have any hope of stopping it and protecting our families, we need someone with your skills. And you need me."

I flash my eyes at Atheer, but either he doesn't see me or he ignores me. A single tear rolls down Taha's cheek. Around us, the wind dies, the dark world surrendering her last breath.

"Damn you, Atheer," he whispers. "I believed in you. Why did you have to go off and betray us?"

"We all make our choices, Taha. We decide how we want to live. How will you?"

After a long, agonizing moment, Taha loosens the bowstring and throws his weapon down. Qayn ducks over and collects it. Atheer nods to me, but I don't budge my dagger.

"Imani, you can let him go now," he says.

"No." I tighten my grip on the hilt. "You may have spared his life, but I have not."

Taha turns his head to me. "You really do despise me that much."

"You tried to *kill* me!"

"I had to."

I toss my dagger aside and punch him in the jaw. "You didn't *have* to try to bury me and an innocent girl alive!"

He staggers and stubbornly rights himself. "I had my orders—"

Curse him, he is a ship that cannot be capsized, no matter the gale. But I will try. "To Alard with your father's orders!" I exclaim, punching him again. "Your father almost got Safiya caught and killed by the prison guards, and you made me endure a night that will haunt me forever! Won't you even apologize?"

He spits blood onto the deck. "Would you even accept it?"

I pull him by his tunic. "No!" I scream in his face. "I will forgive you once you've offered your neck to my blade!"

Tears sting his forlorn eyes. "It's yours," he says quietly. "End my misery like I did your horse's, and we will be even."

My grip slackens. The world is askew again, spinning underneath, spinning away. Wretched, all of it.

"Imani, what Taha did was wrong, but it was a mistake," Atheer is saying. "If you want him to accept my mistakes, you must be willing to do the same for him."

I bite back shocked tears and shove Taha away. "Get him away from me," I gasp.

I need there to be as much distance as possible between us right now—his mere presence injects me with conflicting emotions I cannot sift through, let alone understand. Anger, yes; relief that he has surrendered—but gut-wrenching pity too, for a young man raised and molded by such a hateful man, and a bone-deep regret that things did not turn out better between us.

Farida comes limping across the deck. "You took the words right out of my mouth. Makeen, Muhab, secure our prisoners below." She stops the sailors as they pass her. "And thank you for doing what you did to keep me alive."

Makeen frowns. "You really thought we would abandon you?"

Farida grimaces, shrugging. Makeen raises his hand to his forehead, and Muhab follows suit.

"Storms or the fires of all the hells, we sail together forever, Captain," they say in unison, saluting.

Atheer meets the teary captain in a happy, laughing embrace, kissing the palm of her hand. I stand aside as Makeen pulls Taha's arms behind his back and binds his wrists with rope, Muhab attending to Reza. Taha watches me, heedless of the blood sliding down from the corner of his lips.

"Your brother has doomed us, Imani."

"Shut up already," Makeen grunts, shoving him forward.

Taha looks at me over his shoulder until Makeen forcibly bows his head and takes him belowdecks. But even though Taha is gone from my sight, I know I will never be free of the invisible scar he has left on my heart.

41

I LEAVE AMIRA AND ATHEER ALONE FOR A WHILE AFTER that. I go down to the crew quarters and find my bag that my sister brought on with her. I drink some water, I wash my bloody knuckle, I bandage the wound on my neck. I try to compose myself emotionally, but too many of my seams have split tonight.

By the time I return to the deck, we've reached the end of the Bay and the sailors are dropping anchor. Amira and Atheer have been joined by Farida; they sit at the bow with their backs to me, talking spiritedly. They look so happy and relieved, but for some reason, I don't feel quite ready to participate. I notice Qayn standing by himself on the balcony outside the captain's cabin. And as it always does, something mysterious compels me up to him.

We exchange a nod as I stack my elbows on the rail beside him. I can't help but look to Farida and my brother, conversing with startling ease. Atheer says something undoubtedly witty; Farida puts her hand on her chest and laughs to her heart's content. She has a beautiful laugh, confident, sharp, and energetic, like a vengeful blade. And my brother is so plainly enamored with it; his eyes dance over her face, and his fingers curl with hers. How familiar they are, how vibrantly he shines in her presence, in a way he hasn't done with us for years. I experience a rotten burn deep in my chest.

"He can love Farida and your family equally," Qayn says suddenly.

It is a surprisingly intense hurt I feel. I roll my eyes, hoping my sarcasm will conceal my childish jealousy. "Thank you for the advice, but what do you know about love?"

"It may shock you to learn that in the many centuries I have lived, Slayer, I have loved and, yes, at times even been loved in return."

I expected a smirk and a gleaming riposte, not sincerity. In truth, I am so frayed by the day's events, I hesitate to venture down a path where we discuss anything at length bar the weather. I snort, leaning casually into the rail. "Whoever loved you was surely mad."

"A few, I'm certain."

He is watching the pair too, my sister having curled up and fallen asleep by my brother's side. Farida is gazing into Atheer's blushing face, smiling. He says something, and her grin widens, the corners of her eyes wrinkling. She brushes a stray curl that's fallen across his forehead, saying something quickly and laughing again, except this time it's like she is laughing at him. And Atheer cups her cheek and silences her laughter with a long, tender kiss. When they part, I see the sun peeking over the horizon between them.

Qayn lowers his gaze to his hands dangling off the rail. "The person I loved the most betrayed me."

He offers the statement without warning, and I sense he is seeking comfort in me.

"Nahla," I prompt, and he nods. "She stole your magic, didn't she? Why?"

"She and I were from different societies. Me, a magical being. She, a Sahiran, like you."

I blink several times. "Oh. I didn't realize . . . I thought she was a djinni too."

He shakes his head. "No, and although she and I were very much in love, her people did not accept me. I was different to them, intolerably so, in the same way you in the Sahir feel about the outsiders. That is the way of the world, Slayer. Everyone hates and distrusts what is unfamiliar to them."

I hum softly, thinking of my attitude toward Alqibah when I first learned of it, my desire not to be involved with the rebellion because this land and its people are not mine. Or my attitude to Taha, even.

"It's a very narrow way of thinking," I admit. "What happened then?"

"I possessed much wealth in that time," he explains. "Nahla, who came from poor circumstances, asked if I might share some of my wealth with her and her people. My love for her was great, and I agreed. I built her the First City. I gave her people everything they could desire, and they lived in opulence. But in secret, they were not satisfied. They could not tolerate the possibility that one day I might withdraw my bounty if I chose to. So they plotted to steal my wealth and rid themselves of me."

"They used her," I say.

His brows lower, a fine line forming between them. "They did not *use* her. Nahla, of her own will, chose my fortune over my love. She aided them in stealing from me. She destroyed me."

Though things are still fuzzy around the edges, the pieces of the puzzle begin to assemble a coherent picture. "That's why you let the First City fall to the Desert's Bane," I say. "As revenge."

"Yes. But my fortune was not enough for Nahla. To ensure I could never challenge her people's wicked theft, she took my magic away too, leaving me destitute and powerless."

"How?" I ask, leaning in curiously. "What was the source of your magic?"

"My crown."

My eyes widen. "Oh," I breathe, remembering the ethereal, three-pronged crown he wore in the memory. *That's* why he reacted so strongly to my insult and demanded I never call him *king without a crown* again. "I'm so sorry, Qayn." I hesitate, then reach over and lightly squeeze his hand. "My feelings about the First City's fate aside, you didn't deserve to be treated that way. What happened to Nahla and her people?"

"I suppose they perished eventually, as people do," he says distantly, appraising my hand on his. "I left after she stole everything from me, and when the Swallowing Sands were created, I was trapped, left to aimlessly roam the Sahir."

"I'm sorry," I repeat. "It is not a fate I would wish upon anyone." I sigh, turning my mind to Taha. "Though I fear we may all encounter a worse fate yet. Taha said something earlier that may be true . . . that we are doomed."

"He was referring to the Harrowlanders," says Qayn.

"Yes. What if he is right?" I press my back against the rail. "We don't know the true extent of their might. From what I've seen in this short time alone, they possess an impressive martial force by land and sea, and those among their ranks who are not willingly dedicated to the cause are too afraid to disobey orders."

Qayn shrugs. "And you Sahirans have magic."

"The use of which is limited to the Order of Sorcerers. Not all our warriors are sorcerers; they must undertake a separate, higher level of training. But the Harrowlanders?" I shake my head. "It seems all their men and boys are soldiers, all familiar with conflict and war. It is a staple of their society, whether their common people want it to be or not. They live it, they breathe it."

"And you Sahirans—"

"Don't." I look across at a building on the docks destroyed by the war, its rubble touched dreamy dawn-orange. "We haven't fought this kind of war in a millennium. We have tens of villages and towns scattered throughout the Sahir, full of farmers, hunters, bakers, carpet weavers. Not warriors." I glance down the deck at my brother and Farida, quietly watching the sunrise. "Back on the ship, Atheer said King Glaedric has been having more and more meetings with his military heads since he learned of the magic. . . . They are speaking of invasion."

"You truly fear the Sahir might fall to them," Qayn says.

"Yes." Unease slithers through me and coils around my heart. "Along the Spice Road they went, pillaging. But at the end of the road is a spice unlike any they have known before. And if this is the force they unleashed on a city that doesn't have magic . . . imagine the force they will unleash to defeat us. Imagine what the misra could do for them—they would be unstoppable." I shift my gaze to Qayn. "The only reason Glaedric is not leaping at the opportunity to flood across the Sands is because his preparations are not complete. Once they are . . . I looked into that man's eyes, Qayn. He is cunning and pitiless. Such a combination could raze the world if left unchecked."

"I've no doubt," Qayn says. "But what do you propose?"

"What *can* I? We must warn the Council and pray they have an answer, though I fear that whatever answer they give will fall far short of what's needed."

"What's needed," Qayn repeats softly. He bites his lip, fingers curling around the rail. "I must speak truthfully now. Atheer and I . . . we had a plan."

I study him, though his silk-smooth face is impossible to read. "The plan Farida spoke of. To do what?"

"Save Alqibah . . . defeat the Harrowlanders." His fingers close on the rail. "You see, without my magic, I am rather useless. But when I was powerful, I was *very* powerful."

"What are we meaning here?" I ask, my heart beginning to thud. "More powerful than building the First City?"

He meets my eyes, and I am drawn to his, hungry to know more of him, his memories, his thoughts, his feelings. Eager to return to that palace and explore to my heart's content, even if it means letting him do the same to me.

"Powerful enough to summon you a magical army that could supplement the Sahiran forces," he says.

I exhale a long, whistling breath. "The First City is one thing, but a magical army . . . Not even the djinn of ancient folklore were that mighty."

"So naïve," he mutters. "You didn't know Alqibah existed,

from reading your tomes. Do you really think they cover every-thing and everyone?"

I chew my lip. "I suppose not. Be that as it may, you told me your magic was lost to you forever."

"To *me,* yes." He mulls his words, then clears his throat. "Be-fore Atheer was captured, we were attempting to retrieve it—the crown, that is. The idea was that I would help Atheer free Alqibah of this Harrowlander plague, and he would return my most precious possession to me. I must admit, the going was not easy and we were struggling to make headway. But with you here now, seeing the things you are capable of—" His fingers toy with mine. "My magic could be retrieved in a fraction of the time and with a fraction of the difficulty. So I must ask . . . will you help me, Slayer? I will repay you what you are owed one thousandfold. I will help you save the Sahir. More, whatever you desire."

I look over the sly cut of his lips, the curl of his long, black lashes, the wavy strands of hair wisping down his temples. My pulse hitches, desire flurrying within. "Help you regain your magic in exchange for defending the Sahir. Always a deal to be made with you, isn't there, negotiations to be had. How do I know I can trust you?"

"Aside from the fact that your brother trusts me?" He sighs. "Come now, did I not fulfil my promise to bring you to Atheer? And here he is, safe and happy."

"Yes, that's true," I murmur, glancing at Atheer sitting with Farida.

"And have I not done my utmost to help and guide you?"

"Yes, you have . . ."

"And there is so very much I know about magic—what you

did with your blade tonight is but a taste of the things I could teach you."

I look back at him. "Will that be part of the deal?"

He closes his fingers around my hand. "You've my word, I will make you great. What do you say? Another arrangement for mutual benefit and success?"

I draw a long breath. "All right. I *tentatively* agree to retrieve your magic in exchange for an army. But if I discover you are lying to me—"

"Yes, yes, you'll lop off my head and keep it for—how did you describe it? A pretty souvenir? *Deal.*" He leans in and kisses me on the cheek, and his lips linger dangerously close to mine. Tingles rush through me, my face heating up. I pray he doesn't notice the blush in the early light. He steps back, smiling, and for the first time since we met, something appears in his eyes, akin to the Qayn from memory. Life, emotion—a distant but distinguishable flame in a long night.

I clear my throat. "I'm going over to the others. Why don't you join us?"

His brows lift. "I would like that."

He pads after me down the stairs. Most of the sailors are retreating to the crew quarters for much-needed rest, including Farida, who makes her way over to me.

"I was hoping to catch you before I went down," she says. Behind her, Atheer shifts around to watch us.

I reflexively fold my arms. "Sure, what is it?"

"Well, firstly, thank you for bringing Atheer back to us. To me. I don't think I've been so happy since my father was alive."

I didn't bring Atheer back for her; I brought him back for his own well-being, and my family, and *me*. But he is watching me carefully, and I don't want to argue with someone he loves. I bow my head.

"I'm glad to hear it," I say stiltedly.

Farida gives a tight smile. Something more pressing is clearly on her mind. "Atheer told me what King Glaedric is planning for the Sahir," she says. "I thought of you—what you may do after this, and how much of a *loss* it would be for us if you leave. Of course, you've every right to return home and worry about protecting your people alone, but, well . . . would you consider helping us fight the Harrowlanders too? After all, Alqibah is the doorstep to the Sahir. What impacts us here will impact you there."

I cast my gaze over the water. She is wrong; with Qayn's magical army, we could defend the Sahir and ensure that the Harrowlanders never set foot in it. The foreigners would become a distant, soon-to-be-forgotten problem. But something Auntie said to me before I left Qalia has come back in a new light: *All life is sacred. If we can, we must lay down our own in defense of it.* She was trying to tell me, *all* life, not only Sahiran life. If I turn my back on Alqibah, what society am I helping to create in the Sahir? What would I be acquiescing to if I helped Qayn get his magic back, only to use his army to protect the Sahir alone and nobody else? All our peace and blessings will mean nothing. Atheer was right: light not shared is light diminished. If I decide to go home after this and never return, I am allowing the Sahir's light to ebb. The decay of apathy will find us eventually; at first, it will skulk around the edges, but gradually it will bleed its way in. And when it finally smothers the Sahir's light—the light the Great Spirit charged us to protect—we will live in a land where the only things that matter are status, wealth, and magical might, not humanity, justice, and mercy for all. And I will have had a direct hand in creating that world. Is that really what the Great Spirit wanted for us when it blessed us with magic? I refuse to believe that; I simply cannot continue an existence where such a thing is true. This is a lesson Atheer long ago learned, one I am only getting to. But it is better late than never.

"I will help you," I say, extending my hand. "It is not freedom if the Sahir is safe but Alqibah is not. Like you said, we are sisters, and sisters protect one another."

Farida's eye floods with tears; instead of shaking my hand, she hugs me. Over her shoulder, a grinning Atheer gives me a proud nod.

"Thank you, Imani." Farida steps back and formally adjusts her tunic. "I imagine you have a lot of lost time to make up with your brother. I'll leave you to it." She squeezes my shoulder and limps past, then disappears belowdecks.

I sit down beside Atheer, who has his arm slung over a sleeping Amira. He beams and pulls me against him too. "There she is, my Bright Blade. And who could forget the handsome devil attached to her?" He winks at Qayn. The djinni returns the wink and climbs onto the handrail nearby, where he perches, happily swinging his bare feet in the morning air.

For time uncounted, Atheer and I sit on the bow like that, watching the horizon, basking in the relief and gladness.

"We're together again," I murmur.

He kisses my forehead. "And so we shall remain."

"Do you promise?" I ask. "You won't go away again?"

"Never," he whispers as he watches a seagull silently cross the sky. "Every moment I spent stuck in that cell on Glaedric's ship, I thought of you and Amira, Mama and Baba, Teta, Auntie, Raad, even Simsim with how much he chews through my slippers." He laughs sadly. "I thought of home, and the Shields. The memories we all shared, the new ones we would never be able to make. The pain you must have been going through." He shakes his head, tears slipping down his face. "Forgive me. I never want to endure that torment again, and I never want to put you through it either."

I brush the tears away, even as my own rise to the surface. "It's all right, Atheer. You were trying to do the right thing."

"But I went about it the wrong way," he says. "My apology will not erase months of grief."

A sob erupts from me, and I curl against his chest. Even through my pain, the feel of his warm touch and the sound of his steady heartbeat are magical. He hugs me firmly.

"I only want you to know this, Imani. I recognize what I have done, and I do not expect you to accept my apology, not now, perhaps not ever. But it is blessing enough for me to sit with you again, and to have witnessed how much your magical skill has grown in such a short time. I am so, so proud of you. I can only imagine how much Baba sings your praises to anyone who will listen."

I burst into tearful laughter. "The men at his barbershop must be sick of hearing my name by now."

Atheer snorts, resting his chin on my head. "Never. A better subject than me, I'm sure," he murmurs.

I pull away. "Don't say that. You are the jewel in Baba's crown;

you always have been. You should have seen how elated he was when he heard you might be alive here; it was like the Great Spirit was breathing new life into him again."

"Really?" Atheer swipes a tear before it falls. "I miss the big man. And sweet Mama. Spirits, I miss them so much, it hurts to think of."

I lean against him. "You will see them soon. We all will. But we will not forget what we know now about Alqibah, the injustice here, the people who need help."

"No." He takes my hand. "We are going to change things, Imani, you and I. We will make things better."

"I will be content to try, at least," I say, nodding. "It is the most anybody can do."

He chuckles, his chest shifting against me. "Just to try? How bizarre. Since when did you become so humble and unenterprising?"

I pull away again, feigning an outraged scowl. "What's that supposed to mean? I am both the humblest person in the entire Sahir *and* the best."

He laughs harder, his sad tears transforming to joyful ones. And just like that, we start joking around, the sound of our bliss loud enough to rouse Amira, who joins in. Eventually Atheer asks her how school is going. She and I lock eyes, her lips puckering in a threatening pout that says *Don't breathe a word.*

"Fine," she lies. "I am excelling in every class."

"She barely attends!" I snicker and flop onto the deck, wiping a gleeful tear from my eye. "But honestly, she's somehow gotten cleverer for it. And wiser. It must be some new magic we don't know about."

"That'd be about right with this one," Atheer says, pinching her arm. "She's got the Spirits' luck on her side."

Her worried expression immediately transforms to relief. *Thank you,* she mouths to me, to which I give a small, knowing nod.

We reminisce a little while longer after that, giggling about that time Atheer wore his flower crown for an entire week, to Baba's consternation; and the time when a grounded Amira snuck into the stables at dawn to take a horse for a ride and accidentally released four of them, prompting a half-dressed, shouting Baba to run after them, his arms flailing, while Simsim howled bloody murder at his heels; and the elaborate distraction we devised as children to get Mama into another room while I snuck into the pantry and stole all the pastries intended for some guests, only to realize at the last moment that Teta was quietly sitting in the corner, observing my heist.

Eventually we lapse into comfortable, contented silence, encased in the golden cocoon of our happiest moments. Amira lies down again to nap; Atheer props his chin on my head. I find myself listening to their breathing, coming and going like even tides. It is as lovely as the song of birds floating over the peak of a sand dune. The sweetest sound the world could ever produce. It tells you an oasis is near: water, food, shade. A good place to rest, be safe, and forget your worries for now. So I do.

I cast them out to sea, and I sit with my brother and sister, watching the darkness steadily lift from the world.

ACKNOWLEDGMENTS

Heartfelt thanks to my agent, Peter Knapp, who advocated tirelessly for this manuscript and guided its development over years with a deft and thoughtful hand. For his invaluable help in transforming *Spice Road* into the book it is today, he has my eternal gratitude. Many thanks go also to Stuti Telidevara and everyone at Park & Fine for their continued support in getting *Spice Road* out into the world.

I am also incredibly thankful to my UK agent, Claire Wilson, and her assistant, Safae El-Ouahabi, at RCW, who went above and beyond in giving *Spice Road* the best home I could ask for in the United Kingdom.

My editor, Kelsey Horton, has been wonderful to work with, and it is thanks to her insight that I was able to bring *Spice Road* to its fullest potential. I am similarly grateful to the team at Random House Children's Books—Regina Flath in design, artist Carlos Quevedo, Colleen Fellingham in copyediting, and my publicist, Lili Feinberg, among many others—for all the hard work they've put into sharing *Spice Road* with readers (and presenting it so beautifully.)

To the generous people who have read this book in its various forms, you have my thanks. I must make special mention of Jamar J. Perry, E. J. Beaton, Amélie Wen Zhao, and Ayana Gray for their enthusiasm, critiques, and advice—but most of all, for their friendship, without which the path to publication would have been terribly lonely.

My family keeps the wind in my sails, and to them I owe an immense debt. My wise and witty Mama and Baba, who bought me books and nurtured my love of words as a child (and still do), and my big brothers, Sharief and Saamer, whose steady confidence in my ability as a storyteller helped me weather many storms of self-doubt—thank you for always being there for me.

Lastly, I want to thank my stalwart husband and best friend, Jason, whose contribution to this book is too great for words. Without his love, support, and kindness, *Spice Road* would simply not exist.

ABOUT THE AUTHOR

MAIYA IBRAHIM is the debut author of *Spice Road*. She graduated with a Bachelor of Laws from the University of Technology Sydney. When she isn't writing, reading, or spending time with her family, she enjoys video games, gardening, and expanding her collection of rare trading cards. She lives in Sydney, Australia.